Midnight Maiden

A Noble. An Assassin.
A Girl with a Past...

Kathryn Marie

MIDNIGHT Duology Book One

For information contact :

Kathryn Namenyi

55 Spencer St

PO Box 342

Lynn, MA 01905

authorkathrynmarie.com

Cover design by Celin Graphics

Chapter Header Design by Silver Wheel Press Designs

Developmental Edits by Fiona McLaren

Copy Edits by Renee Dugan

ISBN: 9781734832303

First Edition: August 2020

10 9 8 7 6 5 4 3 2 1

Disclaimer:

This book contains a few semi-graphic scenes of physical and sexual assault. Please be advised.

Dedication

To Elizabeth

Thank you for showing me the magic of the written word.

Chapter One

THE LOUD CLAMORS OF THE VILLAGE CENTER swept across the empty streets as Christiana clung to the shadows. This was her fifth night in the modest village of Rynas, standing in the same claustrophobic alley while the muggy air settled around her. She stared out into the heart of the town, waiting for her mark to appear in the dampened cobblestone streets. For the past five nights, she had been forced to flee without success, her drunken target outlasting the moonlight in the stench of gambling dens where he chose to pass the time. But patience was important in her line of work, so she kept quiet and watched the den doors for any sign of movement.

The large clock tower above the whole city rang out, striking loudly to mark the time. Just past midnight; she had three more hours before she would have to begin her journey back to her cottage. Christiana listened closely, allowing the sounds of the streets to envelope her. Soon, the distinct noises of glass shattering, screaming men, and splintering wood reached her ears. Her stomach filled with fluttering wings as she watched two oversized men emerge from the gambling den's doorway, dragging a sweaty body outside and depositing it on the ground. The form lay still for a few minutes before forcing itself onto its feet to head home. A smirk spread across Christiana's face, adrenaline slowly building in her bloodstream when she recognized the stumbling man as her mark.

Securing the silky fabric of her veil around her face, she waited in her shadowed cover, rubbing her thumb up and down the poisoned dart clutched between her fingers. Her stomach fluttered deep inside as she watched his every movement with bated breath. He stumbled and fell frequently when he attempted to make his way, his uneven gait slowly moving him into her line of attack. When he rounded the corner into the dark alley, she fired the dart with perfect precision, landing right in his neck.

"What the—" he stuttered. "Where the hell did this come from?" He stumbled around in circles attempting to find the culprit.

"I have a message for you," Christiana told him, her voice muffled through her veil as she stepped forward to face him, shoulders pulled back while she watched his face contort in anger. As if that could ever scare her.

"And who are you?" he cracked his knuckles, staring her down.

"I'm the one your eldest son sent to end your life."

"That little nothing isn't smart enough to find an assassin, let alone brave enough to hire one to kill me." He laughed, dropping his fist and shaking his head as if she had told him a joke. "Now why don't you run along like a good little girl? Unless you want to stick around and show an old man a fun time."

She scoffed, crossing her arms against the silk ties of her corseted coat. "As much as a sweaty, drunk man appeals to me, I think I'll pass."

"You disrespectful—" He raised his hand again, but before he could strike her, she grabbed his arm midswing and, with a sharp pivot, pinned him to the wall face first.

"Now, like I was saying, I have a message for you. Your son wanted me to let you know that he may be able to handle your nightly beatings, but he'll be damned if he ever sees you lift a finger to his little sisters."

"Why does my chest hurt?" His moans of anguish echoed off the wall she pressed him against.

A grin spread across her face as the man squirmed in pain under her hands, the poison making its way through his bloodstream. Grabbing his face, she clutched his mouth closed to drown out his agonizing screams. "Please be quiet until I've finished my message. As I was saying, he will not let you lay a finger on his sisters, so he has no other choice but to end your life. For in his mind, his kind and loving father died alongside his mother five years ago and a monster replaced him. And he does not hesitate to kill monsters."

"Please don't do this," he tried to plead, the muffled noise filtering through her fingers. "I promise to never hurt my son again if you give me the antidote."

"Even if I did believe you, you'd still be out of luck. Midnight has no antidote. If an unlucky person's bloodstream comes in contact with it, they're dead. But don't worry, your suffering is almost at an end." She kept his body pinned to the wall, his suppressed cries of pain the only sound in the alley. Soon, they softened to a pathetic whimper before his body went limp.

Dropping the body to the ground, Christiana plucked the dart out of the man's neck and stored it back on her leather gauntlet. Opening the satchel strapped tightly to her right thigh, she removed the vial of poison she had used on the dead man. Opening it, she dipped a paint brush into the opaque, black liquid, and drew her calling card on the man's forehead: a crescent moon. With it, she had now branded him an abuser.

Satisfied with how the case turned out, Christiana returned the vial and brush to her satchel before disappearing back into the shadows to return home.

***

About an hour before dawn, Christiana's stiff legs finally returned her to the cottage. The damp morning mist clung to her face as she approached the stone building, cutting around the back to the open window of the master suite. Swiftly scaling the wall, she climbed through, her body finally flooding with the exhaustion she had ignored during the journey home. Pulling the window shut, she stared out, watching the sun peek over the horizon to greet a new day.

She walked to her traveller's trunk and unlaced the front of her coat. Pulling the satin strings, she released herself from the tightened bonds, letting out a deep breath. A sort of graduation gift her mentor, Marek, had given to her after years of training, the custom-made sleeveless black coat had a tight-laced up corset on her torso, then flared out behind her, cascading with beautiful ruffles reaching down to the backs of her ankles. It was enough to help her blend in if necessary, but gave her better range of motion with the black leather riding pants she wore with it. A thick hood and detachable veil were sewn on as her main way of hiding her identity.

Once the corset was unlaced, she folded it and opened the false top of her trunk. Removing each of her weapons, she gingerly placed them inside the folds of the coat, making sure they were properly sheathed and stored. Finally removing her pants, boots, and gauntlets, she put them back in their proper hiding space, making sure to secure the false top.

Walking over to her plush bed, she picked up the soft nightgown she had removed earlier in the night and pulled it back over her head. Sitting on the edge, she dropped her head into her hands, rubbing her temples and searching for peace. The weight of her sleepless nights coursed through her body, her aching muscles and tired mind begging for sleep. But her racing heart pulsed through every inch of her skin, sending shocks with each miniscule movement. Giving up on getting any sleep before the adrenaline drained out of her system, she walked over to her desk and began to work, her quill scratching against one of her many ledgers as the sun made its final steps back into the daylight.

"Oh, good morning, My Lady," Natalia greeted from the doorway, her mouth gaping as she struggled to keep the tray of breakfast foods secured in her hands. Peeking over her shoulder, Christiana stifled a giggle as she gestured for her lady's maid to drop her breakfast on her desk. Her stomach rumbled in pleasure as she took in a deep breath of steaming, fresh bread and sweet fruits. Jumping right in, she let out a low groan as she bit into the delicious meal.

"Did you sleep at all last night?" Natalia inquired, her sharp features pulled into a frown as she ran a hand over her smooth, obsidian hair.

"Enough," Christiana dismissed, focusing on the food in front of her as Natalia shuffled behind her to prepare for the day. "Please make sure to pull out my travel outfit. I think it is time to return home, I've finished up all of the work I need here."

"Of course, My Lady. I'll let the rest of the household know. We should be ready to leave within the next few hours," she replied with a curtsy, once again leaving Christiana alone with her thoughts.

Returning to reality and responsibility was necessary, her title as the Marchioness of Tagri pulling her back home to her rightful place in society. But a bittersweet pang settled in her soul as she realized once again, an assassin job had come to a close. Her life was a constant battle between the title she was blessed with and the one she had fought for. She adored every moment as Marchioness, but there was something about the way she helped bring peace to other lives as the Maiden—it filled her soul with a gratification she never thought possible. She pushed the saddened thoughts out of her mind as she finished up her breakfast, her body tingling at the thought that a new job would fall into place soon.

7

Chapter Two

"*ANA! YOU'RE BACK!" SQUEALED CHRISTIANA'S* sister, Isabelle. The young girl of thirteen stood up from her chair the minute Christiana entered the library, walked over and threw herself into Christiana's arms, staring up at her older sister with gleaming eyes. Pulling Isabelle to her torso, Christiana stroked her wispy blonde hair, a sense of calm washing through her. No matter what her day was made of, spending time with Isabelle always brought her back to peace.

"Welcome home, my darling girl," her mother, Maria, greeted her. Melting into her warm embrace, Christiana wrapped her arms around her mother. The Dowager Marchioness had aged too quickly from years of enduring her husband's wrath and anger. Lines covered her angelic face and whispers of grey speckled her hair. "How were your travels?"

"Busy as usual." Christiana smiled, closing the door behind her. The modest-sized room instantly wrapped a person in comfort once they crossed the threshold, with the walls of various books, reading nooks, and the floor to ceiling gray stone fireplace crackling in the background.

"Sit, sit. I had tea made for us to enjoy," Maria offered. The three ladies sat at a cluster of rich, evergreen, velvet chairs around a mahogany table.

"What do you need to talk about?" Christiana asked, brow wrinkling as she stared down her mother who happily poured their cups of steaming tea.

"What makes you say that?"

"Whenever you have us sit down for tea it means you have something important to discuss." Taking the outstretched teacup, Christiana stirred in a lump of sugar, refusing to take her eyes off her flushed mother.

"Belle, you should head back to your room," Maria said with a tone hinting it was more of an order than a suggestion.

"Why?" she whined, lips pouting as she stared at her sister and mother for an answer.

"Because this is something I need to discuss with Christiana. You'll understand when you're older."

"But I am older!" she cried. "I deserve to be here as much as she does."

"Belle," Christiana chimed in. "Please go upstairs. I'll stop by soon and we can spend more time together."

"Fine." Dragging her feet as she left the library, Isabelle slammed the door behind her, shaking the tall copper candelabras standing at attention on either side of the entrance.

"What's wrong, Mother?" Christiana asked, the billowing steam filled with nutmeg and orange wafting to her as she took a sip of her tea. She tried to force the liquid down, a lump forming in her throat as she watched her mother's lips pull downward into a saddened frown. So many ideas raced through her mind about what turn this talk would take.

"This arrived for you a few days ago." Maria handed over a sealed letter addressed to the Marchioness of Tagri. The large, bright purple seal caught Christiana's attention; the crest of the Royal Family firmly pressed into the center of the hardened wax.

She reached across the table, placing her teacup in its saucer before taking the thick envelope from her mother's grasp. She stared at it for a moment, trying to keep her hands from trembling as her gaze followed the swirls of her name flourished across the front. She had a feeling this letter would be arriving on her doorstep one day, although a part of her wished it hadn't come so soon. She slipped her finger under the seal and pulled it off to open the envelope, removing a single piece of parchment covered in the words she expected.

It was a simple ordinance: come to court with a partial household to be a guest at the Royal Palace for the summer months. Christiana peered up from the parchment, her mother's hesitant smile showing she already knew what this letter said as well. "They have asked us to send a letter ahead with any necessary items I might need in my apartment by the time I arrive. They're expecting me in three weeks' time."

"You must be excited." Maria nudged Christiana's arm gently.

Christiana folded the parchment. "Why do you say that?"

"You'll get to see Prince Alekzander and Princess Dorina again. After so many years apart." Maria winked.

"My focus going to the palace this summer is to make a good impression on the King and Queen." Christiana tried not to smirk, her fingers gently stroking the wax crest as images of her closest childhood friends filled her memory. "But yes, it will be nice to see them again."

"Well, we'll have to make a list of what we need commissioned. You'll certainly need a few new formal and informal gowns that are proper for the Palace. We can go into town in a few days to the dressmaker," Maria prattled on, although she still could not look her daughter in the eye.

"Is there something else you haven't told me?" Christiana laid the letter down on the table and narrowed her gaze at Maria. She couldn't put her finger on it, but something in her stomach couldn't seem to settle as she watched her mother run her thumb over the handle of her cup.

With a deep sigh, Maria pulled a smaller letter out of the folds of her dress, offering it for Christiana to look at. "Just after that letter arrived, I received one from my old friend Madeleine as well."

"Oh?"

"It seems the King and Queen have more than your presence in mind for the summer. They aren't too pleased with your lack of a husband and feel this would be the perfect opportunity for you to socialize with some prospective suitors."

"What?" Christiana asked, pulling the letter from her mother's hands. She read it over twice, the crisp parchment crinkling between her fingers as she tried her best to will the words on the page to change. But no matter how hard she tried, the dark black ink didn't seem to move. The Queen had told Madeleine it was time for the Marchioness of Tagri to finally secure her bloodline with a husband. After her father's untimely death, they were anxious to have their strongest title finally be solidified with an heir.

"No matter what the King and Queen want, I will not walk away with a husband unless I'm the one choosing him," Christiana said bluntly, her jaw tightening at the idea of what her summer was going to be. She knew between her title and her age of twenty-three, it wasn't typical for a Virian noble like her to be unmarried, but she never cared. Her life was her own, and she always made the best decisions for herself.

"I know, my darling. I'm the last person to force you into an arranged marriage, but the King and Queen will be pressuring you with different men the moment you arrive."

Letting out a laugh, Christiana replied, "You're probably the only one in the Kingdom who doesn't want that."

"I want you to be happy." Maria smiled at her daughter, patting her tense hand until Christiana released the strong fist that had formed on the armrest.

"I know," Christiana replied, handing the letter back to her mother so she could try to relax and enjoy the rest of her tea.

***

Exhaustion etched through all of Christiana's muscles the next day, the constant talk and preparations for her summer plans filling her mind with fog. She had spent all morning with her mother and Natalia, meticulously going through every dress she owned and making a list of what new ones she would need to commission before she left. It made her miss the hours she spent filling out land reports and counting the tax money she collected every season.

By mid-afternoon, she finally found a quiet moment to slip out of her manor house, the tension in her shoulders slowly dissipating as she rode her favorite mare through the forest trees. The mild air tickled her skin when she slowed down to a trot, the whisper that summer was almost upon them. She took in a deep breath, the light scent of lilac enveloping her as she came to a stop in front of a modest cottage at the edge of her property line.

The house was beautiful in Christiana's opinion, more than a place for someone to sleep and eat. The grey and black stone structure stood strong, with long strands of ivy growing at the base. It was surrounded by a circle of evergreen trees, the tall trunks giving privacy that kept this place well-hidden from prying eyes and passing caravans. It was intimate, but the perfect place for Christiana to use as an escape. To her, it was a sanctuary away from responsibility. She approached the front door, her hands reaching for the loosened rock pried into the side of the house. She wiggled it free, a dust cloud puffing out before she reached her hand in to find two parcels addressed to her alias. Pulling them out, she recognized the handwriting on the letters belonged to two of her informants. The best way she found jobs was through five prior clients, one in each territory in the country of Viri. Instead of paying for her services, she retained them as points of contact to help sort through different potential jobs. They helped her do research and solicit proper business, and handled the client before and after meeting with the Maiden directly.

Unlocking the front door and heading inside the house, she made her way into the kitchen, a majority of the limited counter space taken up by her distillery equipment. She removed her leather riding gloves and threw them on the table before opening the letters. The first was from her Banshyl informant, who sent well wishes along with the final payment for her last job. Looking into the pouch, Christiana made sure the full amount was present before storing it in her riding bag. Taking the second letter, she moved over to the fireplace, milling about her space to prepare herself a much-needed cup of tea. As she continued on with her task, she noticed this letter was from Robert, her Palace and Cittadina informant. A grin spread across her face as she ripped into the envelope, eager to read his words.

My Dear Maiden,

I hope all is well in your life. The palace is abuzz preparing for the arrival of the nobles for the summer months. I have recently acquired a new job for you to look at, in the hopes you will be visiting the area soon. I received a letter from someone looking to remove an abusive husband, although they claim to be hiring you for a friend. I have included the original correspondence, detailing the area of the palace where they wish to meet you. I have done some research and discovered the area is occupied by the Royal Family and other nobles, although I was not able to discover the exact occupant of the window.

I know you are wary of working for nobles. However, my opinion is that this job is worth looking into. This person is willing to risk much by consorting with you right under the prying eyes of the nobles. I beg you, Maiden, please look over the attached letter and inform me if you would like to set up a meeting with them upon your arrival. I fear this person might be as desperate as I was when I hired you. I would not be the man I am today without your willingness to work with someone close to the palace. Please consider giving this person the same courtesy you gave me.

Your humble servant,

Robert

With bulging eyes, Christiana reread the letter a second and third time and tried to process what Robert was asking her to do. It wasn't uncommon for her to travel to Cittadina, the town that housed the palace, to take on a job. But she usually hid in her cottage house outside the city to wait for nightfall. She had never taken a job that was located inside the palace itself. It was crawling with guards who would cut her down in a heartbeat, no matter her title. She had received a few requests for a palace assassination in the past, but she never found it worth the risk of exposure.

Taking a seat at the table, Christiana removed the second letter from the envelope, hoping to see what made Robert so interested in taking this job.

Dear Midnight Maiden,

I write this letter in hopes you are the person people whisper about in the shadows. I've been searching for the right assassin to complete the delicate job I have and it seems you might be the perfect fit. A vulnerable friend of mine has been forced into a dangerous situation. Her husband, a noble resident of the palace, has taken to beating her regularly. She has been enduring this pain and torture for the past year, only now bringing it to my attention. She cannot risk corresponding with you for fear her husband will find out, so I agreed to contact you on her behalf.

Maiden, I beg you, please consider taking my request seriously. I know I'm asking a lot of you, to risk yourself and your livelihood by sneaking into such a heavily-guarded place. If I felt there was a better way to save her life, I would do everything in my power to do so, but each time I look for a solution I find a dead-ended road. I fear if I do not act quickly, her husband will take a beating too far one night. I would never be able to forgive myself if I didn't do everything possible to save her, even if hiring an assassin is the only way to do it.

He resides inside the palace year-round, which I know can make an assassination attempt difficult. However, I'm also a resident of the palace, and will be at your full disposal to help you through the difficulty of sneaking in and out. If you are willing to meet with me, you can find my residence through the highest windows along the northwest wall. Please write me back with a date and time to meet, where I can further prove my case to you. I have included a secondary address to send any correspondence to. I hope to hear from you soon.

Sincerely,

The letter intrigued Christiana. This person was indeed willing to risk a lot. If anyone discovered what they were doing, they would be arrested for attempted murder and treason. She stared down at the letter, reading the words once more as she finished the last of her tea, her mind trying to decipher who would force someone to not only consort in illegal activities, but risk exposure so close to the Royal Family.

In the end, it couldn't hurt for her to have one meeting with this mystery person. Marek had been pushing her to go outside her comfort zone recently, claiming her skills would stop advancing if she chose to stay complacent. Maybe he was right and she needed to finally take a risk, a controlled one at least.

Grabbing a fresh piece of parchment and some ink, Christiana began writing a letter to Robert, a surge of adrenaline coursing through her body as she scratched her quill against the rough page. Wrapping the package to Robert along with the other letters, Christiana placed them outside her door for the postmaster to pick up later that day. After a few hours of work, she mounted her horse and began her journey back home to reality.

Chapter Three

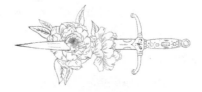

"I PROMISE, THIS IS WHAT MANY OF THE NOBLE** women have asked to commission for their time at court," the dressmaker said to Christiana and Maria. The two ladies found themselves in Christiana's favorite dress shop that day, sipping on rose tea and eating bite-sized pastries as they surveyed a procession of dresses. Christiana knew over the summer she would be invited to multiple banquets and private dinners with different nobles and their families. Although she had appropriate day dresses and a few that would be acceptable for luncheons and parties, she owned nothing quite fancy enough for the lavish events at the palace.

"I believe you, Lauren, but it is too ... outlandish for my personal taste," Christiana remarked as she stared at the bold pink dress the young seamstress had pulled out. Although she loved the delicate cap sleeve and full billowing skirt, the bodice made her nervous. The plunging neckline matched well with the brash color, allowing the young women of court to flirt their way into a rich marriage.

"But many women your age love this design," Lauren urged.

"But most of the women you are sending to court in these dresses are being paraded in front of single and rich noblemen for marriage. I, however, will be attending as the head of one of the strongest households in the country ... and one of only three women to hold such a title. I think that calls for my style to be a touch more dignified."

"Of course, My Lady." Eyes downcast, Lauren scurried back to the racks of sample dresses in search of a better option.

"It wasn't that terrible, Christiana," her mother said from her perch on an elegant, silver satin chair. Sunlight streamed in from the storefront windows, painting the sitting area in the center of the showroom. The cream-colored walls were lined with racks of dresses ranging in every known color, from the soft lavender of a freshly plucked flower to the deepest black of a starless sky.

"No, it wasn't." Christiana helped herself to another serving of tea. "But my reason for attending the palace isn't for the sole purpose of finding a husband."

"Whatever you say, dear." Her mother shook her head and attempted to stifle a giggle.

"How about this, Marchioness?" Lauren returned, presenting another option for Christiana's approval. She held up a deep burgundy dress that took Christiana's breath away. Unlike the first, the color of this matched her personality and needs perfectly, rich but understated. The tight bodice met the full, satin skirt right below the hips and the square neckline cut low enough to be amorous but not ostentatious. This dress was perfect, dignified and grand yet still stunning and flirty.

A smile spread across Christiana's face. "Now *that* is breathtaking!"

"Really?" Lauren's fingers tightened around the padded hanger.

"Of course!" Christiana walked over, running her hands along the fabric, the silky finish soft against her fingertips. "It's exactly what I'm looking for."

"I have a few similar dress designs to this one." Lauren scurried through the different displays, loading her arms with plumes of chiffon, taffeta, and brocade. "They have a few subtle differences, but just as dignified."

"Sounds perfect. I'll take seven gowns all in different colors and patterns. Keep them in deeper tones similar to this one."

"Perhaps you should get one or two of them in a lighter color, Ana," her mother suggested. "You never know what occasion will call for it. Besides, it will be summer. There will be a few days you will be thanking me when you aren't boiling in the heat."

"Fine," Christiana huffed. "Two dresses in lighter tones. Just two."

"Yes, My Lady. Let me get a fitting room all set for you and I can take your measurements." Lauren strode away, an extra bounce in her step as she disappeared into the back room. Christiana sat down in the plush chair next to her mother, closing her eyes and taking in a deep breath to cleanse herself.

"How are you doing, sweetheart?" Maria asked.

"Overwhelmed, honestly. Getting my affairs in order so quickly is exhausting." Not to mention the possible task of a dangerous and potentially identity-revealing client she had agreed to meet with.

"Have you thought about the other matter the King is going to want to discuss with you?"

"I've been ignoring it." The more she thought about it, the more her blood boiled at the idea of her expectation this summer. She had never been opposed to the idea of marriage, even with her parents' destructive one as her only example. The thought of having a constant companion was lovely, someone who would treat her as an equal and support her through hardships and trying times. Unfortunately, many noble men would expect her to submit to them, even with her strong title backing her up.

"I've been considering some of the potential gentlemen they might try to throw your way," Maria teased.

"How do you even know who will be in the castle this summer?"

"I may not attend court anymore, young lady, but I still have friends there. When they heard you were going to arrive in a few weeks, they shared some gossip they thought you might find useful."

"Such as?" Christiana asked half-heartedly as she examined a bundle of fabric swatches sitting on the table next to her.

"Well it seems some of the unmatched gentlemen around your age have already arrived at the palace. A few of them you might even know. Theodore, Earl of Banshyl, Nicholas, Earl of Stroisia, and William, Baron of Tagri," Maria suggested.

"The names sound familiar of course, but I barely remember them." Christiana sighed, throwing the swatches back down on the table so she could rub the tension out of her temples.

"Rowan, Marquess of Banshyl, is already there as well," Maria added with a smile. Rowan was Christiana's equal in title, although he didn't control as much land as she did. But since coming into his title two and a half years ago, Christiana heard reports he was thriving. She hadn't seen him in eight years, but she remembered his passion for helping people was almost equal to hers. She was intrigued by the prospect of spending time with him.

"I see," she answered, trying to hide the smile forming across her lips.

"I thought that would bring some kind of reaction," her mother teased. "There is one more you might want to prepare yourself for."

"Who is that?"

"Edgar will be arriving at the palace a few days before you do," Maria admitted.

"Oh goodness," Christiana groaned, a true headache panging behind her eyes. Duke Edgar Castriello of Tagri was one of the few nobles Christiana had dealt with since her reign as Marchioness began. "He's going to attempt to sweet talk the King into having some of his lands returned to him, I wager."

"Possibly. Luckily, you have legally binding contracts and land titles even the King cannot dispute. Be on your guard, but he is barely a match for someone as strong as you."

"Thank you, Mother," Christiana smiled.

"Are you ready, My Lady?" Lauren asked as she returned to the front room. "I have a fitting room all ready for you." Forcing herself back to the present, Christiana followed to continue the preparations for her palace visit.

***

"There you go, My Lady," Natalia said as she placed the leather riding gloves into Christiana's hands. Although she would be riding in a carriage for the long journey to the palace, she wanted to stay as comfortable as possible, opting for a riding outfit instead of a lighter day dress. Riding outfits were the only appropriate way for a woman to wear a pair of pants, allowing her to settle more comfortably even inside the carriage. Her outfit was a deep navy jacket tightly corseted along the torso before flaring out behind her to the floor. Underneath, she wore a pair of black riding pants and riding boots. It was fashionable, mimicking the look of a proper dress, while also being functional to make riding a horse easier for a woman. Christiana's mentor had fashioned her disguise in a similar style.

"Thank you, Natalia." Christiana squeezed the petite woman's hands. "Can you please make sure the carriage is ready for us? I want to check on one more thing."

"Of course, My Lady." She gave Christiana's shoulder a gentle pat before turning to leave. Christiana let out a sigh, delighted at least one familiar face would be coming with her to the palace. Taking one final look around her suite, Christiana made her way to the other side of the house, to her sister's bedroom.

When her father was still alive, Christiana used to reside in this wing as well, right across the hall. Although they had a ten-year age difference, she had always been fiercely protective of her little sister. After their father's death, it was only proper for Christiana to move out of her childhood bedroom and into the master suite since she was the new head of the household. She may have only been eighteen, but she stopped being a child the day she inherited the title.

Isabelle hadn't taken her move so well at first. When she was young and scared of a storm, she used to run into Christiana's suite and hide in bed with her. She smiled at the memory of her little sister huddled in the giant bed big enough for three people. As the years passed, Isabelle grew strong enough to stay in her own room when she was frightened, but it didn't stop Christiana from protecting her as much as she could.

Christiana let herself into her sister's oversized bedroom, the dying embers from her ivory, stone fireplace the only source of light. The young girl slept peacefully, her even breaths blowing a piece of blonde hair off her face as she snuggled against one of the many blush-colored pillows surrounding her. The sun was barely rising above the horizon, but Christiana couldn't leave without one final goodbye from her baby sister. Sitting on the edge of the bed, she nudged Isabelle awake.

"Hi Belle," she whispered with a smile. "I'm about to leave."

"Please let me come with you," Isabelle begged, still half-asleep. Christiana was convinced this little girl was made up completely of dreams. All she wanted was to come up with new adventures she would one day experience.

"I'm sorry Belle, the invitation was for me. But I'm sure you will be able to visit for a few days over the summer."

"Really?" Eyes widening, Isabelle bounced under the covers at the suggestion, rattling the gauzy canopy hanging above them.

"I can't promise anything, but I'm sure the King might be kind enough to let you and Mother come for a bit, if I make a good enough impression," Christiana joked.

"Well, then make a wonderful impression! For my sake." Isabelle smiled, crawling over to wrap herself into her sister's arms.

Pulling Isabelle close, Christiana stroked her bed-tousled hair from scalp to neck. "Go back to bed, Belle. I'll start writing you letters as soon as I arrive at the palace."

"With as many details as possible?"

"As many as I can fit," she promised. Placing one final kiss on her sister's flushed cheek, Christiana tucked her back under the protective covers. As she listened to Isabelle's breathing begin to slowly even out, warmth spread through her.

She left the room and headed out to join her caravan to the palace.

Chapter Four

THE SUNLIGHT FILTERED THROUGH THE FLOOR-TO
-ceiling hallway windows as Christiana made her way to
the palace throne room. Each step she took felt like
walking back in time to her last visit, the summer before her father's
death and her ultimate rise to power. So much had changed—her life, her
passions. But one thing would remain the same: the secrets she would
have to hide from everyone around her. So many people she used to care
for that she would be forced to lie to. Just as her father had made her do
so long ago.

As per tradition of the summer months, the King and Queen were
hosting a reception for all of the visiting nobles, welcoming them to the
palace. Christiana walked through the expansive hallways, taking in the
familiar scent of the freshly cut flowers that decorated every surface. So
much looked the same—the high ceilings and gold-painted pillars
bringing a lustrous glow to every inch of the space—but something was
different for Christiana this time. Instead of feeling like she was

swallowed by the grandeur, she walked through the expanse with her head held high and shoulders pulled back, commanding the space this time. Her heels clicked on the marble floor, her pace slowing as the sounds of the throne room reception drifted to her.

Rubbing her hand up and down her forearm, Christiana tried to calm her rapid heartbeat as she approached the doorway. The room was filled with people, nobles congregating in groups, their laughter drowning out the string quartet playing quietly in the corner. The excitement was palpable as people reunited for a favorite time of year. Christiana took a glass of wine from a waiter's outstretched hand before making her first lap around the room.

Her head was spinning as she took in her surroundings. Everyone was dressed in their finest day wear, women wearing billowing dresses with modest hairstyles and men sporting fine-patterned doublets with crisp linen shirts. So many people were crowded into the space, but Christiana only recognized a few of them. The King and Queen were the easiest to spot, as they sat on the raised dais housing their large, onyx thrones, overlooking the entire space. A few nobles stood with them, laughing and mingling. Christiana's heart dropped as she saw the young lady standing next to the queen, her curly dark hair and russet eyes unmistakable. Princess Dorina was a vision with her tall posture, showing her rightful place in the chaotic space.

Christiana hoped they would have time to talk this afternoon. They had been close friends growing up, and people always laughed at how they barely left each other's side during the summer. But as time went on and her father changed, Christiana was forced to leave Dorina behind, weakening that strong bond. Dorina was one of the few people she was excited to see again. Hopefully, their reunion would go smoothly.

Christiana began her obligation of socializing with different nobles who approached. Most conversations stayed relatively tame; small talk about the excitement of the next few months. As she said goodbye to a particularly dry pair of Barons, Christiana finally saw one other person she knew she would recognize—but unlike Dorina, this man was an unwelcome part of her summer. The sound of his deep, guttural laugh rang in her ears as she turned to see Duke Edgar casually talking with a few young ladies of the court. Her stomach churned at the mere sight of him, his willowy build and smirking face somehow charming the ladies who giggled with him.

Her heart pounded as she turned in the opposite direction, finding a table to place her drink on in hopes of finding a moment of peace. She pulled in a few breaths through her nose, allowing the cleanse to rush through her body. She sipped at her wine, the burning liquid assisting her with the sense of calm she craved in the moment.

"All alone?" A voice behind Christiana pulled her from her momentary daze. "Or hiding?"

Turning, she came face to face with another childhood friend. An involuntary smile spread across her lips. "Rowan. It's so wonderful to see you."

"And it's always wonderful to see you." He gracefully lifted her hand to his lips, dropping his own glass of wine on the table next to hers. "You have certainly grown since our time in the summer lecture halls."

"Time moves on and people change." Christiana smiled, taking in how much Rowan had matured himself. He still had the same chestnut hair cropped on the sides with wavy strands pulled back from his tanned face. However, his rounded features had chiseled out, defined with a new hint of the years that had passed. His shoulders were relaxed, his emerald eyes glowing as he looked down at her.

"You never answered. Hiding or alone?"

"Hiding. From him." Christiana gestured toward the display of arrogance Edgar was putting on.

"Ah," Rowan sighed, straightening the collar of his sage doublet, the delicate swirled pattern embroidered with gold thread slipping under his fingers. "Understandable. Most people tend to avoid him at these things, to be fair."

"They don't seem to be," she scoffed, her gaze lingering on Edgar's companions—one twirling her auburn locks between her fingers while her friend played with a ribbon secured to the bodice of her salmon dress.

"Well, anyone with common sense. Give it a few years and all three of those ladies will be running for the hills when he approaches." Rowan laughed, his eyes creasing. "When did you arrive?"

"Last night. It took a bit of time to arrange everything." Her caravan had travelled all day, arriving in the early evening to the palace. She was lucky to slip inside without any fanfare and spend the night in her new apartment, organizing things the way she liked. "And you?" She picked up her glass once again, settling into the flow of conversation.

"A while ago." Rowan smirked, picking up his glass for another sip as well.

"Oh?"

"I live here now. Zander offered me residence once I gained my title."

"I see." A thick lump formed in her throat as she struggled to swallow a sip of wine. "And where is the Prince?"

"Away on crown business. His father sent him off a few days ago to check on some things in Stroisia. But he should be back in a few days."

"Ah." Christiana's gaze wandered to the servants milling with freshly filled trays of appetizers while nobles picked at them as they passed by.

"My company isn't enough for you?" he teased, inclining as if he was having trouble hearing her words. She turned herself back toward him, shoulders leaning into his lean build.

"Now, I never said that." She smiled. Her cheeks warmed at his closeness, his infectious laughter causing hers to escape her lips. She was surprised by how comfortable she felt in Rowan's presence, the years apart not wearing on the friendship they once had.

"My Lady?" A young servant appeared beside them. "The King and Queen wish to speak to you for a moment."

"Oh." Christiana's hands bunched into the folds of her slate-gray chiffon dress. This was to be her first time with the Royal Family since gaining her title; her stomach knotted up at the prospect of leaving the comforting confines of her conversation with Rowan.

"You'll be fine." He lightly touched her hand, his eyes encouraging her to stand taller. "But you don't want to keep them waiting."

With a curtsy, Christiana walked away toward the Royal Family for her first formal introduction. She felt the pressure of their gaze with every step; King Lucian's cornflower-blue eyes followed her up the dais, his broad shoulders pulled back. He wore a simple circlet gold crown studded with diamonds, the jewels glittering on his golden-brown curls. His hand clasped Queen Penelope's, her warm brown eyes brightening as she smiled at Christiana. Her black hair pulled to the side, curls cascading down her shoulder, contrasting with the sky-blue brocade of her dress. As Christiana neared, her eyes caught Dorina's, a pang of guilt settling in her stomach as she noticed her delicate eyes were downcast, wide smile faltering.

She dropped into a deep curtsy when she arrived, the stares of the three weighing her shoulders down. She waited; the moments passed as if time stood still.

"Welcome back to our court, Marchioness. You have been missed in our home and we are forever grateful you accepted our invitation to stay with us this summer season," the King proclaimed warmly, allowing Christiana to finally let out a deep breath she'd been holding.

"Thank you, Your Majesty, I'm not worthy of such kindness." She pulled herself up to stand tall in front of her King and Queen. Once again, a servant appeared next to her, placing a new glass of wine in her hand to enjoy with the Royals.

"Nonsense," the King said. "You have done so much for Tagri and even the territories you do not live in. We should be thanking you for all you and your father did throughout the years."

"I may have been young when I became the Marchioness, but I was not about to let that stop me from doing right by the people of Tagri," Christiana responded with a sly smile, her tense fingers loosening.

"You seemed so prepared for it, especially after your father's untimely death."

"He taught me well." She grimaced. "He wanted to make sure I was ready for the task at any age."

"Well, bravo to him," King Lucian saluted as he raised his goblet. The rest of his family joined in, and with the faint taste of disgust, Christiana raised her glass.

"We would love for you to join us and a few other nobles at dinner the day after tomorrow," Queen Penelope offered. "The Prince will be back, and we want to sit down with some of our friends in a more intimate setting."

"Thank you, Your Majesties." She tried to keep her voice level, her spine straight. She knew this invitation wasn't given to just anyone, only to the nobles the King and Queen felt were worth more of their time. It was an invitation her father received every year they attended court and it was one she had been determined to receive today. "That is most generous of you."

"It's also the perfect place for you to begin getting to know the other nobles. You have worked hard these past five years building up your landholdings, but now we think it might be time for you to rejoin society," King Lucian said, a hint of a laugh in his voice. Christiana's stomach squirmed at his words, her spine stiffening. The last thing she wanted to do was to fail at meeting the King and Queen's expectations of her, but she didn't want to put herself in the same position her mother had been in—a forced marriage to a man she barely knew.

"I'm excited to meet all of them as well," she replied, trying her best to sound giddy at the idea.

"I'm sorry to interrupt your privacy, Your Majesties." A tall, slender man appeared to the King's right, his dark eyes surveilling the room.

"Nonsense, Julian." The King beckoned him closer. "Marchioness, may I introduce you to Chancellor Julian Marlow, my right-hand man."

"My Lady," Julian greeted her with a deep bow. "It is an honor to finally meet you."

"You as well, Chancellor," she responded with a slight nod. Chancellor Julian had held his position for as long as Christiana could remember, but she never had the opportunity to meet him growing up. He was certainly too busy to deal with a small child causing a scene.

With a nod, Julian continued, "I didn't mean to interrupt your conversation, but I had a few things I wished to discuss with His Majesty."

"Of course, of course. I'm so sorry to cut this time short, Marchioness, but we'll find plenty of time to talk more as the summer continues. Dorina, my dove, why don't you go with Christiana and help introduce her to more of the nobles?" the King suggested, although by the urgent look in his eye, it was more a demand than a request.

"Of course, Father," Dorina replied, her hand tightening around her goblet as she descended the dais, Christiana following right behind.

"Thank you, Princess, that is kind of you," Christiana said, a chill running up her spine as they made their way through the crowd together.

"My pleasure, Marchioness." Dorina fiddled with the smooth fabric of her dress before looking back at Christiana. "Are you ready to rejoin society?"

Christiana hesitated, her fingers twirling the stem of her glass. "Actually, I am a bit overwhelmed and tired from my journey. Maybe it would be best if I went back to my apartment."

"Oh." Dorina's face fell.

"But..." Christiana reached out. "I'm not exactly sure how to get back. Would you be able to escort me?"

Dorina bit her lip gently, her gaze wandering over Christiana. "Of course. I'd be happy to."

The two ladies finished the final sips of their drinks, depositing the empty glasses on a nearby table before walking out the throne room doors.

Chapter Five

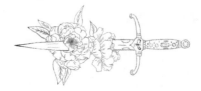

THE TWO GIRLS SLOWLY MADE THEIR WAY BACK to the noble apartment wing. Although she still recognized every part of the palace from the past, Christiana had used the excuse she was lost to try and get Dorina alone. Dorina kept her gaze straight ahead, her hands were twisted together, fingers tugging at the tips of her nails.

"I was excited to see you upon my return," Christiana admitted, warmth spreading through her chest at the memory of all the beautiful times the two of them shared growing up.

"Really?" Dorina halted them in a quiet corner of the mostly-abandoned hallway, her dull gaze bearing into Christiana.

"Of course."

"Then why did you stop writing to me?"

Christiana's balance faltered, forcing her to take a few steps away from Dorina. She knew it was a fair question, one she had hoped would never be asked. After her last summer at the palace, she had cut off all communications with the Royal Children. Her father was a paranoid man and kept a constant watch on all mail that was delivered to their household. Even if she had been lucky enough to sneak a letter out of the house, any reply would have been sent directly to him. Christiana shuddered thinking about what kind of punishment he would have given her if he had caught her.

Pulling in a deep breath, she explained, "Well, my father heavily discouraged it. He wanted me to keep all my focus on learning how to run Tagri and the estates that came with it. After his passing, I became so overwhelmed." She wanted to forgo the lies and explain everything, but she clamped the truth down on her tongue, forcing different words past her lips. "I thought he prepared me well, but I don't think you can ever be prepared for the amount of work that goes into leading a territory."

"I'm sure that's true." Dorina pulled her arms tightly across her chest. "Not that I would understand."

"What do you mean?" Christiana tugged on Dorina's arm as she tried to walk away, stopping her in her tracks. The long, dark stone hall, lined with half a dozen towering mahogany doors, was quiet as they stood there together.

"It's nothing." Dorina leaned herself next to a large tapestry depicting a Virian battle fought long ago. "We just reunited; I probably shouldn't be talking about such depressing things."

"Dorina, we aren't children any longer." Christiana lightly squeezed the Princess's tense shoulder. "If you're having a problem, I hope you know you can come to me about it."

"I know. At least, I felt that way when we were younger," Dorina said. Christiana's gaze fell to the floor, her jaw twitching. "But I also know you might not have time for my petty problems."

"Dorina, please, I want your friendship back. That means being there for you no matter what. If you need someone to open up to, I'm here," Christiana said with sincerity. Marek had always taught her to push unnecessary people away, that it was the first rule of a professional killer. But being back in these hallways, with her old friend standing in front of her, she knew this was one person that was not as unnecessary as she once believed. It was easy to separate her friendship with Dorina all those years ago when they were kept apart. But now that they were reunited, she remembered why they had become so close.

"Really?" Dorina's lips twitched as if trying to break into a smile.

"Of course," Christiana said, forgetting formalities and embracing her friend. "Let's get out of the hallway."

She beckoned Dorina into her apartment rooms. They had only been there a day, but Natalia, with the help of the palace servants, had been quick to unpack all her things, bringing a sense of home to the palace already. They entered the wide common area where dozens of candles brought light into the darkening space as the sun set through the open window, the balsam scent of the palace garden pine grove wafting in. Christiana gestured for Dorina to settle into one of the plush, maroon couches circled around the dark stone fireplace. Taking a bottle of wine and two glasses from the liquor cabinet next to the dining table, Christiana joined her.

"What's happening, Dorina?" she asked, pouring generous helpings of golden liquid into the two crystal glasses and handing one off to Dorina.

"Honestly, it's probably frivolous compared to what you go through." She waved her hand in the air, taking a sip of the cooling wine.

Christiana sat next to her, leaning her arm along the back of the couch so she could face Dorina. "If it's bothering you this much, then it isn't. What is it?"

She let out a deep breath before answering, "I feel out of place sometimes. I'm the princess of this country, and I don't have any actual responsibility."

"That can't be true. Your mother does plenty for this country, why not assist her in her charity work?"

"I'll never be the queen, only the second-born princess." She looked down into her glass, her brow furrowed. "I love my brother, Christiana, and I know he's going to be an amazing king, but sometimes I'm jealous he was born with such a big purpose and I was born to be the pretty daughter who will one day become a wife."

"Well, a lot of noble girls follow that path, it's nothing to be ashamed of."

"You didn't."

"That's different. I was born into a title without the choice of becoming a lady of leisure."

"Would you? If you had the choice?" Dorina asked, although her russet eyes showed she already knew the answer.

"No," Christiana admitted. "I wouldn't. I like having my title and the responsibilities that come with it. I would never want to give this up."

"I wish I had that option." Dorina rolled her eyes, taking a large gulp of her wine to drain the glass. "The constant tea parties and judgmental women I have to deal with is enough to make a girl go mad. You're lucky this summer you'll be able to decline some of those annoying events since you'll be expected to keep up with your other responsibilities."

"Not all of them, though. So at least there will be one non-judgmental person at those parties sometimes." Christiana smiled, trying to bring some spirit back into Dorina.

"For the summer at least."

"Have you talked to your brother about this?" Christiana asked, her free hand tracing patterns into the velvet couch as she kept her gaze on the woman next to her. "I know I haven't seen him in a while, but since he will be king one day soon, maybe he would be open to giving you more responsibilities."

"Possibly. I've never asked. I'm scared of the answer I would get.

He's more open to change than our father, but I also know he respects Father's opinion above all else. If my father disapproved of me taking more responsibility, which I know he would, I'm not sure Alekzander would be as open to it, even when he does become king."

"You'll never know the answer until you ask him," Christiana urged, nudging her friend.

"I know." Dorina's shoulders drooped as she stared down at her hands.

"And if the answer is no in the end, you can start to figure out how you'll break out on your own, something I can always help with if necessary." Christiana wondered if there was a way to find a place in her own household for Dorina, maybe allowing her to oversee a part of her business or even take over responsibilities for one or two of her landholdings. She knew it wasn't traditional for a princess to have that kind of responsibility, but Christiana was the last person to care about the typical traditions for women in Viri. If holding this responsibility made Dorina happy, she would find a way to help her achieve it.

"Really?" Dorina asked with a grin.

"Of course! What are friends for?"

"Thank you, Ana." Dorina set her glass on the table before embracing her once again. "And in return, I'm more than happy to help you this summer."

"With what?" Her eyebrows stitched together as she looked at the Princess.

"Finding a husband, of course." Dorina giggled.

"Oh, please don't bring that up," Christiana groaned, flopping herself farther down onto the couch. "I try my best to ignore it."

"Sorry, but that's going to be impossible this summer if my parents have anything to say about it. I'm not sure whose marriage they are more invested in, yours or Alekzander's," Dorina admitted, taking the pitcher to refill her glass.

Christiana held hers out as well. "I'm surprised they let him wait so long. He's set to inherit the crown in his thirtieth year."

"I know, but apparently Zander negotiated a deal with my parents. He has this summer to pick his own wife without any opposition, or else they'll pick for him." Dorina took a quick sip of her wine. "Personally, I'm surprised my parents even said yes, let alone allowed him so much time. But he was determined. Plus, he's picky about women, so I'm fairly certain Father thought he wouldn't make the deadline."

"Well he doesn't have much time left, only a few months before your parents take over." Christiana leaned her elbow on the couch armrest, weaving her fingers into her curled reddish-brown locks.

"What can I say, my brother is headstrong and determined to marry someone he loves. Honestly, I don't mind, because his delay in marriage has kept my parents focused on his future spouse instead of trying their best to marry me off before he becomes king."

Christiana tilted her head. "What do you mean?"

"A princess's marriage is the decision of the reigning king and not necessarily her parents. So, if Zander gains the crown before my parents can arrange a marriage, technically he gets to choose my husband." Dorina curled her legs onto the couch, her dress spilling over the sides like a waterfall. "And he made me a promise many years ago he would give me the right to choose instead of choosing for me. So, I'm holding out hope my parents stay distracted long enough to hand that power over to him."

"Here's hoping," Christiana replied, clinking her flute to Dorina's.

"But since you're the one expected to be betrothed this summer, please let me know if there is anything I can do to help," Dorina gushed. "I also have the gossip about almost everyone here, so if you ever need advice..."

"Hold on." Christiana stopped her, ringing a bell on the table. A few seconds passed before Natalia emerged from a door off to the right of the common area, leading into Christiana's bedroom.

"Yes, My Lady?" she asked.

"Natalia, can you please inform the kitchen that the Princess will be dining with me tonight, and make sure they send up enough food for both of us?"

"Of course, My Lady, I will arrange everything," she replied with a curtsy before leaving the apartment.

"I think we have a lot more to catch up on." Christiana smiled, and they both erupted into giggles.

Chapter Six

WHEN NOBLES WANTED TO HIRE THE MAIDEN, they always wanted to meet as far away from the palace as possible.

Christiana was curious to meet the noble who felt confident enough to sneak an assassin into such a heavily-guarded location, although something about this whole situation kept gnawing at the pits of her soul. She had been struggling since the day she agreed to meet with this mystery client, wondering if she should have pushed more for a location outside of the palace. She couldn't help but wonder if this was all a trap. She tried to force those terrible thoughts away, knowing she was called for a purpose: to help a victim. That was all she needed to know, the only thing she could let herself think about as she tapped her fingers against the rough cover of her book waiting for Natalia to finish up her evening chores.

"Are you sure you do not want me to bring you anything else, My Lady?" Natalia asked, gathering up Christiana's dinner dress to take to the wash.

"No, Natalia, I promise I'm all right. I want to stay up a little longer and read."

"Of course, My Lady. Can I bring you tea to help you sleep?"

"No, I would like to be left alone for the rest of the night." Christiana smiled tightly. She needed to get Natalia out and dress as quickly as possible or she'd be late.

"Of course. Have a good night, My Lady," Natalia said with a curtsy.

After waiting a few palm-sweating minutes to make sure Natalia hadn't forgotten anything, Christiana locked her bedroom door and made her way over to her trunk. Releasing the top, she removed her favorite outfit from its hiding space. She pulled her nightgown over her head and began to lace up the bodice of her coat. With each pull of the front laces, Christiana felt more and more like herself in a foreign place. Within a few minutes, she was dressed with all her weapons secured to her body. Bringing the veil over her face, she took in one deep breath before opening her third story window and beginning her descent down the wall.

She was lucky enough to have found time this morning to take a long walk around the palace grounds. The daylight had made it easier to find a good route from her window to the one the note had described for her to sneak into. She took her time, footsteps light so she could listen for the passing guards that patrolled the area. She had watched their rotation during the afternoon, committing to memory the narrow timing she had to slip past their defenses. She eventually stood under a red and blue stained-glass window on the northwest wall, at least three levels up. With a deep breath to slow down her racing heartbeat, Christiana began her ascent.

The rocks were cool under her hands from the gentle breeze of the midnight summer air, the rough finish scratching her fingerless gloves. She moved as quickly as possible, counting down the seconds until the next round of guards were expected to patrol past this area, the window getting closer and closer with each tense pull of her tired muscles. She focused only on what was in front of her, looking for nothing more than the next place to grasp and pull herself closer. Like the note had said, the window was unlatched, and she quietly opened it to crawl inside, her stomach twisting into knots as she silently touched down on the floor.

Christiana drew her dagger from its holder in her boot and examined her new surroundings. She had landed in the sitting area of an expansive apartment. The cold stone walls were offset by the glow emitting from the grand fireplace. The room mostly consisted of a large sitting area, hunter-green couches and chairs huddled together to create a welcoming environment. Off to the side was a large mahogany desk with scrolls of parchment strewn across it, several quills, and multiple pots of dark ink. This person must have a good reason to entertain others; the well-stocked liquor cabinet with assorted brandies and liqueurs proved that.

"Thank you for coming tonight," came a voice from the entryway.

Shock rippled over Christiana as she locked gazes with the deep sapphire-blue eyes of her newest client: Prince Alekzander of Viri. She couldn't believe, after all of these years apart, this was the way they were reunited—and he wasn't even able to know.

Panic crawled up her throat, her desire to flee taking over, her fingers wrapping around the smooth hilt of her dagger before sending it sailing toward the Prince. It whirled right past him, lodging into the far wall. She never intended to hit him, but his flinch gave her enough time to dart back to the window so she could disappear.

"Please stop! Don't go yet!" he pleaded. She halted instinctively, her legs already half out of the window. Damn her noble upbringing and her habit to follow those above her; it might be the thing that got her sentenced to death. "I promise I'm not trying to trap you."

"And why should I believe you?" she spat, purposefully lowering her voice an octave. Although only her eyes were showing, she didn't want to take any risks.

"Because I need your help."

Christiana's head spun as she tried to accept what was happening. "I don't think I'm the type of assassin you're looking for." Gingerly, she stepped back onto the floor. "If you're looking to take out a political enemy, hire someone who isn't so selective with their jobs. I only work with specific clients."

"I promise you, the man I'm sending you after is an abuser, if not a murderer. I chose you because I know you'll do this for the right reason, not for the payout."

"And why should the Prince of this fine country have to worry about paying someone?"

"So, we've established you know my identity."

Christiana scoffed. "I make it a point to keep an eye on people who could have me executed." She took a few hesitant steps forward, keeping to the shadows. Although most rooms at this time of night would have been flooded with light from dozens of candles, only a few candelabras were lit, providing just enough flame to illuminate Alekzander.

"Fair enough," he sighed, finally moving away from the bedroom door into the common room. "To answer your question, I don't have to worry about money. But the woman I'm helping is nervous and I want her to feel comforted you're not just a killer."

Crossing her arms, she looked the Prince up and down. "I'm an assassin, Your Highness. If that job title doesn't scream cold-blooded killer, you need to reevaluate your choices."

"Think what you will about yourself, it matters little to me. But the job I need done is a precarious and delicate one. I need someone who is willing to put in the time and dedication to make sure this goes off perfectly. Based on my research, that makes you the perfect choice."

"So, you're not the one being abused?" she asked, her eyes following his every move as he coolly walked around his space. Her fingers tingled as she watched him pour himself a glass of water as if he were casually spending time with his old friend.

"No. An acquaintance came to me in confidence a few weeks ago and admitted her husband had been beating her. She was terrified to talk to anyone about it, but she thought she could trust me to tell the King and get him imprisoned for his deeds."

"Why come to me? Like you said, you can have your father arrest him."

"If it was only that easy." He sat down at his desk. "Unfortunately, the man I want you to take out is one of my father's closest confidants. When I tried to broach the subject, he shut me down and told me to stop listening to rumors. I love my father, he's a wonderful ruler I respect, but his relationship with this man is clouding his better judgment. The only way to save this woman's life is to take matters into my own hands and eliminate the threat he poses to her. That's where you come in."

"Well, isn't that generous of you, Your Highness. A woman comes to you in need and you're willing to risk it all and help her, even if it means hiring me to take him out."

He narrowed his eyes at her. "What's your point, Maiden?"

"I don't believe your intentions are so pure. You must have more than a kind heart to help this lady." The empowerment of her hood and veil rushed through her, emboldening her to speak the words she wouldn't dare speak if they were having this conversation in their usual titles.

"Are you accusing me of something? If so, spit it out, we don't have the time to play coy with each other."

She took a few steps toward his desk, unable to keep to the shadows any longer. "Is she more than an acquaintance? An infatuation, perhaps? Maybe even your lover?"

"You forget who you are talking to, Maiden." His nostrils flared as he ran his fingers through his already-tousled dirty blond hair. "Don't forget, I'm the one who's hiring you, not the other way around."

"And you forget, Your Highness, I don't let just anyone hire me. I'm not scared to speak my mind if I believe your intentions are anything less than honorable. Now answer my question."

"No," he seethed. "She's not my lover or any type of romantic tryst. But when she came to me, desperate and scared for her life, the last thing I was going to do was push her away. I feared she would take her own life if I did."

"I see."

The Prince leaned forward in his chair. "Make no mistake, Maiden, the man I'm sending you after was never my favorite person. I find him to be manipulative and posturing. Now that I know what he does to his wife, it makes me want to rip his head off myself."

Christiana evaluated the man before her. It had been over five years since she last saw the Prince, but she had recognized him the minute he entered the room. His features had sharpened into a more regal quality, and she could feel his anger from this terrible situation radiating off of him like a heat wave. She wanted to believe him, if not for the obvious passion he had against this man, then because she had a level of trust for him already. But she wasn't the Marchioness of Tagri right now, she was the notorious assassin Midnight Maiden. As Marek had taught her so many years ago, emotions had no place in their line of work. Forgetting they existed was the only way to survive. "Who's the mark?"

"Now, see, this is where it starts to get complicated."

"You mean the Prince of Viri hiring me isn't the complicated part?"

"Unfortunately, no. The man I want you to take out is named Julian Marlow. I'm assuming you know the name."

"You mean the Chancellor? Yes, I might have heard about him," she sneered. Of all the people to send her after, all the nobles that could have been marked for death, he had to choose one of the most dangerous. It was widely known that Chancellor Marlow was a well-respected but cautious man. "Do you even know what you're asking? Julian Marlow is a damned war hero. He's been the king's right-hand man for nearly twenty years, and you expect me to waltz up and kill him?"

She ground her teeth, silently cursing her luck. Marlow had never been the typical choice for Chancellor, as the position was usually filled by a higher house of the court. But his military prowess had caught the King's attention early on in his reign, and they had been working together ever since. Christiana's palms began to sweat thinking about the possibility of crossing blades with that man. And now, the Prince wanted her to try and kill him.

"Where is the proof what his wife said is true?"

"I figured it would come to this." He picked up two scrolls of parchment. "These are the death certificates and reports from Marlow's last two marriages. Both women died at a young age of the same cause— a brain bleed." He held out the papers for Christiana to take. Not willing to risk getting too close, she gestured for him to place them on the table in the sitting area. Once he stepped away, she retrieved them and pored carefully over the information.

"It's quite a coincidence they both died of something so uncommon for women their age," she remarked. Marlow's first wife was apparently thrown off her horse and collapsed two weeks later from the brain bleed. His second wife hit her head on the banister when she lost her balance, but didn't die for another three weeks. "Is it common to survive a brain bleed that long? I thought death was instant."

"I'm sure you would know, Maiden." The Prince leaned against his desk, his hot gaze bearing into Christiana.

Christiana rolled her eyes. "Cut the sarcasm and answer my question."

"According to a doctor I inquired with, the likelihood of the women surviving so long after their accidents was slim if the bleed was severe enough to cause death. My theory is they sustained a little damage during their accidents, but their ultimate death was caused by a beating from Marlow." Christiana's fingers tightened around the papers, her nostrils flaring. "He was with both of them when they collapsed and died. I don't have any physical proof, but my theory would match with the timeline of their deaths."

"It certainly does." She scanned the autopsies again. All the words made sense, matching up perfectly with Alekzander's theory. The facts were in front of her, begging her to accept the job. But something held her back. Maybe it was her fear of being caught, or the sinking in her stomach telling her to run away. Or maybe it was the idea of killing for her childhood friend that made her lower the parchment, her suspicious gaze locking with the Prince's.

He crossed his arms. "You still don't believe me?"

"Honestly, I don't know." Christiana threw the pages back on the table, taking a few steps back into shadowed comfort. "I certainly find it odd both of his wives died so similarly. Your theory makes sense based on the accusations against him and the cause of death. However, this isn't proof enough to make me take the job."

"What will, then?" He threw his hands up. "Whatever it is, I'll try my best to get it for you."

"That's easy." Christiana folded her arms and leaned against the wall, trying to relax even as nerves fizzed along her body. "I want to meet her."

His brow furrowed. "Who? Eliza?"

"If that's the Chancellor's wife, then yes, Eliza. If I'm going to believe in this case, I need to hear about it from the victim and no one else. When she is able to convince me, then you have an assassin."

"She's not the easiest to get alone." His fingers rubbed gentle circles against his temples, gaze lowered to the floor as seconds passed. "Marlow makes sure she is watched as often as he can."

"If I was able to sneak into your apartment without getting caught, I think I can figure out how to get to her." Christiana knew this was the only way to make herself at ease over this entire job. It was risky, and her throat dried at the thought of endangering Eliza if indeed Alekzander's suspicions were true, but it was the only way to settle her mind and soul over the idea of killing Chancellor Marlow. "All you need to do is tell me the date and location, and I can take care of the rest. Until then, I'll do some research on my end, but I won't agree to take the job."

"Fine," he surrendered. "Anything else I can do to convince you to take on the case?"

"Just one. I need some kind of reassurance you aren't going to turn me in. Collateral of some kind, if you will."

"Anything specific in mind?" he asked.

Christiana smirked behind her mask. "A letter stating your intent of hiring me, accompanied with both your signature and the Royal Crest."

He frowned, brows creasing together. "That's a bold request, Maiden. We don't make a habit of handing out our crest on a whim."

"I may not know you well, Your Highness," she lied, "but I don't think Eliza is the mere acquaintance you're making her out to be. You may be a kind-hearted royal, but I cannot imagine you would go to the lengths of hiring me for any subject." His posture became more rigid as she continued. "Which means you have a deeper connection with her, even if it isn't a romantic one. Seems to me you're willing to go to great lengths to ensure her safety. Which means I have every right to ensure mine in the process."

Moments passed before he muttered, "There is nothing else you could think of?"

"This is a deal breaker, Your Highness. Either give me a letter of intent now or I leave tonight and never return. Your choice," she replied, staring him down. He stared back at her, his face twisted as the moments passed.

Finally, his gaze dropped, a deep sigh releasing from his lips. "Very well, Maiden."

Returning to his desk, he scribbled out his intentions, describing his reasons for hiring her and the specific job he requested, before signing it with his lavish signature. He finished by pouring a stream of melted wax next to his name and pressing his crest deep into the paper. Once the ink had dried and wax hardened, he folded the paper and placed it on the table as he had before. Christiana retrieved the note and secured it in her boot for safekeeping until she could stash it in her trunk.

"Thank you, Your Highness. I look forward to seeing your next letter. Let me know when Eliza is ready to talk to me." With an overly flourished curtsy, Christiana exited through the open window.

Chapter Seven

THE MARCHIONESS SAT AT HER VANITY TABLE while Natalia continued to poke tiny pins into her hair, the deep ruby gems glittering in the candlelight as they held each meticulously-arranged curl in place. Unlike grand balls, this dinner would be held in the formal dining room. This was not an excuse to celebrate lavishly, but a way for the King and Queen to discuss important matters with their most trusted nobles.

Christiana wished she could absorb this moment as a triumphant one; her chest should be swelling with pride at the thought of being chosen to attend such an intimate gathering. But she could barely control her shaking hands as she dabbed on powder, the loose dust mattifying the sheen of sweat forming on her tense forehead. She tried her best to focus on the task at hand, carefully choosing each product to make herself perfect for such an important night.

"All set," Natalia announced, placing the final curl into the elegant updo she had created, taming Christiana's wave of deep auburn hair in a secured bun above her neck. "Are you nervous, My Lady?"

Christiana's eyes flew open, staring at her lady's maid in the mirror. "Why would you say that?"

"Um, because it's your first dinner with the Royals?" Natalia's jade-green eyes blinked one too many times, brow furrowed as she fumbled to grasp the pearl necklace they had picked out earlier that day. It was Christiana's favorite, the twisted braid of creamy jewels a gift from her mother the day she was officially made Marchioness of Tagri. She hoped it would bring her a needed strength tonight.

Releasing her pent-up breath, Christiana sighed. "Oh, of course."

"It's all right to be nervous, My Lady." Natalia set the heavy jewels on Christiana's décolletage and hooked the clasp at the base of her neck. "But everyone here knows exactly who you are. Your strength will carry you through." She gave her a gentle pat on the shoulder, her kind gaze still holding Christiana's in the mirror.

A weary smile spread across Christiana's lips in reply, words escaping her for a response as she dabbed on her floral perfume she concocted herself. She breathed in deeply, taking in the delicate scent of peonies and orchids, perfectly distilled to wrap her in a comforting embrace. She prayed the comfort would carry her through the entire dinner, though she knew she would need more than a pleasant aroma tonight. The thought of locking gazes with Alexzander's intoxicating blue eyes made her stomach drop.

With the last pin in place and her jewelry properly draped, Natalia helped Christiana step into the gown she had chosen to wear for the evening's events. The high-waisted dress had a beautiful black corset, decorated with a gold filigree pattern that wrapped around her until it snaked down to the ends of the long, satin sleeves. The corset met perfectly above her waist, cascading down into the billowing gold satin skirt. It made her feel gorgeous without making her the center of attention.

"You look beautiful, My Lady," Natalia exclaimed as she scurried around Christiana in a circle, her hands smoothing the skirt and making sure every inch looked impeccable. If anyone was going to make her look perfect for this evening, Christiana knew putting her trust in Natalia was always the right decision.

She examined herself in the full-length mirror, ensuring she was properly presentable for the occasion. For the most part she looked ravishing, each piece of her ensemble meticulously picked out and placed to create her best appearance. But there was one part of her that leaked her true feelings: her eyes. They sang with the fear she had battled since the moment she escaped through the window the previous night. She had spent most of the daytime in her apartment, too scared to even step one foot over the threshold and risk running into Alexzander before she was ready. Based on her rapid heartbeat, she wasn't as prepared as she hoped to be by now.

"Thank you, Natalia," she said. "I'll need one more moment alone before I depart."

"Of course, My Lady." Natalia curtsied and left the room. Christiana put one hand to her chest, the beat of her heart thumping against it like a wild animal trying to escape a cage. She closed her eyes for a moment, pulling in a deep breath through her nose and releasing it slowly through her parted lips. When her eyes fluttered open, she stared at herself one final time before walking out of her room, prepared to face the night with every last bit of her strength.

The walk to the dining room was quiet, uneventful, and too short. Christiana lingered in front of the palace dining hall, staring at the ominous, large doors before her. Then she nodded quickly to the two guards standing watch in front of them and took one final deep breath before the doors opened for her entrance.

"The Most Honorable Christiana Santinella, Marchioness of Tagri," the herald announced as Christiana swept into the room, her shoulders pulled back and her head held high. She accepted a glass of wine from a passing servant who held out a tray and admired the room around her. The high gilded ceilings were ornately decorated with hand-painted murals and the tall, thin windows let in streams of moonlight, complementing the candles set in various places around the room. The long, elaborately decorated table stood in the center, with nobles milling around the edges of the room socializing as they waited for the Royal Family to make their arrival.

Christiana took a few moments to herself, watching the mingling people laugh and enjoy each other's company. Soon, a thin, older woman approached her, already set in a curtsy when she said, "Good evening, Marchioness. It's a joy to see you back in the palace halls for the summer."

"Thank you." Christiana looked over the woman's features, her pointed nose and high cheekbones rang familiar, but the silver-blonde hair showed how long it had been since they last saw each other. But she would know that kind smile anywhere. "It's wonderful to see you again, Madeleine. I appreciate the letter you sent my mother before all this...it's good to come to these things prepared."

"I see your mother couldn't join you this summer." Madeleine straightened herself to eye level with Christiana.

"Unfortunately, no. She had to stay behind with my younger sister, Isabelle."

"Oh, of course!" Madeleine exclaimed. "My goodness, I haven't seen that little one since she was a toddler. How old is she now?"

"Thirteen." Christiana's chest swelled at the mention of her little sister. "And how is your husband, the Count?"

"He is quite well. Unfortunately, he'll not be able to join us at the palace for a few more weeks due to some issues with the farmers at our livestock farm back home. But he sent me and our oldest son along to appease the King and Queen. He knows how I love spending the summer with the Queen."

"How kind of him."

"My son William is here tonight as well." Madeleine gestured to a man hovering in the corner—although boy was a better term to use. His round, chubby face did not match the rest of his lanky body. His arms, thin as toothpicks, looked as if they would snap the minute he tried to pick up a sword. He stood there, alone, clutching a glass of wine in a death grip. It was obvious this poor soul did not do well in social situations. "Would you like to meet him? He was so eager to hear you would be attending."

Christiana blinked her eyes a few times, hoping she could formulate a gracious response. "That is kind, however..."

"However, she has other childhood friends to catch up with as well, Countess," said a deep voice from behind Christiana.

"My Lord." Madeleine curtsied to the newcomer.

"Rowan." Christiana turned to face him, an involuntary smile spreading across her face. "It's so wonderful to see you again."

"And it's always wonderful to see you." He gracefully lifted her hand to his lips, giving her a quick wink before releasing it.

"Thank you for the offer, Madeleine, but I promised Rowan a bit of my time tonight, as our last conversation was cut short. Maybe some other time?" Christiana said with a dazzling smile.

"I'll hold you to that." Madeleine grinned, turning to leave the pair alone.

"Thank you." Christiana sighed in relief the moment she was gone.

"I saw the panicked look and decided I had to intervene," Rowan joked as he tucked her hand in the crook of his arm. They strolled around the room, making their way to a table holding trays of cheese and fresh fruit.

"She's a friend of my mother's. I thought she would be a safe person to talk to tonight, but apparently she had a different reason for approaching me than I thought."

"Of course, the reason being attempting to get her son to marry the most eligible woman in court." He smirked.

"I would hardly call myself the most eligible."

"Take a look around this room." Rowan gestured with his other hand. "How many other single women do you see?" She peered around and slowly realized how right he was. Although there were plenty of women in the room with them, they were either older, widowed, or happily wrapped around their newly-anointed husband. Besides the Princess, Christiana would be the only single woman attending this lovely dinner party.

"Wonderful." Her cheeks flushed, and she tried to calm the jittering tingles spreading through her body with a large sip of wine.

Rowan laughed. "Don't worry, I've taken some precautionary steps to assist you. Lucky for you, my best friend happens to be the Prince. So, I may have asked him to pull a few strings to make sure you would be seated next to me tonight."

"It seems I had nothing to worry about." A coy smile spread across her face as tension released from her shoulders. Some women might be turned off by the thought of a man trying so hard for her attention, but Christiana chose not to look at it that way. Instead she looked back at her old friend, someone she used to know fairly well, and saw a man who wanted to get to know her again. She leaned in closer to him.

"Well, we haven't seen each other in so long, and I have to admit I was saddened when our conversation was cut short the other day. I've heard exceptional tales of the young marchioness who took over her father's already-impressive title and helped it flourish. I needed to make sure the rumors were true."

She turned her head off to the side, trying her best to conceal her growing smirk. "I hope I can prove them right."

"So far, you certainly have, Ana," he replied, addressing her with her childhood nickname as if they had never been apart. His kind smile, enamored gaze, and sweet words were exactly what Christiana needed at that moment.

The bellow of the herald interrupted them. "His Grace Edgar Castriello, Duke of Tagri."

Christiana groaned under her breath as the preening Duke strutted into the room like the king himself. He oozed arrogance, just like the last time she saw him.

Rowan whispered to her, sarcasm lacing his words, "Wonderful, he's coming this way."

"Rowan, it's great to see you!" Edgar exclaimed.

"You too, Your Grace." Rowan bowed to the petty man. Following proper protocol, Christiana bit her cheek and slowly lowered herself into an appropriate curtsy. Even though she held most of the wealth from the duchy, tradition dictated her actions.

"Christiana, don't you radiate through this room," Edgar said with a charming smile.

"Thank you, Your Grace, you're too kind." She straightened and looked him in the eye.

"Nonsense, no woman here can hold a candle to your beauty." He lifted her hand and kissed it. Unlike Rowan's gentle and appropriate kiss, Edgar's rough lips lingered too long for Christiana's comfort.

"Just wait until the Princess and Queen arrive, then no one will be paying attention to me," she said, trying to make light of the situation. Edgar was staring at her with such intensity, she was trying her hardest to appear at ease.

"Ladies and gentlemen of the Court," the Herald interrupted again, "may I present to you the Royal Family: Their Majesties King Lucian and Queen Penelope of Viri, and their Highnesses Prince Alekzander and Princess Dorina."

The Royal Family entered together, the King and Queen in the center with their children flanking each side. Christiana could not stop herself from looking at Alekzander. He stood tall next to his father, confidently surveying the room. His dark blond hair was perfectly slicked back to keep it out of his beautiful, cerulean eyes. She had been so surprised last night, she hadn't taken the time to look at how much he had changed since they last saw each other. He was no longer a boy playing prince, he was a strong man ready to take on the title of King. Her trembling fingers played with her necklace as his eyes found hers, his irises lighting up at the sight of her. Christiana tried her best to keep her muscles loose, reminding herself he didn't know the truth.

"Welcome everyone," King Lucian greeted the room with a toast, a cup of wine already in his hand. "Thank you for joining us, not only tonight, but for the summer season. I look forward to spending this time together learning about the welfare of our country through your eyes and catching up with old friends!" He took a delicate sip. Everyone in the room followed suit. "Please find your seats around the table. I'm sure you are all famished from your long journeys over the past few days."

"May I escort you to your seat, My Lady?" Rowan asked Christiana, swooping in before Edgar could take the chance to ask her.

"How kind, thank you," she said with a smile. They made their way over to one end of the table, guided by an encouraging wave from Dorina as she sat down at the opposite end next to her mother. Rowan wasn't joking when he said he had arranged for the two to sit next to each other; what he neglected to mention was that they would be directly next to the King and right across from Alekzander. Even worse, as Christiana sat down in her seat, she noticed Edgar was casually sitting to her left. Although the Royal Family had agreed to put Rowan next to Christiana, it seems they couldn't stop themselves from putting another "eligible" bachelor to her other side.

As the first course of ginger turmeric carrot soup was served, Christiana sat silently, taking in the conversation. Every once in a while, she felt the Prince's hot gaze linger on her, and she clutched her soup spoon so tightly her knuckles whitened. She kept replaying last night's events in her head. Though she had tried her best to make herself unrecognizable, she feared she had done something to give herself away.

"My Lady, if I remember correctly, your father taught you how to fight with a sword," Rowan said, pulling her from her swirling anxieties.

"Yes, he did," she said with a forced smile, placing her spoon down in the half-empty soup terrine. "He thought it best I learn in the same manner as any male noble would, which included weapons training."

"What is your favorite weapon to work with?" Alekzander asked.

Panic filled her once more, her hands sweating under the table. Was he trying to bait a confession out of her? "A short sword, Your Highness," she answered, making brief eye contact with him. A smile spread across his face. "I always enjoyed the workout I would get when we practiced in the mornings."

"Have you kept up training now that your father has passed?" the King asked.

"Yes, Your Majesty. I have a weapon tutor I continue to work with. He's a retired military man who lives near my estate." Not a complete lie.

"Impressive," Rowan commented. "If you need to keep practicing while away from your tutor, I'd be happy to take you down to the training ring."

"That's kind of you," she replied.

"Now that you have been here a few days, Christiana, how are you finding the palace after all of these years?" the King asked with an amused smile, his posture straight as he leaned back in his chair.

"Overwhelming at times," she admitted. "But it feels wonderful to be back in these halls. It's as if I never left with how well I remember each nook and cranny of the place. Although some halls still seem foreign to me. But of course, I wasn't allowed everywhere last time I was here."

"Well, if you ever need a guide, I've been spending summers here since I inherited my title," Edgar said. "I would be happy to show you around during your free time."

"He has plenty of time on his hands, since his land holdings are some of the smallest in the country. He doesn't have to worry about all of that pesky paperwork," Alekzander retorted, shooting a cold glance at Edgar.

"Don't worry, Your Highness." Edgar's smile stiffened. "I have plans to change that soon."

"Something you aren't telling us Edgar?" the King inquired. Christiana tuned them out, especially since she owned all the land Edgar lost over the years. She could only imagine what terrible plans that man had to con his way back into wealth. Her gut knew there was a chance, a rather large one, she would somehow end up involved in all of it, but she chose to ignore it for now. She had enough stress to deal with tonight; Edgar was the last man she needed to worry about.

"Are you all right?" Rowan whispered to her.

She turned to face him, leaning in to keep the conversation as private as possible. "I've been dealing with Edgar and his attitude for years. It doesn't faze me anymore."

"But you've never had to deal with it in front of the King and Prince." His eyebrows rose as he waited for a response.

"True." She took a moment to look around the table, catching Dorina's questioning stare for a fleeting moment. With a slight nod of assurance to her friend, her gaze moved on, finding a few pairs of male eyes resting on her. She turned to Rowan with a sigh. "We've only had the first course, and already I'm tired of all of the wayward glances directed at me."

"I told you before, you're the most eligible woman here tonight. Every unwed man around this table wants a chance at your hand."

She rolled her eyes. "Stop making it sound like a competition. I'm not a prize pig to be won."

"You're certainly not a pig, but I must disagree on the prize part. You're truly something wonderful to behold."

Christiana looked away so Rowan couldn't see her deep red cheeks, and found Alekzander staring at her once again, his deep blue eyes locking with hers as if he was trying to discover all her secrets. The intensity of his gaze sent a shudder through Christiana's whole body, her skin prickling with the aftershock. She had never had such a physical reaction to something as innocent as a man staring at her.

All she could think was he must know the truth, that it was her in his room last night, hidden behind a large hood and dark mask. He had hired her and was in as much danger of discovery as she was, however, it didn't stop her mind from feeding her lies and convincing her he would find a way to execute her if her found out the truth. Her summer was now so much more than finding a husband she could keep secrets from.

A smile spread across the Prince's face when she stared back at him, prompting her to look away quickly. She tugged at the bodice of her dress, trying to hide the flush creeping up her clavicle, and stole another glance at him.

"Are you sure you're all right, Ana?" Rowan asked more urgently. "You looked flushed."

"I'm fine," she lied. "I guess I don't drink this much wine at home."

"Don't worry, you'll be used to it by the end of the summer."

She tried her best to smile back, glancing over at Alekzander to see if he was still staring. However, he had moved back into a conversation with his father. Her shoulders sagged as a servant placed the colorful spinach, walnut, and cherry salad in front of her.

The rest of the evening droned on without any more incidents, flirtatious or otherwise. The conversation veered toward business talk, which was a more comfortable topic for Christiana. She tried her best to show off for the King, going into detail about her landholding successes and the different ways she had streamlined production over the years. By the time she returned to her apartment, slightly tipsy from wine, her head was filled with all the business she would be expected to accomplish over the next few months. Between staying up to date with all of her usual title responsibilities, being coerced into finding possible courtships, and having to potentially assassinate the beloved Chancellor for the Prince, her summer was going to be more complicated then she originally anticipated.

The only way to make this happen without losing her mind was to pay a visit to one of her favorite people residing in Cittadina.

Chapter Eight

$\mathcal{T}$HE COBBLED STREETS OF CITTADINA WERE
littered with few people, the full moon reflecting light
along their path as they made their way home. Christiana
blended in well, the dark hood of her Maiden outfit concealing her face.
She had left her veil behind, knowing she didn't need to hide from the
one she chose to visit tonight.

She had finally found the time to slip through her window and find
her favorite informant, Sir Robert Donoughe. As a retired military man,
he held decent status inside the Court, working as a temporary secretary
for any visiting nobles who needed assistance. Because of his status, he
kept Christiana updated on the Court and sent her clients from Cittadina.
Not only was he her very first client, he was the only informant in her
network who knew the identity of the Midnight Maiden.

She turned down an empty alley, cutting through the dank, narrow
walkway until it opened up to reveal the long stretch of townhouses
littering many of the streets. It only took her a few seconds to find the

proper one, the deep red brick sticking out in a row of dull, gray stone structures. Christiana took a quick look around, making sure she wasn't being watched, before cutting around to the back of the house to her preferred entrance.

She snuck through the open window of his first-floor study, quietly sliding it closed so his cook and maid wouldn't hear. She looked around the haphazard room with a smirk. During their three years of working together, this place had never changed. Most of his bookshelves were neatly organized with leather-bound novels and political texts, but the large mahogany desk was covered in papers, both blank and scribbled with ink. It seemed to be completely chaotic, but he would claim he knew exactly where everything was.

As usual, Christiana made herself at home, pulling out two glasses and a decanter of brandy from the desk's bottom drawer. Pouring herself a generous serving, she took a slow sip, enjoying the subtle tastes mixing on her palate. She drew in a long, relaxing breath as she settled on the couch and waited for Robert to return home.

Twenty minutes passed before Christiana heard the quiet creak of the front door opening. After a few moments of shuffling, the study door swung wide and Sir Robert strode in. The tall, muscular man didn't even look shocked when he saw Christiana lounging on his couch enjoying a glass of his secret stash. Without a word, he crossed over to his desk, dropped the few papers he had been carrying, and poured himself a similar-sized portion of brandy before sitting in the large chair across from her.

Staring him down, an amused smile spread across her lips. "Not going to say anything?"

"I have had a long day, My Lady. I need a few sips before discussing things." His square jaw set in tension as he lifted the glass to his lips.

"After three years of knowing each other, you still insist on calling me 'My Lady'. I've told you to call me Christiana many times." She lowered her hood so they could talk face to face.

"Apologies, My Lady, but you are a woman of great status and wealth, and I'm nothing more than a lowly knight, titled as a gift."

Her face softened. "A gift for saving the King's life. You deserve everything he has given you for your loyalty."

"That's what most tell me." He sighed, his fingers tracing the intricate patterns carved into the glass. "Now, how was the first meeting with your newest client?"

"Did you know who you were sending me to when you gave me this request?" she asked, leaning back in her chair.

"Of course not." Robert finally pulled his gaze away from his hands to her face. "I knew it was someone in the palace. After investigating what window they directed you to, I assumed it was the wife or child of some noble family. But I have no idea which one."

"It wasn't any noble, Robert. My newest client is Prince Alekzander." His eyes widened. "Excuse me?"

"In all of his glory." She rolled her eyes, biting her cheek to stop herself from muttering a few other choice words. "Someone close to him asked for help with an abusive husband. Apparently, this was his best solution."

"Who is he sending you after?" Robert tapped his fingers against his glass.

"Chancellor Julian Marlow."

"What an honor."

"Tell me about it," she muttered. So much about this situation made her body vibrate with anxiety. Her mind constantly swirled with all the possible ways she could lose everything because of this. Yet nothing compared to the wave of nausea she got whenever she thought about taking on Marlow. He was not a man to be trifled with, making him a mark unlike any other she had faced.

Taking a few minutes to tell him about the meeting, Christiana took a deep swig of her brandy to wet her parched throat.

"Did you agree to take the job?" Robert asked.

"No." She sighed, rubbing her forehead before raking her fingers through her windblown ponytail. "Not yet, at least. All of the evidence he presented seems legitimate and all of it helped make his claim stronger."

"Then why didn't you agree?"

"She wasn't there. The only person I talked to was the Prince. Besides the death reports he showed me, the only proof of the abuse was his word. For all I know, he is using this as a cover up. He could be sending me after the Chancellor because he doesn't like that he has influence over his father or he wants him out of the way when he ascends the throne."

Robert nodded. "Where did you leave things?"

"I told him to arrange a meeting with the Chancellor's wife. If she testifies that she wants this assassination, I'll agree to it. But until I hear it from her, I can't trust his words."

"Sounds like a solid decision. Is there anything you need my help with?"

"I need you to investigate the evidence he gave me. Confirm that the reports weren't forged in any way. I wrote down everything I could remember," she said, setting down her glass so she could pull out the wrinkled piece of parchment hidden in her boot. "I wasn't able to take the death certificates with me, but this has all of the details you'll need."

"Very well." He took the paper from her hands, brow creasing as his eyes darted between the scribbled words. "Did something seem off about them that made you question their legitimacy?"

"Well, no. But I still think it is a good idea to double check."

"Of course." His eyes softened as he leaned over to pat Christiana's leg. A smile crept across her face as she met his gaze. "Anything else?"

"I think that should be it for now." She picked up her glass to take the last sip of her drink, savoring every second of the tingling fire burning down her throat. "I'll be back in a week to talk more about it."

"Of course, My Lady," he replied, and they both rose.

"Thank you, Robert." Christiana smiled and nodded, lifting her hood, her face concealed in the shadows as she climbed back through the window.

***

Late the next morning, while the sun was making its way to the highest point of the cloudless sky, Christiana finally took some time to stroll leisurely around the palace gardens. Her heart swelled at the happy memories this part of the palace stirred in her mind. It had always been a simple time here for her; even after her father began to change and she started to study for her future as a Marchioness, her times coming to the palace were always a necessary relief.

She took in a deep, cleansing breath as she wandered through the different pathways. The warm summer breeze whispered across her skin, rustling the folds of her cream-and-navy day dress, the light fabric dancing around her legs as she admired the beautiful flowers flourishing all around her. She lost track of time and before she knew it, she had made it all the way to the edge of the stone-fenced grounds. A laugh escaped her lips as she finally realized where her legs had instinctually taken her; pricked with curiosity to see if her favorite hiding spot was still standing, she followed the wall to the gorgeous weeping willow she used to call sanctuary. As a child, she would run as fast as she could to this tree, trying her hardest to escape whichever escort was sent after her for the day.

She brushed the feathery branches aside to enter into her safe haven, the inside cooled by the shade of the overgrown leaves. She made her way to the center, running her hands along the rigid bark and looking over every inch of the tree to see if it was as she remembered.

"I can't say I'm surprised to find you back here," came a deep voice from behind her. Pivoting sharply, she spotted the handsome face of Prince Alekzander pushing between the willow fronds. Her palms began to sweat as she tried her best to keep them from shaking uncontrollably.

"Good morning, Your Highness." Christiana swept herself down into a deep curtsy.

"Please, don't," Alekzander pleaded. "We were never the Prince and the Marchioness under this tree. Personally, I would prefer to keep it that way. At least leave one place sacred to our childhood."

Christiana straightened, biting her bottom lip to stop it from quivering. "What are you doing all the way at the garden edge?"

Chuckling, he stepped into the center of the haven. "I come out this way when I need peace and quiet. Even when I try to barricade myself in my office, it doesn't stop a determined servant trying to break down the door and clean. I was sitting against the wall when I noticed a familiar face walking along in the distance."

"You were the one who showed me this tree, if I remember correctly." She tracked him carefully as he leaned against the opposite side of the truck.

"Yes, I did. When you were running away from the nanny one afternoon in the summer. I believe you were seven years old."

"Sounds about right." The tension in her neck relaxed. "I was trying to find the perfect hiding place from her. You were out here reading in the garden."

"I saw you running as far as your legs could take you. When I asked you what you were doing, you told me you were running away and never coming back unless your father fired the nanny." He laughed, sitting down against the tree trunk and tilting his head so the streams of sunlight hit his pale face. At that moment, he didn't look like the future king of a powerful country, but a man looking for solace from the hardships of the world. Everyone deserved moments of peace, even the leaders of countries. "I showed you a real hiding place."

"Too bad we're now adults who can no longer hide." She laughed, her voice finally growing lighter. This tree brought her to a time when life was simple and they could just be Ana and Zander.

"You can sit with me, you know," Alekzander said. Somehow, during the exchange, she had moved away from the tree to the ring of branches. She wished she could enjoy the moment, to be there with a man she once called a friend, but something deep in her mind was yelling at her to flee.

"Actually, I need to leave," she answered, smoothing her hands over the soft fabric of her puffed skirt. "The lunch with your sister and mother is beginning soon and I promised Dorina I would be there early."

"Oh." His voice faltered at her answer. "I didn't mean to keep you."

"Don't apologize, but I should get back." She lowered herself into a deep curtsy. "Enjoy the rest of your day Your Highness." Before he could reply, she escaped the confines of the tree's billowing branches.

Chapter Nine

HE SUMMER HEAT WAS WELL-TEMPERED BY THE large cloth tent erected on the garden terrace. The open walls let in gentle air, filling the entire space with delicate scents of flowers and trees. Christiana drew in a deep breath; the buzzing of all the women chatting around her filled her ears as she fiddled with the handle of the hand-painted teacup in front of her. She and Dorina were sitting alone, enjoying the privacy of the table set at the front of the room for the Queen, Princess, and their chosen guests. Although it was a bit impolite, they were enjoying their own conversation while the Queen did her best to mingle with the rest of the ladies joining them for the afternoon.

"I'm surprised so many people are leaving us alone." Dorina played with the morganite pendant hanging above the scooped neckline of her pale sage dress. "Most of the older women here have sons perfect for your future husband."

Christiana scoffed. "Or at least that's what they would like to believe."

"They've all probably heard the news anyways." Dorina shrugged.

"What news is that?"

"It was obvious at dinner the other night you were fairly comfortable in Rowan's company. People are probably starting to take bets on when the engagement will be announced." Dorina bit her lips to stifle her giggle.

Rolling her eyes, Christiana sipped her tea, the warm liquid dancing on her tongue. "I'm not even sure if he has that idea in his brain."

"Trust me, he does. Why do you think he personally asked Zander to have you sit next to him? He wanted to show you he was interested."

Christiana shrugged. "Or he wanted a familiar face during an uncomfortable dinner."

"Uncomfortable?" Dorina's brow furrowed at the comment. "What was so bad about it?"

"Nothing," Christiana responded quickly, fingers tingling. "I'm not used to them the way you are. I've never attended one before."

"Oh, right. I keep forgetting because you're handling it so well. You're acting exactly as you should, if it makes you feel any better."

"Thank you," she replied, releasing her breath as they changed the subject, the sound of a metal utensil tapping against the crystal glassware interrupted them.

"Thank you, Ladies, for joining us for lunch this afternoon." Queen Penelope captivated the room with her arms opened in greeting. "On behalf of myself and King Lucian, we welcome you to the castle for the summer. It is one of our favorite seasons, as we get to share it with all of you. Please, everyone find their seats, lunch will be served shortly. I look forward to catching up with each of you after the meal has concluded."

"Well said, Mother." Dorina applauded as the Queen approached their table. A fourth lady Christiana didn't recognize joined them, her tight bun and unamused smirk clashing with the serene setting. But since

Dorina and the Queen didn't even flinch at her company, Christiana could only assume she was the Queen's choice for a dining companion that afternoon.

"Thank you, my dear." Penelope smiled, caressing Dorina's shoulder before taking the final empty seat at the table. The servants began milling around the tent like bees, pouring more tea and serving different savory and sweet treats for the ladies to indulge in. Light and pleasant conversation resumed, and Christiana quickly learned the other woman was Duchess Rachella Dorchester of Stroisia. She was there with her husband and children for the summer like all the other nobles. As they enjoyed their second round of treats, a young lady's maid approached their table and whispered something into the Queen's ear.

"Did he say what he needed?" she asked, her eyes narrowing toward the side of the tent as if someone was about to burst through.

"Just that he wanted to talk to her," the maid answered, stealing a glance at Christiana.

"All right, then. Allow him to come over."

Christiana shot Dorina a questioning look, but she simply shrugged as they waited for the mystery man to make himself known. Both of their mouths gaped open quite unladylike when Edgar sauntered into the tent, head high and grinning as he made his way over to the Queen's table with a large bouquet of flowers in his hands.

"Your Majesty," he greeted with a deep bow to Penelope. "Thank you for allowing me to stop by this lovely afternoon."

"And what, may I ask, was so important that you felt the need to interrupt our lunch time?" Her lips pinched together tightly as the room came to a hush waiting for his answer.

"I sincerely apologize for the lack of formality, but after dinner the other night, I couldn't wait to ask a very important question to the Marchioness." He smiled, turning to Christiana. He was starting to make even more of a scene now as he knelt down to eye level with her. The women in the party turned and stared at the spectacle in front of them. "Christiana, would you do me the honor of joining me for dinner tomorrow evening? I think it is time for the two of us to bring things out into the open."

He winked, presenting her with the flowers. Christiana glared at the odious man, but all she could hear was the ooh-ing and aww-ing of the onlookers.

"How romantic!" Rachella squealed. Even Dorina and the Queen were quite taken by the romantic gesture, staring at her with anticipation, silently begging her to accept the offer.

"What a kind offer, Your Grace," was all she could get out. "How about we discuss this further while I escort you back to the palace? If you will excuse me, Your Majesty, I will only be gone a moment."

The Queen's nod was all Christiana needed before she fled the tent, her cheeks on fire with a deep blush. She tried her best not to punch Edgar for making such a spectacle in front of everyone. He followed closely behind her, their steps falling in sync as they made their way inside the palace walls. The minute the doors closed behind them and the prying eyes and ears of the women were gone, she whirled to confront him.

"What the hell was that?" she exclaimed. One of the guards winced at her outlandish vocabulary.

"I thought it was pretty clear." He laughed, crossing his arms behind his back and strolling down a random hallway. "A dinner invitation to talk about a potential courtship, of course."

"Stop it, Edgar." She trailed behind him, refusing to call him by his title. "We both know that was nothing more than a desperate attempt to force my hand. Make it as public as possible so I'd have to say yes."

"Don't you know me well." He stopped in his tracks, his playful face finally twisting back into its true form: the pinched leer of a greed-driven weasel who only cared about appearances. "I knew it was the only way to get you to say yes."

"For goodness sake," she exclaimed, pulling him with her down the hall to a more secluded area. Privacy was necessary at this point. "What will it take to make you leave me alone?"

"Isn't it obvious? I want my land back."

"You mean *my* land." Christiana released him, crossing her arms against her puffed-out chest, her shoulders pulled back as she stood tall against him.

"Stolen land is more like it," he huffed. "Completely undervalued and taken right from under me."

"You act as though you didn't come to me willingly every time, begging me to give you more money in exchange for those holdings. It's not my fault you didn't have them valued before approaching me. If you weren't so desperate to appear wealthier than you are, maybe you wouldn't be in this mess."

While Christiana was growing up, her father had purchased at least half of the dukedom landholdings. It wasn't a secret that Edgar's father, Henry, had developed a gambling addiction and swindled away most of their fortune. Whenever he needed more money to waste, he would go to her father. Henry was so desperate, he would sell most of the land for cheap. Once Christiana and Edgar came into their titles, the pattern of buying and selling passed on.

"Either way, what's done is done." He waved her off and she balled her fists in the folds of her skirt at the gesture. "However, an alliance of marriage between our households will give me the perfect opportunity to put all of those flourishing plots of land back in the rightful hands of the duchy."

She finally halted them, the quiet corner illuminated with sunlight. "Are you so much of a daft idiot that you revealed your entire plan to me? You aren't even attempting to make this seem legitimate?"

"Let's be honest with each other, Christiana, that tactic never would have worked on you." He grazed his fingers up her arm. A snarl of disgust escaped her lips as she shoved him away from her. "You hate me so much, you would never see past it no matter how charming and flirtatious I was."

"Very true," she agreed with him for once, her arms pressed tightly against her chest as she stared at him through narrow eyes.

Waving his finger at her, he continued, "However, you're the only one who sees it that way."

"What?" she said through her teeth, nostrils flaring.

"I arrived at the palace earlier than most of the nobles this season. I wanted to make sure to get plenty of alone time with the King during such an important summer trip. He mentioned he wanted to see the beautiful Marchioness of Tagri raised to a station befitting her power and success. He wants to make sure you only have the best."

"How thoughtful of him."

"But unfortunately for you, there aren't many positions higher than yours. Except, of course, that of a Duchess." He smirked. "Now, he did mention he would be content with you at least marrying someone of equal status if it came down to it. But why should you have to when an eligible Duke is standing right in front of you?" He flourished his arms wide to show himself off to her.

"Why would the King tell you all of this?" Christiana's chest felt tight with hurt, almost like the King had violated her trust with these private conversations.

"You'd be surprised how loose his lips become when you bring him a bottle of his favorite imported brandy." He laughed. "In the end, Christiana, all I have to do is convince the Royal Family I'm the perfect match for you. With their approval and a few grand gestures in public to make everyone swoon over the prospect, you'll have no choice but to accept my offer."

Christiana's blood boiled, rising to the surface as if it would burn her. How dare this cocky, lowlife cretin think he could take control of her? He stood there, staring at her with such glee, thinking he had it all figured out. He assumed in the end, he was dealing with a delicate woman who would never go against the crown and their wishes for her life. It seems after years of dealing with each other in business, he was still so thick he couldn't see past his own selfish behavior.

"Listen to me right now." Christiana stalked toward him, fury and vengeance swirling in her chest. "If you think it will be that simple to force my hand into marriage, think again. In the end, I don't care about the King's opinion, let alone anyone else in this Court. So, if you think anyone here can convince me that marrying a lowlife like you is the right decision, you're even stupider than I thought."

"How dare you talk to your superior like that!" he spat.

"The last thing you are is superior to me," she shot back, pushing him against the wall to pin him in place. "Now get it through your thick skull. I will never marry you. Even if you were the last man on the continent, I would rather be celibate than share a life and bed with the likes of you. You'll never get your land back and you'll never get me. End of story."

"We'll have to see about that, now won't we?" He smirked, not even fazed that her forearm pressed him tightly against the wall. "Anything else you wish to declare?"

"Leave me alone." She released him from his trap.

"Always a pleasure, Marchioness," he mocked, lowering himself into an overly-flourished bow. "It looks like this is going to be quite the entertaining summer."

He sauntered off, laughing to himself as he disappeared down the hallway. Once he was out of sight, she closed her eyes and tilted her head back, trying to inhale as much oxygen into her lungs as possible. Putting her hand against her heart, she listened closely, waiting for the beats to even out. The last thing she was going to do was go back out into a tent full of women with a scowl on her face. She was going to walk in there like nothing had fazed her, showing everyone that the empty gestures of a petty man would never be strong enough to force her will.

After a few more cleansing breaths, she pulled her spine up, held her head high, and rejoined Dorina and the Queen for the rest of the planned afternoon.

Chapter Ten

THE MORNING MIST HAD FINALLY DISSIPATED
when Christiana made her way to the palace stables.
Blackbirds and robins flew overhead, their loud chirps
ringing out as they woke to enjoy the warm breeze. She pulled in a long
breath, staring out into the horizon, the sun peeking out from its hiding
place behind the soft tones of burnt orange and lavender sprinkling the
sky. The crunch of her boots on the dirt path coaxed her to spend an hour
or two galloping through the woods with her mare, Willow.

Christiana had been struggling to find restful sleep for a few days
now, her mind constantly buzzing to bring her peace when the moon was
in the sky. The constant, low hum of anxiety ran through her body
whenever her thoughts lingered on Alekzander and the possibility of
such a dangerous case. She was trying to find any excuse as to why she
should say no, even though she was still waiting for Robert's research to
be completed. Whenever she tried to distract herself, somehow her mind
ended up filling with Rowan's emerald-green gaze. Memories of the

welcome dinner, and the kindness he had shown her, sent a flutter of wings floating through her torso. Yet even thoughts of him made her mind spiral, nothing calming her enough to find peace at night.

Finally giving up on finding tranquility, Christiana realized she needed something to help stimulate her tired mind; a ride with her favorite mare always brought her back to center.

Halfway to the stables, she slowed at the heavy clanging of metal and turned in the direction of the swordplay sounds. The noise drew her like a child to candy, her arms tingling as she hurried to discover the source. When she turned the corner, her eyes blinked furiously, taking in the sight before her.

Standing alone in the training fields for the soldiers, the Prince was practicing the art of sword fighting with a well-armored training dummy.

Although she should run in the opposite direction, Christiana stood planted to the ground, her arms crossed as she watched Alekzander's rough display. Instead of dressing in proper military garb, he enjoyed the muggy morning in simple pants and a sleeveless tunic, most likely to keep from overheating while putting in such a vigorous workout. His focus was perfect, his eyes never leaving the dummy, as if it were the most dangerous opponent he had ever faced. He jabbed, parried, sliced and blocked, each move made with perfect precision and a gracefulness many soldiers would envy. Christiana could almost feel the vibration of the sword up her own arm, as if she were the one blocking his heavy sword when it made impact.

His strong arms contracted with each hard and precise strike against the dummy, his muscles singing in strength. Under all those thick and proper dress clothes, Christiana never realized how in shape the Prince was. Sweat formed along his forehead, the droplets slowly falling down his angular, pale face, the light of the sunrise dancing off his skin. Without realizing it, Christiana stood there for a few minutes, watching him continue his morning workout. It wasn't until he turned around to grab his waterskin he even realized he had an audience. Grinning, he waved her over.

She wiped her sweaty hands down the sleek fabric of her leather riding pants and walked closer to the Prince, trying her best to come up with any excuse for her blatant staring. Her hands began to shake with each step, and she closed them into fists, the vibrations finally dissipating only when she raked her fingers through the low ponytail hanging over her shoulder.

"Good morning, Christiana," the Prince greeted. "What are you doing out so early?"

"I hadn't been sleeping well the past few nights, Your Highness," she admitted, halting a few feet away from the arena. "I decided an early morning ride would help to wake me up before having to bury myself in paperwork for the rest of the day."

"It doesn't tire you out even more?" he asked, taking a long swig of cold water. A few drops escaped down the sides of his lips as he gulped.

"I guess you'd expect it to, but not for me. The adrenaline rush I get when galloping through the trees and jumping over fallen logs helps keep me awake. Sometimes tea isn't enough," she joked, her hands braced on the rough, unfinished wood of the ring. "What about you?"

"I get up at this time every morning." He closed the top of the skin before hoisting himself over the side of the ring, joining Christiana on the outskirts. "It's the only time I can have the practice yard to myself. The rest of the day it is either crawling with soldiers or the other nobles who have taken over to duel each other."

He sauntered over to a cluster of nearby tree stumps and took a seat to rest. She couldn't stop herself from slowly following, though she kept a few steps of distance between them. "Why not practice with the other nobles?"

"I do," he answered. She raised her eyebrows, pulling her eyes open wide. "Does that surprise you?"

"Why so much effort in training?" She tilted her head off to the side, waiting for an answer. "I understand wanting to know how to fight, but why the dedication of a soldier?"

"The truth?" he asked, and she nodded. "I could be like every other king before me and learn the bare minimum. To know about fighting yet never practice it. But one day, when I was about twelve or thirteen, my father took me out to the training yard to watch the soldiers practice. As I watched them, I realized how talented they were, how much effort and dedication they put in, like anyone else learning a new skill they were passionate about."

Blinking, she asked, "That's a good thing, isn't it?"

"Of course it is!" He threw his arms in the air. "But how can you respect someone and follow their orders when they don't even try to understand what you go through? When you work so hard to make yourself strong, how can you blindly follow someone who refuses to do the same?"

Her stomach fluttered. "I suppose it would be difficult."

He leaned back, his hands resting on the back of the jagged tree trunk. "Exactly. When I become King, I want my soldiers to know that I not only learned about strategy and war, but also how they fight and protect our country. I don't want them to blindly follow me because I inherited a title. I want them to follow me because they respect and believe in me."

Christiana stared down at the Prince, her tense shoulder blades relaxing as she watched the hard-set determination settle across his face. She stood in front of a man who looked like he felt the weight of his impending reign on his shoulders like the palace itself. The strength of his passion wove into each word he spoke. Christiana's heart fluttered at the idea of a King who would listen to the people and the real issues plaguing them every day.

"That's unorthodox, Your Highness," was all she could say.

"We're moving into new times, Marchioness." He picked up a rag cloth from a satchel sitting on the ground, rubbing the soft material up and down the steel of his sword to clean off the specks of dirt and hay that had settled on the sharp edge. "Times in which I'm unsure our generation will be so willing to follow blindly. Don't get me wrong, I respect my father. He has spent his reign working hard to keep peace between our country and those surrounding us. However, I fear the people within our own borders are more restless than my father likes to let on. It's time for the King to stop focusing on the fear of invasion and begin listening to what his people have to say."

"But isn't it better to focus on both issues instead of isolating one?"

"Absolutely." He nodded, his hand hovering over the blade for a brief moment as he looked up at her, eyes soft. A smirk spread on his lips before he continued his sword care. "I'm lucky my father has kept me involved with international relations for a while now. I have a decent relationship with all our bordering countries, which makes me confident I can keep the peace my father worked so hard to build. I don't plan on neglecting that responsibility, just shifting some of the dedicated time from it to some intercountry affairs needing to be settled."

"That is a beautiful sentiment, Your Highness," Christiana responded, gooseflesh skimming down her arms. He was ready to be King, to listen to his people and try his hardest to help them.

"I know, I know." He laughed, throwing the cloth back in his satchel before sheathing his long sword. "It's certainly a dreamer's dream."

"Of course it's not, Your Highness," she replied quickly. "It shows how much you love your people."

"Really?" He stared up at her, eyebrows pulled in close.

"Yes. You want to listen. That's something people have been ready to see for a long time."

He slung his bag over his shoulder, the contents rattling as he stood. "What makes you say that?"

"Things I've heard from some of my tenants. I know they have certain complaints and gripes, but they feel like it's pointless to even bring them to my attention. They believe the King loves them but doesn't listen to them."

"Well, hopefully I can change that point of view. I hope one day my people will trust me enough with the issues in their lives that they find important."

The chiming of the clock tower rang out in the palace to tell everyone it was seven o'clock. Soon, the large building would begin buzzing with servants bringing their masters or mistresses breakfast, while the nobles prepared for the different activities they had planned for the day.

The loud clang snapped Christiana into attention, making her acutely aware of how close Alekzander had drifted. No longer was he sitting on his stump, but a mere two feet away from her. Soft pinpricks covered her entire face and her pulse sped up at his relaxed stance.

"I-I should be on my way." She fumbled over her words, turning away.

"Would you like an escort?" he offered, his swift gate catching up beside her.

"Oh, no, I'm fine, Your Highness." She weakly tried to brush him off. "I wouldn't want to keep you from your day. Have a wonderful morning." She dipped herself into a swift curtsy and walked in the opposite direction.

She bit her lip, trying her best to forget the pained look in Alekzander's eyes when she turned to walk away.

***

"I'm back!" Christiana exclaimed, shutting the door to her apartment. The strong scent of the forest pine needles clung to her as she removed the sweaty riding gloves and mud-spattered riding coat. The heavy, silver damask fabric clung to her, peeling down her arm like a second skin. The refreshing morning air had revitalized her spirits, her shoulders sagging down as she rubbed the final bit of tension from the back of her neck. Even with the awkward encounter with the Prince, her head was clear to face the rest of the day.

"I'll take those, My Lady." Natalia scurried in from the doorway of Christiana's bedroom. A fresh pot of strongly-brewed tea sat on the large dining table, the warm scent mixing with the sweet smell of the fresh-baked pastries next to it. Handing off her clothes to Natalia, Christiana scraped a chair away from the table, settling herself and pouring a large helping. "I've already drawn you a bath. It's all set in your bedroom when you're ready."

"What would I do without you?" Christiana teased.

Her maid's full lips pulled into a smile. "You'll never have to find that out. This also came for you this morning." She freed an envelope from the folds of her apron, a delicate script scrolled across the front with Christiana's name.

She took the cream-colored parcel from Natalia's outstretched hands. "Thank you. I'll be a moment."

"Of course, My Lady." Natalia curtsied, disappearing back into the bedroom.

Christiana flipped the envelope over, a smile spreading across her face when she recognized the crest pressed into the deep navy wax. She ripped it open, her pulse hitching as she read the request for help. With a final sip of her tea, she made her way to the bedroom, the swirling scents of citrus welcoming her as she prepared for her unexpected afternoon plans.

Chapter Eleven

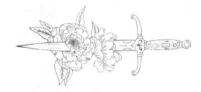

T HE MORNING TICKED BY QUICKLY, AND Christiana soon made her way down the long, marble hallway of the public corridors, her favorite leather-bound notebook in hand. She arrived at her intended doorway, the bronzed plaque on the outside noting its contents as the library. Pushing her way through, Christiana lost her breath at the expansive space.

The tall, echoing room occupied one of the castle's towers, the cylindrical shape and high, vaulted ceilings lined with rows of books. Long staircases led up to the levels with different couches and desks, allowing people to explore the dozens of subjects and sections without having to climb all the way back down to the ground floor. For such a grand room, it didn't seem to get much use. All the books were lined up with no holes or missing texts in sight.

"Thank you for agreeing to help me." Rowan sighed, smiling as Christiana joined him at the table.

"Of course! I'm more than happy to help. What seems to be the problem?"

"Well." He shuffled the stacks of paper in front of him. "I acquired this livestock farm in Banshyl a few weeks ago, and for the life of me I cannot seem to figure out what any of these reports mean!"

A chuckle escaped Christiana's lips as she set down her notebook and picked up random sheets of parchment. The scraggly handwriting was almost illegible, as if a child had written all the reports. "Who did you buy this from?"

"Baron Jorah."

"Ah." In his late eighties, Jorah struggled to lift a feather, let alone write smoothly with a quill. "Well, it may be a bit of a headache, but we should be able to decipher everything in a short time."

"Honestly, it's not just the handwriting that's giving me trouble."

"Oh?"

"This is my first livestock farm," he admitted. "And I've absolutely no clue what any of this means. I was hoping you'd be willing to talk me through everything? I know you have experience with a couple of farms."

"Of course, I can help!" she exclaimed, her heart warming that he thought of her first. Her eager hands collected the papers, meticulously sorting them into the proper piles to help with her lesson. A boyish grin plastered on Rowan's face as he watched her, and she watched him in turn. He was a man with a warrior's build; with the right glare, he could intimidate anyone. But when he smiled, a childlike quality softened his face, coaxing a contagious grin across hers.

"All right, I think the best way to start is for us to decipher everything first. Once we know exactly what each page says, it will be much easier for me to go through and explain their purposes." She handed him a stack, pulling the rest toward herself. She flipped her notebook open, her wispy quill feather flowing in the air as she dipped the pointed edge into the ebony ink pot on the table. Silence fell over them, brows furrowed as they transcribed the scribbles.

Dropping her quill for a moment to rub out a particularly tight hand cramp, Christiana looked over to see Rowan's posture had sagged, his spine curved as he feverishly wrote. Her cheeks relaxed at the sight.

"What?" Rowan asked, snapping Christiana to attention, his amused face pinched together as he waited for her answer.

"Nothing." She shook her head, her fingers tapping against the ledger in front of her. "I think it's funny you find all of this so difficult, but stitching up wounds and treating illness is an enjoyable time for you." She knew well he had gone off to become a physician a long time ago, one of the main reasons they hadn't seen each other in eight years. The other being her own seclusion for the past five.

"What's exciting about a bunch of numbers written on a piece of paper? Now, the blood-pumping rush of adrenaline you feel as you're stitching up a wounded leg in hopes of saving a person's ability to walk? Nothing can compare." He chuckled, shaking his head as he looked down at the stacks in front of them. "My father...he was always better at this than me."

"I never got to tell you how sorry I am about your parents." Christiana reached out to touch the top of his hand. It had been a shock for the entire Court when the news spread. The Marquess and Marchioness of Banshyl had been traveling around the country when their carriage was attacked by road bandits. Although they were well-guarded, they were outmatched by the number of men who led the attack. The Marquess fought his hardest, but he was overcome. The bandits took Rowan's mother with them and her body turned up a few days later on the side of the road. It was unheard of for nobles to be attacked so brutally.

"Thank you," Rowan said, the glassy glaze of tears covering his eyes. Although it had been two years, the whisper of his pain rang in his darkened gaze. "It wasn't fair. If they had been sick or something, I wouldn't have left home for so long. But they were healthy and strong, they didn't deserve to die the way they did."

"That's why you moved into the palace?"

"Yes." He nodded, looking back up at her. "I couldn't stay in our estate for long. It was so...empty and quiet without them. Zander came to visit me one week and noticed how I was struggling. He forced me to pack everything up and we travelled back here that same week. I haven't left for very long since."

She shuffled the papers in front of her to start on the next stack. "That was so kind of him," she observed, unable to look up at Rowan as her cheeks blazed at the mention of the Prince.

"That's Zee for you." He laughed, returning to his own work. The silence settled back over them. An hour or two went by, the pair losing track of the time as the candles shrank around them.

Jotting down the last number, Christiana dropped her quill and rubbed the back of her neck. Rowan stretched his long arms above his head, and she reached across the table and pulled his stack to her, examining everything he had written. "Your handwriting is almost as bad as Jorah's!" The letters pushed together so close, she had to squint to make them all out.

"No, it isn't!" He snatched the paper from her grasp.

She laughed. "I could barely read it."

"Well, at least I can read my own handwriting, so it doesn't matter."

"Fair enough. So, are you ready to learn what each report means?" His playful expression gave her the faint hint he wasn't as ready as she was.

"You know what would be extremely helpful?" he asked, leaning slightly over the table. The hairs on the back of Christiana's neck stood up straighter at the sudden closeness.

"What would that be?"

"If you took a walk with me in the garden. The fresh air will help me refocus."

"I thought you wanted to learn." She smirked. "A walk in the garden is a distraction."

"How about I make you a deal." Her eyebrows rose as she waited for him to continue. "A thirty-minute walk in the garden together, then we can come right back here and I will be the picture of a perfect student, focused and ready to learn." His eyes danced with glee as he waited for her response.

She couldn't stop herself from laughing, shaking her head as she answered. "Fine."

Rowan bolted out of his chair, his lean arm outstretched to her. She placed her hand in his, allowing him to pull her upright and escort her out of the dimly-lit room into the bright summer day.

Chapter Twelve

THE SUN WAS DISAPPEARING BEHIND THE
horizon by the time Christiana left the library, her
notebook firmly in hand. A smile crossed her lips as she
thought about the hours spent with Rowan this afternoon, both in the
library and outside in the garden. She had nearly reached her apartment
when a figure disappeared through a large door ahead; she recognized
the dark chestnut hair, perfectly quaffed around his angelic face.

Without thinking, her pace picked up, the clicking of her heels
rhythmic as she approached the same doorway. She pulled in one more
deep breath, her hand twitching as she grasped the bronzed handle and
pushed the gallery door open.

The room was expansive, covered in different paintings of the Royal
lineage from over the years of Viri's existence. The only form of light
filtered in through the window, the moonlight bouncing off the elaborate
frames illuminated by a handful of candelabras meticulously placed
around the room.

She stood in one of the many dark corners, pretending to look at a painting, while she finally put eyes on the one she had followed. Every inch of her hummed, needle pricks dancing along her arms as she watched with a hunter's focus. He was clearly lost in his own thoughts, the long day creased through his tense face and balled fists clenched behind his back as he slowly walked around the gallery. She barely knew the man, but still she struggled to believe what he was doing behind closed doors would force someone to send the Maiden after him. She stood there, her neck tensing as she hoped and prayed he would finally see he was not alone. Minutes ticked by, her eyes narrowing to the side as she followed his movement, each of his steps slowly gaining on her. Finally, she snapped her eyes back to her painting, the sound of his shoes approaching in a more determined manner.

"Marchioness?"

She turned to him with a smile, feigning surprise that she wasn't alone. "Chancellor Marlow," she greeted as Julian approached the corner, his forest-green doublet partially undone and shoulders slumped.

"I didn't mean to disturb your examination of the paintings, My Lady, but I'm not used to people being in this area of the castle often."

"Oh," she replied, the hairs on the back of her neck prickling when he stood next to her. "It's quite all right, Chancellor, I was just admiring the Royal Family's first portrait together." She nodded at the large, gold-framed painting on the wall. The paint was slightly cracked in places, the portrait about twenty years old; Dorina was a small babe, tightly clutched in her mother's smiling arms. Alekzander, at only six, stood proudly next to his father, his unruly curls and shining eyes perfectly depicted by the talented artist who had meticulously crafted the piece.

"Ah yes, I was there when it was created. I was in my position about a year when this piece was commissioned." His face softened with a smile.

"You've been with this family for a long time."

He looked down at her. "I have, and I'm lucky to have been a part of it. I got to watch the Prince and Princess grow up and assist their father with growing this country into its true potential. Something I felt passionate about from a young age."

"Really?" Christiana took in the extra bit of height the Chancellor gained as he straightened his spine.

"That's why I joined the military when I was only a teenager." A fact Christiana had already known, and wished she could ignore; but this side of him added a whole new level of danger to the marks she typically handled. "I loved this country, and I had so much pride in it. I wanted to do all I could to keep it flourishing. And for a merchant's son, all I could do was fight."

He held himself with pride, beaming. And though Christiana had been in her line of business for many years now, learning how perfect abusers were at hiding in plain sight and convincing others they were not capable of such dreadful acts, she couldn't stop a thread of doubt from creeping into her thoughts. How could someone so dedicated to helping his country be capable of such terror?

"An admirable story, Chancellor. I didn't know you were from a merchant family." She didn't want to see him in such a kind way. She didn't want to admire him for all he had done when a despicable charge was placed against him. Yet she couldn't help it; he was convincing, that's for sure. Maybe a part of her was giving into the beautiful story because she wanted to believe it was Alekzander who was lying. Unfortunately, that fact would make her life much easier this summer.

"Oh yes," he continued as they started a slow walk around the gallery. "My father was a well-known wool merchant. He wanted to train me in the craft, but I was too interested in politics and war strategy to pay attention."

"Was he understanding of your decision?" Perhaps his potential role as an abuser stemmed from an abusive childhood. The more Christiana fought abusers over the years, the more often she found it came from them being abused as well, although that wasn't always the case.

"He was." He smiled, and her face fell. He was not making this easier for her. "He could tell my heart wasn't in making and selling products. He also had my younger brother to pass the knowledge down to, so he was just happy his legacy continued on."

"How kind of him." She already could tell why so many women fawned over the Chancellor. Although he was well over forty, the years had been kind to him, even with his stressful job. His dark hair was peppered with strands of white and his rounded face was softened by his charming smile and kind eyes. If what Alekzander said was true, she now understood why he felt the need to hire her. No one would ever believe this kind, loyal man could hurt someone he claimed to love.

"And how are you enjoying your time here, Marchioness?" Julian asked, the weight of his eyes burning into Christiana's neck.

"So far, it is exactly how I remember, but it feels completely different...if that makes sense." She laughed, her voice hitching up an octave as she tried to nonchalantly dab away the bit of sweat below her earlobe.

"As in it looks the same, but the way you now live your life is completely different?"

"Exactly." She looked up at him, his charming smile forcing a flutter to escape her heart.

"Well, I know you have a lot of...expectations this summer." Christiana silently scoffed as he continued. "But I hope you have as much luck as I've had."

"Oh, you're married?" Christiana asked with false intrigue.

"Yes, for almost three years now." He gave her a sideways glance, eyebrows creasing.

Her stomach flipped at the sight, realizing this was information most people already knew about him. "Forgive me." She laughed, the back of her neck prickling. "I've been away from Court for so long, facts are starting to blend together."

"Of course." He shook his head, the muscles in his face relaxing as he sighed deeply. "My darling Eliza. She is the kindest woman I've ever met. Her beauty rivals your own." He winked, and Christiana struggled to conceal a smirk.

"You're too kind." She looked down, watching their feet come to a stop by the front door.

"Speaking of which, I need to meet her for dinner shortly. I'll leave you here, Marchioness."

"Please, call me Christiana."

"Christiana." He smiled, giving her a deep bow and a gentle kiss on the hand before straightening. "Enjoy the rest of your night." He left her speechless in the gallery.

***

All the information was staring at her, cleanly written on pieces of parchment strewn out on Robert's desk. The lamp on the edge brought clarity, allowing Christiana to read every word over and over again. She hunched over all of them, fingers tapping on the hard, wooden surface as she tried to process everything he had discovered for her. The death certificates, the Chancellor's household past, everything she needed to catch the Prince in a lie.

"Not what you wanted to hear?" Robert leaned over her from behind as she continued to stare at the papers.

"That everything he told me was the truth?" She banged her fist against the desk, the crack of the impact ringing through Robert's study.

"At least you know his intentions are pure."

"Well, maybe I didn't want them to be!" she burst out, rubbing her head as she walked away from the desk; she couldn't look at those words any longer. She paced back and forth, trying to calm her racing brain as it struggled to process exactly what she was getting herself into.

Robert leaned his hip against the edge of the desk as he watched her.

"I apologize if this wasn't the answer you were looking for."

"That's not it." She halted, massaging one palm with the other hand. "If this poor woman is going through all of this, of course I want to help her. That's all I want to do. I just wish the Prince wasn't involved at all. The idea of having him so close to me all the time is unsettling. That, matched with the hardest mark I'll ever have to target, makes me concerned I will end up making mistakes along the way."

"You are wonderful at your job, My Lady." Robert finally broke away from his perch, taking her by the shoulders and leading her to the chairs surrounding the hearth.

She allowed him to push her down by the shoulders into the comfortable confines of the plush cushions. "My concern is if they match up well enough to the Chancellor. It would be easier if the Prince was a scoundrel trying to use me. Then I could tell him to do something inappropriate to himself and spend the rest of the summer focusing on other tasks."

"Fair." Robert chuckled. She could hear him roaming around the room behind her, shuffling different objects, but she couldn't focus on what they were. All she could see was the haze of her vision tunneling as her mind, and heartbeat, refused to slow down.

"I don't know if I can do this." She dropped her head in her hands, leaning her weight onto her legs and struggling to pull air through her nose.

"First thing you need to do is breathe," Robert instructed, inhaling loudly through his nose and exhaling through his mouth. She tried her best to mimic him, the calming oxygen flowing through her system. "Next, you sip on this." He handed her a large glass of brandy, her hands happily wrapping around the cool crystal as the first sip of liquid sizzled down her throat. He sat in his seat across from her, relaxing back in his seat with his own glass. "Let's talk it out. What are you most concerned about? Besides the Prince's involvement."

Christiana took a moment to let her world refocus, the spinning room and her blurry vision finally righting. She stared down at her hands, mindlessly rubbing her thumb across the glass as she tried to focus on the most important concerns she had about this job. "How am I supposed to kill him? Let's start with that."

"All right, let's go through your arsenal." Robert nodded with the calm of many years of military training.

"Most of my poisons are out of the question, including Midnight." She sighed.

"Why?"

"Midnight and a good portion of my poison supply are intravenous drugs. The ability to get close enough to him to administer them is a highly improbable risk, one that would most likely force me to engage in a fight I would lose. It risks my identity and my life too much."

"All right." Robert nodded, his eyes drifting around the room. "Which means a direct assault is also out of the question."

Christiana grunted at the suggestion. "Absolutely."

"Do you have any ingestion-style poisons?"

"A few, but I don't use them often. The risk of hurting other people in the process is too great. Especially in a palace where poison tasters roam the kitchens constantly for checks."

"Too bad you can't slip him something at an event," Robert suggested.

"I wish." Christiana grunted. "It would certainly make my life easier."

There were multiple reasons why this would never be an option. First, the risks of exposure were too great. The Chancellor could share his cup with someone, poisoning the wrong person; or if she slipped it to him at a formal event and he died there, everyone in the room would be considered a suspect, including herself. She couldn't risk herself getting caught up in an investigation. Second, she refused to let her life as the Marchioness cross paths with her life as the Maiden. She was one person, but these parts of her were separate for the safety of both identities. Slipping him something as the Marchioness would set off an entire chain of events she wouldn't be able to stop.

"Research what you have and see if they are plausible options." Robert's encouraging gaze and kind smile filled Christiana with warmth. "There is always an answer, My Lady. You'll find it."

"I hope so," she scoffed. "Although for all we know, this may be for nothing. I still need to talk to Eliza before I agree."

"About that..." Robert trailed off, snapping Christiana's head up, her brow creasing as she waited for him to continue. "This came today. I was going to give it to you after showing you the evidence, but it seems the conversation took us somewhere else." He held up an envelope, the name of one of her aliases scrawled across the front. She grabbed the letter from his grasp, tearing into it. The words were perfectly written, but she couldn't stop herself from skimming most of the letter, her eyes focusing on two words scrawled at the end:

"Tomorrow night."

Chapter Thirteen

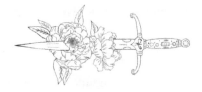

T HE NEXT NIGHT, FAR PAST WHEN THE CASTLE
was asleep, Christiana crept through the darkened servant
hallways to the one meeting she had been waiting for.

The narrow areas twisted and turned, making it seem like an
entirely different palace. Sconces lit the dim space, a handful of candles
burning in each brass fixture lining the stone walls. The passageways
were obviously created to be efficient and hidden, the exact way a
servant should be. Her stomach twisted as she slowly made her way
through them, listening closely for the faintest sound of footsteps. She
silently chastised herself for not exploring more, her movements
hindered when she found herself dangerously close to some patrolling
soldiers on duty. Her hot breath strangled underneath her mask as she
took deep inhales to keep her head clear.

The letter had given her detailed instructions on how to get to the
Chancellor's private apartments, leading her directly to a servant
entrance within Eliza's bedroom. Making a mental note to wander

around these hallways more each night to get a better understanding of the layout, she continued on cautiously, her steps blending in with the heavy footfalls of the patrolling soldiers. Eventually, after evading them, she made it to the wooden door hidden in a dead-end passageway.

She pushed it open, the soft sound of scraping wood against the stone wall filling her ears. She confirmed the only sounds radiating through the space were the crackling flames from the fireplace before slipping inside, securing herself behind the large wardrobe to wait for Eliza to appear. She peeked around the edge, her eyes adjusting to the dimly-lit room as she took it in; the layout was similar to her own, with the large four poster bed, oversized stone fireplace, and the dressing table perfectly arranged in one corner. But this space was different; filled with personal touches of a couple who spent the majority of their year residing in this room. The bright quilt on the bed had been custom-made, the gold pattern matching the intricate frame housing a large wedding portrait hanging above the fireplace.

Her stomach began to turn as the minutes ticked by, her hand rubbing it gently to calm the constant movement. For the first time in a while, she was conflicted about the outcome of a client meeting. If Eliza was telling the truth, she would want nothing more than to help this abused woman finally find some peace. But accepting the offer came with a whole set of new risks. If she was a normal assassin, one who didn't hold a noble title of her own, she would probably consider this job a much-needed challenge. In an odd way, she still did; it was a test of the past five years, her time to prove what she had learned. But there was too much on the line for her desire to prove herself to get in the way of her future. This was her last chance to settle her mind, and her soul, with the fears holding her tongue from saying yes.

The loud creak of the bedroom door rang through the room. Christiana pulled her spine straight up at the padding of bare feet against the wooden floor. Although she was sure she had only heard one set of footsteps enter, she was still frozen, waiting for the right moment to reveal herself. The person moved around before the distinct noise of a groaning bed notified Christiana the young lady had sat down.

"Hello?" she spoke weakly. "Are you here yet?"

"Eliza?" Christiana asked in her tenor-styled voice, stepping out from behind the dresser so the petite woman curled on the bed was in her view.

Christiana tensed as she looked her over. Her plump lips and wide doe-like eyes softened her high-cheekboned face. There was something about her that rang familiar, but Christiana couldn't quite put her finger on it. She had spent so many years trapped in the isolation of hiding in plain sight, the faces of other nobles tended to blend together. She was now starting to separate them all and remember who everyone was.

Eliza looked over Christiana, taking in every inch of the shadowed assassin. "Yes, you must be Midnight Maiden."

"I am, but you can call me Maiden for now." Her hands twitched in the folds of her jacket's skirt. "Thank you for agreeing to this. I wanted to hear everything from your perspective before deciding if it was the right choice to take the job."

"Are you considering not taking it?" Eliza tucked her legs to her chest, her slightly curled blonde hair spilling over the tops of her knees.

"I want to hear the truth from you. I cater to a specific clientele and I needed to make sure you fit that profile, so can you tell me about your husband?"

Eliza's eyes fell flat, emptying of every emotion. "He's heartless."

"I know it's hard, but I need more details than that. So, I'm going to ask you some questions, all right?" Christiana desperately wanted to reach out to Eliza, to sit on the bed next to her and rub her back while she explained what was happening to her. But she forced herself to stay in place, pretending her feet were nailed to the floorboards so she wouldn't take even one step toward the young woman.

"Fine," Eliza agreed, curling her hands into her soft nightgown.

Christiana took a deep breath, her voice softening. "Was this your first marriage?"

"Second. My first husband died about four years ago of sickness. So the answer, Maiden, before you ask, is yes, it was a happy marriage. I loved my late husband." Her chin twitched.

"How soon after your wedding to the Chancellor did the abuse begin?" Christiana's chest swelled, her skin burning all over. She didn't have much time to give the Prince an answer, but her heart splintered with each painful question she had to ask.

"About nine months after our vows. At first, he was kind to me. It gave me hope we could one day find a special place in our hearts for each other, but I could tell we were both still heartbroken about the deaths of our previous spouses." She bit her lip briefly, her face creasing. "After a while, he started to become easily irritated. His temper would flare at even the smallest of things."

"Eliza..." Christiana began, her voice cracking. But her words were lost as Eliza continued.

"Our cook had burned our dinner one night. That was it. That was all it took for his...temper to finally boil over. He said it was my fault. I should have done a better job at running the household." Her hands grasped onto her nightgown for dear life as she squeezed her legs against her chest. Bile rose in the back of Christiana's throat as Eliza's story continued. "He said I needed to be punished and, for some reason, I agreed to take the punishment. He told me to stand up and he stripped my nightgown off of me before restraining me to the bedpost. He proceeded to lash me ten times with his belt against my back. He took his time with each one, waiting for blood to rise to the surface before dealing the next."

"I'm so sorry," was all Christiana could mutter, her hand instinctively rubbing the base of her throat as she tried to process the whole story. She hated every minute of this. She hated having to put Eliza through reliving such a disgusting memory. Silent tears dripped down Eliza's face, the droplets of water reflecting in the low candlelight next to the bedpost.

Eliza shook her head, bits of tears flinging off her face as she stared up at Christiana. "Afterwards, he didn't ignore what he had done. He helped me clean my back up and even applied medicine every day until it healed completely. He was so proud of how well I took the punishment. I wanted to be sick from his happiness in all of it, but I knew there was nothing I could do."

Christiana swallowed a giant lump in her throat, her voice and mind betraying her. "I'm sorry. I know that is a pathetic thing to say when I made you tell me that story." She squeezed her eyes shut for a moment, trying her best to regain her composure. "I just wanted to get all of the details about the case."

"If you want details, here they are," Eliza spat, turning around and pulling her nightgown down to her waist, the fabric draping downwards to reveal puckered skin covering the entirety of her lean back. The lines crossed her flesh in no specific pattern, the coloring changing from a red-rimmed white to a deep, bluish purple. This poor woman had spent the better part of two years taking brutal punishments and having to bite her tongue after every painful lash. Christiana had seen some horrifying things in her past, but she had never seen a person take such disturbed pleasure in the whole experience. Her entire back flushed with a white-hot burn, her own scarred skin flaring at the sight of Eliza's pain.

"Thank you for the proof. I believe you now." Her gaze fell to the ground as she took a few deep breaths, waiting for the burning in her own scars to dissipate.

Eliza pulled her nightgown back up, her hands shaking as she tied the lace strings back at the nape of her neck. "I can't do this anymore. I don't know how much more I can take before..."

"Before he goes too far?" Christiana concluded. It was what she always feared her father would do while she was growing up.

"Or I end it myself." No tears, pain, or sadness filled her voice. She said it so naturally, as if she was listing off errands she needed to run the next day. Go to the market, have lunch with friends, kill myself before my husband gets home. She had been living with the shame and terror for so long, she finally felt backed into a corner with few options: either Christiana killed him or she would kill herself.

Christiana bit the inside of her cheek. She wanted to run to Eliza, to wrap the poor woman in her arms and hold her to help the pain go away. But she knew that would be a futile attempt at comfort. She would instead do everything in her power to stop the devious man Eliza was forced to call her husband. Her soul settled deep within her, the steady beating of her heart giving her the answer she had been looking for over the past few weeks. "You don't have to worry about that anymore."

Eliza's gaze flew up, her eyes wide. "So does that mean you'll do it? You'll help me?"

"Yes."

"I have one request." Eliza stood up on shaking legs, her arms clutching the bedpost for support.

"Anything." Christiana's chest tightened.

Eliza's jaw tensed. "Make him suffer. Make him suffer the way he made me suffer."

***

The cold, hard stone bit through Christiana's hands as she climbed the palace wall for the second time. The rough ascent screamed at her muscles, her brain already exhausted from her conversation with Eliza earlier that night. Finally reaching the proper window, she peeked down to make sure the guards had yet to rotate back around the grounds before she slid the glass pane open and slipped through into the large space. The dark room welcomed her, most of the candles blown out to prepare for her arrival.

"Good evening, Your Highness." Christiana crossed her arms and leaned on the stone wall deep in the shadowed corner by the window. In the Prince's letter, he had requested she come by his room after her meeting with Eliza, to formally accept or deny the job. It took all her willpower to leave Eliza alone, forced to spend more days tied to that terrible man.

"Maiden." Alekzander looked up briefly from his desk, his hand furiously scribbling, filling the pause with the loud scratching of his quill against the rough parchment. "So, do we have an answer?"

"My services are yours." She tried to keep her voice level, the tingling of her cheeks making it hard to move her mouth at all.

"Wonderful." The news pushed him out of his chair to the front of his desk. Christiana took a few tentative steps forward before stopping, her heart beating faster.

"My typical fee for this type of job is fifty kultas." Alekzander raised his brows at the mention of Viri's highest form of currency, the large golden coins only traded among the high merchant class and the nobles. Christiana rarely made her fee so high, allowing less-wealthy clients to pay any amount they could afford, usually resulting in a mixture of the bright silver pratas and the dingy copper kupari coins. However, she didn't need the Prince knowing she was a bargain. "Half is due now and the other half will be collected once the job is completed."

"And where do you expect me to get this money?" he asked, although he was already rummaging through his desk drawers, the clanging of metal giving away exactly what he was doing.

Christiana rolled her eyes. "Doesn't matter to me as long as it ends up in my hands."

"Very well." He tied a leather pouch shut, strings hanging heavily from the tips of his fingers, the coins forcing the bag to slowly shift back and forth. "But here is a counteroffer for you. I will give you twice that amount, fifty kultas now and another fifty once the job is done. But to get this amount, I must be your only client."

"Excuse me?" Christiana balked. She knew when she first considered this job she wouldn't have the time to take any other clients. If she was going to have this job be successful, she would need to dedicate as much time as possible to figuring out the best way to end this man's life. But that didn't stop her blood from boiling at the Prince's demand, her fists balling at her sides as she stared him down, his gaze equally unwavering.

He crossed his arms, the pouch disappearing into the folds. "I don't need you running away or taking another job and drawing this out longer than it needs to be. I want this done and I want this done right. Which means I need your undivided attention."

"Bold ask, Your Highness. Asking me to give up potential forms of income for one man."

"A dangerous man."

"All the people I go after are dangerous."

"I may not know your entire client list..." Christiana snorted at his words. "But my guess is none of them were as skilled as Julian."

She huffed. "Your point?"

"Seems to me that could make him your most dangerous mark yet." The bag swung from his fingers, beckoning her to accept. "You seem skilled enough to know he'll need all of your attention. I'm just giving you a bit more incentive not to be tempted by anything else."

Honestly, she had no idea why she was even hesitating; the money didn't matter to her. What mattered was helping Eliza and making sure Julian couldn't put one more mark on her. "We have a deal."

Alekzander, with his head held high in triumph, walked over to the same place he had been dropping all their exchanges—the coffee table off to the side. He looked up at her, his sapphire eyes dark with emotion. "How long will it take?"

"I'll need the entire summer." Her hand ticked as she waited for him to walk away from her fee so she could grab it and run. The suffocating room was starting to close in on her the longer she spent in Alekzander's presence.

"The whole summer!? Why so long?" His jaw clenched, forcing his chiseled cheekbones to protrude even farther.

"I told you in our last meeting, Your Highness, sending me after a war hero is not an easy task." Her toes wiggled in her boots as she tried to hurry the conversation along. "I need the time to investigate. Lay low and find a way to infiltrate his everyday life to administer the poison. It is going to take a lot of time and a lot of energy to figure out the best way. Understand?"

"Fine." He walked away, and a breath of air escaped her veil-covered lips as she released her fists. She glided over to the table, peeking in the purse before she dropped it in her favorite hiding spot: her boot.

"You know how to get in contact with me in case of emergencies," she said, making her way to the window escape.

His fist banged on the hard wood of his desk, the loud noise forcing her to whip around to face him again. "I won't get any updates? You won't tell me your plans?"

"No." She frowned. "I don't need you hovering over every moment of my planning process. Besides, it's going to be long and slow, but that's what I'm trained for."

His chin dropped to his chest, a sigh escaping his lips. "Very well. I'll let you know if anything comes up."

"Your Highness." She couldn't stop herself from curtsying, her ruffled jacket sweeping down with her as it billowed against the movement.

"Maiden." He crossed his arms again. With one more shadow-covered nod, Christiana jumped out of the window.

Chapter Fourteen

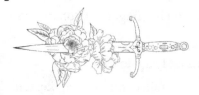

"**T**HANK YOU FOR MEETING ME HERE,"
Christiana welcomed Robert as he rode up to the
front door of her Cittadina cottage house. After
taking a few days off from Maiden duties, her dreams plagued with
images of poor Eliza tied to the bedpost, it was time to sit down and begin
formulating a proper assassination plan. After formally accepting the
offer from Alekzander, the only way to complete this job properly was
to set up a new base of operations like the one at her manor back home.

"Of course, My Lady." Robert dismounted his horse and brought it
over to the stable to settle in before following Christiana inside the house.
It had been almost a year since she had last been there, the collecting of
dust on every surface telling the true time. The common room was
sparsely decorated with one couch, a table with two chairs, and a kitchen
area off to the side. Beyond that was supposed to be the bedroom,
although Christiana rarely slept on the threadbare mattress.

"This needs to be more than a hideout for the summer." She

rummaged through her satchel, pulling out a crumpled piece of parchment. "I've made a list of certain items I'm going to need stocked here, mostly ingredients and things to build a brewing area. Is this something you can handle for me?"

"Of course, My Lady," Robert answered, taking the list from her. Everything on there was fairly simple to obtain, and it wouldn't raise suspicion if he bought it all at the right places. "I'm confused, though. It seems you have everything figured out here. Was this the only reason you wanted me to come?"

"I'm happy it seems that way, but I feel like everything is about to come apart at a moment's notice." She raked her fingers through her hair, twisting a piece around her fingers as Robert's concerned eyes settled on her.

"Is there anything I can do to help?"

"Actually..." she trailed off, sitting herself down on the couch, gesturing for Robert to join her. His eyes narrowed as he took his place by her side. "I know you've been my informant for many years, your help is invaluable to the workings of my double life. But with such a...delicate job, I think I need you a bit more involved."

"How so?" His brow furrowed.

"I want to hire you as my personal secretary for the summer. It means you can spend time with me in the palace and help me keep my lives separate. Since you know about both so well."

His mouth hung open. "Oh...My-My Lady, that is very kind. But..."

"Please, Robert? I would of course pay you for this position. I have an offer all ready. And you can start as soon as you close up any current jobs. We can be as flexible as you need."

"That's not my concern, My Lady."

"Then what is?" she asked, trying to make eye contact with him.

"Well, you and I have never crossed paths in society, before or after your father's death. I'm concerned about what people will say if they start seeing us together without any real explanation."

"Ah, yes, of course!" she said, grabbing her satchel and digging through it to grab a handful of parchment paper. "But I already have that figured out. I started asking around these past few days for a recommendation for a temporary secretary. To no surprise of mine, your name came up often. I even got written recommendations from a few past clients of yours." She handed the pages over to him, his eyes wide as he took in the kind words that had been written about him. "See? I've spread it around that I'm looking to hire someone. When you join my employ, no one will be the wiser as to why you're really there."

"It seems you've tightened up all of the loose ends." He smirked, his broad shoulders relaxing as he handed the papers back to her. He ran his fingers through his hair, still cropped as if he hadn't retired from the military years ago.

"Is that a yes?"

"Of course, I will help you this summer, My Lady." A weight lifted off her chest when he smiled down at her. "You know I would help you in any way I can."

"Speaking of that, come with me for a moment." She led him to the back of the house instead of the front. The property, set with the two-stall stable, also had a pasture ring for the horses to enjoy. However, she knew of a better use for it now that she had decided to attempt assassination on a well-known war hero. She leaned against the ring, old training swords already propped up against the weather-worn wood. "I need you to train me."

He came to an abrupt halt, arms falling limp at his sides. "Excuse me?"

"I need you to fight me and train me like you learned in the military."

"My Lady, you're already trained in multiple weapons. I'm not exactly sure how I can help you with that."

"With this job, I'm expected to fight and win against a trained soldier. I've sparred plenty of times, but battled?" She shook her head. "That's something I've never even been trained for, not against a sword at least. You're an amazing soldier, Robert. You could teach me how."

"I'm nowhere near as good as Chancellor Marlow." He shook his head. "Besides, why would you even attempt to fight him? I thought we discussed it would make more sense to poison him?"

"Of course, it does. But my mentor always taught me to be prepared going into any job. If for some reason I become trapped, I need to learn to fight my way out," she explained. "I'm a master at my daggers and throwing knives, but those are long range weapons. They would never hold up against someone who is a master with a sword. I'm good with a sword but not nearly as good as a soldier."

She could see the hesitation in his eyes. He had spent countless years working with her, but this was the first time she had asked him to pick up a weapon and fight.

"Please," she begged. "I can't do this without you, in more ways than one."

"Fine. But I hope you realize, if we do this, I'll treat you like any other soldier I used to train. When entering a ring, all titles and honors are left on the outside." He jumped into the ring, removing his riding jacket to expose his thin, linen tunic. He picked up one of the dull swords from the wall, making sure it was the proper weight for him. "Are you sure about this?"

"Of course." She smirked, happily following him into the arena, ready to practice as she had so many years ago. Picking up her sword, she let him lead her into a long string of fights lasting well into the sunset.

***

A few days later, Christiana was still sore from the intense training Robert put her through. She was trying her best not to walk too stiffly, her muscles screaming with every gentle movement as she and Dorina walked back to their apartments from the palace dinner.

"Why don't we go and play a game of cards?" Dorina suggested, the balls of her feet bouncing as she looped her arm through Christiana's.

"I don't know, Dorina." She tried not to groan, her foggy mind screaming at her to say no. "I'm not in the mood to go into a crowded game room." It wasn't entirely untrue—the public game room was the most popular place for nobles to continue the evening after a long dinner.

"Neither am I, so we can go to the private one in the Royal Wing. Nice and quiet because no one can go in without an invitation," she offered, her eyes pleading.

With a deep sigh, Christiana nodded, letting the excited princess drag her down the hallway toward her family's part of the palace. It had been many years since Christiana found herself in this secluded part, not including the few meetings she had with Alekzander over the past few weeks, although her typical entrance was not typical for most people. A group of guards stood up straight as the two girls entered the wing with its seemingly-endless stretch of gray stone and elaborate tapestries. The doorway to the game room was already open, the sound of melodic laughter drifting down the hallway to welcome them inside.

"Well, hello boys!" Dorina greeted. Christiana's heart fell as she took in Alekzander and Rowan sitting at a chess table, deeply in the middle of a match. Their bright smiles and infectious laughter filled the room, and they turned toward the entrance to see who was invading their privacy.

"Christiana!" Rowan exclaimed, standing abruptly from his chair to greet her. She plastered a smile on her face as she tried her best not to slip her gaze toward the Prince.

"Hello, Rowan," she greeted, allowing him to give her a quick kiss on the hand before he returned to his seat. "Alekzander." She pushed herself downward into a curtsy, staring tentatively at the floor as she raised herself again.

"Hello, Sister," Alekzander greeted Dorina with a smile, his eyes softening as she approached to give him a kiss on the forehead.

"Christiana. What are you two doing here?" His gaze flicked to her, a smirk across his face as he nodded in greeting.

"We were going to play a few rounds of cards. Why don't you two join us?" Dorina offered, sitting herself at one of the large round tables, already shuffling a deck of cards between her nimble fingers. Christiana sat beside her, praying the sweat forming on her forehead wouldn't completely ruin the cosmetics she had worked so hard to paint on her face for the evening.

"I would love to." Rowan smiled, taking a seat on the other side of Christiana, placing his half-full cup of wine on the table in front of him.

"Well, since my chess partner abandoned me, I suppose I will as well." The Prince laughed, retrieving two extra goblets from the liquor cabinet in the back before returning to the group's table. He poured from the jug of red wine he and Rowan had already started to consume, placing the glasses in front of Dorina and Christiana. She could feel the heat of his arm against her cheek, his towering form leaning over her as he placed the goblet by her hand. She breathed in to stop her racing pulse, the lingering scent of cedarwood embracing her even after he took his seat across from her.

Dorina dealt the cards and the four friends engaged in a few rounds of games they hadn't played together in years. Laughter filled the room, the other three dominating the conversation while Christiana sat quietly in her own seat. She wanted to be included, wished she could find a way to open her mouth and engage with three people she couldn't stop herself from caring about. But every time she felt Alekzander's gaze on her, words seemed unable to escape her lips.

"Goodness, Christiana, I don't remember you being this bad at playing." Dorina laughed as Christiana threw her cards down in defeat, the only one who had yet to win a round.

"It was never my strong suit," she teased herself, taking a sip of wine and letting out a more relaxed laugh. The second glass was helping her nerves.

"That can't be true." Rowan grazed her hand for a moment before pulling away, the warmth of his touch lingering on her fingers.

"It is," Alekzander answered, smiling at Christiana. "You and I used to play all the time. You always struggled to keep your cards a secret."

"Did I?" she challenged, internally laughing at the idea of her struggling to keep a secret from people.

"You twitch your nose." He pulled the newly dealt cards to his chest and arranged them in his preferred order.

"Excuse me?"

"Your nose." He looked up at her. "You twitch it when you have a bad hand."

"I do?" He nodded. "How did you notice?"

"I've always noticed things about you." He shrugged, setting her cheeks on fire at the mention. Her hand stroked the base of her throat, her eyes unable to focus on the cards in front of her. She couldn't stop her mind from wondering if he had noticed anything particularly distinct about the Maiden.

"Zee has always been a shark at noticing people's card tells." Rowan laughed, cutting the tension.

"It's a skill I've come to hone over the years." He smirked, once again taking the winning hand as the rest of the cards were gathered up.

Laughter came from down the hall, deep voices growing stronger before a nearby door swung open. Christiana's ears perked up, recognizing one of them as Julian. She bit her lip; these were moments she couldn't let pass through her fingers.

"Another round?" Dorina asked, though everyone's eyes were starting to glaze over at the late hour.

"I think it's time for me to take my leave," Christiana said. "I don't think I can keep my eyes open any longer."

"All right," Dorina pouted. "But would you be able to stop by my room tomorrow afternoon? I have a surprise for you!"

"Of course," she replied, curtsying to the group before she turned to leave.

"Would you like an escort back to your apartment?" Rowan offered, standing up next to her, hope filling his eyes.

"Oh, no, please." She gestured for him to sit back down. "I wouldn't want to keep you from the fun. I will see everyone another time." She walked briskly out of the room and closed the door behind her. She didn't need them to see what was about to happen.

She walked a few steps away, her friends' voices dissipating with the distance. She waited a few heartbeats, leaning against the wall, her hands holding her up as if she was struggling with something. Footsteps approached as she lifted her skirt and pretended to fiddle with the heel of her shoe.

"Marchioness?" She looked up to see Julian a few feet away, his face creased with confusion. "Are you alright?"

"Oh, yes, Chancellor." She let her skirt fall as she stood up straight, a dazzling smile across her face though she yearned to attack him right then and there. This was her first time seeing him since her meeting with Eliza, her fingers twitching at the mere sight of his suave features. She forced her anger to her depths, remembering this act was all to help Eliza. "My shoe slipped off my foot while I was walking. Maybe I shouldn't have had that last glass of wine!" She giggled, the sound like sand on her tongue, rough and unwelcome.

"Please, let me escort you back to your apartment." He held his arm out, kind eyes beckoning her to accept.

"Oh, I wouldn't want to bother you..." she trailed her sentence off and took a few steps back, wanting to seem like this was the last thing she wanted.

"I insist." He stepped closer, arm still outstretched for her to grab hold of.

"Thank you." She grasped his arm above his elbow and could feel the thickness of his muscles even under the heavy fabric of his plum evening coat. He might be well into his forties, but clearly he wasn't relaxed with his workouts.

Silence fell over them for a few moments, their steps muffled by the carpets lining the halls of the resident apartments. Knowing she only had a few more minutes with him, she took a deep breath. "So, Chancellor, ever since our last conversation, I had a thought."

"Oh?" He looked at her, eyebrows raised. "Please, do tell."

"Well, you were so kind to me." She paused, nodding in appreciation. "And you spoke so highly of your wife...Eliza, right?" She hesitated around Eliza's name, wanting him to think she was impaired, hoping it would lower his guard.

He smiled, patting her hand. "Yes, Eliza."

"Well, she sounds lovely, and unfortunately I don't know many people here anymore because I've been gone for so long." She tried to make her words come quicker than usual, even slurring a bit to make her seem more inebriated than she was. He held her hand tight, keeping her pulled close. She had to force herself not to pull away, his touch like shackles trying to weigh her down. "I would love to have her over for tea sometime next week! To get to know her better."

"What a kind offer, My Lady..."

"Christiana, please, I insist." She batted her lashes at him, her skin crawling with every action. She kept repeating in her mind: *this is worth it.*

"Christiana." He laughed, shoulders shaking slightly. "Honestly, the two of us would love to have you over for dinner some time! I know Eliza would love to meet you."

"How thoughtful of you." She kept her smile bright, but suspicion creeped in. It was expected of an abuser that he wouldn't allow his wife to come to her apartment alone, insisting he be with her. She had taken that into account, knowing that trying to get close to Eliza would mean her being able to observe Julian up close as well. She could maybe find some piece of information leading her to the perfect assassination plan that eluded her. But she had a nagging feeling he would do whatever it took to keep Eliza away from her.

"However," Julian went on, and she bit the inside of her cheek, ready to express fake disappointment with whatever excuse he was about to come up with. "I'm leaving tomorrow for about a week. I have some business to tend to in Astary territory."

Christiana's heart dropped to the pits of her belly. This was not good news. "Oh, I see."

"When I'm gone for more than a few days, Eliza insists on coming with me." He looked off down the hall, eyes dazed. "We hate being apart for so long. With my job, if she didn't travel with me, I would never see her!"

She forced herself to laugh with him, knowing it was far from Eliza's decision to go on these trips. "Maybe some other time, then." She kept her voice even, her insides squirming as she realized what this trip would do to her investigation. She wasn't going to get anywhere anytime soon if he wasn't in the castle long enough for her to observe him.

"Here we are." He stopped them in front of her apartment door. "Now that you are back at court, may I give you a piece of advice?"

Christiana's spine straightened. "Of course."

"Image is important here and rumors can destroy it." His icy gaze held her. "Make sure to remember that when you make important choices."

"Thank you." Was all she could respond, her nerves twisting inside of her. What was he trying to imply?

"Always a pleasure, Christiana." He removed her hand from his arm and gave it a gentle kiss.

A shudder ran up her spine and she fought not to vomit at the sound of her name on his tongue. "Have a lovely evening, Chancellor."

She let herself into her apartment, closing the door behind her and collapsing against it, every muscle in her body tense. "Natalia!"

Natalia appeared instantly, her steps hurried as she walked from Christiana's bedroom. "Yes, My Lady?"

"I need a bath." The hour was late, but every inch of her felt dirty. Her skin was crawling from being near Julian, as if his vile personality was contagious.

"A lavender and jasmine one, if I had to guess." Natalia gently grabbed Christiana's arm, guiding her to the couch.

Christiana tilted her head. "What makes you say that?"

"It's your favorite scent when you're this tense." She forced Christiana to sit down, her hands on her hips. This woman knew Christiana's needs even better than she did. "I even know how to make it better."

"Oh?"

"I'm going to send down for some chocolate cherry truffles for you to enjoy while you soak!"

"Your words are music to my ears!" The tension in her shoulders already began to release at the mere thought. She knew she had to find a solution to her Julian problem, but that problem was best tackled tomorrow.

Chapter Fifteen

AS PROMISED, CHRISTIANA FOUND HERSELF IN front of Dorina's room the next day, her stomach knotted at the surprise waiting behind the closed door. After one deep breath to try and loosen the uncomfortable feeling, she swiftly knocked, and a young servant girl promptly opened the door to reveal a beaming Dorina at her side.

"Thank you for coming!" she squealed.

"Well, you said it was a surprise." Christiana gave her a narrow glance, moving into her apartment, splashed in warm sunlight through the windows that made up the far wall. The entire room was perfectly decorated for the princess, the dusty blue-and-gold accented couches surrounding the floor-to-ceiling fireplace to invite people in.

"Well, Father told us a visiting ambassador from Amarglio will be coming to the palace in only a week's time. So, Father has decided to welcome Ambassador Renald with the first ball of the season!"

"A ball?" Christiana gaped, practically falling into one of the plush seats in the common area.

"Isn't it exciting!? The first ball is always great fun and to keep with tradition for visiting dignitaries, it will be a masquerade."

"Oh, lovely." Christiana groaned. She had done so much to prepare for potential balls, but the one thing she forgot to purchase was a decent dress to pair with a theme and mask.

"I also figured you wouldn't have anything to wear for a masquerade," Dorina said as if she had read Christiana's mind, "so I had our family dress designer make some options for you to try on. She'll be here any minute with them so you can make a decision."

"Really?" Christiana delicately reached out to Dorina.

Dorina's eyes glimmered. "Of course. It's your first ball as a titleholder, you deserve to hold your head up high in style. I want you to enjoy every minute of it."

"Thank you, Dorina." Christiana stood to embrace her best friend. The kindness Dorina held in her heart, not only for Christiana but everyone else, seemed boundless sometimes. It made her feel lucky each day she decided to let Dorina back in her life.

Another knock at the door interrupted their embrace. "Princess Dorina!" A tall, thin woman greeted them with a beaming smile as she entered, her dark hair pulled back in a tight bun, most likely to keep it from falling on her face while she worked. A procession of servants right behind her carrying at least a dozen dresses.

Dorina let out a melodic laugh. "Hello, Alda, thank you for helping us."

"My dear child, I'm at your disposal. Now, this must be the famous Marchioness that has the court buzzing." She smiled, turning toward Christiana, whose stomach retightened at the woman's intense gaze.

"It's nice to meet you, Miss Alda," Christiana rasped.

"Let me have a look at you." Alda skipped a formal greeting to begin circling her like a hawk, dissecting every inch of prey before swooping in. Christiana's scalp prickled as Alda continued, "The Court whispers do you absolutely no justice, My Lady. Wait until we get you in one of my gowns, the vultures won't be able to control themselves."

"Well, don't you have a high opinion of the Court," Christiana remarked as Alda pulled her toward the bedroom, Dorina quietly in tow.

"I can't say it's my favorite place. Now strip to your underthings so we can start putting my beautiful creations on that wonderful body of yours." She turned her back on the girls and walked over to the line of dresses.

"That bit about it not being her favorite place is an understatement," Dorina remarked. She stood behind Christiana to help her unlace her dress, whispering in her ear, "Alda hates court and all the odious people that come with it. Her words, not mine. She only stays nearby because of her relationship with my parents. She's been styling them since my father's coronation thirty-two years ago."

"Impressive," Christiana remarked as she shimmied out of her dress, the light fabric puddling at her feet. She watched Alda move methodically between the sea of fabric, her long fingers flying with purpose. She finally decided on the first dress and brought it over for her. Christiana groaned at the bright raspberry-pink fabric, but she was too overwhelmed to question Alda's decision. She allowed the maids to lace her inside as she became a bright pink poof before their very eyes.

"Absolutely gorgeous," Alda gushed, moving around Christiana to fluff every little part of the skirt's large circumference. "I knew that color would look beautiful with your porcelain skin."

"Stunning," Dorina commented from her bed, stifling a laugh by biting her plump lower lip. Christiana couldn't stop herself from pushing hard on the skirt, trying with all her strength to make it lay flatter.

"What exactly am I supposed to be?" she asked, staring at the gold-and-pink mask a young girl had placed in her hands.

"Isn't it obvious? You're a peony flower! Freshly bloomed for the summer season."

"Ah, yes, now I see it." The short ruffles making up the full skirt did resemble the delicate petals of a peony. "However, I can't say I'm much for flowers. And bright colors such as these, for that matter."

"But you need to stand out!"

"And why is that?"

Alda's scrawny hands encapsulated Christiana's shoulders, giving them an encouraging shake. "You are the most eligible woman in this court right now. You need to make yourself shine through the entire party, leave no head unturned."

"Oh, for goodness sake," Christiana whispered under her breath. She already had to deal with everyone else pressuring her to make a decision, the last person she needed it from was the dressmaker. "I appreciate the concern, Alda, but I would rather be comfortable with what I'm wearing when meeting these men, which means wearing a dress better fitting my style."

"Very well." She huffed. "Let me see what else we have."

"Attracting a man?" Christiana questioned Dorina, whose laughter had finally erupted from now that Alda's back was turned. "Is everyone entitled to an opinion of my love life?"

Dorina shrugged, playing with the soft silk quilt laid perfectly on her large canopy bed. "Maybe not, but it doesn't stop people from having one. It doesn't matter anyway, I'm sure it's easy to ignore now."

"What do you mean?"

"What with you spending time with Rowan, I assumed you had made up your mind quickly."

"Of course not!" Christiana gawked. "I've been helping him with paperwork and clerical nonsense. He's still learning and I offered to help."

"Please, Rowan had all of that figured out the minute he took over. His father did train him before his apprenticeship with the physician. He's a smart man; he didn't forget any of it. He's using it as a reason to spend time with you."

She stared at Dorina. "Are you sure?"

"Look, I care about you, so trust me when I tell you you're sometimes difficult to approach. Some people find you a bit..." Dorina trailed off.

"A bit what?"

With a hesitant look in her eyes, Dorina answered, "Closed off? Rigid?"

"Oh." Christiana dropped her head to look at the floor as she tried to absorb that.

Alda rustled over just then with another large dress. Not even paying attention to their conversation, she diligently helped Christiana into the new dress, this one as bad as the first. Although the black-and-burnt-orange coloring was a better choice, it was the huge wings that sprung from her back and the large wing-shaped mask that gave her concern. At least this time she was able to identify the costume as a butterfly. Not willing to explain again, all she did was shake her head before starting to remove the dress.

"I know you're not like that, Ana." Dorina picked up their conversation once Alda walked away again. "But not many people know you as well as I do, especially men. It's been so long since you were last here, and you come off a little too formal sometimes. Rowan was just trying to find a common subject to help you relax around him."

"How do you know all of this?" Christiana asked, leaning against the hardwood post of Dorina's bed, arms crossed as she rubbed her upper arm.

"I may have overheard Rowan telling Zander his plan," she admitted.

"Dorina!" Christiana pretended to scold, but she was secretly pleased her friend was finding out such valuable information.

"Well, they shouldn't have been talking about it in a public place. Granted, they thought the hallway was empty for the night, but I guess you never know when a young princess decides it's a good idea to take a late-night walk around the Royal Family wing."

"Oh, my goodness." Christiana laughed, shaking her head. She was once again distracted as Alda came back with the third dress. She didn't even need to put it on to know she would never like it. The skirt was made up of multiple pastel colors. It was probably supposed to be a mythological creature of some sort. "Alda, may I choose the next dress?"

"Oh, well..." Alda's face creased as she tripped over her words, her fingers rumpled in the bright fabric.

"Please?"

"Of course, My Lady." Alda bowed her head.

Christiana looked over all the dresses. Most were brightly-colored, covered in frills or emulated some kind of pretty character, all far too girlish for Christiana's personal style. However, there was one dress, hidden behind two others, that she was interested in taking a better look at.

"May I see the one on the end, please, the blue one?" she asked, directing a maid to pull it out. The dress was stunning, made from a midnight-blue velvet. The flowing sleeves and square-cut neckline seamlessly fell right into the tight, simple bodice embroidered with a silver moon. But it was the full skirt that took her breath away. The dark blue chiffon was perfectly contrasted with the shimmering sparkle of minuscule jewels, reflecting the light with each delicate movement. They were placed perfectly, arranged like the stars in the night sky. "Now, this is exactly what I'm looking for."

"I didn't make that one, My Lady," Alda confessed, her lips tightening into a straight line. "It was designed by my daughter, Lorraine." She nodded to the corner of the room, where a tall yet angular woman stood silently. Christiana hadn't even realized the young woman was Alda's daughter at first, but the closer she looked between them, the more she saw the resemblance—the dark hair and deep brown eyes specifically. Not wanting to step in her mother's light, she held her silence, squirming under Christiana's gaze.

"I would like to try it on."

"Of course, My Lady," Lorraine answered, wide-eyed as she took the dress over and helped Christiana step into the luscious fabric. She worked silently and efficiently, lacing up the back.

"It's perfect, Lorraine," Christiana complimented when she stared back at herself in the mirror. "I especially love the mask." She gazed down at the delicate silver mask in her hands. It wasn't too big, just enough to cover her eyes and most of her forehead, woven together in a filigree pattern.

"Thank you, My Lady. I wanted something that complimented the dress without distracting from it."

"Well I love it. I can't wait to wear it to my first ball here at the palace."

Lorraine's eyes filled with tears. This could be her first sale, let alone from someone so prominent in the noble court. Christiana's heart warmed as she watched the young lady pull at the dress, finding a few places where it was too loose. "I think it will need to be taken in a little. Do you mind if I pin it now? I can have it completed by the end of tomorrow."

"Wonderful," Christiana agreed, and Lorraine set to work. "So, who else will be attending the ball, Dorina?"

"Everyone who is staying here for the summer of course, unless there is some kind of emergency elsewhere. Father typically invites other prominent members that choose to stay at their own estates during the season. Some come and others choose to politely decline. And of course, the entire council will be required to attend, since the reason for the ball is a matter of the Crown."

"Including the Chancellor?" she asked, looking over at Dorina, whose smiling face fell at the mention. "I had heard rumors he was away from the castle right now."

"Of course, he comes to all of these affairs no matter how small. My father practically demands it. Julian seems to have a way of charming visiting dignitaries." Dorina slid off the bed to have a closer look at Christiana's gown.

"He seems like a charming man in general."

"I guess," Dorina shrugged. "I don't know him well, to be honest. He's always treated me very formally. Whenever I try to start a conversation of substance with him, he dismisses me and claims it's too complicated for me to understand."

Christiana's face creased, her fingers tingling at the idea of her best friend's pain. "Doesn't that bother you?"

"A little," she admitted, her jaw clenching. "But he's not the only one who treats me like my head is stuffed with clouds. He's just the only one who does it in a condescending manner. Everyone else laughs as if I'm making a joke."

"I'm sorry, Dorina."

"It's all right. To be honest, I've always felt unsettled around Julian. It must be me because every other woman at this court positively swoons when he walks into the room. Probably a clash in our personalities that puts me off." She shrugged as if to push off a pesky bug, but Christiana felt differently. She always knew Dorina had the ability to read people; it came with her upbringing as the silent child people tended to forget could actually hear. Christiana trusted her opinion on Julian more than anyone else in the court, even Alekzander.

"There," Lorraine announced, clasping her hands after she placed the last pin. "That should do it, My Lady. I will have it delivered to your apartment once I finish with all the alterations."

"Thank you, Lorraine," she replied as she carefully removed the garment from her body. With a deep curtsy of both formality and appreciation, Lorraine and Alda left, their line of servants and dresses following in their wake.

"Our first ball together in over five years!" Dorina giggled, bringing over Christiana's day dress to help her put it back on. "I still can't believe it's been so long."

"I know," Christiana mumbled as she stepped her bare foot into the dress. Dorina pulled the fabric up and began clasping the trail of buttons that made up her corset. As she felt each cinch and pull of the tightening dress, Christiana's mind wandered to her last ball at the palace.

The first ball of the summer season was always an overly lavish one in Christiana's opinion. She wasn't even sure what was being celebrated tonight as she stood in a corner of the large ballroom with her parents. Isabelle, still too young to attend, was left behind, making Christiana the center of her father's attention tonight.

"Here you go, my darling." Francis Santinella offered her a wine goblet. Taking it from his hands, she sipped, surprised it was filled with water.

"Thank you, Father." Her typical monotone reply to most of her father's words.

"Smile," he ordered, a tight grin spreading across his own face. "This is a happy occasion. You're having a good time."

"Of course." She smiled back even though it was the last thing she wanted to do. She felt alone, her mind closing in on itself as she tried to ignore the dozens of people slowly circling around her. Her garish, poofy blush dress felt like it was swallowing her alive, making her writhe her shoulders around as she tried to get comfortable. "May I go and find myself some food?"

"Yes, my dear. But don't take so long that I have to come and find you." He said with a smile, but his words dripped with the loom of a threat.

She walked into the throng of people, a weight lifting off her chest with each step she took away from him. Although she didn't want to get into trouble, she took her time when she finally reached the food table, surveying all her options and carefully picking out what she wanted.

"Don't you look beautiful!" came an excited voice beside her. Dorina pushed herself past a few people to stand next to Christiana, smiling broadly.

"Thank you, so do you," she said formally, curtsying to the Princess. She looked absolutely radiant, with her cream-and-gold dress accenting her brown eyes.

She clutched Christiana's arm, tugging as she bounced on the balls of her feet. "Are you hungry? Or would you like to come and dance with me?"

"Actually, I was picking up some food to bring over to my parents. I should get back to them." She yearned for time with Dorina, her hands desperate to clutch her friend while they enjoyed a dance together. But this year was different. Her father had made his decision clear on their carriage ride here: she was to stay away from the royal children. If she lingered here too long, she would pay for it later tonight.

"Oh, come now!" Dorina jostled her lightly. "They've gotten to spend time with you for most of the summer already. They can spare you for a bit so we can spend time together."

"I'm sorry, Dorina. But I can't." She tried to turn away, back to her parents' corner, but a strong grip stopped her, Dorina grabbed her arm to keep her from leaving.

"But why?" she asked, hurt eyes staring at Christiana, full of questions.

Her hand grasped Dorina's, her head racing as she stared into her best friend's eyes. She knew she couldn't say the words out loud; she wouldn't dare speak them in such a public place. But if she could get Dorina to understand, to see what was happening to her behind closed doors, maybe, just maybe, there would be hope for her life and for her friendship.

Her grip tightened on the princess's, trying her best to speak her real thoughts through her eyes instead of her mouth as she stuttered, "I just..."

"Christiana," came her father's stern voice from behind her. Her stomach quivered at the sound. Tears threatened to escape her eyes, wanting so badly to show Dorina what was happening with their family. But all she could do was use every ounce of strength to keep her tears concealed, making

sure not one escaped down her cheek.

"I have to go," Christiana said, releasing her grasp from the Princess's hand and allowing her own to fall limply at her side.

"But, Ana..." Dorina started, taking a step closer.

"I'm sorry," she whispered, shaking her head as she walked back into the seclusion of a crowd that was now her life.

Tears threatened to escape Christiana's eyes as the memory flooded back. That moment she could have reached out, could have opened up to the girl who always stood beside her. But she had walked away instead and played into the hands of her father, keeping away from the one person who had never stopped caring about her.

Dorina tightened the final buttons of her dress, smoothing the billowing sleeves hanging down her shoulders. Without even a glance, Christiana reached up and caught her hand, grasping it the same way she had five years ago.

"I'm sorry," was all she could manage, her eyes downcast at the floor.

Dorina's grip tightened around Christiana's cold fingers. "For what?"

"For walking away. For never explaining what happened that summer. For still not explaining. And for going silent for so long." Her tears fell freely now, dripping down her face onto the wispy fabric of her dress, darkening the fabric at the touch of her pain.

Dorina's free arm encircled her waist to pull her backward into an embrace. "I always knew you kept secrets from me, Ana. I've known that since we were young girls. But it never mattered to me, because when you did come to me, it was because of our friendship and nothing more. It still doesn't matter. All I care about is that you finally returned to me, with nothing more than your desire for the connection we once had. As long as you still want it, this bond can never sever."

"Thank goodness." She turned to embrace the one girl who would never leave her side.

Chapter Sixteen

THE NOTE FROM ROWAN HAD CHANGED THAT morning. The same scrawling handwriting and the typical navy-blue crest, but the words were completely different. After two weeks of working together, Christiana teaching him about his new land, he had moved on from work and instead invited her for an afternoon horseback ride through the forest. She tried to settle her knotting stomach while she hurried to meet him, remembering what Dorina had told her a few days ago during her dress fitting. If Rowan's intentions were as obvious as Dorina made them seem...

She couldn't stop her palms from sweating inside her leather riding gloves as she approached the large stable. Rowan was already standing by the entrance with their horses saddled, but Christiana's steps faltered when she noticed two crossbows sitting on a bale of hay next to him.

"I'm so happy you were able to join me today." He beamed.

She tried to match his excitement, but she couldn't tear her gaze away from the weapons. "Are you expecting some kind of danger during our ride?"

"Oh, no." He laughed with her, picking one of the bows up with the matching case full of bolts. "I thought instead of a regular ride, we could do a little hunting while we're out, add a bit of excitement to the afternoon."

"Oh." Christiana's pulse sped up as he tried to hand her the crossbow. The muscles in her shoulders tensed, her fingers tugging at each other to stop them from shaking.

His eyes narrowed. "Is something wrong?"

"Um." She tried to formulate an excuse, her mind racing. "The truth is, I don't enjoy hunting. I'm sorry."

"That's all right." His shoulders slumped, eyes downcast. "Though I have to admit, I'm surprised." Disappointment was written all over his face, his fingers fiddling with the reins.

It had been five years since Christiana successfully shot an arrow. Her last few memories handling a bow were not pleasant ones, forcing her to remove the weapon from her repertoire. She hated disappointing him like this, but trying to use the bow would not be the relaxing afternoon they both wanted.

"I know." She took Willow's reins from Rowan, greeting her favorite mare with a gentle scratch behind her ears. "I'm not good with a bow and seeing as it's the primary weapon for hunting...it makes it difficult to get into the sport."

"I guess that's fair."

"You should still hunt, though." She mounted, her plum riding jacket flowing behind her as she adjusted herself comfortably. "I'd love to watch and keep you company."

"Are you sure that won't be too dreary for you?" Rowan pulled himself up in his own saddle, his steed a few inches taller than her mare.

"Absolutely not! It'll be exciting." They pushed their horses from the stable, past the threshold of the forest, the lush greenery welcoming them as the soft sunlight filtered through the thick leaves. "Besides, I don't think I can ever consider time spent with you dreary."

"Oh, really now?" He shot her a sly grin.

She rolled her eyes. "If we can get through hours of paperwork and I still enjoy your company, then yes, I don't find you dreary."

"Well, what an honor." He puffed his chest out playfully, a look of mock pride across his face. Christiana couldn't stop herself from laughing, reaching out to nudge him as their horses trotted next to each other. This was one of the many reasons she loved being in Rowan's presence. Things had yet to be tense between them. She always felt a level of comfort with him that a lot of people's company lacked.

The next hour went by in a blur, falling between complacent silence as Rowan focused on shooting, and easy conversation. Christiana's fingers twitched at each shot he took, her chest stirring with a longing to join in. Although she didn't hunt with arrows, she had gone hunting with Marek many times in the past few years using her throwing daggers as her weapon of choice. It was a way for him to teach her how to hit moving targets with her long-range weapon. She wished she could have brought her knives, but they weren't the most acceptable weapon within the nobility.

She was content enough with just riding through the forest while she watched Rowan. Her favorite part was the smell of the crisp air blowing against her skin and through her hair—a freeing feeling she craved. She didn't feel an obligation to the Crown, to her title, to her assassin life or anything in between. She could be alone and free from everything weighing her down. Even if for a few fleeting moments, she was able to take a step back and be a perfectly normal woman.

She didn't crave it much, but sometimes it was all she wanted.

They finally decided to take a break in the afternoon, their horses gleaming with sweat from the warm summer air surrounding them. They came across a stream, the gentle sounds of the current and the dense, bright foliage creating a relaxing environment. They dismounted their horses and led them over to the cool stream to take a well-deserved drink.

"Would you like to sit?" Rowan pointed at the large, flat rock they stopped by. It was the perfect size for both of them to sit on and enjoy the breeze blowing off the stream.

"All right." Christiana nodded, following Rowan over to the hard surface. The cool stone seeped through the thick material of her riding pants, and she leaned backward, letting her mind wander far away.

"Water?" Rowan offered a dark brown waterskin. With a smile, she accepted, pulling a few gulps. "Have you enjoyed these past couple weeks back at the palace?"

"For the most part." She shrugged, her arms falling to rest her elbows on the stone. "It has only been a month, though."

"That's true, although you must be excited for the masquerade," he hinted, looking down at her.

"Yes, I am." Her ey tyes narrowed at him.

"Speaking of the ball. I have something I wanted to ask you."

"All right." Her stomach knotted again at the direction the conversation was going.

"I was wondering if...you would let me escort you to the ball tomorrow night?"

"Really?" She tilted her head, her fingers scratching at the rock.

"I've enjoyed getting reacquainted with you over these past few weeks working together," he explained, his hand reaching out to touch the top of hers. "I'd like to be able to spend more time together outside the library walls. Learning about each other instead of the price of a cow."

She pulled herself upright, her brows creasing as she tried to think of the right words to explain the churning deep in her stomach. "I've enjoyed it too, Rowan. But...the truth is we barely know each other."

"I know that."

"There's so much about me you don't know yet. And honestly, I'm not sure when I'd be ready to talk to you about it." The amount of secrets filling her head, her past and all the complications in her present life, made her head spin at even the prospect of explaining them to Rowan.

"I know that, too," he soothed, his hand stroking her upper arm, the heat from his palm soaking into her skin through her embroidered half-sleeve. "I'm not asking you to bare your soul to me at this moment. I'm not even asking for a courtship yet. I know you have your own life, one that you've lived on your own for a while now. When I spend time with you, I feel a comfort I can't say I've been lucky enough to have with many women over the years."

"I feel that too." And it was true. Every moment she spent with Rowan over these past few weeks, his kind smile and warm gaze always brought her a moment of peace in such a chaotic place.

"Well, then, we shouldn't ignore it. I see potential between us, Christiana. I think this could be something lovely if we take a chance to explore what it could be." The tip of his pinky caressed hers, their hands still placed on the cold stone. The softness sent a chill through her.

"I see the potential too," she admitted, but she couldn't ignore the tightening of her chest. The man in front of her was amazing, honest, and kind, and had been her first choice even before arriving at the palace weeks ago. She thought it would be an easy choice, but an emptiness deep in her stomach stirred now that the moment had finally arrived.

"You do?" His eyes gleamed, his smile growing so large it touched the tips of his defined cheekbones. He had yet to move his hand from her arm, grip tightening as he refused to take his eyes off of her.

The pang of guilt grew deeper in her stomach, eating her from the inside. She couldn't bring herself to match his excitement, no matter how much she wished she could. But her options were limited and the comfort Rowan brought her was one in a million. She couldn't deny him just because something felt off.

"Just an escort?" She pursed her lips, leaning back to escape Rowan's grasp.

"That's it. A walk from your apartment to the ballroom. After that, the night is yours to spend it how you want. Although I do hope you will save a dance for me." He winked, breaking the tension forming in her shoulders when she smiled back at him.

"I think I can promise you more than one dance," she teased.

"We can take this slowly." He slung the waterskin back over his shoulder before standing up, reaching out to help her. They made their way back to the horses, who were happily staring off into the sky, their muzzles dripping with fresh water from the stream.

Their laughter filled the air as they rode back to the palace, mixing with the sound of the chirping birds and the crushing of branches below their horses' hooves. Soon enough, the stables came into view, and two stable hands ran over to them, taking the reins. Christiana and Rowan dismounted and allowed their horses to be taken away.

"Shall we practice for tomorrow?" Rowan teased, his arm outstretched.

"Practice does make perfect." Christiana laughed as they began their long walk back to the palace entrance, her hand in his arm.

"Look who finally returned." The Prince made his way across the lawn in Rowan and Christiana's direction, and her heart began to race at the sound of his deep voice. He wasn't alone, a young woman next to him, and Christiana dug her nails into the light green fabric of Rowan's jacket. "How was your ride today, you two?"

They both bowed properly to him before rising into an informal conversation. "Quite enjoyable." Rowan smiled.

"And you, Marchioness?" Alekzander inquired, turning his gaze to Christiana.

She hoped her reddened cheeks were masked by the sweat of a long ride. A tight smile spread across her lips. "An enjoyable ride, Your Highness."

"I can't see why," sniffed the young lady. "The sun is beating down so heavily, I'm surprised you were even able to breathe while you rode through the forest."

"Christiana, may I introduce you to Elaine Dorcaster, the daughter of the Duke of Stroisia. Elaine, this is Her Ladyship, the Marchioness of Tagri."

Christiana nodded. "Very nice to meet you, Elaine."

"You as well, My Lady," she said with a formal curtsy.

"We were on our way back to the castle. Would you care to walk with us?" Rowan asked politely.

"Of course," Alekzander responded. "We were heading toward the gardens anyways."

"We're expected to join his family for afternoon tea soon," Elaine bragged, wrapping her hands around Alekzander's arm as if trying to claim him like a prized horse. Christiana's nose wrinkled at the pointed comment, taking in Elaine as she talked. Her heart-shaped face perfectly matched her onyx hair and bright green eyes. Although she was more on the petite side, at least two or three inches shorter than Christiana, she made up for her lack of height with a commanding presence.

"How lovely," Christiana mocked, pretending it was the most interesting thing she had learned all day.

"The two of you are welcome to join us as well," Alekzander offered.

The last thing Christiana wanted to do was spend even more time with him. Just walking with him now in the presence of others caused her nerves to try jumping out of her body. Sensing her hesitation, Rowan rescued her from an awkward situation. "A wonderful offer, Zee, but I think Ana and I have neglected our responsibilities enough for the day."

"Of course, they can't join us, all covered in dirt and sweat. It isn't proper," Elaine sneered.

"You're absolutely right, Elaine," Christiana agreed over the crunch of gravel under her boots. Sounds of sword fighting drifted to them, the soldiers practicing off in the training ring she had caught Alekzander in. "I would never want to offend the King and Queen with the natural ramifications of taking a ride through the forest."

"Well, you wouldn't sweat as much if you had a proper summer riding outfit." She nodded to Christiana's half sleeved jacket. Although it was proper for women to always wear a sleeve of some kind, it was considered respectable to wear sleeveless riding outfits during the hotter months of the year. However, Christiana always preferred ones with sleeves to keep the jagged scar on her upper left arm covered. The last thing she wanted was for people to question how she got it. "If you need help finding a good designer to make you a proper one, I would be more than happy to suggest one. She's talented when it comes to creating exquisite equine outfits."

"Thank you, but I've always preferred to have a sleeve for myself."

"Why on earth would you want to add more fabric to an already hot outfit?" she scoffed.

"Just my preference is all." Christiana tried to keep her jaw loose, her eyes trained ahead as the palace turrets took shape in front of them. She had plenty of reasons to wear modest outfits, her station and her desire to hide scars being the most prominent. However, she refused to stoop to Elaine's level and show off in front of the men.

"Well, it seems this is where we should part," Rowan interrupted, stopping to the group near the palace entrance. "Enjoy tea with your family, Zee."

The Prince turned away with a smile and a sneering Elaine following beside him.

"Well," Christiana said to break the silence. "She seems like an interesting girl."

"Yes, that's one way of putting it." Rowan walked slowly toward the door. "Another way is self-entitled and bratty."

"I didn't want to be rude if she was in such high respect to the

Prince."

"Zander is having a hard time finding someone by himself. Elaine is his parent's pick, so he humors them by spending time with her. Besides, he knows time is running out and this could possibly be his wife in a few months. He figured he would start to get to know her and hopefully learn to handle her quirks. He's still hopeful, though, that he'll meet the right girl."

"I'm sure he will," Christiana agreed politely. All this talk about Alekzander's future wife made her shoulders squirm. She was ready to change the subject.

"Christiana?"

"Hmm?" she responded as they entered through the palace doors.

"Is there something happening between you and Zander?"

Christiana came to a halt. "Um, what makes you say that?"

"I don't mean to be intrusive." Rowan looked at her. "But I couldn't help but notice there seemed to be tension between the two of you."

With a light-hearted laugh, she answered, "Well, a little tension isn't a bad thing. We haven't seen each other since I was eighteen and we haven't had much time to talk now that I'm back."

"Are you sure that's it?"

"Rowan, out with it. What aren't you saying?"

"I've noticed this...tether between the two of you ever since the royal dinner at the beginning of the month." Christiana looked down as he continued, "I meant it when I said I see potential between the two of us. But I don't want to try something if ultimately your heart is drawing you somewhere else."

Christiana sighed, her heart pounding in her ears as she thought of the best way to explain what was happening between her and Alekzander. She didn't want Rowan to worry, especially since the mere idea of her and Alekzander made her chest tighten as if it was smothered in a vise. She knew why her tension was so apparent when she was around the Prince, but what was Rowan seeing from Alekzander? She had been so focused on her own unease, she assumed all the tension was one sided.

A shiver ran up Christiana's spine. She banished her thoughts of what it could be, turning her attention back to Rowan. "Trust me when I say the life the Prince leads is far from compatible to the way I live mine." Her voice hitched slightly. "He's a wonderful man, and a future king I look forward to following one day. But I don't want the life he can offer. I'd rather follow the potential we both see."

"Are you sure?" Rowan asked once more, his smirk quirking at the edge of his lips.

"Yes," she said firmly, wrapping her arm in his and guiding them deeper inside the palace walls.

Chapter Seventeen

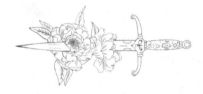

HE EARLY-MORNING SUNLIGHT WAS FINALLY streaming through the small kitchen window when Christiana threw another journal on the floor of her tiny cottage. The first ball of the summer was looming over her, the lush occasion only hours away. Yet she couldn't help but find herself buried in all her assassin notes, her hair free-flowing down her back as she crumpled it through her fingers at the roots. Only a week after formally accepting the job, she had yet to crack the best way to administer a poison to the Chancellor.

She had been forced to put her investigation on hold all week, a skirmish in Stroisia keeping him away from the palace past his intended absence. She had wanted to try and get some insight into what he did all day and if there was ever a moment where she could find a weak spot. Plus, she needed to find the right meal to administer the poison; that was if she could even find a poison to use. The deep throb of a headache settled in her left temple as she began reading her third journal, the scrawl from her poison training with Marek blurring in her tired vision.

Trying to rub the tension out, she could not seem to focus on the words in front of her, the black ink bleeding together like droplets of water had fallen on the worn pages. She slammed the book shut, her hands tingling at the need to be productive. She pushed herself out of her chair, moving slowly into the kitchen. Her hands began to settle as she gathered together glass jars from the cabinet, the dried herbs and flowers gently shaking against the edges as she placed them on the clean counter.

Her arsenal was perfectly stocked, since she'd made sure all of her poison vials were filled completely before leaving for the summer. But she couldn't sit around any longer, the buzzing of her skin and the tingling at her fingertips begging her to move and be productive. The only thing she could think of to refocus her mind was to try and brew a vial or two of something. She didn't really care what it was as long as it kept her hands busy.

She began pulling out ingredients to make extra vials of a few poisons. Her lips twitched into a smirk when she realized she had instinctually pulled ingredients for two of her favorites.

She started with the easiest, spending the next hour making the first poison Marek had taught her to brew: Amnesia. The ingredients flowed together as they steeped in boiling water, clear liquid turning milky white to show it was finished. Amnesia was one of her favorite poisons, a sleep-inducing drug that erased the last few hours of the victim's memory. Whenever she needed to do a bit more 'research' into a mark, Amnesia helped her interrogate people for information without risking their big mouths telling others about it. It was also the first poison she ever administered to another person.

She moved on to her next brew: Crimson Fire. It was Marek's signature poison when he killed as the Crimson Knight, and one of the last poisons she learned with him. Years of training finally gave him confidence in divulging the secret recipe he had concocted decades ago.

She rarely used this recipe, her own signature poison Midnight being her typical choice for her cases, but she always made sure she had a vial of Crimson Fire on hand to be prepared.

It seemed she would have an overstock now.

A soft knock rattled the front door, almost drowned out by the rough sounds of dried leaves grinding between Christiana's mortar and pestle. She brushed her dusty hands on her plain black riding pants before pulling the door open to reveal Robert's face.

"Good morning, My Lady," he greeted with a small bow before entering the common area. His brown riding pants and matching sleeveless tunic were the most casual thing Christiana had ever seen him wear.

"Good morning," she grumbled, her voice still graveled from the frustrated grunts she had been making during hours of research.

"You look a bit tired," he observed, dropping his satchel on the small kitchen table and sinking in Christiana's abandoned chair.

"Couldn't sleep last night," she replied, the stone pestle back in her hand as she ground a handful of flowers into a fine powder. She and Robert had plans to meet early that morning to get some more sword training in. However, after a few hours of waking up consistently drenched in sweat, her typical nightmares plaguing her, she had decided to start her day earlier than intended and ride out to the cottage for some research. Research that turned out to be useless.

"Are you sure you want to train then? It's all right if you need to rest before tonight's event."

"I need to stay busy." She dropped a pot of water on top of the stove, the heat of the fireplace forming beads of sweat at her hairline.

"By researching, I see." Robert picked up one of her journals from the floor, dusting off the cover and placing it back on the table. "Having any luck finding a plan?"

"None." She slammed down a wooden board on the counter before pulling out a sharp knife. Taking a bundle of dried herbs from one of the small jars, she roughly chopped them, the constant clicking of her knife helping to push her frustration out of her hands. "All of my ingested poisons are fairly fast-acting. Which means they won't get past his poison testers without detection."

She scooped up the herbs, the popping sounds of the rolling boil on the stovetop alerting her that it was time to start cooking her concoction. Her hands methodically worked, her brain instinctually leading her movements as she perfectly measured and stirred all the plants together. The scratching of her wooden spoon against the cast-iron pot lulled her into a trance.

"Aren't there some poisons that will not cause symptoms until a few hours after ingesting?" Robert suggested, fiddling with the worn strap of his satchel while he watched Christiana stare into her pot.

"There are, but none in my arsenal unfortunately."

"Really? That's a bit surprising."

"To be honest, not many of my clientele are of noble birth." She dropped a few more logs on the fire to help lower the flames a bit. The herbs were mixed and simmering; all she needed to do now was wait for them to infuse and distill before the poison would be potent enough for use. "Even when I have, they've never been as heavily guarded or as well-trained as the Chancellor. I always found a way to make a more direct assault work."

"Ah." Robert sighed.

She sat next to him. "Besides, I've always needed fast-acting poisons so I could get home quicker without my family questioning my whereabouts. If I tried anything that took time to kill, people would begin to question me."

"Have you considered asking your mentor? Maybe he has something he didn't teach you."

"I sent him a letter last night," she admitted, her thumb mindlessly tapping against the table. She was lucky the two of them still consistently talked. She needed to bring in all her resources for this job, and Marek was the biggest resource she had access to. He wouldn't be able to do much to help, but maybe he could at least lead her in the right direction of a plan.

"So." Robert straightened up in his chair. "How long does that poison take to distill?"

"At least two hours." She peeked over at him, her stomach churning a bit at the smirk rising across his face.

"Then, let's start today's lesson." He led her out the back door, the overcast sky welcoming them as they jumped over the side of her small training ring. They took a couple moments to stretch, Christiana raising her hands above her head, her tightened triceps screaming in relief at the taut stretch.

They went on for an hour, with Robert poking Christiana's sides and jamming the dulled tip of his sword into every weak and exposed spot she left open. She could feel the dark purple bruising already forming on her pale stomach by the time they dropped their practiced swords to take a water break. She picked up her waterskin, leaning against the rough fence and consuming half of its contents.

"After this break, we'll work on some strength training. Arms and core," Robert said, his arms dangling over the side of the ring as he looked out into the thick wooded area.

"Why?"

"Stronger core means a stronger and more planted stance. Strong arms mean an ability to not only hold a sword longer but take harder blows."

"That's fair." She dropped her chin onto the top of the ring, the scratchy, unfinished wood rubbing against her sweaty skin. A deep frown weighed heavily on her rounded cheeks.

"What's wrong?" Robert asked, the burn of his gaze biting into

Christiana's back as she stared mindlessly around her land, not really observing anything in particular.

"Just tired."

"It's more than that. When you're tired, you get snappy. Today you're quiet."

She breathed in deeply, realizing just now how well Robert had picked up on her traits over the past year. They had been working together for almost three, but it was about twelve months ago that Christiana had revealed who she really was to him. Ever since then, he had taken his job as her informant to a whole new level.

She shook her head, a deep sigh escaping her lips. "I'm just...frustrated is all. It's never taken me this long to figure out a plan, let alone find a poison to kill the mark with."

"Ah."

"Plus, with Julian away for the past week, my poor investigation has been at a standstill for too long." She dropped her forehead onto her hands, her eyes throbbing from the sunlight.

"His secretary's name is Tobias, right?" Robert asked.

"I think so." She had learned a few details about Julian from idle gossip around the court.

"I've met him a few times in passing. He's a particularly nervous gentleman, but nice enough."

"So?"

"So, I could probably find a moment or two to strike up a conversation with him."

Christiana's head shot up, meeting Robert's gaze. "Really?"

"He's a secretary, and I'm your temporary secretary now. It isn't too odd for the different administrative workers in the castle to talk now and again. I'm sure I'd be able to handle it."

"Oh, Robert. That would be perfect!" She wanted to lunge at him, give him a great big hug of gratitude, but she kept herself planted, her elated smile enough to show her thankfulness.

"Of course." He smiled down at her. "Anything in particular you need me to fish for?"

"If you can just figure out a time for me to go and...interview him. If anyone is going to have information on Julian's daily life, it would be him."

"Is that it?" His face creased. "I can certainly try and fish for more information."

"No, it's too dangerous for you to ask questions. If you start asking about Julian and then a few weeks later he ends up dead?" Her insides churned at the thought of Robert being accused of the murder. She needed his help, but she would do everything in her power to keep him out of harm's way. This was her job and she would do the real dirty work when necessary. "Just find out when I can interview Tobias privately. That's all I need."

"I'll do my best."

"Thank you, truly." She grasped his upper arm, giving him a tight squeeze.

"You can give your thanks by doing some push-ups with me. Come on." He pushed himself away from the ring's edge, walking into the center again and dropping to the ground. Christiana let out a long groan, dragging her legs to join him. At this rate, he would send her to the ball tonight barely able to walk.

Chapter Eighteen

THE SECONDS ON THE MANTLE CLOCK TICKED
through the room as the corset pulled tight against
Christiana's ribs. The midnight-blue fabric fell around her,
perfectly hugging every curve of her body. She felt absolutely stunning,
the twinkling of the jewel-encrusted skirt shimmering lightly in the
delicate candlelight of her bedroom.

She let out a shaky breath as the final tug screamed against her torso,
Natalia securing the last button at the top of her shoulder blades. Her
first ball had finally arrived, the summer months in full swing with the
gentle sounds of excited nobles walking to the ballroom wafting through
the crack of the doorway. She kept her shoulders pulled back, the flowing
sleeves of her dress dancing around her pale arms as she moved back
toward her dressing table for the final touches on her evening look.

"Time for the mask!" Natalia squealed, picking up the delicate piece
from the table's edge. She gently placed it across Christiana's face, the
silver matching perfectly with the light dusting of glitter tapped across

her eyelids, delicately framing her storm-blue irises. Christiana adjusted the mask to sit comfortably on the bridge of her nose before Natalia tied it, hiding the black strings in the folds of her elaborate updo.

Christiana's lips tilted into a small smirk as the mask conformed to the shape of her face. The feeling of concealment was so natural, even this delicate disguise for no more than the fun of the evening, that it stirred a weird leap in the pit of her stomach. She picked up the lipstick sitting in front of her, dabbing on the deep red color to finish off the entire look the two ladies had created that evening.

A light knock came from the front door, and Christiana's stomach fluttered as Natalia left the bedroom to invite the guest inside. She looked down at her hands, her fingers gently tugging the base of her thumb while she listened to their incoherent voices through the thick bedroom door. With one final look in the mirror, she pulled herself up from the small bench, lightly smoothed the chiffon of her skirt, and glided into the front room.

Rowan was a vision, his entire outfit elaborately embroidered with gold stitching across an all-black vest and coat. The delicate pattern flowed into different musical notes and patterns of sheet music. His cream-colored mask covered half of his face, hand-painted black notes swirling around his eyes, a large treble clef painted up his right cheek to complete the look of a musical composer.

"Don't you look radiant!" He beamed, eyes trailing every inch of her.

A small blush crawled up her cheeks at his intense gaze. "Thank you." She smiled, walking toward him. "You look very handsome yourself."

He took her hand, placing his typical gentlemanly kiss on top of it, then moving it securely to the crook of his arm. "Shall we?"

At her delicate nod, they joined in the stream of people in the hallway, following the flow of the current down the dozens of steps to the main halls of the palace proper. The delicate sounds of strings glided through the open space, beckoning all the guests to enter the large, double-doored entrance when the ballroom came into view.

The entire ballroom screamed opulence, with gold decor and creamy pearls covering almost every surface, glittering as they reflected the soft candlelight. Servants passed around trays of delicious wine fizzing in celebration. Different stations around the room served delectable food, ranging from fresh meat pies and spice-scented vegetables to an impressive display of sweets towering with decadent chocolate and fresh fruit tarts. The room was filled with masked guests, an array of colors and disguises surrounding Christiana as Rowan led her into the throng. She picked out all different types of costumes, ranging from very obvious animals and mythological creatures to more ominous themes that were cause for guessing.

"Would you honor me with your first dance of the night?" Rowan whispered into her ear, the small hairs along the back of her neck standing up at the feeling of his hot breath against her earlobe.

"I would love to." She smiled, allowing him to lead her to the center of the dancing. He twirled her around the minute they joined in, her skirt reflecting off every surface as the crystals moved with her. Her smile grew, instinctual laughter singing from her lips as she remembered the steps for the waltz. Her heart fluttered at the vibrations of the music flowing through every movement and step. She looked up into Rowan's smiling face, his green eyes glinting as they moved in tandem. When the song came to its final crescendo, he gave her one final spin while rounds of clapping rang through the hall.

"Let's find a drink," Christiana suggested, trying to pull in air, the thick heat of people filling her lungs. They walked to the outskirts, Christiana's eyes wandering to find Dorina off to the side, waving the two of them over to join her.

The Princess looked gorgeous as always. Although Alda was not Christiana's favorite designer, her skills were undeniable. Her large dress was made of beautiful soft pink fabric, the long sleeves and bodice decorated with delicately blooming flowers that spread down to her full skirt. Her cream-colored mask swooped across her eyes and up the left side of her face, meeting perfectly with the fresh flower crown woven through her dark, curly brown updo.

"You look breathtaking!" Christiana beamed, hugging her friend. "Springtime?"

"Yes, to match the rest of my family." She nodded over to her parents and brother, talking to a group of nobles close to the throne dais. The Queen's summer-themed dress was a delicate cream stitched with a burst of gold threads heavily concentrated on her torso, then dissipating like sunrays down her skirt. The King contrasted with the winter season, his jacket and vest a rich cobalt blue embroidered with silver thread detailing patterns of falling snowflakes and icicles. Christiana's gaze lingered a moment on Alekzander's ensemble, the season of fall the perfect fit for his skin tone and features. He wore a knee-length coat and matching vest of deep burgundy stitched with gold thread woven into the patterns of different falling leaves. The details were so precise, it looked as if a slight wind would make his whole outfit come to life.

"Fun." Christiana smiled, accepting a full glass of sparkling wine Rowan handed her. She took a small sip, the popping of the delicate perlage fizzling down her throat.

"Predictable." Dorina smirked, her own wine half-consumed as she clinked the thin crystal against Christiana's glass. "But I love the dress so that's all that matters."

"The night seems to be successful so far," Rowan observed. "Is that the Ambassador?" He nodded to the tall, olive-skinned man standing next to Alekzander, his boney fingers clutching a small plate of food while he laughed with the prince.

"That's him, Ambassador Renald. I had to escape his dull conversations. If I had to hear one more talk about how amazing the new

King will be when he takes the throne, I was going to garrote myself with my own flower crown." Dorina rolled her eyes, pouring the rest of her wine into her mouth before replacing the empty glass with a fresh one.

As she took another sip, her other hand raised above her head, waving someone over to join them. "Eliza! Over here!"

Christiana's heart dropped into her stomach, and she looked over her shoulder to see Eliza's wispy blonde hair bobbing toward them, a bright smile spread across her pink cheeks.

"Princess," Eliza greeted, falling into a small curtsy before Dorina pulled her into a tight hug. Christiana's brow creased against her mask.

"I know you've met Rowan, Marquess of Banshyl." Dorina gestured to Rowan, who took Eliza's hand for a quick peck as she curtsied to him. "But I'm not sure if you've met Christiana, Marchioness of Tagri."

"It's very nice to meet you, Marchioness!" Eliza curtsied. "I'm Eliza Marlow, Chancellor Marlow's wife."

"It's wonderful to meet you as well, Eliza." Christiana nodded, taking in the full splendor of Eliza's costume. The pure white bodice was embroidered with silver snowflakes, the elegant details melting into the thick satin skirt, the pure white darkening into an ombre of deep silver at the hem. Her silver mask wove around her eyes like a flurry of snowflakes.

"She's more than just Julian's wife, she's basically our cousin!" Dorina giggled, tapping her shoulder against Eliza's. Christiana's breath caught in her throat as a small wince twitched across Eliza's face at the contact.

"Cousin?" Christiana questioned.

"Oh, you didn't know?" Dorina smiled, looping her arm through Eliza's. "Eliza was first married to my cousin Fredrick before he passed away three years ago."

"Oh," was all Christiana could say, her heart thudding against her ribs as a rush of cold spread through her veins.

She knew there was something about Eliza that rang familiar when they first met. She hadn't known Fredrick well, but she had socialized enough to meet his wife once or twice when she still came to court. She had accused Alekzander weeks ago that Eliza was more than an acquaintance, and she had been completely right. Eliza wasn't just another subject; she was family.

The music tempo picked up swiftly as a new song rang through the room. Dorina rose on the balls of her feet, touching Rowan's arm. "Rowan! Dance with me, please?"

"Your wish is my command, Princess." He laughed, allowing the dainty girl to pull him away. "I'll be back," he whispered into Christiana's ear and shot a quick wink in her direction before turning to his new partner.

Christiana turned back to Eliza, a weary smile on her lips as they stood in silence, sipping their wine. She cleared her throat, trying to think of something to break the tension, but each time she looked at the beautiful young lady all she could think of was the jagged scars perfectly concealed behind the thick fabric of her dress. Her fingertips tingled, wishing she could reach out to Eliza, show her she was not alone in the struggles she was forced to face behind closed doors. But all she could do was stand there, the silence screaming between them.

"My darling!" Julian's alluring voice carried above the music, his deep pink lips pulled into a smile as he approached, his dark gray and silver costume perfectly matching his wife's—the storm cloud to her snowfall. "I've been looking all over for you." He planted a gentle kiss on her forehead and wrapped one of his long arms around her waist. Christiana looked at Eliza, her kind smile straining to stay plastered across her cheeks.

"Hello, Marchioness," Julian greeted Christiana. She kept her own smile firmly planted as she pushed herself downward into a curtsy.

"Chancellor," she said, raising herself back up, shoulders pulled back as she faced him.

"Thank you so much for keeping my precious wife company. Work never seems to stop for me, even on such a joyous occasion." He laughed, and the two women politely joined in. "Now that I'm back, would you care to dance, Eliza?"

"Oh...um..." she stuttered, fingers tugging as she looked up at her husband.

"Actually, Chancellor," Christiana swooped in, "I was going to ask if you would care to join me for this song?"

"Oh!" Julian exclaimed, his posture straightening. "I would be honored, My Lady." He offered his hand, and her tight fist against her side relaxed to grasp it. He led her into the group of bodies, tugging her close against him as his right arm encircled her waist. Her stomach churned at his warm breath against her cheek, their movements flowing with the music as they began the steps of the next dance.

"You look positively exquisite tonight, Christiana." His grip tightened around her waist, lifting her quickly in the air before placing her back down on the balls of her feet.

"Thank you," she forced herself to say, keeping her movements light as they circled around to the flow of the melody. Though she had taken this dance for one purpose—to give Eliza a few more moments of peace—she realized this might be a new opportunity to find a way under his protective shield of privacy. "Eliza is as lovely as you described her to me. I hope you both enjoyed your trip?"

"Oh, yes." Julian nodded, bright eyes contrasting against the deep grays of his mask. "She loves traveling with me when it is a trip longer than a few days. I always find a way to show her the different areas in between work."

"How lovely." Christiana's cheeks hurt from forcing a smile. Every inch of her skin crawled the longer he held her close. "Now that she's back, I would love to reextend my offer to spend time with her."

"That's very kind, but she is usually quite tired after travelling, and with all of the excitement of the delegation right now, I just don't think it is the best time." Christiana's shoulders sagged at the excuse. It was all a web of lies he had perfectly woven. No one ever realized how truly dangerous something so beautiful could be until it trapped them inside. "But I will of course let her know you're thinking of her."

"Thank you." She would get nowhere with this man, a fact that shouldn't surprise her. He was a military man and an abuser, he had the ability to hold secrets through even the longest torture sessions, she would bet. She refused to go to Eliza about any of this and put her at risk of her husband finding out the truth; and Alekzander was absolutely off limits for Christiana's own safety. She just had to have hope that Robert would find a time for her to get the Chancellor's secretary alone. Tobias was her best option to figure out a hole in Julian's perfectly-planned life.

She silently counted the seconds until the dreadful dance finished, resigning the rest of their time together with uncomfortable silence. Julian's eyes never left her face, and heat crawled down her arms as she refused to take her gaze off the thick fabric encasing his shoulder. Not soon enough, the song came to a close, Christiana gently pulling herself out of his grasp with a small nod of thank you.

"Now, if you'll excuse me, My Lady, I must return to my dear wife." Julian bowed.

"Of course." She curtsied back and took off in the opposite direction, desperate for another glass of wine. She found a passing servant the minute she exited the dance floor, grasping one of the chilled glasses and downing almost the entire thing to stop her cold fingers from shaking.

"How about blessing me with the next dance?"

Christiana groaned as she removed the glass from her lips, turning to find Edgar standing right behind her, his arms crossed against his chest and a deep smirk set on his lips.

"Funny," she sneered, trying to walk in the opposite direction, but his steps were close on her heels.

"It wasn't a joke. As your potential suitor..."

"Ha!" she burst in his face, whirling back to him.

"...I have a right to dance with you."

"Get this through your head, when it comes to me, you have zero rights." She took the last sip of her wine, the bubbling liquid barely down her throat before she deposited it on a servant's tray and wrapped her hands around a fresh flute. She could not seem to catch a break tonight when it came to her companions.

Edgar shook his head, an obscene laugh escaping his lips. "I don't think the King would agree with you."

She glared at him. "Stop using such a weak excuse."

"It isn't weak," he replied, moving forward so there were just inches between them, his torso barely grazing hers.

"Christiana! There you are!"

Her muscles seized as she turned to see Alekzander strolling over to them. His eyes glistened as he approached, and Edgar finally took a few steps back so Christiana could let out a breath of air.

"Your Highness." She curtsied, her legs shaking as she stood back up.

"I've been looking all over for you. Our song is about to play," he teased, the shimmer of his golden mask accenting the gold undertones in his dark blond hair.

"Excuse me?"

"Don't you recognize it?" He gestured up into the air, the beginning of a slow song starting to ring through the ballroom. Memories flooded Christiana's mind, the one dance she and Alekzander always practiced together growing up. The two of them, twirling in the hallways as a quartet practiced during the day for an evening event, their laughter filling the empty space.

Her cheeks burned as she looked up at his smiling face. "Oh, of course I remember."

"Then, may I have this dance?" he asked, his hand reaching for hers.

"Oh..." She stared down, her fingers twitching at her side. Something deep inside wanted to share this nostalgic moment with her childhood friend, but the small voice in the back of her mind stopped her. It wanted to know why he was so desperate to get her close. Was it because he was close to figuring out the truth? Her mind spun from both men in front of her and the wine running through her veins.

"Unless you'd rather dance with the Duke here?" He nodded over to Edgar, whose rigid stance and pursed lips showed just how displeased he was by the Prince's interruption.

The only way out was through dancing with one of them. So she forced herself to look up, a smile on her lips. "I would be honored, Your Highness."

He smiled back, and with a deep breath, she clasped his hand, allowing him to lead her out onto the dance floor. It began slowly, the two circling around each other. She remembered the steps perfectly, as if she was once again the child Alekzander talked about. But this time was different. They were no longer two children playing pretend; now they were two grown adults with more responsibility than they could imagine.

"I was happy to see you and Rowan accompanying each other this evening," Alekzander said, attempting to break the ice between them. "He's lucky to have such a beautiful partner on his arm tonight."

"Thank you, Your Highness." Her legs shook beneath the thick folds of her dress as she forced them to keep moving, the other dancers swirling around in a blur of colorful fabrics. "He's very lucky to have a friend like you in his life as well." It was true; for all the anxiety Alekzander instilled in her, she admired him as the caring friend, loving brother, and kind-hearted prince he was. She only wished she could express it to him fully without fear standing in her way.

"I'm sure I'm the millionth man to mention it, but you do look absolutely stunning tonight," he said as he spun her around, pressing her back against his chest while they stepped to the rhythm. Her breath hitched when they touched, her body flooding with the heat of his closeness. She wasn't sure she would make it through this dance without fainting.

"Thank you, Your Highness."

"I mean it. Your beauty only matches your wit." The strong scent of cedarwood enveloped her as his hands firmly held her against him. She didn't know if it was the wine or the anxiety, but she could get lost in his intoxicating scent. "You've spent half a decade running an estate and working so hard to prove that you belong where you now are. We recognize everything you have sacrificed for the good of the Kingdom. I hope you realize you've earned it."

When they came face to face with each other once again, his left hand pulling her close to him, she boldly asked, "Then why are your parents so keen on finding me a match?"

She had tried to hold back her sharp tongue, but couldn't seem to help herself. She wasn't unhappy at the prospect of marrying, but ever since her father's death, she developed a stubbornness to control the life she had finally gained back. The idea of anyone telling her what she needed to do to make herself happy, royal or not, put her on edge.

"I'm sorry if my parents made you feel pressured to move things along quickly." They separated for a brief moment, her eyes wandering around the glittering room and hoard of people before he pulled her back into his embrace. "If it makes you feel any better, I'm in the same boat as you and not enjoying it myself. I understand how daunting it can be with a ticking clock hanging over your head."

Her face creased at his response, looking over their clasped hands. "Thank you."

"I'm sorry if you felt any pressure from me as well," he continued.

"I'm trying to understand the animosity that seems to be between us and I can only imagine I did something to cause you great pain."

"No, Your Highness, that isn't it at all." Why she felt the need to clarify was beyond her. It would make her life easier if he thought it was something as trivial and childish as too much pressure.

"Then why?" he asked, staring down at her.

"I wanted people to see how strong I was without the favor of my childhood friend, the Prince," she explained weakly.

"I don't think anyone was going to question you on that." He laughed.

"Still, you can't go into battle unprepared. You must face it with every piece of armor secured and every weapon sharpened. It is the only way to survive."

"You are certainly your father's daughter," he complimented with a smile, and she tried her best not to wince. So many people thought those words must fill her with such pride, but they had no idea what inner turmoil brewed inside her whenever they were spoken in praise.

Firmly grabbing her hips, Alekzander lifted her into the air and began to slowly spin. She stared down at him, trying desperately to keep the happiness in her eyes, not sure exactly how to respond. But for the first time, she felt like she didn't have to say anything at all; it was different, the way he was looking back at her. The intensity mounted as he studied her deep steel irises, as if they held secrets he had been deciphering for months and he was trying to strip her down until he held her very soul in his hands. She expected to feel unsettled and exposed, but she couldn't look away.

"Is there something the matter, Your Highness?" she finally asked when he set her back on her feet to finish the last few steps of the dance.

"It's just your eyes is all. They're so hauntingly beautiful," he answered, still not tearing his gaze away.

"You're too kind, Your Highness," she replied as the rest of the partygoers clapped for the end of the song.

"If you'll excuse me, My Lady, I must return to keeping Ambassador Renald company." He bowed before turning away from her. Dazed, her head spinning from the combination of wine and dance, she slowly walked off the dance floor as well.

Chapter Nineteen

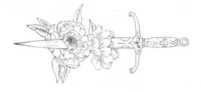

THE BALL WOUND DOWN AS MORE AND MORE nobles left the large room to return to their quarters. The sounds of long goodbyes and saddened hugs rang out as if all these people were leaving for a long journey instead of walking just upstairs to rest off the evening. The music continued to play, but few people were dancing, most likely exhausted from all the wine, food, and exciting activity of the night. Christiana lingered in the ballroom, her head feeling fuzzy from all the sparkling wine she had enjoyed.

Her feet ached from the hours of dancing in heels, the throbbing pain crawling up her swollen ankles and forcing her to find a secluded corner in the back of the room, where the large windowsill cushion welcomed her. Her feet screamed in happiness when she released the pressure of her body weight from them, a small groan of pleasure escaping her lips as the numbness settled in. She tried her best to keep herself upright, though all she wanted to do was lean her head against the window and close her eyes, her fuzzy focus lulling her into a few moments of rest.

"Are you all right?" Alekzander's voice roused her at his approach, his mask dangling from his fingertips, his wavy locks finally free from the confines of his styling cream to gently frame his face.

"I think so," she replied with a smile, removing her own mask and setting it down beside her. She could not muster up enough energy to run away from him like she had been ever since their intense dance, finding solace in Dorina or Rowan. She didn't know if it was the wine, her aching feet, or both that kept her rooted to her seat when he sat beside her.

"You probably shouldn't have had so much to drink," he teased.

She giggled just a bit, wondering why she found his comment so funny. "It wasn't that much."

"Your glassy eyes are saying something different." His eyes took in every inch of her. For the entire summer so far, she had felt so uncomfortable with the idea of him being too close to her. But she couldn't help but be drawn in now, allowing him to stare as much as he pleased. It was as if an unknown entity kept her still while he examined her thoroughly.

"What?" she asked at last.

"How have you been enjoying the summer?" His gaze still locked with hers, forcing a warm blush against her pale skin.

Her breath caught in her chest, her teeth gently biting at her lower lip. "It's been wonderful, Your Highness."

"Alekzander," he corrected, his eyes never leaving hers.

"Alekzander," she repeated, stuck in the trance of his stare, his body heat absorbing through her dress and sending a shiver up her spine.

"Have you done anything special?"

"Um, besides working?" Her brow creased as she struggled to form coherent sentences in her mind before speaking them. "I try to spend time with your sister and Rowan, of course."

"Of course. I'm glad the two of you have been getting so close." The sternness in his voice didn't match the statement. "Anything else you've been doing this summer?"

It was like he was trying to get her to confess to something. Wasn't this something she should be concerned about?

"No, Alekzander. What would make you say that?" She leaned back a little, her brow creasing as the fog in her brain began to dissipate. Her heart raced when she finally realized just how close she was letting him get.

"No reason." He shrugged, his shoulders slumping a bit, his rigid posture finally relaxing out but his gaze still holding her by his side. Silence fell over them, the room melting away as if they were back under the safety of the willow tree.

"Why are you looking at me like that?" Her shoulders squirmed the longer he stared, the movements of her skirts knocking her mask off the ledge and onto the floor.

His eyes softened. "I'm just...remembering." He paused for a moment, leaning down to pick up her mask and handing it to her. "Remembering what you were like when we were growing up."

"Seems so long ago," she mumbled, finally breaking free of his gaze to stare down at her finger twisting into the freed ribbons of her mask.

"That's because it was." There was something about the deep breath he let out, as if he was letting go of something else entirely. His eyes wandered, taking in the dwindling scene in front of them. "You've changed."

"For better? Or worse?" She wasn't sure if she would like his answer, but she hoped the haze of alcohol softened the blow if necessary.

"You're stronger." He tilted his head a bit, a wistful look overtaking his features. "Many would consider that better."

"I certainly do." That was one thing she would never apologize for. Her strength had gotten her through the last five years, it was what kept her going every day.

He nodded. "So do I."

Christiana's throat went dry, her breath trapped inside. She stared at Alekzander, his back now hunched as he leaned his elbows on his knees. She felt it again, the jolt inside her at his closeness. She had been so scared of it before, trying her best to ignore it and push it away, but now a small part of her wanted to reach out, to bridge the distance she had put between them since the summer started. She knew it was dangerous, that he couldn't find out the truth.

She curled her fingers into the gauzy fabric of her dress, forcing them to stay put. A weight crawled up her neck while she debated if she should flee or stay exactly where she was.

"Alekzander..." she started, trying desperately to break whatever was pulling them together.

"I should go and help my parents say goodbye to everyone," he said abruptly. "Besides, it looks like someone else is ready to talk to you." He nodded to Rowan, approaching them, then stood up and gave a small bow of respect before disappearing through the crowd.

She stared after him, her skin tingling as she tried to remember every word they had just spoken. She had no idea what he was trying to get her to confess to, but her paranoid head could only think of one thing: her identity.

But she logically knew that couldn't be it. It had been two weeks since Alekzander had last seen Maiden, and she hadn't said or done anything tonight for him to draw such a conclusion.

Trying to shake off the situation, she blinked a few times to refocus her eyes and turned to Rowan, smiling in greeting.

"Would you like an escort home?" He offered his outstretched arm.

"Thank you, I would love one."

All else aside, she had loved the evening, especially getting to know Rowan better. They had shared several dances, swirling through a crowd of people while they laughed and rediscovered the connection they once had so many years ago. The comfort she felt in his arms was soothing after such an intense dance with Alekzander, the lightness in her chest a welcomed distraction to keep her mind from focusing on what he had meant by 'hauntingly beautiful eyes'.

"I'm so happy I was able to be with you at your first ball." He laughed as he supported her through the hallways, quiet and well-lit with rows of candles. They only passed a few servants along the way to her apartment.

"Me too. You're quite the dance partner," she teased, her grip on his soft jacket tightening as she stopped herself from stumbling over her own feet. She was trying her best to seem graceful, though her legs felt separate from her body whenever they tripped and stumbled. Before the two realized it, they had reached their destination.

"I live here." She giggled again, gently tapping against the door.

"Yes, you do." He chuckled, his smile filled with amusement as he stared down at her.

She looked up at him, her body swaying as it tried to find its equilibrium. "Did I thank you yet for the escort?"

"Yes." He laughed again, gently rubbing the back of his neck before he removed the mask to expose his handsome features.

"Well, I'm going to say it again. Thank you." She leaned against the threshold to try and steady herself, stomach churning.

"Are you all right?" Rowan grasped her upper arms, his strength helping her shaking legs to steady themselves.

"Yes." Her hazy eyes tried their best to bring his strong face into focus so she could admire him. She always knew he was a handsome man, and she'd heard the giggles from other women all summer, whispering about his classic features. But after all of their talk about a potential courtship, she had never taken time to wonder if she was actually attracted to him.

His eyes creased. "Then why are you looking at me like that?"

"I like looking at you," she cooed, enjoying the moment, biting the corner of her lip to stop it from quivering.

"Oh, well, thank you. I certainly enjoy looking at you as well," he teased, stepping a bit closer, releasing her arm to rest his hand on the wall above her shoulder.

She broke eye contact, at the warm rush spreading through her chest. "Stop it."

"If you get to do it, then so do I."

"Fair," she conceded, not really feeling the need to win that argument.

"It seems tonight was successful." His breath whispered across her flushed cheeks, a shiver rushing down her spine at its gentle caress. "So, I have a question to ask."

"And that is?"

His eyebrows rose. "Do you see the potential for a courtship between us?"

She looked over his whole face, her gaze resting on his gentle smirk. "There is just one more thing I need to see before I can give you a proper answer."

"And what is that?"

Instead of answering him verbally, she grabbed his doublet in her fists and pulled him forward, crashing his lips to meet hers. It seemed abnormal to have forgotten something most people would consider important, and in the fog of her many glasses of wine, her brain deduced that the only logical way to test any attraction was to kiss the man standing in front of her.

Although her brazen action made him tense, he quickly composed himself, his body melting into hers. Their lips moved fluidly with each other, like a current. She couldn't help but notice just how soft and alluring his felt against hers. Satisfied with her research, she pulled away, his stunned face staring down at her.

"What was that?" he purred, a smirk settling on his rosy lips.

"I wanted to know what your lips felt like." She shrugged, mouth still burning from the heat of his.

"Satisfied?" His brows twitched up.

"Yes, thank you." She fiddled with the doorknob behind her.

His eyes swirled with desire as he bit his bottom lip. "Always my pleasure."

"Goodnight Rowan," she murmured, leaving him in utter shock when she closed the door.

Chapter Twenty

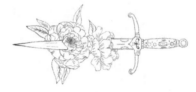

THE KNOCKING AGAINST HER SKULL WAS THE first thing that Christiana felt before opening her eyes the next morning. Sunlight streamed in through the window, and she squinted against her burning irises while she tried with all her strength to pull herself up. Her brain felt full of cotton, the events of last night blurring together like the dancers that swirled around her all evening. She collapsed back against her soft pillows, allowing the feathers to devour her as her head sank inside. She pulled the covers over her face, surrounding herself with darkness as she tried to clear her brain enough to process exactly what had happened.

"Good morning!" came Dorina's too-excited voice from the bedroom doorway. Christiana let out a loud groan, the slam of wood against stone shaking her pounding brain.

"Go away." She refused to reveal her face, stomach churning at the rattling of trays entering the room and the smell of steaming hotcakes.

"Never!" The bed groaned as Dorina laid down next to her. "You need to eat and hydrate yourself, all of which I have brought you." She tugged on the thick quilt, forcing it out of Christiana's weakened grip to expose her face. She smiled down at her, face too amused at Christiana's suffering.

"What is wrong with me?"

"You have wine sickness," Dorina said, pouring herself a cup of tea from one of the two trays laying at their feet.

"What?" Christiana finally found the strength to pull herself up, rubbing her eyes to try and focus her blurred vision.

"You drank too much." Dorina handed the second cup of tea to Christiana, her shaking hands wrapping around the steaming cup so the warmth spread through her fingers.

"And you didn't?" She blew on the tea before taking a tentative sip, her stomach heaving. "How come you don't feel like this?"

"Because I've been going to these types of parties for years. I know how to keep this from happening." She bit into a piece of toast, the crisp edges dropping crumbs into Christiana's bedsheets. "Did you at least have a good time?"

Christiana sipped her tea, giving herself a moment of peace to try and think about everything that happened the night before. Her escort to the party, her different dance partners, and the walk home...

"Oh no..." Christiana's eyes flew open, her hand shaking so hard it barely held on to the delicate teacup.

"What's wrong?" Dorina snatched the cup from Christiana's grasp before it gave out.

"Oh, no, no, no..." she chanted, dropping her head into her hands as her cheeks lit on fire from what she had done to Rowan the night before.

"Christiana." Dorina shook her, alarm filling her voice. "What happened?"

"I did something stupid last night."

"What did you do?"

"I kissed Rowan when he walked me back." She peeked over to Dorina; the princess's mouth hung open and she stared wide-eyed at the confession.

"Really?"

"Yes." Christiana groaned, rubbing her temples.

Dorina's eyebrows wiggled a bit. "How was it?"

"It's not funny!" Christiana threw a pillow, a few drops of tea spilling at the impact.

"Oh, Christiana." Dorina gently stroked her arm. "This is a good thing! Why do you look like you want to run away and never come back?"

Christiana stared down at her shaking hands, trying desperately to decipher the emotions swirling through her head and chest. She had been so fuzzy with the taste of wine last night, she had only focused on the touch of his lips and the warmth of his body pressed against her. It was certainly a lovely experience, albeit a tad sloppy from their clumsy movements.

Yet something stirred deep within her, doubt mixed with confusion rushing through her tired limbs.

She wanted so badly to remember that kiss like it had been perfect, but she struggled to find peace with it. Somehow, this moment with Rowan felt...lacking. She always heard that kisses and intimate touches were supposed to send fire and lightning through a person, to awaken their body in a way no other encounter could. But when she remembered that moment, the feeling of his lips on hers, she felt a seed of dread rooting inside her at having to face him again. "I'm just embarrassed. What does Rowan think of me now?"

Dorina smiled kindly. "Honestly, he's probably walking on air. I highly doubt he thinks any less of you. He probably can't wait to see you again!"

A weary smile spread across Christiana's face in turn as she looked up at Dorina, the comfort of her friendly touch filling her heart with warmth and settling the stirring within. She had so much hope in her connection with Rowan before the ball started. She had walked into that room proudly on his arm, wistful thoughts of a potential future for the two of them swirling in her mind. So why, after starting to form a connection with him, did this moment seem to falter?

One explanation could be the wine, her overindulgence and impaired memory and judgement possibly ruining the moment. That was the only explanation that didn't end with her heart aching.

"Besides that, did anything else interesting happen?" Dorina asked, her arm wrapped around Christiana's shoulders as she handed her teacup back.

Christiana's mind instantly went to her encounters with Alekzander, her heart racing at just the idea of how close she let him get last night. He had set her skin on fire during their dance, the anxiety-ridden movements forever seared into her brain. The comment he made to her at the end of the dance, about her eyes, made her pulse skip a beat. What had he meant when he called them hauntingly beautiful?

Then there was their conversation before Rowan escorted her home. The words were blended together in her mind, the conversation barely registering, but that nagging voice she always tried to suppress told her what she was most worried about: that somehow Alekzander had recognized her as the Midnight Maiden. The odd comments and probing questions lining up with the thing she had been so concerned about all summer. But she forced that idea to the back of her mind; it had been a few weeks since the last time Alekzander and the Maiden saw each other. He had no reason to suspect her just by her eyes.

"Christiana?" Dorina's voice broke through. "Where did you just go?"

Christiana's gaze jolted from the bedspread and she shook her head to clear it of the unwanted memories. "Sorry, this sickness is getting the better of me."

"Then let's fix that." Dorina pulled the trays closer for them to enjoy their breakfast. Each bite tasted like ash in Christiana's mouth while she tried desperately to forget the entire evening.

Chapter Twenty-One

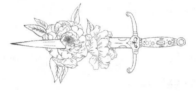

*T*HE CLANGING OF HEAVY METAL RANG THROUGH the trees as Christiana and Robert sparred, the mid-morning sun beginning its ascent to the highest point in the sky. They had been training hard for a full hour, determination gripping her body as she pushed through exhaustion. Sweat dripped down her face when he advanced on her, luring her closer to the outer edge of the training ring. She blocked each swift blow, trying to push him away from her. Her exhaustion and heavy breathing overtook her body and Robert's final blow forced the sword out of her hand. His dull blade pressed against her neck in victory.

"My match again," he declared, lowering his weapon from the tender spot.

"Damn it!" she screamed, punching the wooden slats of the training ring.

Multiple training sessions had gone by and she was still unable to beat Robert. Her heart pumped loudly in her ears, the memory of each defeat flooding her head. A voice crept into her forethought, trying to root itself, whispering that she was a failure. Her fingers trembled as she grasped them into fist and her breath sped up. She tried to push the dangerous voice away, but it wouldn't stop.

"Breathe with me," Robert consoled, touching her lightly on the shoulder. He started breathing loudly himself, in through his nose and out through his mouth, coaxing her to mimic his actions. Reluctant at first, she pulled air through her nose to bring her rapid heartbeat down. With each release through her mouth, the rush of air pumped through her bloodstream, her tunneled vision slowly widening. The voice drowned out with each calming exhale, finally dissipating from her mind.

Robert gripped her shoulder gently and gave it a quick shake. "Let's take a break."

"No, I'm fine. Let's go again," she spat, her muscles dancing in anticipation of the next fight.

"Well, I'm tired, so I'm going to rest. You might as well join me."

"Fine," she grudgingly agreed, shoulders slumped as she walked over to the two bales of hay they had stolen from her stable to use as a seat. She pulled her waterskin off the ground and took long sips, her dry throat screaming in pleasure at the cool water. She hadn't realized how drained she was until she relaxed into the soft hay.

"You're getting better," Robert commented. "You're lasting longer with each fight. Your stamina is improving and your blocks and blows are quicker."

Her fingers twitched. "But I'm still not winning."

"It takes time. You need to be patient."

"That's the thing, we don't have unlimited time. The weeks are going by so quickly and I have yet to figure out how to kill Julian." She had been pouring through all her recipes for weeks, trying to find an ingestion-based poison to use. She had even received a letter from Marek with a list of different poisons, their effects, and the process they took to kill. But none of them were slow-acting enough to get past both of the Chancellor's tasters.

"You'll think of something." Robert seemed to have an unlimited amount of belief in Christiana's skills as an assassin, but as the weeks went by with no plan, she had begun to doubt herself. She wasn't sure if she was overthinking everything, but the more she researched into different poisons, the more she considered Julian the unkillable man.

"I feel like I'm running out of time." She sighed, wiping the dripping sweat from her face onto her soft tunic. The cloudless sky hung above them, the beating of the sunrays suffocating her throughout their morning workout. It was hardly better now that they rested.

"The summer isn't even halfway over," Robert reminded her. "You don't have to start worrying quite yet."

"Why did Alekzander have to do this to me?" she groaned, leaning her back against the wooden ring, the hard surface scratching against her thin tunic.

She had cursed the Prince's name for weeks now. Not only because of the impossible mark he chose to send her after, but because of the uncontrollable reactions she had toward him whenever he was close by. She could always return the money and deny the job—that thought had certainly crossed her mind during particularly frustrating research moments. Yet she always pushed forward, desperate to find any way to kill this man...not because she didn't want to admit defeat, but she refused to leave Eliza in her time of need. Each time she thought about quitting, she remembered that night in Eliza's room. The scars crossed up her slender back, the desperation in her eyes, the gentle sobs of her pained tears. Those memories pushed her forward, they reminded her why she was doing this.

"He's doing what is right for one of his subjects," Robert tried to explain.

"Stop trying to be logical. I'm not in the mood." Christiana rubbed her temples.

Robert shrugged. "You never know, Julian could drop dead one day this summer, making it easier for you. Especially with the way he eats."

"What do you mean?" Christiana asked. She had been watching the Chancellor every chance she got, and nothing seemed off about his diet.

"He loves salt. He salts his food every single time he eats a meal."

"Wait, what?" Christiana straightened up sharply. "How do you know this?"

"A lot of the soldiers talk about it. Apparently, he sustained some kind of injury in the field years ago that stole part of his ability to taste food. Adding salt is the only way for him to enjoy it."

A laugh burst from her lips. "That's it!"

"What is?" Robert asked.

"Come on, get up." She dragged him up and after her.

"Where are we going?"

"To work on the poison! I think I need you to buy a few ingredients before I can begin, though."

Robert tugged her arm backwards, stopping her in her own tracks. "Christiana, stop. What is going on?"

"I realized something. Why should I poison him when he could poison himself?" she asked with a giddy laugh. Her chest felt like it was going to float away, her head spinning as she started making mental lists of what she needed to complete this plan.

She pulled Robert inside and explained her plan.

***

Later that afternoon, after giving Robert an extensive list of herbs and ingredients to track down, Christiana finally returned to the castle for a quick clean up, full of newfound excitement to work on her marchioness paperwork. The scratch of her quill was the only sound in the quiet room, her brain running through different numbers and integers. Anxiety had clouded her mind for so long, now that she finally had a base of a plan for Julian, she could sit down and focus on something else. She followed a great work momentum for two hours, her mind racing as she tried to catch up with her mountain of land reports.

"My Lady?" Natalia interrupted her with the clinking of coins in the leather pouch she dropped on the table.

"Yes?"

"This arrived for you." Natalia handed her a folded piece of parchment with no seal or formal envelope. Christiana took it, her lips and brows tightening at the rough parchment under her fingertips. Only her name was neatly written across the front, no extra flourish to be seen. She flipped it over, the closure set with ivory wax and a plain seal pressed into it. She bit her lip as she removed the note, her finger tapping against the edge of the paper while she read it. Her shoulders slumped, relief rushing over her as she realized how harmless this little invitation was.

She dropped her quill and shook her head with a laugh. It was a simple invitation, informal and easy to say no to, but after working for a few hours she decided a break was necessary. With a quick thank you to Natalia, she was out the door and down the hall.

The warm air welcomed Christiana as she walked out the double glass doors into the garden. The midafternoon was abuzz with many nobles walking around the expansive lawn or sitting on blankets together. Her heeled shoes sunk into the gravel path as she walked, her wandering gaze searching for her companion for the afternoon.

She came across the rose grove quickly, peeking inside to find Dorina sitting on a stool, her hands diligently working with a long paintbrush gripped between her fingers. Her face was concentrated on the large canvas in front of her where bright pink and green paints meshed together. She walked closer, the vision of Dorina's artwork coming to life as she detailed a large rosebud.

"It's gorgeous," Christiana commented.

"Thank you," the Princess smiled, leaning back to take in her canvas, a smile gracing her lips. "You've been preoccupied for a few days. Finally feeling better?"

"Much."

"Good, because fresh air is always a great way to rejoin society. I had the servants set up an easel for you as well. Join me." Dorina gestured to the second stool, canvas, and the set of clean brushes and untouched paint situated right next to her.

"Oh, no, no, no." Christiana waved her hands, taking a few steps back.

"Oh, come now, painting is fun! It's a wonderful way to capture nature and relax."

"Maybe for people with artistic talent." Christiana laughed.

Dorina peeked at her, amber eyes glittering in the sunlight. "You can't be that bad."

"Oh, trust me, I'm that bad." She remembered all of the painting and cross-stitching lessons her mother had tried to give her growing up, long before her difficult marchioness training began. She always hated every moment of it, the patience and silence making her want to burst at the seams with untamed energy. Even worse, she never understood how people could look at something as simple as a flower and find a new way to interpret it. She thought it was beautiful how someone could look at a rose, and in their own mind morph it into a new figure, capturing the internal beauty; but when she looked at it, all she saw was a flower.

"Well, just let your hands play with the paint. It doesn't have to be perfect." Dorina waved her hands, a splatter of blush paint flicking across the bright green grass.

"Says the girl who has a perfect painting in front of her," Christiana grumbled, sitting reluctantly on the stool.

"I promise, if your painting is offensive, I'll burn it."

"Every last inch." Christiana picked up a paintbrush at random, its flat bristles perfectly manicured, the white strands sticking straight up like a soldier at attention. She dipped the end lightly in the lavender paint and touched it to the blank canvas, her brows furrowing as she tried desperately to make a decent outline of the rose petals. Her fingers latched around the brush, knuckles going white as silence fell.

"So." Dorina broke her concentration. "Have you talked to Rowan since the ball?" A sly grin spread across her face as she narrowed her eyes at Christiana.

"Unfortunately, no." Christiana's stomach flipped. "He sent me a letter the next day, though. He had to travel to Banshyl quickly, his new livestock farm had some kind of emergency."

"Ah," Dorina exclaimed.

"I think he said he was arriving back today." She hadn't thought to seek him out—partially because she had been busy with work and partially because she wasn't sure what she was going to say ever since her drunken goodbye to him.

"Oh, he did. He had breakfast with Zander and I this morning when he got back." Dorina bit her lip.

"Then why did you ask if we'd spoken?"

"Wanted to see your reaction," Dorina teased. "Oh, and look who's coming this way."

Christiana whipped herself around to find Rowan walking toward them, a smile on his face, with Alekzander right next to him. "Dorina," she hissed, her stomach now sinking deeply, as if rocks had settled inside. Her pulse throbbed against her throat, making her fingers tingle.

The Princess shrugged, the light green fabric of her loose skirt billowing. "You have to face him sooner or later. Might as well be around other people."

"Sounds like hell," she mumbled before the two men were in earshot. She plastered a smile across her lips, hoping her eyes wouldn't give her true feelings away.

"Hello, ladies," Rowan greeted informally, the privacy of the empty grove allowing him to forsake the typical greeting. With a smile on his full lips, Alekzander wandered over to his sister's side.

"Rowan," Dorina nodded, her teeth biting her lower lip to stop from giggling.

"Hello," he murmured to Christiana, his body heat radiating onto her arm when he halted only a few inches away, grinning down at her.

"Hello," was all she could say, her eyes catching his. She still had no idea what had been missing in their kiss a few nights ago, or why it had been gnawing mercilessly at her heart ever since. But when he stood so close, with her heart pounding in her chest, she wondered if maybe the alcohol had impaired her senses, dulling her enjoyment.

"So, gentlemen," Dorina interjected, "what do you think so far?" She pointed to her painting, the rose's detailed beauty leaping off the canvas.

"Gorgeous as always." Alekzander smiled at his sister, circling around her to stand between her and Christiana's easels. Her skin pricked furiously as he moved closer, his back turned to her while he studied Dorina's work.

"You certainly have a talent, Dorina," Rowan added, his head tilted up to talk over the top of Christiana's. "And yours, Christiana, it's...abstract."

Her shoulders slumped, her bright blob not fully taking shape yet. "I told her I wasn't good at this." She peeked over at Rowan, his encouraging smile bringing a slight blush to her cheeks.

"The colors are pretty." Alekzander's deep voice came from her other side, his gaze now plastered on her canvas.

Not only was she trying to ignore her kiss with Rowan, but she was also trying not to overreact to the one dance she had shared with Alekzander the other night as well. She wouldn't sleep well tonight if her anxious brain didn't stop overthinking everything.

"Thank you, Alekzander." Her skeptical glance revealed his eyes now fixated on her. She stared up at him, his brows creased while he studied every inch of her face just as he had done during their dance. Her spine shivered, the intensity flowing through her as she desperately turned away.

"I'm sure your father wasn't as concerned with art as he was with learning math," Alekzander commented. Christiana's jaw instinctually tensed at the mention of Francis.

"I suppose," she mumbled, dipping her brush in the sky-blue paint to try and salvage any part of her painting. She felt his eyes lingering on her, a gleam of sweat forming along her hairline with each passing second under his scrutiny. Her brush hesitated a few inches from the canvas as she turned to look at him, their gazes locking, her mind once again entranced by his stare.

All too suddenly, Alekzander tore himself away and took a few steps back, his boots crushing the gravel beneath them. "We should go." A breath released from Christiana's heavy chest as the distance between them grew.

"Are you sure?" Rowan asked, his gaze flicking to his friend while he kept close to Christiana's side.

"We shouldn't disturb their concentration any longer. Besides, we promised some of the other men we would meet them for cards in twenty minutes, remember?"

"Oh, right." Rowan's smile fell into a frown. "I'll hopefully see you soon?" He looked down at Christiana, his emerald eyes swirling with hope.

Christiana's chest swelled, and she smiled. "Of course."

Rowan leaned down, his lips brushing against her earlobe. "Hopefully by then you'll have an answer to the question I asked you a few days ago?"

She kept her eyes trained to her canvas, her upper lip twitching at the comment. "You'll have to wait and see."

"I look forward to that day," he replied before backing away to rejoin

Alekzander. Christiana turned herself around, her body freezing at the sight of Alekzander's cold stare trained on her. It wasn't until Rowan slapped him playfully on the back, something he said breaking the Prince's tension, that his face once again softened. Blond hair dancing, he shook his head in laughter at the comment. She watched the two men disappear through the vine covered archway.

"Dorina." Christiana turned to her best friend. "Is something wrong with your brother?"

"Stress, probably." Dorina shrugged, her eyes turning to Christiana. "He tends to get sullen when he's overthinking things. Why do you ask?"

"Just making sure," she said brushing it off, ignoring the cold blood running through her veins as she tried to forget that deadly stare he gave her.

Chapter Twenty-Two

THE LETTER HAD ARRIVED TWO DAYS AGO, handed to her by Robert at the end of a particularly annoying training session at her cottage. Ever since, Christiana couldn't shake the nausea that overcame her with each breath or movement. She tried her hardest to bring normalcy to her life, but just like every day since the ball, she couldn't shake that deep, gut-filled feeling something was about to change.

The letter bore no seal, free of any ties or connection, like most of her client letters. The paper felt like lead in her hands when she first ripped into it, the Prince's request for another meeting scrawled on the page. She had asked him to stay away, to let her do the job he had hired her to do; he was only supposed to message her if it was an emergency. The amount of terrible thoughts filling Christiana's mind at that moment was terrifying, and only multiplied after. She had no idea why he wanted to see her, but fear consumed her as she tried to dress herself for the meeting.

She focused her thoughts on her shaking hands, wishing they would sit still for a moment so she could finish securing her leather gauntlets. Every time she put this outfit on, her strength swelled to the surface, this disguise giving her permission to show her true self. But in three years of wearing it, she had never felt more fearful. She wanted to rip the clothes off her own back and disappear under the protective covers of her bed. But something pulled her forward, forcing her into her alter ego's black covering. She wasn't going to let her own paranoia get in the way of helping Eliza.

She finally secured the last buckle of her gauntlet against her hot skin, her arm already sweating from the weight of the leather cuff. She counted her daggers and throwing knives one last time, making sure every single defense was properly stored and accessible before opening her bedroom window and beginning the descent she had learned so well. She moved quickly, keeping to the palace walls as she moved in between shadows to avoid soldiers on patrol. She finally made it to the Prince's window, taking her time to make the climb. She pulled in a deep breath of the fresh air before climbing through, the stifling heat inside already making her cheeks sweat under the thin fabric of her veil.

"Thank you for coming tonight on such short notice," he greeted her from his large desk. Tonight, he wasn't busy working; he leaned back in the tall chair, his arms tightly crossed as he watched her enter his apartment. "Honestly, I'm surprised. I figured you would need a couple days to travel all the way out here."

"What can I say, I like to stay in the area when I'm trying to kill someone," she responded, sticking to her normal shadowed corner of his common room.

His brow furrowed, pulling his eyes tightly together. "Then why am I sending the requests so far away?"

"Do you think I'm stupid enough to have you send them somewhere I reside?" she scoffed, her spine stiffening as the tension of the room crawled into her shoulder blades.

He shrugged. "It seems like a waste of time."

"I'm sorry if you don't like my postal methods, but is that why you wanted me to come here tonight?" Her lips pulled tightly against her teeth.

"Of course not." His rigid posture pulled him out of his chair and he moved forward into the room. Christiana dropped her arms to her side, her thumb brushing against the bulge of her weapons through her coat's ruffles.

"Then explain yourself, or I'm leaving," she snapped, her palms sweating as she followed him with her eyes. He paced the room, his gaze trained to their movements. She bit the inside of her cheek, the metallic taste of blood on her tongue distracting her while she waited for him to speak.

He finally stopped in his tracks, staring at her coldly. "When I hired you, I was expecting secrets."

"That's kind of what a person gets himself into when he chooses to hire an assassin." She tried to keep her voice steady. She could already tell he wasn't here to talk about Eliza or the case at all. She was trying her best to keep her thoughts untangled, but her anxiety threaded them together like a ball of yarn.

"I'm aware. You have a life outside of my employ, and to be honest, I never wanted to know what you did during the daytime."

"Very well..." Sweat formed on her brow as he began pacing again, his eyes never leaving her still form in the dark corner. He laced his fingers together behind his back.

"But that didn't stop me from guessing, from thinking about what must have brought you to this job in the first place." His pacing brought him closer and closer to her shadow, forcing her to take a few steps to the side. "Maybe you worked in a tavern and were finally finished with drunk men groping you. Perhaps you had fallen on hard times and become a street walker. Or perhaps it was a family business."

She pulled her trembling chin up. "Are you expecting me to tell you if any of those are true?"

"No, not at all. Like I said, I didn't want to know the truth, because the truth of who you are is dangerous. That mask and hood were not only your best friends in this room, but mine as well." He pointed at the disguise covering the identity of a person he had known since childhood. Her hand flew up to her face, the veil's soft fabric still perfectly placed across the bridge of her nose to fall down the lower half of her face.

"So why don't we continue with that?" she croaked, her voice finally giving out on her.

He stalked her like prey around the edge of the room, his feet moving methodically to end up only a few feet away from her. She had never let a client get this close, the pounding of her heart reminding her how badly she wanted to escape.

"Because unfortunately I cannot ignore your hauntingly beautiful eyes anymore."

The blood drained from her face, a chill running over her sweaty skin.

"You can remove the mask now, Christiana," he challenged, his chin lifting and his slit-like eyes staring down at her.

"I don't know who that is." She backed as far away from him as possible. Unfortunately, he had positioned her to move in the opposite direction of her escape plan, her back stopping against the hard-stone wall. He was certainly an expert strategist if he was able to distract her that well.

Her chest tightened when she considered her options. She pulled her stiletto from her belt, the tip shining in the dull candlelight as she held it out in front of her, desperately trying to keep distance between them.

"I wouldn't do that if I were you, Ana." His hand reached for hers, and she jerked her shoulder back. His arm fell to his side, a smirk pinching at the edge of his lips. "I have multiple guards standing watch by my door tonight. Even a slight sound of a struggle and they will come rushing in here before you can consider jumping out that window."

"What do you want?" She forced her voice to stay low but refused to sheathe her weapon. It was the only thing keeping her from falling apart, the smooth metal fitting her palm perfectly.

"The truth. Take your mask off."

"I don't know who you think I am." She tried to formulate an escape plan, her eyes darting around the room. But she couldn't ignore the one tall obstacle blocking her from every possible way out. "I can walk out of here and you never need to know the truth. Just as you've wanted from the beginning."

"I can't do that anymore." He shook his head, his wavy hair breaking free of its leather strap, a few strands framing his face. "I can never unsee what I saw the other night. I know it's you, Ana. I would know those eyes anywhere."

Her free hand clawed at the stone behind her, her jagged fingernails scraping against it as if she could claw her way out of the situation. "Please."

"I'll make you a deal." His face softened as his gaze met hers.

"No." She shook her head violently, her hood slapping her face.

"Remove the mask..."

"No!" She extended her arm out all the way, the dagger visibly shaking as she tried to recover her strength.

"And I step away from the window," he bartered, his hand pointing to the still-open way she had entered.

She looked at him, her dagger-wielding hand faltering as she considered her options, which were few at this point. If she tried to fight her way out with force, the guards would seize her and she would have to answer for all her crimes. Or, she could trust him, willingly admitting to the future King of Viri that one of his powerful nobles was also a professional killer. Even if she was able to escape tonight, she could never guarantee he would let her walk away. But if training with Robert was any indication over these past few weeks, she was barely ready to fight one trained soldier, let alone a handful of them.

Taking a deep breath, she lowered her dagger, storing it back in its proper home on her hip. She stepped toward him slowly, the weight of her feet dragging along the plush carpeted floor. She wasn't exactly sure if she was making the right decision, but she had to take a risk; hopefully she was choosing the right one. Their eyes caught, the intensity of that gaze drawing them together like a magnetic pulse until she stopped in front of him, their chests barely touching. Her numb fingers slowly reached up to her face and clutched the soft fabric, but she couldn't bring herself to pull it down.

Her eyes closed, wet tears forming at the edges. The warmth of his large hand on hers brought her back to reality, his eyes never leaving hers as he helped her pull down the fabric. She fought not to collapse under the pressure of his gaze as he took every inch of her in for what felt like the first time. She had never felt so exposed and vulnerable in her life, even when she was being beaten to a pulp by her father. The moments passed agonizingly slow as her childhood friend realized he was finally getting to see the real her.

"Please," her voice shook, her eyes flitting to the window. She had held up her end of the deal and she was praying he would do the same.

His feet shifted forward for a brief moment before he stepped aside with a sigh. She darted for the escape and vanished quicker than smoke disappearing in the wind.

***

Christiana clutched her shaking arms around her torso, her legs carrying her through the empty streets of Cittadina as if they were separate from herself. The summer night's warm air engulfed her, but she kept pressing forward, trying to force her mind to forget what had happened. Her thoughts blurred together, dizzying her with confusion.

Alekzander knew who she was. He knew the truth she had hidden from so many people for the past five years. The look on his face was seared into her mind, branding her for the rest of her life. His eyes were so full of questions, each one desperately trying to find an answer. Her heart twisted at the memory and her mind left her body, her steps taking her to the one place she would feel somewhat safe while she retreated within herself.

No one was in sight, the evening quiet except for a few hollers and loud noises when she made her way past a busy tavern. Her hood was pulled up still, the fabric covering her wet face in a private shadow all her own. She had yet to refasten the veil, the limp fabric resting against her chest and catching the tears she shed. Every part of her shook as if it was a cold winter night; the summer warmth did nothing to bring her comfort or ease the chill.

Her focus finally returned when she found her way through the quiet neighborhood, most of the houses dark with the late hour. It was well past midnight by now; she'd lost track of the time the minute she stepped into Alekzander's room. She let out a shaking breath at the sight of the red townhouse, her lungs contracting when she noticed the dim light of burning candles in the windows. She feared Robert would already be asleep, but she had taken a chance knowing he struggled to find peace in the dreamlands most nights. She found herself at his office window, peering in to find him sitting by the low flames of the hungry fire. She tapped on the glass, and he jumped at the sound, looking up to see her standing outside.

"My Lady?" He pulled the window open and helped her inside. "What are you doing here?"

She clutched at his forearms, her weight bearing against them both as she tried to keep her legs from collapsing. "Robert..." her voice shook, "he knows."

"What do you mean?" His eyes widened as he wrapped her arms around her waist to support her.

"The Prince. He figured it out, he knows it's me." She let Robert lead her to the tall wingback chair stationed behind his desk. She crumbled into it, her legs finally releasing the agony of carrying her here.

Robert bent down so he was eye level with her. "How is that even possible?"

She couldn't form the words in her brain, let alone speak them out loud. All she could do was shake her head, the weight of her fear crushing against her shoulders as she tried to process what happened. Her body rocked back and forth in the chair, the creaking of the legs breaking the silence. Her skin crawled as if a million eyes watched her; nowhere seemed safe enough in her mind.

"I don't...he..." she stuttered at last. "I went to his room and he was trying to get me to take my mask off. He said he figured it out by my eyes. I don't know how this happened! He's only seen me as the Maiden twice. I thought I was careful!"

"My Lady, you need to breathe." Robert put his hands on her shoulders, trying to steady her. She hadn't realized how labored her breaths were, her lungs burning at the lack of oxygen. She lifted her head, Robert's eyes catching hers as he breathed loudly in and out, his usual way of coaxing her back to equilibrium. She followed his lead, pulling in air through her nose. She held it for a few seconds, the pressure of her full lungs bringing her dizzy thoughts back into focus before she let out a breath slowly through her cracked lips.

Her heart steadied, pulse beating against her neck as she allowed clarity to settle on her exhausted mind. Reality set back in, the true weight of what happened hanging on her back.

She wasn't safe anymore. A leader of this country knew her identity, knew the real face behind the mask of the Midnight Maiden. There weren't many assassins in Viri, only about a dozen players staying active in her field of choice. But those who did hold a career were dangerous, and all of them were on a wanted list by the Crown. Her life was even more in danger than it had been when her father was alive.

Not only that, but her contacts in her assassin life were now at risk. She not only had Marek, but she'd met and worked with a few of Viri's other assassins over the years. She knew information and the channels people had to go through to get their attention. If she was ever captured, she risked being interrogated, the chance of exposing others too great. She had known this for years, but it had never felt likely until the risk of exposure turned into actual exposure. She was lightheaded thinking about what they would do to find out every little dirty secret she held inside her mind.

"I have to leave." She shot out of the chair, pulling her veil off her neck to wipe her drenched face free of sweat and tears.

Robert rushed to the window, using his body as a barricade to keep Christiana in the room. "What do you mean, leave?"

"I have to run. I can't stay here. I can't even go home! I'll be putting Isabelle and my mother at risk." She took a few steps back, her mind racing as she began to pace. "I need your help, Robert. I need provisions to help me survive for the next few days. Food, blankets, some clothes. I can walk as far as possible and stop at a village to restock when necessary."

"No, My Lady, you can't disappear!"

"I have to!" Her hands clutched at the base of her sternum, the rhythmic pull of each breath helping to keep her heart under control. "Don't you understand what I said? He knows who I am! I'm not safe anymore."

"Running away isn't the answer!" He approached her, his steps wide as he moved swiftly to her side. She looked up in his eyes, a mix of concern laced with calm. "Go to the cottage for a few days."

She shook her head, heart skipping a beat at the idea of being close to the palace. "No, it isn't safe."

"The house is under an alias, remember?"

She had forgotten that detail for a moment. After securing the land under her title, she had pretended to sell it to someone else so it would be put under a false name. "Yes, that's true," she mumbled.

"Go to the cottage." Robert moved around the room, stopping at his desk to pull out a piece of parchment and ink. "I'll write a letter to Natalia now, saying there was an emergency at one of your wheat farms. You and I had to go immediately to see them and will be gone for a few days. This will buy you some time."

Christiana shook her head again. "She won't believe that."

"Do you trust her?"

"Of course."

"Then she won't question it. If it's what you said, she'll take your word for it." He finished the letter, blowing on the parchment to help the wet ink dry faster.

"There are too many weaknesses in that excuse. People might see through it." She scratched her scalp through her tangled, knotted hair. Even though she didn't have to give a detailed reason to leave the palace for work, it never stopped people from gossiping. The other nobles would all too eagerly speculate what took her away. Although Christiana knew they could never guess the truth, their lies would not be much better.

She had no idea why she was worrying about her reputation when her actual life was at stake, but her noble upbringing probably had something to do with it.

"That's true," Robert said. "But it's the best excuse we have. We have to hope no one will take the time to think about it."

Her stomach churned at the plan. She could think of a dozen different holes and questions at the idea of it. She had never willingly entered into a plan so weak before; however, she had never been at risk of exposure before either. "All right."

"I'll send this out now." Robert lifted the folded parchment, his seal pressed deeply into the black wax securing it closed. "Go to the cottage and I'll come by tomorrow morning with some food. You have clothes there, right?"

"Some plain clothes for training." She pulled her hood back over her face.

"Perfect. And remember, if they find you there, you have the Prince's letter of intent stashed there, which means you can use it against him if all else fails."

Her shoulders released some tension, her mind finding comfort in the fact she had asked for that so many weeks ago. It might be the thing that saved her life in the coming days.

"Go," Robert urged, pushing her toward the window. "I'll be by tomorrow morning."

She pulled the windowpane up, the warm air rushing against her skin. "Robert?"

"Yes?" He turned to her, his face creased.

"Thank you."

His smile warmed her heart as she climbed out the window and back into the dark streets.

Chapter Twenty-Three

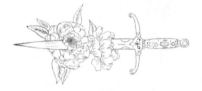

TWO DAYS WENT BY IN THE COTTAGE, AND Christiana's murky mind spiraled with each moment that passed. She woke up on the third day, her eyes heavy with lack of sleep after a few hours of nightmares. She pulled herself up, massaging her tender temples to release some of the tension, and peeked out the bedroom window. The dark clouds of a summer storm swirled in the sky as the sun desperately tried to break through.

She finally felt enough energy to swing her legs over the side of the bed, her feet shuddering at the uneven stone floor as she walked to the corner where a bucket of cold water waited for her. She dunked a hard piece of unscented soap inside and lathered it in her hands before she touched it to her bare torso. She didn't care that the water was cold, that the soap dried her soft skin out, or that the mattress made her back ache. She didn't care about any of the missing luxuries she was so used to in her daily life, because all she could think about was if her life was going to end today.

Robert had visited her each day, bringing food and other provisions she would need to survive. Each time, he came with an update from the palace, giving her information on when she should expect her impending arrest. But he had yet to report a warrant was out for the traitorous Marchioness. She knew this was likely because of her own incriminating evidence against the Prince, his letter of intent still safely hidden away. Yet this fact didn't bring her any comfort, her chest constantly smothered by the heavy pressure of something unknown.

Finally cleaner, she dressed quickly in fresh clothing and wandered into the common area. She dropped her hands to the wooden counters of her distillery, the rattling of glass jars filling the room at the impact. She pulled in a few deep breaths through her nose, trying to drag her mind out of its typical panic. She had done so many chores over the past few days, cleaning anything and everything in sight. She needed to find a new distraction to make it through another twelve hours of consciousness.

She eyed the different plants in front of her, dropped off by Robert the day before. They were a few of the ingredients she had needed to start the poison she planned to use on Julian.

Shoulders sagging, she pulled the jars of herbs closer, her cutting board and knife already cleaned and sharpened. She wasn't even sure if she would need this poison anymore; her job was most likely terminated and her alter ego destroyed. She had no use for any of the equipment around her or the different jars littering the cabinets and counters. But she couldn't stop herself, the rhythmic sound of the knife against the wooden block lulling her into a trance, allowing her to escape into the deepest parts of her mind.

The creaking of the front door behind her brought her back to her surroundings. "Excuse me, My Lady," Robert greeted her.

"Come in, come in," she answered, her back still turned as she poured the freshly-chopped greens back into their jar. "Can you come and help me chop some of these?"

A few moments passed, the hairs standing up on the back of Christiana's neck as she waited for Robert to move closer. "I'm sorry, My Lady, but he made me."

"Who did?"

"Me." Alekzander's deep voice sent a shudder down Christiana's spine as she slowly turned to face them. The two men stood in the threshold, the Prince with his arms crossed and Robert leaning against the doorway.

"What are you doing here?" Her stomach dropped at the sight of Alekzander's dark blue eyes, surrounded by creased lines.

"I wanted to talk." He displayed his hands openly in front of him. "That's it, I promise. You fled my room before we could say anything."

She closed her eyes, her lip swelling as she bit it tightly between her teeth. She pulled in a deep breath, her heart trying desperately to break free. "You can leave now, Robert."

"I'm so sorry, My Lady." He hung his head low, his tall form shrinking with every passing second.

"We will discuss it later. Now leave us," she ordered, fixing him with a cold stare.

Nodding slightly, Robert left the room and closed the door behind him to give them some privacy. Christiana refused to say anything, her shoulders tightly pulled back, shoulder blades barely touching. As Alekzander's loyal subject, she was forced to tell him the truth, but she would be damned if she told him anything unless asked.

Alekzander took a few steps closer, blinking a few times. "I didn't bring anyone else with me."

"Why are you telling me that?" She crossed her arms against her chest and leaned against the hard counter, refusing to take her eyes off of him.

"To help you feel safe. I don't want you to think I came here to take you away." He stopped at the kitchen table, his fingers drawing a nonsense pattern on the wood. "In truth, I wouldn't be able to without incriminating myself. I did hire you, after all."

"True." She narrowed her eyes at him. She wanted to believe him, but something deep inside still kept every inch of her at attention.

"All I want is the truth." He moved forward again slowly, his steps echoing in the cozy space. "I want to ask you questions and to finally get some answers. Ever since you arrived at the palace, I could tell you were keeping something from me. I never dreamed this was it, but here we are."

"What did you think my secret was?" Christiana asked, her head leaning toward her shoulder as she waited for his explanation.

"Honestly, I wondered if you didn't want me to be King." He sighed, his body falling into one of the chairs at her table. "I was so excited when my parents announced you would be coming back to the palace for the summer. But the minute you arrived, I knew you were keeping me at arm's length...and it broke my heart."

A lump formed in her throat. "It did?"

"Of course, it did." His face softened. "You were the one I was most excited to see this summer."

Her limbs filled with lead as she let the weight of his words fall on her. She wanted to explain everything, but the tight bonds around her heart kept her from telling the truth. They lingered there as the seconds passed, staring at each other. She didn't know how to move forward anymore.

"I felt the same way about seeing you," she finally whispered—her first truth to him.

"I'm not angry at you for keeping this secret," he said eventually. "But now that I know, I want to understand more about your life."

She took a deep breath, her arms finally relaxing at her sides, and joined him at the table. "All right, but I can't promise I'll answer all of your questions."

"That's fair," he replied, his eyes following her as she sat warily on the edge of the other chair. His brows pulled inward, his face contorting. "How? Just how...did you learn all of this?"

"I hired a mentor to teach me." Marek's kind face filled her mind.

"Can I ask who?"

"No." She leaned back, her hands gripping the edges of the chair until her knuckles turned white.

"Very well." He hesitated, his index finger tapping against his upper arm. "What made you want to learn?"

Her lips pursed off to the side, her mind racing with the multiple reasons her father gave her during her long childhood. She thought she was ready to open up to Alekzander, to repair a bond with an old friend, but her heart and mind weren't making it easy for her. She could feel the gates closing around her, their iron-clad locks tightening on the secrets of her past. She didn't know what to say; all she could do was stare at him, her eyes blank.

"You won't tell me that either?" His shoulders sagged at yet another unanswered question.

"I'm sorry," was all she could push through her lips.

His head fell to his chest, his left hand rubbing circles against his forehead. "I guess I can't blame you. But I wish you'd realize you aren't in danger around me."

"It's not that easy."

"Why not? You trusted me once, didn't you?"

She looked at him, his eyes begging her for an answer. She thought back to their time together years ago, when they were young and uninhibited by the pressures of Viri. She had once considered him a close friend, a person she could spend countless hours with. But did she ever really trust him? She had spent most of her life harboring shameful secrets and dangerous truths, too focused on keeping them concealed to even consider if he was worth confiding in.

Even now, there were only two people in her life she considered trustworthy: Marek and Robert. Two men who understood her struggles and accepted her for them. But it had taken years of knowing them to even begin opening herself up. Could she put herself through the pain of admitting her secrets to yet another person? Did she have that kind of strength left within her?

"I know you want me to trust you," she began, her eyes dropping to the table. "But you don't understand how much...darkness it takes to make a person ready for this kind of job. That kind of darkness...it isn't easy to show to just anyone. I know we were friends once, but that was so long ago. I've changed a lot since."

"I know that." He reached for her hand and she pulled it away, letting his fall limply back on the table. She returned to the distillery to rummage through one of her upper cabinets.

"I'm not the same girl you once knew." She stretched her arm up, her hand feeling around the dusty top shelf before encountering the crisp piece of hidden parchment. She pulled it down, clutching it to her chest as she returned to the table.

"I never said you were." He watched her sit down. "All I said was I wanted to get to know the woman you've become."

"I don't easily trust people. Why do you think I asked you for this?" She held up the folded piece of paper, the bright purple wax sitting proudly on the outside.

"My letter of intent and seal?" His eyebrows furrowed.

"Yes." She dropped it, her fingers holding it down to the table so he couldn't reach for it. "I needed this to feel protected. I didn't trust you and I needed insurance for this whole case."

"I see." His shoulders sagged, a deep frown setting on his face. "So, I'm assuming this isn't you returning it to me?"

"I'm sorry, I can't." Her fingers tightened around the parchment.

"Not until this case is over. You promised it to me, and I'll hold onto this safety until the last moment."

The parchment was rough against her hand as she pulled it close to her chest again, a rush of relief flooding her body at its closeness. She wished she could give it back and move forward with him. But nothing would stop her from wondering if her safety was truly stable with each morsel of knowledge she let him gain. She couldn't risk herself or her network because of a childhood friendship.

"Keep it." He sat back in his chair. "For as long as you need."

Her eyes went wide, meeting his steady stare. "Excuse me?"

"Keep it. Even past when you close the case, if that's what you need."

"But...why?" Her eyes narrowed again.

"I'm not going to stop working toward showing you that you can trust me again, but I can already tell it's going to take time. So, if having that piece of paper close to you is what will make you feel safe around me, then it's yours. I trust you, so I know you aren't going to use it against me unless you absolutely have to."

Her jaw went slack. She couldn't believe how open he was being, how he was willing to let her hold an incriminating document against him in her possession for an unspecified period of time. Her fingers trembled, the paper crinkling under her tight grasp. She wanted to reach out to him, her arm trembling, but she refused. "Thank you."

"It comes with one condition, though," he said.

Her heart picked up speed again. "And that is—?"

"That you at least try to spend some time with me for the rest of the summer?" He smiled. "Give me a chance to show you that you can trust me."

She could feel the twitch of a smile on the corner of her lip, a warm fire spreading through her chest as her gaze caught his. She remembered all the time she had enjoyed with him once, and the pain she had felt earlier this summer when she realized she had to stay away from him. It had been a heartbreaking decision, and now he was giving her an opportunity to gain it back. She could see how their friendship was meant to develop without the interference of others keeping them apart. She tried not to let her daydreaming wander too far, a slight whisper in the back of her mind telling her his tender gaze and affectionate words meant so much more than she even realized.

She silenced that voice as best as she could. They were friends, even if her heart was trying to convince her otherwise.

"All right." She smiled, her heart settling in her chest at the thought of being around Alekzander again. Her fear wouldn't disappear as quickly, but the only way to overcome it was to work through it, which meant spending time with him. She sat up straight, remembering the exciting news she could finally share with him. "Actually, since you're here, I might as well tell you one thing."

"Really? And what is that?" He chuckled.

"I finally figured out a plan for the...task you've asked of me." She stood up slowly to return the piece of parchment to its hiding place.

Alekzander straightened up in his chair. "Without having to fight him?"

"Yes, thankfully." She rummaged through one of the other cabinets, the different-sized vials filled with multicolored liquids. She waved to Alekzander, beckoning him forward. "Eliza's only request was that he suffer for what he has done to her. So, I think this will work best." She pulled out one of the vials, brimming with a murky white liquid.

"Purgatory?" Alekzander read the label, standing only inches away from her.

"It's the name of the poison. Once administered, the victim will fall into a deep, hallucinating coma for about three days before the body and heart stop from exhaustion. It's said each victim spends those days reliving all of the sins they committed during their lifetime."

"Certainly, it sounds like suffering. Do you use this one often?" He leaned his back against the edge of the counter.

"Not really," she answered, mimicking his stance. "Unlike most poisons, this one can only be administered by ingestion. It makes it difficult to give it to people in an inconspicuous manner without risking the lives of others around them."

His smile faded, a deep frown setting on his lips. "Well, how are you going to give it to Julian? He has two poison testers to check all of his food."

"I thought of that already. What makes this poison extra special is it comes in two different forms: a liquid one," she said as she grabbed the bottle from his hands, "which is the easiest and most common form. However, I was taught to brew it into a solid, crystalized form. Once complete, it looks exactly like salt."

"Seriously?" His eyes widened.

"People always assume poison is added to food before it gets to the table, so no one will ever suspect it's in the salt dish. We'll have to make sure to give it to him during a private dinner, or one with his wife."

"That would certainly work." He looked down at the floor, his gaze dark as he stroked his chin lightly.

"The only complication is, I don't have any of the crystalized form already made. And it takes at least three weeks to make a batch."

Alekzander shrugged, crossing his arms. "Having to wait a few more weeks seems like a small price to pay to make sure this is done correctly."

"I agree," she said with a slight smile, relief finally seeping in as she explained the rest of her plan.

Chapter Twenty-Four

*C*HRISTIANA WOKE UP THE NEXT MORNING, comfortably snuggled in the folds of her four-poster bed's soft, heavy quilt, sunlight streaming through the tall window of her luxurious bedroom. She was able to take a bath, drowning her body in the warm water scented of jasmine and rose petals; she was able to sit at her large dining table, her mind fully clear from a good night's rest and a warm breakfast happily filling her stomach. She felt revived from the dead, her limbs relaxed from the tension she had built up over the past seventy-two hours.

It would still take time to trust Alekzander, their friendship far from repaired after the years apart. But the air had shifted, the prospect of change filling her chest. She wanted to believe she could one day have his friendship again, some happy memories of her past filling her present. And although she was skeptical, she couldn't help but feel for once that she could be hopeful for a piece of her immediate future, too.

As she was finishing the last of her morning tea, a hard knock came at the front door. Christiana dropped her book on the table to answer it, finding Robert's kind face on the other side. They had a lot of work to do this morning, for both of her titles.

"Come in." She moved back to the table, Robert firmly on her heels.

"So, are we..." he trailed off, hesitating to sit down.

"We are fine." She smiled softly. "Though I'm sorry you had to implicate yourself in the whole exposure."

"I have faithfully stood by the Maiden's side for three years now, My Lady." Robert finally sat down at the table next to her. "He tracked me down at my townhouse. I know I didn't have to say anything—to him I'm only your assistant, after all—but he made a compelling case he wasn't going to harm you. I followed my gut telling me that bringing him to you meant bringing you back to the palace."

"I guess your gut was right."

"I've always put my trust in it." A smile quirked at the edge of his lips, his broad shoulders slumping against the seatback. "Now that the last few days are behind us, are you ready to work?"

"Natalia is doing a few chores in the laundry, so why don't we catch up on some Julian progress?" Christiana leaned forward, pulling her stack of notebooks closer and picking up her favorite quill. The white and black feather slipped through her fingers with ease, the silky wisps tickling the edges of her fingertips.

"Very well." Robert shuffled a few of the parchment pieces he had carried into the room with him and finally settled on the correct one, scanning it. "As you saw, most of the missing ingredients for the poison are in. A few more came last night and I stashed them at the cottage."

"Perfect."

"The most difficult ingredient to track down was Golden Chain."

Christiana sighed. She wasn't surprised by that; the bean-like capsules were not commonly grown in many gardens. It was an important ingredient in the poison, the main cause for the coma she was planning to put the Chancellor in.

"No luck?" she asked, still playing with the ends of her quill.

"Not at first, but I found an apothecary a few villages over that sells it. He's doing a fresh harvest of the plant late next week and can send us what we need then. I've already put in the order and given payment. We should have the pods soon."

"Wonderful!" Christiana clapped her hands, fingers rubbing against the soft flesh of her palms. "Any news on Tobias?"

Robert sighed deeply. "Unfortunately, no. I tried talking to him last week, but he found a reason to excuse himself. I told you before, he's a fairly nervous fellow."

"Pity." Christiana's shoulders sagged, her heart dropping to meet her stomach.

"However, we were both invited to a cocktail party at Alastair's house over the weekend," Robert added. Christiana's brow wrinkled at the name she didn't recognize. "He's another secretary in court. He holds these parties once a month for all of the administrative people to help them relax. That, and he's a gossip."

Christiana laughed quietly, showing teeth through her amused smile. "I see."

"I'll try again." Robert shrugged. "Maybe a few glasses of wine will be useful in this as well."

"If I haven't said it before, thank you for the extra help with this." She leaned forward, her fingers brushing his as she gave him a smile.

He had risked so much for her over the past few weeks, her heart swelled thinking about his loyalty. She knew Robert's life had been relatively quiet ever since he left the military. After everything he went through with his older brother, and the weekly beatings that ultimately led him to hire her, he deserved the peace he had craved for so long. Now, she was asking him to risk all of that because her illegal activities needed his unique touch. She never went a day without being thankful for the friend she had gained during such dark times in both of their lives.

"You're welcome, My Lady." He smiled back. "I believe that is the last update I have with that particular job."

Christiana leaned back in her chair, pulling the top journal off the stack in front of her. "Perfect. Should we move on to updating my financial ledger?"

"Of course." Robert grabbed the chest that had been sitting on the corner of the table. Christiana's spring harvest had been successful this year, both her grain and vegetable fields producing fruitful products. After a few weeks of her farmers selling their wares at many markets around Tagri, they had sent over her profit, the families already keeping their share from their hard work over the season. The last of the payments had arrived a few days ago; now Christiana and Robert had the menial task of counting all her profits and tracking them.

The next two hours flew by with the clanging of the many coins against the table while Christiana counted. She kept track of each pouch; a tag attached to each with the landholding parcel number. The falling coins clashed with the scratch of Robert's quill tip, his blocky handwriting meticulously filling up the ledger when Christiana gave him the right numbers.

"That's the last of it." She sighed, dropping the final pouch of coins back into the chest with a heavy clash.

"Fantastic." He laughed, shutting the ledger with a loud thud.

"I think that's enough for today. We both deserve a break after the stressful days we've had this week." She pushed herself up from the chair.

"There is one more thing I need to give you before I go." Robert hesitated, his eyes downcast as his fingers played with the edge of the table.

"Oh?" Her brows creased.

"This came for you a few days ago." He offered a letter. "Natalia handed it off to me last night after you arrived back at the castle."

"Why didn't she give it to me herself?" Christiana took the parcel from his fingers.

"I think she was scared," he admitted.

Christiana turned the envelope over to open it, bile crawling up her throat as she saw the moss-green wax pressed into the page. "Ugh, why is he writing to me?" she spat, her hands yanking the Duke of Tagri's crest open. She pulled the piece of parchment out, Edgar's handwriting littering the page.

My Dear Christiana,

The news of your travels back to Tagri have reached my household, my fingers tingling as I write this letter to you, eagerly awaiting your arrival back to the palace. As I have mentioned many times this summer, I think a union between our households is in the best interest of us both. And although you have brushed off such thoughts without a care, I think you will find it is best to reconsider my offer.

We both need something from the other person, and a decent conversation will help us move forward with this prospect. I ask that you sit down with me for a lunch upon your return. I think you will find my argument for our courtship quite compelling if you choose to open your stubborn mind and listen to my offer.

Please write me once you arrive back and we can set up a time and place to meet. I look forward to your impending reply.

Sincerely,

Edgar Castriello, Duke of Tagri

Her stomach churned at his words, his arrogant demeanor wafting off the page like rotten fruit. "I hate him." She threw the parchment onto the table like it was on fire.

"What does he want?" Robert asked, his hand mindlessly organizing his scrolls as he prepared to leave.

"To give me a courtship proposal over lunch. Over my dead body will I ever meet with him." She crossed her arms, looking over to Robert for his support. But he stared intently at the table. "What is it?"

"I know you won't want to hear this, but..." he trailed off for a moment. "It may be in your best interest to take the meeting."

"Excuse me!?"

"If you go and listen to the formal proposal, it means getting everything out in the public and in the open." Robert stood up, gathering his things in his arms. "You already know you want to say no. So, all you have to do is listen to his terrible words for a few moments before denying them. Once you do that, this whole thing will be put to rest and he'll hopefully leave you alone because of his wounded pride."

She looked over at him, her lips pursed as she considered his words. He had a valid point. Edgar had kept bothering her and pushing her nerves up until this point because he had yet to give a formal proposal. But Virian culture was fairly strict when it came to courtships; once a lady denied a man's offer, he couldn't propose again without looking like a petty and desperate fool. Edgar was too prideful to make a foolish spectacle of himself after she publicly said no.

"Fine." She sighed. "Can you draft me a letter before you leave? Tell him I can meet him in a few days, make him suffer longer. I'll sign it and send it out once I return." Her feet were already moving her toward the escape of the door.

"Where are you going?" Robert turned to ask her.

"To find a decent distraction from this horrible idea," she mumbled, shutting the door behind herself.

Chapter Twenty-Five

*C*HRISTIANA WENT TO THE ONLY PLACE SHE FELT
any amount of comfort the past few weeks.

She nodded to the two guards standing watch at the
entrance to the Royal Wing, men already used to seeing her walk down
the long hallway. She hurried to the familiar door, hand balled into a fist
as she pounded it against the wood.

Seconds passed, her impatience stirring in her stomach as she hit
the door again. She didn't want to return to her room yet, her fingers
already twitching at the thought of her lunch with Edgar. She needed
someone to pass the time with, and she needed them now.

"Christiana?"

The back of her neck tingled at that deep voice. She turned slowly
to find Alekzander's head peeking out from behind his own door.

"Oh, I'm sorry, Alekzander," she said with a quick curtsy. "I didn't
mean to disturb you."

"You didn't." He pushed the door open wider, his whole body

coming into view as he leaned against the frame. "I thought you were knocking on my door. Are you all right?" His head tilted to the side, a wayward curl falling on his forehead.

"Yes, I ..." she trailed off for a moment, not used to the steady beat of her heart while conversing with him. "I wanted to see if Dorina was busy. I need a distraction and I thought a game of chess would be a good one."

"Oh, well, she's with our mother right now. They have some planning to do for her birthday ball."

"Oh, of course. It was just an idea anyway." Christiana waved her hand, her heart falling as she realized she would need to go back to the loneliness of her apartment. She had gotten so used to having companionship over the summer, she was surprised to find being alone was not as enjoyable as she once thought.

She turned to leave, Alekzander's baritone stopping her in her tracks. "But if you want some company, I could use a break from work. A chess game with you sounds like a wonderful way to relax."

She pivoted again to find a playful smile dancing on his lips as he waited for her to respond. "I'm not sure..."

"You did say we could try to be friends again," he murmured, stepping closer to her. A smile tried to break free of her tense lips at those words. She had promised him to put in some effort, and her own aching chest showed her how badly she wanted to try.

"That would be wonderful." She paused for a moment before adding, "Zander."

His childhood nickname rolled off her tongue for the first time all summer. His grin grew wide across his face, the tops of his cheeks pinching when his eyes narrowed. He offered his arm out to her, her hand grasping the crook of his elbow as he escorted her to the empty game room. She let go when they entered, drifting over to one of the corner chess tables. He wandered in the opposite direction, stopping at the liquor cabinet.

"Would you like a drink?" he offered, already pouring himself a serving from a large decanter. "There is plenty of wine to choose from."

She pulled out the marble white chess pieces from the bottom drawer, placing them with a click on the board. "I wouldn't mind a glass of what you're having."

His head jerked up, eyes wide. "Whiskey? Really?" A laugh escaped his chest, the deep, infectious sound drawing out Christiana's own.

"It's my favorite liquor. One of the few I keep back at my estate in Tagri."

"Hm, you are full of secrets, aren't you?" He winked, his hand outstretched with a generous serving. She shook her head as she took the drink, her lips parting to allow a sip to rest on her tongue.

Her senses exploded, the lingering taste of honey-soaked apples and rich butterscotch dancing on her taste buds as the burning liquid slid down her throat. "What is that?" Wide-eyed, she studied the deep, rich amber swirling around in the crystal glass.

"The prized whiskey of Amarglio," Zander said, placing his own glass next to the board as he began to set up his obsidian pieces. "Although the Ambassador was an arrogant bore most of the time, he did come with a few barrels of this delectable treat. It was well worth the hours I was forced to spend with him."

Christiana took one more sip, savoring the flavor against her tongue as she finished placing the last of her pieces. Once the board was set, Zander nodded, and she picked up her first piece and moved it. Silence fell over them for a few moments, a handful of moves acted between them as the board became a mixture of black and white.

"So." Zander broke the silence. "What forced you to find solace with my sister this afternoon?"

"A disappointing invitation," she mumbled, moving her rook a few paces. "Seems Edgar isn't going to let me go as easily as I hoped."

"I would say let him down easy," Zander moved his castle forward three paces, "but I know how infuriating that man can be even when he's not flirting with you. So, if an accident occurs while you're with him, I'm sure I could convince my father to look the other way."

Christiana looked up at him, stifling a giggle at the smirk on his face. "I'll keep that in mind."

They played a few more turns, Christiana taking a moment to study Zander's pinched face while he stared down at the board. This moment felt surreal to her. After weeks of avoidance, paranoia, and fear cutting short all her moments with him, she was in awe over the way they were settling in together today. Warmth burned deep in her soul, something she hadn't felt for five years. Her mind wandered as she waited her turn, trying her best to remember the last time the two of them had spent any real time together.

Christiana was thankful that on the bright summer day, her father pulled away on a morning hunting trip with a handful of other nobles. It finally gave her some time to breathe away from his suffocating presence. She knew right away where to spend her free time: in the comforting confines of her favorite willow tree. She had been reluctant to come here all summer, afraid her father would discover her childhood hideaway. He was determined to discover every secret she had, but she refused to let him have this sacred one.

"I'm surprised to see you out of the palace." A familiar voice wove between the branches, one she hadn't heard much this summer. Opening her eyes, she looked up at Alekzander, a happy smile spread across his face.

"Finally got a morning to myself," she admitted, shoulders tensing at the sight of him.

"Good for you. You deserve it since you've been working so hard. You seem to be even busier than me," he teased, relaxing next to her with his back propped against the trunk. A lump formed in her throat and she wondered if she should walk away. But something kept her planted to the

ground, her back firmly set against the tree trunk.

"My father is determined. I'm lucky yours decided to take everyone out today," she said. "Why didn't you go with them?"

Looking out into the distance, he sighed. "I didn't have time. I have to prepare for something."

"Are you all right?" she asked, sensing his melancholy.

"My father is sending me to one of the borders for the rest of the summer."

"That's too bad." Christiana played with the hem of her dress, saddened she wouldn't get to see him longer.

"It is. Especially since I've barely gotten to see you this entire time."

"That's not true." she argued, her cheeks warming. Her father had been successful at keeping them away from each other, but somehow, she still felt comfort knowing her friend was close by, even if she wasn't able to talk to him every day.

"Did I upset you?" His eyes turned to her, his shoulder only an inch away from hers.

"No, no." She blinked the tears in her glassy eyes. "I'm going to miss you is all."

"Yeah?" he asked with a boyish grin.

"Well, don't laugh." A whisper of a blush heated her cheeks, the warmth spreading down her neck.

"I'm not, I promise." He touched her shoulder lightly, his thumb rubbing circles along the silk-covered skin just above her newest bruise. Unable to control herself, she grimaced, jerking away from him, and his glee evaporated into a frown. "What? What did I do?"

"Nothing." She tried to smile, her shoulder still nursing a dull pain.

"It's not nothing, Ana, I hurt you. What happened?" His eyes were filled with concern as he stared her down.

"It's embarrassing. I was riding yesterday morning and I fell off my horse. I must have hurt my shoulder more than I realized," she lied.

Two nights ago hadn't been easy on Christiana. Her father returned home from dinner, angry to see his daughter reading a book instead of studying. He had dragged her from her comfortable bed and banged her body against her bedpost one too many times, spreading a dark purple bruise over her entire shoulder.

"You should go see the court physician," Zander suggested.

"No!"

"Why not?" His brow creased.

"Because I told you, I'm fine. It will heal in a few days."

"If you're sure..."

"I am." She stood, dusting her skirts off. "Now, I need to go."

"Don't leave, Ana," he pleaded, "I'm sorry, I didn't mean to embarrass you. Don't leave."

"You didn't," she lied once again. The truth was, it wasn't only the pain making her flinch away from him, but something unknown that coursed through her at his delicate touch. Growing up together, she had always felt a spark whenever they came in contact, nothing she ever paid attention to. But for the first time this summer, that spark had grown into something completely unexplainable. It was as if it had finally ignited the intended flame and it was now burning through her entire body. She didn't know what to do. The only thing she could think of was to get as far away from him as possible. "I need to get back to work. If my father returns and I haven't studied at all, he'll kill me."

"All right. But I leave next week. Promise me you'll say goodbye before I go."

"Of course," she promised. With a saddened curtsy, she left the comfortable willow tree to return to the castle.

She stared over at Zander now, remembering that moment under the willow. She had forgotten about that fire deep within her, her lack of proximity to the Prince over the years pushing it to the deep corners of her memories. A lingering thread whispered through her chest still. She hadn't noticed it until today, deafened by her fear the most, but now it was unignorable. He sat across from her, his brow creased in concentration as his curls once again tried to escape his quaffed style. She wanted to reach out, to see if that blaze between them was still there. All she needed to do was touch him...

"Are you all right?" Zander pulled her out of her longing curiosity, staring at her with blatant concern.

"Yes, sorry. Lost in my own thoughts." She shook off the memory and grasped the smooth marble piece to make her next move. She needed to stop wondering what could have been between them all those years ago. Even if she felt that slight pull, she couldn't say for sure if he felt it too. False hope in past feelings wasn't going to help her.

As if he could read her thoughts, Zander smirked. "Since we're finally spending time together, why don't we take the time to...reacquaint ourselves?"

Her stomach rumbled at the idea. "What did you have in mind?"

"A game of questions. Each one I ask, you get to ask one back." He reclined in his chair, his hands folded and his eyes challenging her to the new game.

She smirked as well, intrigued by the idea of learning more about Zander, although she wasn't ready to be so open about her other life. "Do I have a right to not answer?"

"Of course." He nodded, swirling his whiskey and taking a sip. "And I promise to keep all...unwanted topics off the table. Deal?"

"Fair enough. Go ahead and ask." She leaned forward to reach across the chess board, her next move capturing one of Zander's rooks.

"Let's see..." he contemplated his first question, his fingers tapping together as he stared at her. "What's your favorite color?"

She couldn't stop herself from laughing, his easy question not at all what she expected. "Burgundy."

"Dark color." He moved his next piece, picking up the bishop he captured from her.

"What can I say, I like dark things." She smiled, and his grew when they briefly made eye contact. "My turn. What's your favorite weapon?"

"Well, depends on what kind of weapon we are talking about. For swords, I prefer a well-balanced longsword. Broadswords are too clunky for me and I prefer the thin blade. If we are talking archery, I like a crossbow."

She nodded, biting gently at the inside of her tender cheek. She wasn't surprised by his answers, but she liked how knowledgeable he was about the different types of weapons. The nape of her neck prickled as she took a sip of her whiskey. "Your turn."

"What is the greatest lesson you have learned over the past five years?" His face turned downward at the board, but his eyes looked up at her.

She thought over her years of work, both as the Marchioness and as the Maiden. She had been forced to stand up for herself and fight for the sanity she almost lost during years of brutal punishments and mind-bending torment. She wondered what lesson, what piece of her life, was the greatest.

A smile played at her lips. "Never be afraid to fail." Marek's lesson danced on her tongue. "It's through failure that we can find our greatest successes and achievements. Plus, failures make our success more enjoyable."

"Quite inspiring." The Prince nodded, his cheek twitching.

"Thank you." She smiled back at him. "Same question to you."

He did not hesitate. "Don't always take life seriously."

"Excuse me?"

"It's true!" he defended. "I'm forced to feel the weight of many people's well-being and lives on my shoulders every day. I'm expected to protect their lives as my responsibility in the future...a job I'm excited and happy to accept. But that doesn't mean I need to take every moment of my life as a serious moment. I would die under the crushing weight of the responsibility if I didn't make a joke or be silly every now and again."

Her mouth fell open even more. She had changed a lot over the past five years, but she had never realized the ways he had changed as well. His kind heart and sense of duty had grown exponentially, his mind prepared for his future. But somehow, he had also allowed himself to hold on to some of his boyish charm to help him through it all. She didn't know why she was so drawn by such an answer, but her hips shifted forward, her torso leaning over the chess board.

"That is..." She hesitated for a moment. "A surprising yet profound discovery."

"I have those every now and then," he joked, their laughter finally breaking free. Christiana hadn't laughed like this in so long, belly shaking, muscles contracting with giggles.

She felt giddy, a rush of euphoria spreading through her limbs at the sound of his infectious laughter. She finally realized what her fear had been masking these past couple weeks: not only did she want Zander back in her life, she longed to be closer to him. She wanted to know him, all of him, the light and the dark. The walls around her heart quaked for a moment, a piece of her wanting to break them down. She refused to let them fall, but for once she wasn't scared at the idea of being vulnerable. Not when it was Zander sitting across from her.

"Sorry to disrupt the fun." The King's voice interrupted them from the doorway, and Christiana's laughter halted in her throat, her legs forcing her up to greet him.

"Your Majesty." She pushed herself into a deep curtsy, her legs shaking as she bowed her head to conceal her dark pink cheeks.

"Oh, please sit back down, Christiana." Lucian waved his hand at her, and she collapsed back into the soft chair. "We were here to play a round or two of cards."

"We?" Zander's neck craned at the door.

"Hello, Zander." Voice sultry as ever, Julian moved on the King's heels into the room.

"Julian." Zander spoke through tightened teeth. His one hand hid behind the chessboard, his knuckles white.

"My Lady," Julian greeted Christiana, eyes sparkling as he nodded at her.

"Chancellor." She kept her voice steady, her stomach twisting at his close proximity. Her skin crawled at the memory of his arms around her at the masquerade.

"So, what was so funny?" The King asked, shuffling a deck of cards he pulled out from one of the cabinets against the wall.

"Oh, reminiscing about some childhood memories." Keeping her voice light, Christiana quietly slid her hand across the table, making sure it was concealed from view by the chessboard. She touched Zander's tight fist, softly stroking his knuckles until she felt the pressure release.

"You two certainly were close back then," Julian spoke up. "It's wonderful to see you spending time together again."

Christiana's gaze met the King's, his face twitching at his Chancellor's words. She frowned, unsure why the King would flinch at their spending time together. "We certainly think so." She shot them her most charming smile, keeping eye contact with both of them.

"Well, let's not disturb them." The King pushed himself away from the wall. "Come, Julian, we can play in my room."

"As you wish, Lucian." Julian smirked, a quick wink twitching against his face toward Christiana before the two left the room.

Zander's hand finally unraveled under hers, the tight muscles releasing. They looked up at each other, deep sighs escaping their lips as silence fell over the room.

Chapter Twenty-Six

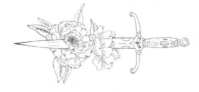

THE NEXT WEEK PASSED QUICKLY, AND BEFORE Christiana truly felt prepared she was dragging her feet to the second-floor conservatory for her fateful meeting with Edgar. The sound of bubbling water reached her ears as she rounded the corner, bright sunlight filtering through the glass walls. The large fountain was situated in the center of the room, surrounded by bright blooms, assorted flowers, and a handful of metal tables and chairs, all of them empty except one covered in fresh fruit and assorted cheeses and meats. Christiana's chest tightened, a scowl twisting her lips as she spotted Edgar staring out the windows.

She walked over to him, feeling like chains encircled her feet and slowed her pace. His head whipped to the side, a devilish grin spreading across his face as he stood up to greet her. He looked like a peacock in his bright blue doublet with its ivy-green stitching. His amber hair was slicked back, showing off his sharp features.

"Thank you for joining me." He pulled her chair out, the light chiffon fabric of her navy dress draping over the sides when she sat. "Took you long enough to accept," he mumbled in her ear.

"Let's get it over with, shall we?" She crossed her arms, the weight soothing against her boiling heart.

He returned to his seat, his face curved in amusement as he stared her down. "Please, help yourself." He gestured to the food arranged on the table.

"No appetite." She frowned, her stomach rumbling in disagreement. She was starved, and silently chastised herself for not eating before she left. The food smelled delicious, the sweet fruit and salty meats mingling in the air. She would love to indulge, but she wasn't in the mood to draw this out any longer than needed.

"If you say so." He leaned forward, picking up a piece of toasted bread and a slice of cheese and taking a large, cracking bite. His smirk stayed steady as he chewed, his slow movements taunting her.

She rolled her eyes. "So, you had a proposal for me?"

"Eager to learn more about it?" He drizzled a stream of honey over his next piece of cheese, the sticky liquid dripping on his fingers as he shoved the food in his mouth.

"Eager for something," she mumbled. "You said it was worth listening to. So out with it."

"Very well." He wiped his hands and face on his napkin and leaned back in his chair. "I think we both have something to benefit from a prospective marriage."

"I know you certainly do." She still couldn't come up with anything he could offer her that would entice her into marriage.

"You're right, I want my land back and the power and wealth along with it." He nodded. "But I know one thing you currently have that you would most likely have to give up in any other marriage."

"And what is that?"

"Your privacy." He smirked, his eyebrows raising to his hairline as his eyes locked with hers.

Her heart dropped to the pits of her stomach, a bead of sweat forming along her jaw as it tightened. "What makes you think that?"

"I know you think I'm an idiot, Christiana, but I'm quite good at noticing certain mannerisms and habits in other people. You've stayed away from court for the last five years, basically choosing to seclude yourself from society. You obviously like to live your own life. A life I have no intention of disturbing."

"Except binding yourself to me for the rest of it," she muttered through closed teeth.

"Binding our households and titles through marriage doesn't mean we have to bind our lives together." He flicked his hands. "I'm even willing to add to the marriage contract my full agreement to give up any control on all of the land that will be under our joined title."

Her eyes bulged, her mind trying to process the words. "You don't want any control over the decisions? You would allow me to hold all the power?"

"Why not?" He shrugged, his shoulders relaxed against the back of the chair. "Fact is fact, Christiana: you took depleted lands from my family and turned them into flourishing profits. I wouldn't know how to run any of that. Why disturb perfection? Besides, I couldn't care less about the responsibility."

Her veins boiled along the surface of her skin, her fingernails scratching against her forearm. "So, basically, you want all the benefits of a wealthy title without the responsibility of holding it?"

"As if you don't enjoy every moment of running your own title?" he accused. Her tongue tasted blood from biting the inside of her cheek. "You walk around this place with your head held high because of your achievements. Do you think most husbands would let you keep control of power once your land was in their grasp?"

Christiana's mind froze. She had spent the past few weeks flirting with the idea of a courtship with Rowan, her answer still due to him about the prospect. She realized, with all the conversations and time spent together, she never once asked him how he wanted to merge their lives together. She couldn't help but wonder if he expected her to give up her power like many of the other men would.

She shook the image of Rowan's face out of her mind, his plans not the ones she should be worried about. The smug look dancing across Edgar's face made her pulse quicken. She processed his words, her body still from the shock that they made a bit of sense. But the man in front of her was a pest, one she had been swatting away from her face for years now. The idea of entering such a life-long contract with him caused bile to rise in her throat. Now she was happy she hadn't eaten anything, her stomach churning at the thought of him kissing her intimately.

"What about heirs?" she shot back. "We'd be expected to produce a few."

He laughed, the sound forcing up the hairs along Christiana's neck. "If we are smart about it, we can make children quickly. We could get away with lying together only a dozen times if we do it correctly."

"Wonderful." She shuddered, the vision of Edgar lying on top of her making her want to bathe for the next hour.

"You never know, I could surprise you. Maybe you'll enjoy being intimate with me." He wiggled his eyebrows at her.

"You're disgusting."

"Just being honest." He laughed. "Anyway, once we produce a few children, we can stop. And we can go on with our lives however we each see fit. I won't even care if you find...pleasure with someone else. As long as you take care to not find yourself in any compromising situations."

Her mouth fell open once again, his words sending chills down her spine. Her blood felt as if it was leaking through her skin, the rage forcing its way out of her. She closed her fingers around her thumb, the white knuckles grasping it in a tight fist. She tugged it inward, the joint pain distracting her from the odious man before her. She could not believe the audacious things he was saying right now, every word and phrase laced with such selfish and loathsome motives.

But that wasn't the only thing causing her emotions to spill out. She should be worried about other issues, but they were easily dismissed. She wasn't even worried he might know about her secret life. He was observant, but he wasn't smart enough to put those secrets together. The person she was quite mad at was herself. For a few short moments, a fleeting thought, she wondered if this was the life she wanted to live. Besides the disgusting prospect of lying with him, his argument had persuaded something hidden deep in her mind. She could have privacy, control, and enjoy the life she had spent five years building. She could disappear for days on Maiden cases, Edgar never once worrying or asking why she was missing from the house. She would continue to grow their holdings, maybe becoming the richest Duchess in Viri.

She felt the pull of the temptation, realizing how logical this decision could be.

But her heart screamed in her chest, trying its hardest to pound thoughts into her brain. She had been raised in an unhappy household, her parent's marriage and her father's destructive behavior almost destroying their family. How could she, in good conscious, even think about bringing children into an unhappy marriage? She knew love was not the only reason to choose a husband; too many other responsibilities loomed over her. But that didn't mean she should give up hope. Even if she didn't fall madly in love with her future husband, she should at least show her future child that finding a kind, caring partner was more important than personal comfort. She could never subject her future heirs to have to claim Edgar as their father. That thought was as disgusting as the idea of lying with him.

She looked up at him, her stone-cold stare meeting his amused eyes. "Anything else you would like to offer?"

"I think that is enough to prove my case." He smirked.

"Wonderful." She placed her hands firmly on the table, pushing herself to stand over him. "That means I can officially give you my answer to this courtship proposal."

"Go ahead."

"Absolutely not!" She slammed her hand in the table, plates rattling at the impact. His face fell slack, eyes wide. Her smirk returned at the pleasure of watching his disbelief manifest.

He rose to meet her, leaning forward so their faces were inches away. "You will never receive an offer as good as mine. Think carefully about what you would be giving up with everyone else."

"A proposal from a rabid dog would be more welcomed than anything you offered me today." She shook her head, straightening to leave the room.

"You will regret this!" he yelled after her.

"I regret nothing," she yelled back, not even looking over her shoulder to see his response as she left the fuming duke behind.

Chapter Twenty-Seven

CHRISTIANA'S SKIN STILL CRAWLED WITH EACH STEP she took away from the conservatory, the large main hallway finally coming into view as she hurried back to her apartment. She chastised herself with every stride, her heart beating her mind to a pulp for even humoring the idea of marrying Edgar. She would be disappointed in herself for a long time over that falter in her moral compass.

Currents of boiling blood ran along her arms, the distraction of her thoughts clouding her mind and vision. She didn't even realize until it was too late that she was about to collide with Alekzander.

"Careful there." He caught her by her upper arms, smiling down at her.

"I'm so sorry." She shook her head, pushing the last half an hour out of her brain as she looked up at him. She'd instinctively grabbed his forearms for balance, the broad muscles tense under her hands.

He bent, his eyes desperately trying to make contact with her lowered gaze. "Ana, are you all right?"

"I'm fine." She dropped her arms, his grip loosening as she took a step back. "Just a long morning."

She moved around him, his steps falling in next to her. "Are you going back to your apartment? Let me escort you."

"Zander, you don't have to..."

"If not for your safety, then for the others around you?" His eyebrows rose, gaze sparkling as he tried not to laugh.

She pushed his shoulder back lightly, a giggle escaping her lips. "Fine." She shook her head, once again placing her hand in his outstretched arm.

"So, what is bothering you?" he asked as they walked.

"Nothing."

"Liar."

"How can you tell?" She looked up at him, no longer focusing on what was in front of her as she allowed him to guide her steps.

"Because your fingers are gripping my arm so tightly, I think you've cut off my circulation."

Her cheeks flushed. "Oh, I'm sorry." Her fingers loosened on his dark brown coat.

"It's quite all right, I can handle it." He smiled at her. "But what caused such rage?"

"I just finished having lunch with Edgar," she mumbled, her eyes straight ahead again, refusing to acknowledge the amused look that must be across Zander's face.

He let out a deep breath. "Oh, that's right. You told me about it last week. I see it went well."

"He's lucky he walked away with all of his limbs intact," she grumbled, her neck screaming from the tension she had built up. She was going to need a long, hot bath with lots of lavender and luxury oils to release some of this build up in her strained muscles.

"I told you I would have looked the other way if he hadn't," Zander teased.

"Apparently, I have more control than I thought." She smiled up at him, his grin matching hers.

"At the cost of your own peace, by the look of it. Are you sure you're fine?" His pace slowed as they turned the corner down the hallway leading directly to her apartment door. Servants milled about, putting out fresh floral arrangements on the marble pedestals lining the walls in between each door, the sweet smell of gardenias and roses mixing with the air around them.

She let out a deep sigh of relief, the push of air through her lips calming her speeding heart. "I'll find something to release some of this energy this afternoon."

She jerked back, Zander's sudden stop making her feet stumble. She looked up at him, his face bright as his eyes darted across the carpet. "I have an idea!" he exclaimed. "Do you have anywhere you need to be right now?"

"Well, no..." she began.

"Wonderful." He released her hand from his arm, the limb falling with a whack against her thigh. "Go and change into one of your comfortable riding outfits and I'll meet you outside the palace doors in twenty minutes." He turned around, his quick steps pulling him away from her.

"Zander, I don't know..."

"You need to release all of that negative energy, and I have the way to do that." His voice rose to reach the distance he had put between them.

"True." She shook her head.

"Then trust me, all right?" He looked back at her, the intensity of his dark blue gaze locking her in a grip. A week and a half ago, he had told her he was going to show how she could trust him. It looked like he was trying to do just that.

"Twenty minutes." She nodded, her feet moving quickly back to her own apartment.

***

Twenty minutes later, Christiana was outside the palace, her hair neatly restrained behind her neck and her simplest riding outfit fitted on her body. She had no idea what Zander had planned for them, or why he was so convinced it would be helpful. But she stood outside, the tall palace looming behind her while she waited, her foot tapping against the dirt path.

"Ready?" Zander's voice signaled his arrival behind her, his doublet and black leather pants traded for a plain tunic and cotton pants.

Christiana's brow creased, curious why he wasn't in a riding outfit as well. "I guess..."

"Let's go!" Excitement laced his voice as he grabbed her wrist and dragged her behind him. Her feet followed, falling in step with his hurried pace.

"Where are we going?" Her stomach churned at what he could possibly be thinking.

"Not far, I promise," he replied, not even turning back as he kept his determined pace. A few moments later, he slowed them down, a few feet away from the soldiers' training arena. For the most part, the area was abandoned, only a few men practicing on their own with the many dummies.

"Zander, what are we doing here?" Christiana asked, although it was an obvious answer. He had already moved over to the side of the large practice ring, his hands mindlessly skimming the different practice weapons lined up against the wooden posts. Her hand twitched at her side, all of her willpower keeping her from joining him.

"You need to burn off negative energy," he explained, a long sword balanced in his palm as he checked the weight. "What better way than in the ring?"

Christiana's heart leaped at the idea of training. She had always found working with her weapons a great way to refocus the mind. She had spent countless hours at her secret cottage back home, throwing her daggers against a target while she worked through a problem, each throw perfectly timed and filled with her frustrations and angers of the day. She released the terrible energy and allowing the adrenaline rush to wash over her in peace.

But it had been a long time since she had done any type of sparring with someone that wasn't for training purposes, like her fights with Robert. She bit her upper lip, her mind racing at the idea of raising a sword against the Prince. "I'm not sure if this is the best idea. Won't soldiers or other nobles be here soon?" Her stomach churned at the idea of an audience.

He looked over, then made his way back to stand in front of her. "Soldiers aren't set to come back for training for another hour. Most of them are eating lunch if they aren't on patrol duty. As for other nobles, they tend to fight later in the evening, when the sun isn't as bright. Trust me, we won't be interrupted for a while."

"I'm not sure if this is the best idea." She tried to turn away, but his warm palm wrapped around her wrist, once again to stop her in her tracks.

"Are you telling me you don't enjoy putting all of your anger into your weapons? Because I do not mean to offend, but that is hard to believe." His lips teased a smile, his blue irises lighting up.

The tips of her fingers tingled, itching to wrap around the hilt of a sword. She felt her rage build, all of Edgar's comments and smug looks from earlier this afternoon racing through her memory. "Very well," she replied. His smile burst at the seams, pushing his cheeks up.

She made her way over to the arena's side, finding a short sword hidden behind a few broadswords. She picked it up, the cool metal sending chills up her arm as she felt the weight perfectly balanced on her palm. Zander was already in the center of the ring, his feet dancing back and forth as he swung his blade to warm up. She threw the sword over the side, hoisted herself up, and dropped lightly on her feet inside the ring. Zander watched each step she took toward him with an amused smile.

"I don't know how I feel raising a sword to you." She smirked, stretching her back out before taking her fighting stance.

Zander's eyes twinkled as he took his own ready stance, and they began to slowly circle in step, weapons raised. "Why? Because I'm your Prince?"

"No," she whispered. "Because you're my client."

He threw his head back in laughter, his shoulders falling as he kept his feet moving. "Well, aren't you going to attack?"

"You're the one who literally dragged me down here. Shouldn't you be attacking first?"

"I'm not the one who had to spend an entire meal with Edgar. You have the most fuel to burn."

She stopped, Zander halting his steps as well. Birds chirped in the treetops as they stared at each other. "I told you, I'm uncomfortable lifting a sword against you."

"You were serious?" He straightened, his face twisted in confusion.

"A bit," she admitted. Her stomach wasn't settling well at the idea of fighting with him. Their friendship had rekindled well over the past week, but though she had hoped since he found out her identity, the odd current lingering between them would start to dissipate, the opposite was happening: the more time they spent together, the stronger the current formed. She was trying not to think about it, to focus on Rowan instead, but somehow thoughts of Zander kept creeping in. This wasn't the way her heart was supposed to act.

Christiana considered sparring and fighting an intimate experience, having only ever done it with three other men: her father, Marek, and

Robert. She wasn't sure if she was completely ready to share the experience with Zander, especially since she was barely accepting that her feelings toward him had begun to shift away from mere friendship.

"Well, then, don't look at me like Zander. My name is Edgar, and I'm the overly quaffed Duke of Tagri." He preened around the ring, his hips moving in the most unmanly and unnatural sway.

Christiana's laughter burst from deep within her chest, fingertips touching her lips as she tried to control it. "What are you doing?"

"I'm getting you in the mood to fight." He laughed with her, continuing his show. "I'm going to force your hand in marriage and take all of my money and land back. And what are you going to do about it?" He came up right next to her, his strong build leaning over her, their bodies only inches apart.

A smirk settled on her lips, her mind remembering all of the disgusting things he had said to her at lunch. "Oh, I have a few ideas."

She raised her sword above her head, her body pushing her anger through her hand and into the weapon as she brought it down for its first blow. The impact of her sword against his pushed into her, enveloping her body in chills as she continued her attack.

Their laughter was infectious, filling the ring as she kept pushing forward, each thrust and parry filled with the words Edgar spoke today. She allowed her rage to build before every hit, guiding her movements and solidifying her strength. Zander danced perfectly with her, their steps in tune as he blocked enough to keep her moving forward. He never once tried to take the offensive stance, allowing her to force her rage out of her body and into his sword.

She ignored all the training Robert had given her so far this summer. She kept herself wide open, her core was loose, and she didn't care that each strike wasn't perfectly timed or planned. She kept throwing her sword toward Zander, her mind and body filling with such lightness, she was surprised she didn't float away into the sky.

After a few minutes of this odd fight, Christiana backed Zander into a corner, his body pressed against the ring as their swords impacted. A yelp escaped her lips as he wound a tight grip around her sword-wielding wrist, his strength yanking her in, their blades never losing contact with each other.

Their breaths were shallow and labored, both of them already covered in a layer of sweat under the high-hanging sun. She stared up at him, once again enamored with the man in front of her. She could not tear herself away from him, his cerulean eyes staring down at her. Her lips trembled, the sparks finally igniting in her chest and setting her heart ablaze as she instinctually grasped his sword wrist as well.

"So," he murmured, "feeling better?"

"Much." Her gaze fell to his full lips, a lump forming in her throat as she tried to swallow. "Thank you for suggesting this."

"Of course." His head leaned closer, his hot breath brushing against her cheeks. "I'm always here if you need me."

The loud chime of the clock tower rang through the open air, striking one o'clock for the entire palace's ears. Christiana jumped, her skin crawling as she finally realized how close she was standing to Zander. She released her grip from his wrist, his own hand following suit as their swords finally unlocked.

She cleared her throat loudly, trying to make that pesky lump dissipate as she took a few steps backwards. Zander pushed himself away from the fence, a smile on his face and his eyes glistening. Her heart tried desperately to escape her chest, the loud thud ringing in her ears as she put distance between them. Whatever had transpired here was the final proof Christiana needed. Her heart was trying to take control; she was no longer just friends with Zander, she was becoming infatuated with him. This was never part of her summer plans, her mind screaming at her to escape this feeling.

"I should probably get back to work." Her arms fell limply at her side as she continued to back away. She needed distance from him.

"Of course." He nodded. "Drop your sword. I can clean them both before I leave." He gestured around, as if there was a large mess for him to clean up.

"Are you sure?"

"Absolutely." He smiled. A deep flush crawled down her neck at the sight.

"Thank you for...whatever this was." She flicked her hand, jumping back over the side of the ring. She pulled in a few more deep breaths, her heart finally slowing down when she put distance between herself and the Prince.

Chapter Twenty-Eight

HEAVY RAIN PELTED AGAINST THE TALL GLASS windows, dripping down the panes. Christiana once again found herself in the calming library, her usual companion by her side, relaxing in one of the soft couches. Rowan had been quiet for a long time, his face buried in a large book while Christiana tried her best to focus on the words in front of her.

A crack of thunder hit against the palace walls, rattling the tall candlesticks and many bookshelves. Tension built in Christiana's stiff neck, her nerves rattling in reply. "How are you able to focus so well through all of this?" She dropped her book into her lap, the hard cover hitting gently against her thighs.

Rowan peeked out over his book. "It's easy." He smiled. "I find the rain peaceful, easy to get lost in."

"Peaceful?" Christiana exclaimed. The bright shock of a lightning strike briefly illuminated the room before disappearing back into the black clouds.

"Of course, how can you not?" He laughed.

"Easily." She picked herself up from the couch and dropped the book on the table in front of her, wandering around the room to stare out one of the windows.

Rowan pushed himself up as well, his fingers placed between the pages of his book to save his spot. "I don't think I've met a single person who doesn't like the rain."

"Well, now you have." Christiana tilted her head to shoot him a quick smirk before focusing her gaze back out the window on the heavy rain and thick fog. For so long, she had hated the rain. Thunderstorms always scared her as a child, but as she got older the hatred grew deeper.

"What about it do you hate?"

"It makes me feel trapped." She felt claustrophobic during any kind of storm; rain, hail or snow. The idea that she would be forced to stay in one place, the dangers of the outside too great for her to risk, made her feel imprisoned. When most people saw beauty in nature, Christiana saw a jailer.

"Interesting take on the subject." She felt Rowan come up behind her, the loom of his head above hers.

She scratched mindlessly at her arm. "I don't like being forced to stay inside all day."

"That's fair." Rowan's hot breath fell down the back of Christiana's neck. "One positive that comes from the rain is the extra time we get to spend together. Alone." His hand trailed down her shoulder, catching her hand against her arm.

"True," she whispered, her breath catching in her throat as a shiver ran down her spine.

So much had changed recently, between her mishap after the masquerade and everything developing between her and Zander. But that didn't stop how she felt when she was actually with Rowan. He brought a calm to her life, he made conversation easy and the tension in her shoulders loosen. Something might be brewing inside her, some underlying infatuation for the Prince rising to the surface, but it wasn't anything she was ready to act on. Zander was her friend, but the dangers he held were never worth the risk. Besides, she had no idea if he felt the same toward her.

She had known what kind of match she was looking for when the summer began, and Rowan was everything she had hoped for and more. He held the future she wanted and he wasn't afraid to express how he felt about her. Her heart raced under her ribcage, the pounding a reminder of how she was starting to care for him in return.

She turned, his body pressing her against the window. She let out a shaky breath, her eyes closed as she felt the warmth of his skin seep through her silk dress. "Will you finally give me an answer to my question?"

Her eyes opened to lock with his. She wanted to smile; she thought she would be ready to say yes when he asked. But she couldn't stop a creep of doubt from entering her mind, Edgar's damned words ruining the moment. She had one more thing to clarify with Rowan before she could give her honest answer.

"There is..." She trailed off for a moment. "One more question I have to ask before I can tell you my answer."

His face fell, a deep frown pulling down his sharp features. "Very well?"

"If our courtship led to marriage," she said as her heart skipped beats at the words, "and we drew up a marriage contract, would you expect me to give up my control on all my lands?"

Rowan's face contorted and Christiana couldn't read exactly how he felt about the question. Her fingers tangled in her skirts; was she asking too much of him? He was a kind-hearted man, but he had expectations for his future as a titleholder—maybe controlling the family estate was one of them. Maybe it was an expectation he was unwilling to part with.

A lump formed in her throat as she stared up at him, desperately waiting for his answer.

After a few moments, he let out a sigh of relief, a laugh escaping her lips. "Really? That's your question?"

"Well, yes."

Her face lit on fire when he laughed again. "Oh, what a relief." He shook his head as his shoulders fell. "Of course, I wouldn't take that away from you. I know you love your work and you're extremely talented with it."

She lowered her gaze. "Thank you. So, how would we—?"

"I thought," he interrupted, his hand tugging at her chin to lift her gaze back to his, "we could share the responsibilities. Work together as partners."

"Partners?" Her heart swelled at the word, her hand reaching up to graze his.

"Of course." He smirked, his face lowering a few inches. "Isn't that what a marriage is?"

Her mind exploded at his words, her lips trembling as his brushed against her warm cheek. Everything he spoke was exactly what she needed to hear. She had been scared of his answer, her mind wandering to dark places for no reason while she convinced herself he would let her down. But he did exactly the opposite, he offered her something she had wanted for many years: an equal and caring marriage. The exact thing she had realized while listening to Edgar's heartless proposal.

Everything she wanted was standing right in front of her.

"You don't know what those words mean to me." Her stomach filled with flutters, her labored breaths forcing her chest to rise farther out than normal. "So, is this your courtship proposal?"

He pulled back a few inches. "Oh no, this isn't it."

Her shoulders sagged, her chest falling. He was going to make her wait. "Why not?"

"Trust me, I have a plan. You'll know it when it comes."

"Fine." She rolled her eyes.

"But, if you need a taste, let me give you one." He bent his head, and as his lips approached her breath hitched against her heart.

Their last kiss had been sloppy and hungry, Christiana overtaken with the desperate need to know what it was like. This was controlled, his lips moving against hers like they had done it countless times. A soft moan escaped from deep in his throat, and her legs grew weak, their trembling making her want to collapse against him.

After a few seconds, he pulled back, his eyes closed as his lower lip trembled. "How was that?"

Her gaze fell, her hands planted against the wall behind her as she tried to find the right words to say. "Perfect," was all she could force out, her mind racing as she tried to understand why her heart wasn't burning bright from that kiss.

***

An hour later, Christiana drifted mindlessly back to her apartment, her head filled with so many more questions from her encounter with Rowan. She had been ready to say yes. Her head was prepared and approved of the man in front of her. She knew her answer. So why did her heart seem to lack the same drive?

He had said all the right things, everything she wished for in a prospective suitor. A kind man who cared about her, who wanted to be her partner but also respected her privacy. Rowan was everything she had ever wanted, yet something still kept her from igniting at his touch. Her heart cared for him and was drawn to him in some way; she enjoyed every moment in his presence and always felt peace when he was near. So why was she still clashing with herself over this?

She tried to shake it out of her mind, reminding herself she had settled on a decision. She ignored her dropping heart; its unpredictable ways were never a good compass for what was a smart decision. She would be excited when he officially asked her, and she was ready to tell him yes. Her heart would have to catch up once the courtship began.

She pushed her apartment door open, the room illuminated with dozens of tall candles to counteract the dreary, dark skies outside. The distinct scratching of a quill filled the room, Robert bent at her dining table while he wrote in one of her ledgers, a pot of fresh tea sitting in front of him.

"I didn't think you would be here this late." She sat down, pulling the teapot to herself as steam whispered from the spout.

"An inquiry from one of your farmers came in today. Their plow broke and they need a loan to replace it." His head stayed down, his eyes darting across the pages in front of him.

"How much?" She brought the full teacup to her lips, blowing on the steaming liquid before taking a sip.

"Three Kultas." Robert sighed.

She wrinkled her brows together. "That much?"

"It's from Reynolds, the farmer on your second largest wheat plot." He pointed to the large map of Tagri in front of them, detailing each of her properties. The price now settled in Christiana's mind; he needed a strong plow to make it through the amount of land he managed.

"Draw up a loan contract with my typical payment rates and interests." She leaned forward, her thumb drumming against the table. "Once he signs it, we can send him the money."

"Do you mind if I draft it at home and bring it back tomorrow for approval?" Robert looked at her, eyes half-lidded with weariness.

"Of course not." She smiled.

He stood, rubbing his broad shoulders and collecting his things. "One last thing, this arrived to your alias. You might want to open it soon, before Natalia returns."

He handed her the envelope, the handwriting on the front making Christiana's heart skip a beat. She took it from his grasp. "Thank you."

"Have a lovely evening, My Lady." He bowed, letting himself out of the room. Though she knew full well she was alone, she still looked around her space before pulling the folded piece of parchment from the envelope and reading Zander's script inside.

Dear Maiden,

If you have a moment tomorrow night, I would love the chance to converse with you again. My window will be open if you're interested in joining me.

Sincerely,

Z

Christiana's pulse raced, her hands trembling as she clutched the note to her chest. She had no idea what he wanted or why he was making her sneak into his room. She should say no, try and distance herself again until she got this annoying infatuation out of her mind.

But the tug of her heart engulfed her, the answer apparent as she walked herself over to the fireplace, the flames devouring the piece of paper as she threw it inside.

Chapter Twenty-Nine

THE NEXT NIGHT WAS CLEAR OF STORM CLOUDS, the grass still damp from two days of rain. The mud stuck to Christiana's boots as she rounded the corner of the palace, gazing up at Zander's open window while the full moon shined brightly down at her. She peered around, once again ensuring the guards were still changing shifts before she began to climb. She took her time, her mud-caked soles slipping a few times. She finally made it to the top, her aching arms pulling her up through the window. She dropped down onto a long towel already placed below, an imprint of her soles stamped on the white linen.

"Glad you could make it." Zander smirked from the couch, his long legs stretched out and a glass goblet twirling between his fingertips. For the first time, with candles lit all around the room, Christiana was able to see the beauty of Zander's apartment. There were a few personal touches, a family portrait hanging on the far wall and an array of swords in a locked cabinet glistening through the glass-front doors. The hunter-green couch looked plush, a gold swirled pattern surrounding his family crest stitched into it.

She kept herself by the window, her lips pulled down as she took in his relaxed posture. "Why did you need me back so soon? Did something happen to Eliza?"

"No, she's fine." He waved his hands, legs swinging off the couch as he sat up. "She's anxious, but she trusts me to do what's right."

She narrowed her eyes. "Then what's this about?"

"I thought, after being able to spend a few times in public together, you would feel comfortable talking in a more private setting." He joined her by the window, his shoulders relaxed as he grinned.

"You did?" She looked up at him, her heart pounding against her chest. She had been happy to spend time with him ever since he learned her secret, but wary to be close after their playful sparring match. Though her mind urged her to leave, she stayed exactly where she was, peeking up at his face.

"You seem to relax more when you aren't concerned about other people overhearing us." His eyes softened. "Which is understandable. We don't have to talk about anything you don't want, but I thought you would feel...safer meeting in a place with complete privacy."

The back of her neck tingled at his concern for her comfort. "That's true."

"You said you wanted to trust me again." He touched her arm, the heat from his palm seeping onto her bare skin. "What better way to build that than a drink and some conversation?"

His smirk was once again infectious. "All right." She nodded, her brain screaming at her as she finished wiping her feet on the towel, removing as much dirt as possible. She walked deeper into the room, shaking her head to release the ominous hood still covering her face. "But before I sit down, I need to remove all my weapons."

"You can put them on the dining table," he suggested, gesturing to the one in the corner while he returned to his couch.

"Just promise not to get scared," she teased as she walked to the table, the heavy weight of her weapons pressed into her thighs.

"I promise." He chuckled, picking up a decanter and the empty glass sitting on the table by the couch. She pushed the folds of her open coat aside, the leather straps of her belt creeping down her legs in full view. She felt Zander's hot gaze watching her as she removed each knife, dagger, and hidden dart from the many holsters and pouches strapped along her legs.

"You certainly came prepared." His hand hovered over the glass, the decanter patiently waiting to pour out its contents. His eyes were wide, a twinkle of mischief swirling within them while he watched her walk over.

She stood in front of him, her shoulders relaxed. "I could hide more if I wanted, but I didn't feel the need to completely arm myself today."

"Happy to hear you feel relatively safe around me." He wiggled his eyebrows and handed her a glass.

She covered her mouth to hide her laughter. "I'm starting to." She sat on the couch, the dark green velvet enveloping her and rubbing softly against her coat. "But when I sneak around like this, I need to be prepared. I have no idea what's going to happen when I leave."

"Very true." He lifted his refilled goblet to his lips and Christiana mimicked his actions.

The dark liquid danced on her tongue, its familiar taste mixing in her mouth. "Is this the same whiskey as the other night?"

"You said it was your favorite liquor." He smiled.

"You listened." She stared down into her glass, her jaw relaxing as she watched the liquid swirl against the crystal edges.

"I told you I did." He shook his head, his index finger tapping against his glass.

"It's good to experience proof sometimes." She laughed, taking another sip. She stared at the large fire as silence fell, the crackling flames singing into the open air. She thought through all the conversations they have had over the past few weeks, each one different and important to her. Her brow creased, remembering one accusation she had made the first time she saw him again.

"What is it?" His head tilted to the side.

She waited a few beats, wondering if she should ask this tonight. Her curiosity won. "Can I ask you something?"

"Of course." He propped himself up, his arm resting on the back of the couch.

"I found out Eliza was married to your cousin." She peeked over at him, his hand reaching up to stroke his chin. "Is that the real reason you are going to such lengths to help her?"

"Who told you?" His cheek bulged out as his tongue pressed deeply against the inside.

"Dorina. I met Eliza briefly at the masquerade." She kept her eyes on him, her posture pulled straight up as his face creased.

"It's not like it's a secret, but yes, she was married to my cousin Fredrick for a few years, before he died of an infection." His voice deepened, the usual amusement gone from his face.

"I remember him." Fredrick had been at least ten years older than her, but he was always kind. She didn't remember many details, but his snorting laugh was a unique one and it brought back a few amusing memories.

"It was three years ago, when he and Eliza had been visiting for a few weeks. When I was...saying goodbye to him, he asked me to make a promise. He asked me to take care of Eliza and keep her safe." He peered over at Christiana. "He loved her with his whole heart. The hardest part about losing his life was the knowledge he was leaving her alone."

"Zander..." Christiana reached out to him, her fingertips brushing against the ends of his sleeve.

"My parents thought they were helping her by arranging a marriage to Julian." His hand pulled away from hers. "I hated it, but I thought she would at least be safe, married to such a powerful man. It meant she would be in the palace more; I could keep an eye on her." His hands balled into a fist, the knuckles rapping against the couch as he continued, "She seemed happy enough. She always smiled and was by his side at most events. I thought she was all right."

"You don't have to..." Christiana tried to interrupt, her heart aching as she watched the painful expression play across Zander's tight face.

"When she came to me, when she showed me the bruises and cuts, I wanted to vomit. She was one of the kindest people I had ever met, and he was trying to destroy her." His eyes were empty as he talked, their gaze nowhere as glassy tears filled the corners. "I had never felt like such a failure as when I realized what was happening right under my roof."

"You are not a failure." Christiana grabbed his hand. He tried to tug away, but her grasp kept him trapped. "Zander, look at me." His gaze rose, her eyes searching his as she continued, "People like Julian are masters at hiding what they do to others. And the victims are even better at it than the abusers. You did not fail."

"I broke a promise...to Fredrick, to Eliza." He shook his head, his hair slapping his face with each movement.

"Hey." She shook his arm, his gaze returning to hers. "You are not responsible for the decisions other people make. What matters now is you're trying to help her. You're protecting her like Fredrick asked of you."

"That's true." His fist released under her grasp, her shoulders sagging as he took a long gulp of his whiskey.

She stared at him, her heart breaking at how distraught he was over the whole situation. A tether broke in her chest, an invisible strand wanting to reach out to Alekzander. He had told her something terrifying, something he obviously held deep inside and told no one. He had told her a secret; he trusted her to hide it. She felt the pull to finally open up to someone, the sensation so foreign to her, it had only happened with two other people in her life. A lump formed in her throat as she tried to take a sip of whiskey.

The time to jump was now.

"When you came to my cottage a few weeks ago, you asked me a question." She stared down at her hands, shaking as she formed the next sentence in her head. "I think I'm ready to answer it now, if you want to ask me again."

His spine straightened up. "Are you sure?"

She let out a deep sigh, her heart steady when she answered, "Yes."

"What made you want to learn to be an assassin?"

"I wanted to stop my father from hurting me and my family any longer." She refused to look up at him, studying the gold swirl embroidered on the carpet under the couch. She felt the heat of his eyes on her, imagining vividly what he looked like right now, but she couldn't bring herself to look up.

Moments passed, tears threatening to escape her eyes as she waited for his response. Her pulse beat faster, her mind trying to convince her this was a mistake.

"You...never deserved that." His hand grazed her gooseflesh-covered arm. "I have questions, but I won't ask them if you aren't ready."

Her heart swelled at his response. She finally looked back at him, her eyes locking with his compassionate gaze. "Thank you. I don't think I am right now."

"Very well." He gave her hand a squeeze. "You trusted me with something."

"You gave me a good reason to." She squeezed his fingers back before he pulled away.

"I will admit," he said, keeping his eyes locked with hers, "the thought had crossed my mind a few times, ever since I found out who you really were."

Her shoulders fell at the weight of his gaze. "You did?"

"I was only guessing, but I felt in my soul it was true." His fingers danced against the back of the couch, the light tapping drifted off. "I couldn't think of another reason why you would start this business, especially with your particular clientele. I wanted to be sick, thinking about someone hurting you. I never wanted you to feel unsafe ever again."

"You want to protect me?" she whispered.

"Always," he whispered back, still staring at her, even when she tried to look away in fear of crying in front of him. "I don't want you to feel scared ever again."

Somehow, during the conversation, Christiana had moved herself closer to Zander, pulled into the protective shield he was building for her. He had learned one of her darkest secrets, and still he wanted her to be safe from harm.

Gently grabbing her chin, he lifted her face, forcing her to look at him. She stared into his eyes, swirling with desire as his gaze bore into her. Her heart sped up at the sight, his magnetic pull drawing her closer.

"I need to leave," she said abruptly, a cold sweat brushing over her, the shine covering her arms and throat. She dropped the half-full glass of whiskey on the table, her legs shaking as she stood.

"Are you sure?" He followed her to the corner table, his glass still in his hand as he watched her sheath her daggers. "You haven't been here that long."

She reassembled her weapons, being as quick as she possibly could. Her fingers trembled as she tried to fit the long points into the narrow casings. For weeks, she assumed her constant buzzing around him was fear, but now that he knew the truth, fear was no longer the excuse. Her desire to be close to Zander was growing stronger and she wasn't sure if she could stop it anymore. A part of her wanted to be more than friends, even though she could name dozens of reasons why he could never be right for her. Even worse, it seemed he was as drawn to her as she was to him—or so her heart was trying to tell her.

She needed to banish these feelings. There was no place for a romance with the future King of Viri to fit in her future plans.

"Yes, it was wonderful to spend time with you tonight." She secured the last dart on her gauntlet, the leather casing rubbing uncomfortably against her skin from the moisture collecting underneath. "I've truly missed this. But I have a lot to do tomorrow, so I should go."

"All right. I'll see you soon, then?" Zander asked, his steps matching hers as they walked to the window. Her hands hesitated on the handle as she looked up at him.

"Of course," she answered, attempting to smile at him before she left him behind.

Chapter Thirty

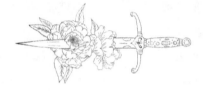

THE SOFT CANDLELIGHT SURROUNDED Christiana while she worked diligently through the night. Isabelle had been asleep for hours and her parents had yet to return from their dinner with some other nobles. Although she wished she could go to sleep and enjoy some peace in their quiet apartment, she would be in a tremendous amount of trouble if she didn't finish the work her father assigned her before he left.

Dropping her quill, Christiana stood up and walked over to the window to let in some fresh air, hoping the cool summer night breeze would revitalize her tired body. She took in a few deep breaths before pulling herself back to the desk, her father's invisible chains forcing her back into her seat. The call of different animals soon filled the night, and a sense of peace washed over Christiana as she scratched her quill against the pages.

She finally felt like she was back in a good rhythm when the front door of their apartment slammed open. Anger radiated through the walls, and her lungs refused to pull in full breaths as her chest shrank. The bedroom door flew open and her father forced his way in, face blood red as sweat formed on his brow, her mother slinking close behind him.

Christiana wanted to run; her legs tingled at the sight. She wanted to jump out the open window and escape as Marek had taught her. But her father's eyes, the whites dwarfing his stormy pupils, paralyzed her in her seat. He charged at her, like a wild animal attacking fresh prey as she gripped the seat of her chair, her head spinning as she sat there and waited.

"Father..." she tried to say, but it was too late. He grabbed her by the throat and dragged her out of her chair to slam her against the closest wall. He pinned her against the hard surface, his shirt bulging at his contracting muscles as his grip tightened, her breath trapped inside her throat. The room was closing in on her, the rage in his twisted face filling every inch of her with unadulterated terror.

"You incompetent idiot!" Hot spit spewed across her face as he yelled. Out of the corner of her eye, Christiana saw her mother run to the open window, desperate to shut their problems away from the world. Once it was latched tightly, Maria stared blankly outside, unable to turn around until the horrid moment was over.

She never came to Christiana's rescue. It was more important to protect their secrets from society than to save her own daughter.

"Fath... I ca..." she tried to say, but nothing escaped her lips. Spots formed in her eyes, blocking half of her father's face from view.

"Shut up!" he screamed again, his free fist making strong contact with her eye. The pain radiated through her whole face, shaking every bone. His grip opened wide, dropping her to the floor like a ragged doll. She scratched at the wooden boards, her fingernails broken and bleeding as she tried her best to draw in deep breaths. All she wanted to do was escape, to claw her way out if she had to, but her attempts were futile. There was no escaping his clutches this time.

"What did I do?" She stared up at him, touching her tender neck. Every moment of the past few days ran through her head, desperately trying to find what she had done to hurt him this time.

He crouched down to meet her eyes, his knee an inch from her face. "You went against my strict orders and talked to the Prince! After I told you to stay away!"

Her cheeks heated at the memory of her encounter with Zander at their favorite willow. It wasn't planned or on purpose, but it had been one of the happiest and most terrifying moments of the whole summer. She hadn't been able to stop thinking about his touch since then, trying to understand what had changed between them to cause her body to react so intensely to something so small. She had yet to discover the real answer.

"How?" Tears welled up in her eyes, the first escaping down her cheek when she shook her head.

"The Prince was at dinner tonight and told me about it. You lied to me!" He stood, his posture straight, his boot slamming into her ribs. An agonized scream escaped her lips as bone rattled against her thin skin. He didn't stop, the hard leather making contact with any part of her body it found.

For years, she had detached herself from the brutality, escaping within her mind. She would find a safe place in the dark, thinking of moments when she had felt bliss. It always made the punishments go by faster, although she never understood why. But today, for the first time, she refused to escape within herself. She lay there on the ground, curled up into a helpless ball, and felt every single moment. Every time he made contact with her body, she let herself feel how deep the pain ran, how hard he was willing to hit his own flesh and blood. She let it burrow deep within her, until it reached the tips of her soul. His darkness surrounded her, trying its best to engulf every bit of light she had left.

But she refused to let him win. She refused to let him take everything she worked so hard for. Christiana wished she could show him the true person she had become, despite his cruelty—what she had chosen without him. She had the strength and the ability to finish everything, take his life away and extinguish the anger from his eyes once and for all.

But it wasn't the right time. She couldn't let her own anger get in the way of the plan she had been working on for so long. If she did, she would get her revenge but lose everything else. Everyone in the castle would learn about the young heiress who killed her own father. No one would even care she was a bloodied pulp herself; she would still be the one convicted of murder.

At last, he reached reach down for her, his steady fingers curled out for her to grasp. She wished she could stand alone, but her aching muscles were too weak to move anywhere. She pulled in a deep breath, her hand touching his cold fingers as he pulled her to her feet.

"Make sure you clean yourself up before you go to bed," he ordered.

"Christiana?" Someone yelled to her from a distance, her head lolling back and forth against the tree trunk behind her. "Christiana?"

Her shoulders shook as a warm hand jostled her. Her eyes finally peeled open, the bright sunlight burning so badly she squinted. Rowan's blurred face came into her vision, pinched as he knelt down next to her. "Are you all right?"

"I think so." She pushed herself up, her head slowly trying to process when she could have fallen asleep. She had wanted nothing more than to spend a day to herself in the fresh air before her busy afternoon, her legs taking her to the safe confines of the willow tree's branches. "I must have fallen asleep."

"Are you sure you're well?" His head tilted. "You were shaking when I found you."

A light sheen of a cold sweat coated her body, a typical symptom of her nightmares. Her mind felt heavy as she tried to remember what exactly her dream was about. "I'm fine. How did you know I would be here?" she asked, her fists clenched into the folds of her dress.

"When I stopped at your apartment, Natalia told me you went out to the gardens." He smiled. "She may have mentioned you like to frequent here at times."

"Oh." She stared down to count the blades of grass around her. She didn't want to make him feel unwelcome, even if she desperately needed a moment away from others. "Would you like to join me?"

"Always." He stretched out next to her, his head leaning against the trunk a few inches away from hers. They sat in a comfortable silence for a few moments, enjoying the warm sun and peaceful surroundings. "Are you hiding from someone in particular?" He knocked his shoulder against hers.

Her face turned towards his, the kindness along his relaxed expression twisting her heart. "Responsibility." In reality, she had been desperate for a moment alone, her thoughts never calming since last night in Zander's room.

"I think we all need those moments." He grinned.

"Yes." She sighed, her mind wandering as she stared at him. Her brow creased when something occurred to her. "Wait, you went by my apartment?"

"Yes." His brows pinched together.

"Just to see me? Or did you need something?" The words sounded harsh, but she was too curious for her own good not to ask.

"Since you ask," he said as he pushed himself up straighter, his torso turning toward her as he grasped her hand next to him, "I did want to ask you something..." His gaze trapped her, keeping her from looking away.

"Hello, you two." Zander's unmistakable voice interrupted them, Christiana's eyes breaking away from Rowan's to seek him out. He stood only a few feet away, his hands tightly clutched around a handful of branches as he witnessed what Christiana could only assume looked like an intimate moment. Her chest tightened in a vise grip, as if she had been caught in some illicit activity.

"Hello, Zee." Rowan bit his lip as he and Christiana stood up. "What are you doing here?"

"Enjoying the day like everyone else." Zander shrugged, walking closer to them.

Rowan's mouth gaped open, his brow creased. "Well, of course. But if you don't mind, I kind of needed to..."

"Hello, Ana," Zander cut his best friend off, his head tilted as he gave her a warm smile, stoking the embers of her heart's fire from the other night.

"Hello." Her voice shook, barely able to rise above a whisper. He stared intensely at her with what she could only interpret as jealousy.

"Is there something you needed?" Rowan asked, jaw clenching.

Zander shrugged. "Nothing really. Just thought I would come over and see what two of my favorite people were up to."

"Well, we would prefer it if we could have a moment alone, if you don't mind." Rowan folded his arms, the muscles taut as his chest pushed them forward with each deep breath.

"Is that what you want, Ana?" Zander asked.

The two men stared at her, waiting for an answer. She felt pulled in two different directions, like the rope in an intense game of tug-of-war.

"I'd love to spend time with both of you." Her words drifted off, her mind unable to pull proper sentences together. She couldn't handle this right now. Her legs shook as she backed away to the edges of the tree, her eyes never leaving them. "But I have plans to meet Dorina and help her plan her birthday ball."

"But Ana..." Rowan pleaded, taking a few steps toward her. Zander gave a look of brotherly concern behind him, a shudder crawling up her spine at the sight.

"I'll see you both later," she said quickly, rushing away as ladylike as she possibly could, leaving the two men in her wake.

***

Christiana's mind finally cleared that evening, distracted by the details that went into planning a large ball. She had spent the last few hours in the empty, daylight-filled grand ballroom with Dorina, helping her pick out everything down to the table linens and glassware. Event planning wasn't Christiana's forte, her patience never staying still long enough for her to get through the long list. But Dorina had been so excited to share this with Christiana, she couldn't stop herself from saying yes.

Finally, after debating between three different types of serving trays, the two girls strolled back to Dorina's apartment, the Princess bouncing on her feet as she explained the dress she was about to be fitted for.

"I can't wait for you to see it!" Dorina giggled, her head nodding to the guards as they rounded the corner into the Royal Wing, their arms linked.

"You're going to be stunning." Christiana smiled.

The sudden, harsh sounds of indistinct shouts drifted down to them from the end of the hallway. They both stopped, their faces drawn as they looked for the source.

"Where is that coming from?" Christiana asked, her arm going limp and slipping out from Dorina's.

She took a few steps forward. "I think from Zander's room." Her pace quickened, Christiana close behind.

As they approached, Zander's door flew open. A red-faced Rowan emerged, slamming the door behind him, the frame rattling as the latch banged back into place.

"Rowan?" Dorina's shoulders tensed, her eyes following him as he barreled away from the door, nostrils flaring when he passed them.

Christiana grabbed his arm, his feet stopping as his head whipped toward her. "Are you all right?" she asked.

He yanked his arm from her grasp, pins piercing her heart at the sight of his cold stare. "I'm fine," he seethed through gritted teeth. "I have to go." He stalked off, fists still balled at his sides when he disappeared around the corner.

Christiana's chest tightened, the sting of his angry glare crawling up her spine. She turned back to wide-eyed Dorina. "I haven't been around for a few years, so things may have changed. Do they typically fight like that?"

"Never." Dorina shook her head slowly, her gaze still fixed on Rowan's path. Seconds ticked by, the two women frozen in place while Christiana tried to figure out what could have happened. Dorina turned at last, her fist pounding against the door. "Zander! Open up!"

A few moments later, it creaked open, Zander emerging when Christiana walked over to stand next to Dorina. "Can I help you?" He smiled, his face not nearly as angry as Rowan's.

"What just happened?" Dorina's mouth gaped open.

"Nothing." Zander shook his head. "I had to give Rowan some bad news. He didn't take it well."

"That's it? Are you all right?"

Zander patted his sister on the shoulder, his grip tightening. "I'm fine. Give him a few days and he will be, too."

"If you say so." Dorina narrowed her eyes at him before she turned away.

Christiana studied Zander, his body relaxed as he reached to shut the door. She stopped him, touching his hand. "Are you sure everything is all right?"

"I promise." His eyes softened. "Everything is going to be fine." He shut the door, a wink sneaking across his face before the latch clicked.

Chapter Thirty-One

THE SWEET SMELL OF CHAMOMILE WAFTED TO Christiana when she took a sip of tea, a groan escaping her lips as the warm liquid seeped down her throat. She had spent the past three hours at her cottage, prepping all the ingredients for the Purgatory poison until every single one was chopped, drained, diced, and properly stored in her cabinets.

She was finally making progress and doing the job she was hired to do. After the Golden Chain pods macerated for a few days, the ingredients would be ready to mix and blend for the crystallization process. She hated how tedious this recipe was, how drawn-out Eliza's suffering would have to be. She had to keep reminding herself it would all be worth it in the end.

A creak came from the front door, and Christiana opened her eyes to find Robert walking through the doorway. "Hello, My Lady." He smiled.

"This is a surprise." She grinned back at him. "What are you doing here?"

"I was on my way back from a hunt with a friend." His face was covered in sweat and tanned from a day in the forest-filtered sun. "I thought I would come and escort you back to the palace."

"Are you alone?" She narrowed her eyes.

"Of course. My friend had to ride ahead for guard duty."

She smirked. "Then I would love a riding partner today." She finished the last sip of her tea, a few stray leaves sticking to the bottom of the cup as she placed it back down on the table. She stretched her arms up, rolling her muscles before packing up her riding bag.

"Before we leave, I also thought I should pass this off to you." He handed her yet another alias envelope, Zander's writing neatly scrolled on the front.

Her pulse raced as she peeled it open, quickly scanning the words. "He wants me to meet him again. Tomorrow night."

Her brow furrowed and doubts raced through her mind, telling her all the reasons she shouldn't go. She didn't know if her heart could handle another private meeting with him; sneaking around was too dangerous; she was too busy with the investigation; and above all else, she needed to keep her distance as her desire for him grew stronger. But something deep in her soul ached to be at that meeting.

She shoved the letter to the bottom of her bag, the strap thrown over her. With Robert on her heels, she raced to the stables where Willow happily chewed on a bale of hay next to Arrow, Robert's brown-spotted horse. She tugged her tack off the wall, methodically placing it on Willow, her thoughts elsewhere.

"There's one more thing I wanted to talk about," Robert said, Arrow's soft muzzle rubbing against his cheek as he fed him a treat.

"And that is...?" Christiana peered at him over Willow's curved back.

"I found a moment to talk to Tobias the other night." She snorted in laughter at his sly grin. "He told me he usually works late on Thursday nights in the Chancellor's office."

"That's helpful." Her hands tingled at the thought of moving forward with her plan. It had been weeks of preparation—the time for action was finally coming upon her.

***

"Looks like the Prince is once again training with other nobles," Robert pointed out upon hearing the clanging of swords in the distance. When the arena came into view, they found Zander in a tight fight against a panting nobleman.

"You go on ahead, I'll meet you back at my apartment," Christiana mumbled, her feet changing direction, bringing her closer to the ring like she was sleepwalking.

She stopped at the edge, arms leaning against the top as she watched the match. A handful of other nobles mingled around the ring, some men with swords in their hands ready to take the next fight, a speckling of ladies dotted among them. Zander was locked in the heated battle, his tunic soaked and a smear of dirt across his cheek, probably from tripping while trying to gain the offensive.

Zander pushed his young opponent, backing him into a corner of the ring. The two locked swords and struggled to gain an advantage. Zander looked up from the intense struggle and laid his eyes on his newest audience member, their gazes locking.

Her breath hitched in her chest. A grin spread across his face. He took his opponent's wrist with his free hand and whipped him around so his back was now against the fence. Using it as leverage, he pushed the young man off and unlocked their swords. Before the noble could react, Zander resumed his offensive attack, disarming him in less than five moves.

"Good fight," the Prince said, offering his hand to the fallen fighter.

"Not good enough to beat you." The young noble laughed, wiping strands of sweaty auburn hair off his shining forehead before accepting the peace offering.

"Well, I had to show off, it seems we are lucky enough to have the Marchioness of Tagri grace us with her presence today." Zander turned to Christiana and offered her a bow. She responded with a deep curtsy, a tense smile spread across her face. "Coming back from a ride, My Lady?"

"Yes, Your Highness," she answered, feeling the eyes of the crowd descend on her. The smothering weight sent a shiver up her spine.

Zander approached, his dulled sword slung over his shoulder. "Rumor has it, Marchioness, you are fairly skilled with a blade yourself."

"Yes, Your Highness, I am."

He stopped in front of her, his voice loud enough for the entire audience to hear. "Care to prove it?"

Her stomach fluttered. "What do you mean?"

"A combat fight, between you and a noble of my choosing." He gestured to the group of men behind him. "You hold a title of power stronger than many who have been fighting with me here today. You have every right to try your hand in a mock combat."

Murmurs ran through the crowd of men, while the women off to the side stifled their gasps. It was completely unheard of for a woman to be welcomed into a challenge ring. But Zander held his ground, staring at Christiana while she contemplated her decision.

She couldn't stop the smirk from spreading up her face. "I accept your challenge, Your Highness." She climbed over the fence, her fingers tingling as she eyed the row of practice weapons off to the side. "Who would you have me fight?"

"Let me see..." Zander turned his attention to the group of men, rubbing the back of his neck as he scanned the crowd. "I choose Edgar." The whispers grew even louder at that proclamation.

"I accept, Your Highness," Edgar said, a wicked grin plastered on his face as he entered the ring. He and Christiana made their way to opposite sides to pick out their sword of choice.

She grabbed the well-balanced short sword from the armory, the same one she had used sparring with Zander a week ago. Her fingers stretched around the hilt as she pulled in a few breaths to calm her inflamed heart. She would have to ignore Zander if she was going to win.

"I need to tell you something." His whisper was in her ear, his hot breath tickling her neck.

"What?" She turned to face Zander, who looked around to make sure no one else was standing close by.

He bit his bottom lip before continuing. "Ever since word started spreading about the...denied courtship proposal, he began bragging about how he never thought you were worthy enough to be his wife."

"Excuse me?" she seethed, her blood boiling at the words

"He said it was pressure from the King that made him even ask." Zander lowered his gaze. "He's trying to make people believe it was his decision to let you go."

Christiana's vision went red, her mind spinning at Edgar's stupidity. "I'm sorry, but how do you know all of this?"

"Dorina may have mentioned it to me." He looked over his shoulder, and Christiana finally spotted Dorina among the ladies standing to the sideline.

"I'm going to kill him." Her muscles tensed, the sword hilt biting into her bare palm as she squeezed it tightly.

"No, you're going to do something even worse." He put his hands on her shoulders, heat seeping down them. "You're going to knock his pride right from under him."

She could imagine the look on Edgar's face when she came out of the ring triumphant, a laugh escaping her lips. She wanted to see that face become reality. Her hand relaxed around the sword and she looked up at Zander. "Why do you care?"

"Because I care about you." His shoulders sagged, his head tilted and his eyes gentle. "I thought that was obvious. All I want is to see you happy, and I know putting Edgar Castriello in his place will bring you an abundance of joy."

"It certainly will," Christiana agreed, her vision tunneling on her opponent as she took long strides to the center of the ring. Edgar already waited for her, his chosen broadsword in hand. It made Christiana's choice look like a twig ready to be snapped in half.

"On my call, begin." Zander took his place on the other side of the ring, surrounded by the other men. "First person to disarm their opponent is the winner. Shake hands."

Edgar outstretched his, waiting for Christiana to take it. She did, his bony fingers wrapping around hers. "Good luck, Edgar."

"Thank you, Christiana, you as well." He pulled her closer by their clasped hands. "Thank you for giving me the opportunity to put you in your place. I look forward to showing everyone here how weak you really are."

He planted a quick kiss on her cheek to spur more gossip through the crowd, then released her hand and took his defensive stance. If he thought he would intimidate her so she would make reckless mistakes, he was sorely mistaken.

"Begin!" the Prince called.

Edgar lunged for Christiana, seizing the upper hand with the first offensive attack, his sword thrusting toward her tender ribcage. She didn't miss a beat and blocked the attack with ease, the first impact of metal on metal screaming into the air. She let Edgar continue his offensive moves, showing off for the crowd that he had the advantage. It would make his defeat even more embarrassing.

Christiana took this time to study him, her mind racing for a weakness as her arms blocked each blow. It took only a few moments before she noticed with surprise that the time between his attacks was slowing down, an extra beat added between each to let him recover. The match had only just begun; even an opponent with mediocre skills should last longer than this.

She twisted around, her dwarfed sword taking a blow from above her head. Her eyes stopped on the hilt of Edgar's weapon, her brow creasing when she noticed his sword hand begin to tremble. That was his fatal mistake—he chose a sword too heavy for his wrists to handle. He probably assumed he would have disarmed Christiana by this point and wouldn't have had to fight with the sword for too long.

She allowed him to get in a few more strikes, his sly smirk hiding the tension of pain in his eyes. When he took a wide swipe from the left, Christiana ducked underneath and slid on the ground behind him. Rising quickly, she kicked him in the back, hard, before he could regain his composure. Knocking him off-balance, she grabbed his shoulder and whipped him around to face her, throwing a few swift attacks. He was able to block all of them, but barely. The quicker she moved, the harder it was for him to control the heavy blade.

With one final upward sweep, Edgar's wrist gave out. Knocking the blade out of his hands, she pointed hers at his neck, ending the match.

The crowd erupted while Christiana stared down Edgar, his dead eyes refusing to keep contact with hers. The men clapped with shocked enthusiasm, and Christiana noticed a few nods when they stared at her. The women cheered more demurely, their heads tilted and plump lips pursed. But Christiana didn't care about any of that. Her chest swelled with pride, her head spinning as the sounds of the crowd faded around her. For the first time, she didn't have to act a certain way to appease others. She was able to show everyone who she was—or at least a part of her.

"Congratulations, My Lady." Zander grinned as he approached. Edgar backed away, his shoulders rounded as he shrank into the corner.

"Thank you, Your Highness." Christiana's shoulders relaxed, her sword dropping to her side.

His eyes sparkled when he stood in front of her. "I bow to your talent."

The crowd murmured as they watched the Prince lower himself to her. He grabbed her free hand, sparks shooting up her arm as his lips pressed against her sweaty knuckles.

Everything disappeared around them, Christiana's vision tunneling to the man in front of her when he straightened up, his hand still grasping hers. The practice sword slipped, the heavy metal falling to the ground. That pull stirred once again, the invisible tether begging her to move closer, to feel him against her. She stared into his eyes, his intense gaze baring into the depths of her soul.

A loud clamor came from the arena's side, where Edgar threw his sword and jumped over the ring to join the other nobles, their faces pinched as they stared at Christiana and Zander. Christiana pulled her hand away, blinking rapidly until her surroundings came back into view.

"Thank you, Your Highness." She cleared her throat, her gaze falling to the ground as she walked to put her sword away. "I should be heading back inside, but thank you for this invigorating opportunity." She gave a curtsy before vaulting over the fence, her legs trembling as she touched down on the other side.

She walked as fast as her tired feet could carry her, her heart racing as she entered the palace and immediately made her way back to her apartment. Bile rose in her throat, her head spinning as she barreled through the door. Robert was nowhere in sight, but her travel bag was neatly placed on the table.

She dropped her hands to her knees, her back hunching as she leaned against the closest wall.

"Are you all right, My Lady?" She felt a soft touch on her shoulder, Natalia bending down to look at her concealed face.

She pulled in a few more deep breaths, her head settling. "I'm fine." She picked herself up, her legs slowly moving to the table where she sat and rubbed her temples slowly, trying to calm herself down.

A knock at her door pulled her out of the daze, the angry pounding radiated through the room. She wasn't surprised that Edgar crossed the threshold the minute Natalia opened the door.

"I don't believe you were invited in," she sneered.

Anger rolled off him as he slammed his hand on the table. "What were you thinking back there?"

"That a stupid, weak little man was trying to prove a point." She stared up at him, her arms crossed. "A point I easily crushed under my sword."

"Do you know what you did to me?" he fumed, his fists balled at his side as he stalked to her side of the table.

"I proved I'm stronger than you." She stood up, her chest grazing his as she stared into his eyes. "That the big, powerful Duke of Tagri couldn't even beat a weak girl like me."

"You embarrassed me!"

"You embarrassed yourself by picking a weapon too heavy for your wrists to handle," she snorted, pushing her way past him and farther into her common room, the candelabras freshly lit as the sun began to set through the open window.

"You shouldn't have done that." His eyes followed her every movement as she leaned herself against the back of her maroon couch. "You could have made this easier on everyone by accepting the marriage at the start. Now it seems I must put you back in your place. And when people get hurt in the process, you'll have only yourself to blame for it."

"The words of a coward do not, and will not, scare me. Now get out of my apartment!" She whipped her hand in the air, pointing him toward the door.

"Gladly," he seethed, slamming the door behind him, leaving Christiana alone with Natalia to control her own anger for the rest of the night.

Chapter Thirty-Two

ZANDER'S FACE LIT UP BEFORE HER BOOTS EVEN hit the floor that night. He sat on his couch again, a glass in his grip as he leaned his elbows on his knees. One of his legs shook, trembling the dark amber whiskey against the crystal glass. Her heart began to pound again, her feet like lead as she removed her hood.

"Thank you for coming." He rose to meet her with tentative steps by the edge of the couch.

She could hear the sound of her pulse deep in her ears as she dropped her gaze. "Why did you ask me to come tonight?"

"I thought we could talk again." Her fingers mindlessly scratched at her leg, desperate to keep moving as she followed him slowly to sit on the couch. "I poured some whiskey for you."

He offered the extra glass already on the table, and her mouth watered at the memory of the smooth taste. She wanted to grab it, but her mind screamed at her; this was not a safe idea. "Zander, if you want to spend time with me, you can ask me in public." Christiana walked toward the couches empty-handed. "I don't know how I feel about you asking me to risk myself every time you want to talk."

He frowned, sitting back down on the couch opposite her. "I like having privacy. I don't get to have that with a lot of people. And if I'm being honest, I did have a selfish reason for tonight."

"Oh?" Her heart raced, her stomach dropping.

He stood again, his steps clicking against the floor as he went to his desk. The scratching of a drawer rang out, his hands emerging with a long wooden box which he brought back to the couch. It landed in his lap, both of them staring down at it.

"What is that?" She couldn't tear her gaze away from the mystery before her.

"It's for you." He placed it on the table, sliding it over to be in front of her, biting his lip.

She ran her hands along the smooth surface of the polished box and pulled in a deep breath, not sure why she was nervous to open something so small. But her heart beat so deafeningly, she could barely hear anything else as she unlatched the side, pulling the cover up to reveal its contents. Her jaw unhinged, her mouth gaping open as she stared inside.

She reached in and pulled out a sapphire-encrusted silver dagger, her hands tingling as she twirled it in her hand. It was delicately crafted, the blade thin, well-balanced, and sharp. She could use it for many purposes, from throwing to hand-to-hand combat. But what shocked her the most when she looked it over were the details on the hilt. The grip was sized perfectly to her hand, the smooth surface comfortable under her grasp. The pommel was gorgeously decorated with a swirl of dozens of sapphires.

Her breath shook as she looked over to Zander, his hands running through his hair. "Zander..." she stuttered., "Who...how...What is this?"

"A gift." He smiled, his shoulders pulled back as he tentatively slid a few inches closer to her.

"For what?" She couldn't seem to move, her muscles locked, the dagger still clutched in her hand, the blade pointed up. She darted her gaze between the enthralling weapon and the man in front of her.

He reached out, taking her empty hand lying limp by her side, his warm touch igniting her arm in tingles. "I wanted to give you this as a...courtship gift. To show you my intentions of where I hope our relationship could go."

"Oh, Zander." She dropped the dagger on the table, her hand giving out as spots formed in her vision. She clutched the side of the couch, trying to form words. She shouldn't be surprised. She should have seen this coming. The fire inside her had been growing for so long, far before he knew the truth about her life. But she had been denying it so fiercely, she had never taken the time to notice he was feeling the same desire.

"This is why I wanted to do it in private." He touched his hand to her shoulder. "I wanted to be able to talk...about everything, without worrying if other people would overhear."

"Most men give jewels to send that message, not weapons," she mumbled, trying to stop her gut from twisting into a million knots. Shocks ran up her limbs, her legs pushing her up to pace, trying desperately to release the energy.

"For most other noble girls, that would have worked, but I wanted to show you that I knew you." His eyes tracked her with every step around the room. "That I listen to you, remember everything you tell me, and want to get to know more about you. I didn't want to give some empty gesture, I wanted it to mean more than that."

She stopped in her tracks, hands held over her chest, protecting her heart from him. "Zander...this is all extremely overwhelming."

"I understand that." He stood, his long steps bringing him to stand a few feet away. "I know you aren't the sort of girl to jump into the unknown, but...I can't deny that I've been drawn to you for weeks now.

I kept away at first because I thought that's what you wanted."

"Well..." His distance was the exact thing she had wanted when the summer began. She couldn't believe how much had changed since then; she never would have believed they would be standing here today.

"But when the truth came out, when you started to trust me again...I thought you might be feeling the same things I have."

Her mouth ran dry, her mind unable to form sentences. She didn't know what to do, what to say; all she could do was stand like a statue in the middle of his common room, her body fighting against itself, her heart and mind battling over what to do.

Her head was telling her all the reasons why she could never court him. She would be forced into the light and lose her privacy. She would not only be marrying a man, but the future King. If she was at risk of exposure when she started working for him, this was a whole new level of danger. Just because she was drawn to him didn't mean they were right for each other.

But her heart was saying something completely different, the bonds connecting them stronger than they'd ever been. She had been drawn to him for so long, but always denied what any of it meant. Staring at him now, his sparkling sapphire eyes, lopsided smile, and unruly blond curls making her stomach flutter and her heart jump, she didn't wonder anymore. He made her laugh, he noticed the little details about her, and he brought her the acceptance she never knew she needed. He stood in front of her, not a Prince, but a man baring his own heart.

"What about Rowan?" she couldn't stop herself from asking. Zander's face fell at the mention of his best friend's name, his shoulders sagging. "Is this why you two got into a fight the other day?"

He nodded, his eyes downcast. "I wanted to talk to him about it. I knew he was planning on asking you too, and I couldn't surprise him like that; it wouldn't be fair."

Christiana remembered the cold stare Rowan had given her when he walked away that day; she had never seen him so angry. But she couldn't blame him. She had been telling him she was ready to say yes to him, and now his own best friend was trying to compete with him for her heart.

"He doesn't deserve this." Her heart splintered when she realized the pain she must have caused him.

"No, he doesn't. And it's killing me slowly, knowing what I'm doing to him." Zander walked forward to gingerly lift her chin, his face a few inches away from hers. "But I would never have lived with myself if I kept this a secret from you. You deserved the truth; you both did."

She leaned forward, her lips trembling as she felt his warm breath against her forehead. Her body swayed, his arm wrapping around her to steady her stance. Her forehead fell against his warm cheek, a groan escaping his throat.

"Zander..." She shook her head, weak from the internal struggle. "I don't...I..."

"Do you want me to stop?" he whispered in her ear.

She knew what she wanted, and she knew the truth. "No."

"Good." He dipped his head, his hands on the sides of her face as he brought his lips to meet hers. Something deep inside her exploded, white-hot fire crawling through every inch of her. Her body took control, hands wrapping around his neck to pull him closer. Tingles enveloped her when his hands ran down her neck and shoulders to wrap around her hips.

Seconds passed before he pulled away, leaving her lips swollen from pressure. A smirk spread across his face, his eyes closed as he leaned his forehead against hers. "I've been wanting to do that for weeks."

Shallow breaths escaped her lips. Her heart fell as he returned to the couch, her body burning for him to touch her again. She fell against the wall behind her, the cold stone helping her spinning head. She clutched at the folds of her ruffled coat, the thick fabric rough between her fingers, and she glanced down, her heart dropping when she saw the truth; yet another logical reason not to say yes. "What about this?"

"What?" He tilted his head.

"This." She gestured to her cloak and hood, her hands shaking. "I don't plan on stopping. Becoming an assassin gave me the strength to begin healing myself. The Midnight Maiden is as much a part of me now as the Marchioness of Tagri."

"I knew this side of you when I presented that dagger." He smiled, playing absently with the velvet of the couch. "I wasn't scared away by it."

"How are we supposed to hide my...night-time activities from everyone? I don't know if I can become Queen of this country."

"Of course you can," Zander said. "I think you're exactly the type of Queen this country needs next."

She liked the idea of helping the country in a more...legal manner. But she also knew she couldn't give up being the Midnight Maiden; Viri's abused needed her, and she would be there for as long as possible. She couldn't abandon survivors because her heart was trying to take control of her.

"But have you thought this through?" Arms crossed, she approached him. "I'll be under constant watch with guards around me all of the time. I don't know how I'd be able to sneak away."

"Christiana, I understand the obstacles that would come with a courtship between us, but we can figure them out together." He reached out to her again. The electricity between them was palpable, setting her skin tingling, but Christiana couldn't let mere attraction aid her in making a potentially heartbreaking mistake. She took a step back, her arm jerking away before he could get too close.

"I don't know what to say right now, let alone think about...this!" She shook her head, her mind once again in control, smothering the fire in her heart. She couldn't put him in that position; she couldn't force him to take that risk. It had been hard enough to think about lying to Rowan for the rest of their lives; it was crushing her soul thinking about the risks she was asking Zander to take. "I need time to figure out what exactly this would mean for me."

"Ana." He sighed, his chin falling to his chest.

"Please?" The weight of fatigue spread through her body. "You've had the luxury of time to think. Please, give that to me now."

His head tilted, his eyes pinched. "Would that make you happy?"

"Yes." She nodded.

"Fine." He stood himself up straight, his arms crossed as he watched her walk toward his bedroom window. "You're right, you deserve time to process all of this."

"Thank you." She kept her eyes locked with his, the cool summer air rushing inside as she slid the window open. They glanced at each other for a few fleeting seconds before she disappeared.

Chapter Thirty-Three

THE LETTER CAME EARLY THE NEXT MORNING
while Christiana was still in bed, unable to move from the
night before. She should have expected it; Zander had
admitted he talked to Rowan about his offer, about the situation the three
of them were cornered into. But receiving the note still made her heart
sink.

Now she pushed the library doors open with clammy hands, her
palms slipping against the wood as they swung wide.

She walked inside, looking around in the dim, welcoming light, her
stomach filled with rocks as she searched for Rowan. He was alone at
one of the tables, staring out the windows with his arms crossed. She
swallowed, her throat closing as she approached him, her legs shaking
with every step.

He turned his head, catching sight of her when she reached the table.
"Thank you for meeting me here."

"How could I say no?" She tried to smile, but his cold stare made it drop. She sat on the edge of a chair, her hands tapping against her knees while she waited for him to talk. Instead he gazed at the carpet, his head shaking like he was debating himself. "Are you going to say anything?"

"I'm trying not to say something I'll regret," he mumbled.

Her heart dropped. "You can say whatever you want." She wiped her sweaty palms along her dress, the chiffon bunching under her palms. "I'm sure I deserve it."

His head continued shaking as he turned to her. "You lied to me."

"What?"

"I asked you weeks ago if there was something happening between the two of you." He leaned his arms on the table, staring at her. "I told you I didn't want to start anything if your heart was somewhere else."

Tears threatened her eyes already. "I know," was all she could say.

"Why did you lie to me?" His mouth pinched inward, a hard line across his face.

Her pulse picked up; she wasn't ready to have this conversation. She was barely ready to accept her feelings for Zander inside her own mind, and now she had to speak everything out loud. She hated it, but she knew she had no other choice.

"It wasn't a lie." She looked over at him. "I meant what I said; the life he offered was not a life I wanted."

"So, when did it change?"

She knew the exact moment; after he had accepted her as the Maiden, when honesty was finally established between them and a new trust began to build. But she couldn't tell Rowan that; she had to lie to him again.

Bile rose in her throat. "It was after the masquerade," she said, trying to keep the lies as minimal as possible. "I wanted to spend time with Dorina, but she was busy. Zander found me and offered to keep me company. We spent the afternoon playing chess and...reconnecting."

He kicked his chair out as he stood up, storming to the window.

"How did it progress from there?"

"Rowan..." she didn't want to tell him any more; she didn't want to hurt him any more than she already had.

"I want to know." He turned his head, his profile illuminated by dull light. "I need to know...if this is worth it anymore."

She closed her eyes, her lips trembling. "We kept finding ourselves spending time together. We sparred once, when I was particularly annoyed at Edgar. And we found other times to..." she tried to think of the best way to explain their private night in his apartment, "talk and enjoy each other's company."

He nodded with every word, his face reflected in the window. She tried to decipher his expression through the blurred glass. "Have you kissed him too?"

His voice cut through her, her stomach churning at the idea of talking about something so intimate. "Rowan..." she groaned.

He turned around, his gaze pleading. "Have you kissed him?"

"Yes." She choked on the word, pressure slowly building in her chest. "When he asked me to court him last night."

He huffed, dropping himself back into his chair. "So, he beat me to it." He reached into his coat, emerging with a velvet pouch. He twirled it in his hands, staring down at it.

"I'm so sorry," was all she could say.

"I saw a life with you."

Her stomach twisted. "I saw that life too. And I liked it."

"And now?"

"Now...I don't know anymore."

She couldn't bear to look at his face as she spoke these terrible words. They tasted like ash on her tongue, pathetic, weak, and worthless in light of the situation. She had felt comfort with Rowan since he first smiled at her at the welcome reception. She had imagined the partnership he offered, the quiet life they could have, far away from the palace. She could live with hiding her alter ego, finding ways to sneak out. She thought about how excited she would be to return home to a man who cared about her.

Yet she had doubted for weeks, ever since her drunken mistake. She could never find what was missing or what was holding her back from saying yes. The answer hadn't emerged until she started spending real time with Zander, when the fire and the tether grew between them. That spark was missing from her intimate moment with Rowan. He was kind, and the kiss was beautiful, but it didn't ignite her the same way Zander's presence did.

But did she need to be ignited? Did she need the passion? She had never dreamed of it, never thought it would be a part of her life. But it wasn't just the passion that drew her to Zander, it was the honesty as well. She never realized the weight of a secret until it was lifted from her shoulders. Would she be able to start a life with Rowan knowing now how it felt to have true candor in a relationship?

His head fell in his hands. "He's talked about you a lot since you arrived at court," he admitted. "But I hoped it would pass, especially if he saw how interested I was. I know it's selfish of me, but how could I compete with a prince?"

"You aren't competing with the Prince." She leaned forward, her hand itching to reach out to him. "I don't see Zander that way, just as I don't see you as a marquess."

"That does make me feel a bit more at ease." He chuckled, offering the velvet satchel over the table. "Open it."

Its surface was soft under her sweaty fingertips. She pulled out a diamond pendant, the beautiful white gold carved into a filigree pattern, the center decorated with clusters of black and white diamonds. It was stunning, the dark jewels perfectly suited for at least a dozen outfits in her closet, complimenting them with its beauty.

"Oh, Rowan." She touched her hand to her throat. "It's beautiful."

"It's no dagger, but I thought you would like it."

The walls started closing in. "He told you about that?"

"When he told me he was going to ask," he admitted.

The pendant bit into the soft flesh of her palm as she clutched it close, trying to stabilize herself while the books and shelves spun around her. Nothing about this summer was going as planned. Christiana had lived the last five years according to her plans and ultimate goals, keeping her sanity intact. Now that this plan was crumbling around her, she sensed one of her fits approaching, the darkness in her mind filling with lies.

She needed to get out of here. The lack of oxygen made her body so light, she felt as if she was about to float away. She couldn't let him see her like this, to see her weak. It wasn't fair to him to keep another secret, but she couldn't subject him to this part of her.

"I'm sorry, you don't deserve any of this." She placed the pendant on the table and stood, her skin tingling, every inch numb. "I'll understand if you want to withdraw any...notion of courtship you might have considered offering."

He stood as well, grasping her arm. "Do you want me to?"

"I don't think so," she spoke truthfully, and tried to tug out of his grasp, hoping he didn't notice how shaky her arms were. "But like I said to Zander, I need time to think and I'll understand if you don't want to wait."

She took a few steps back, trying to put distance between them, the pressure of her chest building so abruptly, it felt ready to explode. She couldn't let him close, she didn't want him to see this side of her yet, if ever. It was her darkest secret and she would keep it in the hidden depths of her mind, shielded from as many people as possible.

His gaze felt hot as he stared at her, his face creased. "We've put a lot on you...you deserve time to think."

"Thank you." She nodded, rushing to the door. Her cosmetics melted off her face, her throat constricting under an invisible garrote.

"Take this with you." He held out the pendant after her. "I hope to see you wearing it one day soon, because I know you'll come to see how well suited our lives are together."

She snatched it from his grasp, giving him one last glance. "I hope so too. I do."

She rushed from the library, running to the safety of her apartment.

Chapter Thirty-Four

WO DAYS PASSED AFTER HER HEART-WRENCHING
conversation with Rowan, and Christiana hid herself in
her apartment from both of them, refusing to leave until
she found a sliver of clarity. But after restless nights of
tossing in her bed, hours of pacing her apartment, and countless failed
distractions, she had yet to decide what she wanted.

By lunchtime on the third day, Christiana's skin felt numb from the
tiny pins pricking at every inch of her. She sat on her couch, bare feet
lying across the fluffed cushions, staring at a book. Her eyes couldn't
keep focused, the words blurring together. She leaned her head back, the
armrest fitting perfectly in the crook of her neck as she stared at the
cream, carved ceiling. Seconds felt like hours as the mantel clock ticked
by, her head spinning as the faces of two men competed for her attention.

A soft knock broke the silence, Christiana's book falling from her
grasp as she turned to watch Natalia answer the door.

"Princess Dorina is here to see you, My Lady," she said from the doorway.

"Dorina, what are you doing here?" Christiana pushed herself up and swung her legs down to the floor.

The Princess smiled brightly as she drifted toward the couch, her spring-green dress swirling delicately around her. "Just wanted to stop by for a moment. I'm not interrupting, am I?"

"Of course not." She smiled. "Please come in."

"Thank you." Dorina flopped down on the couch, her legs curled under her so the hem of her dress spilled over the side of the couch. She turned toward Christiana, her head tilted. "I also wanted to share a surprise with you!"

"Oh?" Her voice strained and she leaned away a few inches. She wasn't sure if she was ready for yet another shock.

Dorina grasped Christiana's hand, her gleeful smile trying to break free. "I sent an invitation to my birthday ball off to your mother and sister!"

"Really?" Christiana's fingers clutched Dorina's tightly, her smile pinching her cheekbones, and when the Princess nodded Christiana pulled her into a tight hug. "Thank you, Dorina."

Dorina pulled back after a few seconds, her hands still clutching Christiana's. "Of course. Besides, I figured you might need your mother."

"Why?" Christiana narrowed her eyes.

"Well, with everything that's happened over the past few days..." She looked down, trailing off when Christiana let out a loud groan.

"Oh, Dorina." Christiana dropped her head in her hands. "Please don't tell me your brother sent you here to fish for information?"

She forced Christiana's hands down from her face. "Of course not! I came here out of my own curiosity."

"Even better." Christiana slumped against the back of the couch, a few curls falling from her pins and rolling down her shoulder. She had been trying to sort through her mind for days and barely got anywhere;

she wasn't sure if she could have an actual conversation about the whole ordeal quite yet.

"I wanted to know if you're all right." Dorina squeezed Christiana's shoulder. "Those two idiots put you in a...complicated situation."

Christiana scoffed. "Complicated doesn't even begin to describe it."

"You can talk to me, you know." Dorina settled in, their heads a few inches apart as they leaned against the back of the couch.

"But that's the thing...I don't think I can." Heart aching, she peeked over at Dorina.

"Why not?" Dorina's shoulders fell.

"Your brother is one of the men trying to court me."

"True, but..." Dorina began, pulling herself up.

"But nothing." Christiana straightened as well, their shoulders knocking together. "I know you care about Rowan too, but Zander is your blood. Even if I talk to you about it, you'll probably have a biased view."

"Can you blame me, though?" she asked, her eyes aglow, "If you pick Zander, you and I might be sisters-in-law!"

"I know." Oddly enough, that was one of the many reasons Christiana saw herself choosing Zander, knowing she would always have Dorina by her side. "But I can't let that sway my decision. I need to make this about me. Not anyone else."

"I know." Dorina sighed loudly. "Let's not talk about them. How are you doing with all of this? I may love my brother, but I care about how you're doing as well."

"Honestly? I'm terrified," she finally admitted aloud. "I care about both of them. I know I feel differently about each of them, but it doesn't make it any easier to pick one. I feel like I'm barely keeping it together while I decide."

"It's to be expected, Christiana." Dorina patted her knee.

"But they're both so desperate for an answer." Christiana shook her head, her eyes tracing the pattern of her large carpet. "Going into the summer, I thought I knew what I wanted, but all of this has caused such a mess in my head."

Dorina furrowed her brow. "Your head? Don't you mean your heart?"

"What?"

"Look, you can go back and forth in your head for days and get absolutely nowhere, because this isn't a decision your head can make for you. Your heart is the one that holds the real answer. I think the longer you ignore it, the longer you're going to feel unsure."

"I don't want to lose one of them," Christiana said, a few tears finally slipping down her face.

"I know." She wrapped her arm around her friend's shoulders and offered a handkerchief. Christiana took it, dabbing the smooth fabric against her wet face. "Chances are, you will. But that doesn't mean you can't find something beautiful in this ugly situation. You need to think more about what you could gain from it and less about what you'll lose."

"I never thought of it that way," Christiana mumbled, mulling over Dorina's words. She had spent most of her life calculating and learning everything, always believing her head held every answer possible. But for once, she had to ignore the constant barrage of her thoughts and listen to something even stronger—her feelings.

"You're going to make it through. You're too strong not to." Dorina offered an encouraging smile.

Christiana dropped her head onto the Princess's shoulder, her wet cheek staining the fabric of her dress. "Thank you."

"Of course." Dorina shook her, and Christiana's sniffles died down as the tears stopped flowing. "You look like you need a distraction. I have my birthday cake tasting in my room soon. Want to join?"

"Yes." Finally smiling again, Christiana wiped the tears from her face. "That sounds perfect."

"Let's go." Dorina rose with an outstretched hand. Taking a hold, Christiana leaned on her friend as they left the apartment.

***

Dorina always had the best distractions. After an hour of indulging in tiny cakes, the two ladies sat in Dorina's apartment, steaming cups of tea in front of them while they chatted over nonsense. Christiana's heart finally lightened under the warm summer breeze spilling in through the open window, the rustle of leaves singing to them. She finally felt like laughing after two days of constant battles in her mind and heart.

She was lucky to have a friend who was willing to stand by her side, even when a member of her family was involved.

A slamming door interrupted their pleasant conversation, two voices drifting under the cracks of Dorina's doorway. Christiana's chest tightened, her fingers trembling around her cup while she silently prayed the voices were not the two that instantly came to her mind.

Dorina's eyes narrowed at her door, the angry voices growing louder, closer. "That sounds like Zander."

"And the other is Rowan." Christiana shot up out of her chair and bolted for the door.

Dorina was right behind her. "The game room."

Their skirts swished around their legs as they hurried down the hall. Christiana's vision tunneled on the closed door, the screams finally coherent when Dorina pushed inside.

"You are selfish!" Rowan shouted across the room. Zander leaned against the back wall, his arms crossed against his chest, his pained stare never leaving Rowan while he paced the room, one hand tapping his leg, the other swishing through his brown hair.

"I wanted to be honest," Zander argued, his voice rumbling from deep in his chest.

Christiana was frozen in the doorway, eyes wide as she watched the events unfold. She wanted to look away, she wanted to shut the door behind her and pretend they weren't ruining a distraction-filled afternoon. But something kept her there, her feet creating roots as the tension of the moment crawled into her muscles.

Somehow, the two men had yet to notice they had an audience—or didn't care. Rowan shook his head. "An excuse to be selfish. But you're used to getting your way, so how could I have expected any less?"

"What would you have preferred I do, Ro?" Zander threw his arms up. "Never tell her how I feel? The two of you get married and I pine after your wife for the next forty years?" His legs moved him forward, the gap between the two men closing. "Tell me how that would have been any better."

"You would have gotten over her," Rowan mumbled, Christiana's heart jerking at the comment. She wasn't exactly sure why it had hurt her, but she felt Dorina's hand on her shoulder, Christiana peeking over to see her best friend's stone face, staring at the two men.

"Would *you* have?" Zander challenged, face-to-face with his friend.

Silence fell, their eyes never breaking from each other. Christiana's arms shook; her heart didn't break for Zander or Rowan individually this time, it now broke for the friendship she had come between. She had caused chaos and she couldn't watch it any longer.

"Stop," she pleaded, stepping into the room, Dorina right on her heels.

"Stay out of this, Christiana," Rowan spat, his eyes never leaving Zander, his jaw tense. "This is between us."

Christiana scoffed, her nostrils flaring when she halted beside them. "You're fighting over me. So, unfortunately, it does concern me."

"It's not just about you." Zander was the first to break eye contact, his gaze moving to Christiana. "It's about me betraying him."

"Oh, he can finally admit it," Rowan sneered.

"I never denied it," Zander shot back, turning back to Rowan. "What I denied was doing it maliciously."

"What other reason is there?" Rowan took a step forward, his chest puffed out. Christiana instinctually put her arms between them, pushing them each back a step.

"Rowan, stop."

Zander's hands balled at his sides. "Wouldn't you rather she picked you because you're her first choice, not her only choice?"

Rowan's eyes went dark, his jaw locked. His body shook, muscles contracting under the tight fabric of his day coat. Christiana's heart sped up; she had never seen him look so enraged. She hated that look; she didn't want it anywhere near her again.

She should have seen it coming, but her body was too frozen in fear to react in time. She stumbled backward a few steps when Rowan barreled past her, charging at Zander and grabbing him by the front of his doublet, dragging him close. "What did you just say?"

A loud bang came from behind all of them. "Enough!" Dorina screamed, slamming an empty silver pitcher against the table a second time. All three of them stared at her, Rowan loosening his grip on Zander while he gaped at the fuming princess. "Rowan, let my brother go and step away from him!"

Rowan's hands fell to his sides. Zander brushed himself off, smoothing his wrinkled outfit.

"And Zander," she said turning to him, pointing sharply, "you may have been honest, but it was your honesty that caused this whole disaster. So, take some damned responsibility for it!"

Zander nodded, his head hung low.

Christiana stared at Dorina, her mind swirling as she dropped the pitcher back on the table. She always knew Dorina had a certain blaze inside her, but this was the first time she saw it burst through. She couldn't stop herself from smiling, her chest warm.

"Now," Dorina continued, striding toward them, "why don't the two of you *apologize* to Ana for causing her even more stress, and quietly leave. And maybe stay away from each other until this whole situation is settled, hm? Probably wise to think over how you can repair the twenty-year friendship you are currently tearing to shreds."

"Sorry, Christiana," Rowan mumbled, peeking up to look at her. Her mouth tightened as she watched his painful gaze dart back down.

"I'm sorry, Ana." Zander looked over as well, his hand twitching at his side as if he wanted to reach out to her. Her arm prickled at the memory of his touch.

"It's all right," she said to both of them.

They both left silently, heads hanging as they disappeared through the door.

Dorina wrapped Christiana in a hug, the tight squeeze settling her churning stomach.

"I know this is your decision," Dorina whispered into Christiana's ear. "But I think for all of our sanity, making it sooner rather than later is best."

Christiana sighed. "I know." Her cheeks turned to flames as her peaceful afternoon disappeared into the past.

Chapter Thirty-Five

HE HOT SUMMER SUN PELTED CHRISTIANA'S back as she counted out each push-up, her muscles screaming, sweat drenching her sleeveless tunic. Robert was right there next to her, mimicking her movements and speed, continuing the muscle training he had rigorously pushed her through all summer.

This was usually her least-favorite part of training with Robert, but today it was a welcomed distraction from unprecedented circumstances. Her mark was dangerous, her assassination planning ran at a snail's pace, and her courtships tangled her mind and heart together. Each time she shoved her face away from the ground, her biceps shaking, she forced all her frustrations out of her body and into the earth, trying her best to find clarity

"Done." Robert grunted, dropping onto his haunches.

Christiana collapsed to the ground, dirt and sweat smearing across her cheek before she flipped herself onto her back. Fluffy clouds danced across the bright blue sky for her to enjoy. She should be happy. She should be excited that in a few days, she would be reunited with her mother and her dear Isabelle. Yet all she could do was beat her fists against the soft ground, her body unable to sit still while all her anxious thoughts swirled.

"What's wrong?" Robert asked, dropping her waterskin by her side.

"Nothing." She shook her head and sat up, unscrewing the cap from the brown leather casing and pouring the cool water down her parched throat. Robert glared at her, his eyes never leaving her face. "What?"

"Tell me what's wrong." He pulled Christiana to her feet. "We both know you're lying."

"I hate men." She grumbled, her mind spinning at the memory of Rowan shoving Zander in the game room yesterday.

"I've come to learn most women agree with you." He laughed as they hopped over the ring, Christiana's tired calf muscles pushing against her when she dropped down on the other side.

They walked to her cottage. "I didn't need this. I didn't ask for this. I knew my noble obligation and I was ready to move forward. Then Zander had to go and create chaos within that plan!"

"Are you going to try and convince me that you weren't excited when Prince Alekzander told you how he felt?" Robert asked, opening the door for her.

"Stop it." She walked inside and dropped onto the threadbare couch, her limbs melting into the cushions. "It doesn't matter if I was excited, Zander is complicated."

"Obviously." Robert sat down next to her. "Becoming King is never an easy task."

"I may be a noblewoman, but I was never like the others. I never dreamed of becoming Queen."

"In all fairness, you're probably the most qualified out of all of them." Robert chuckled.

"That's what Zander said, too." Christiana rubbed her temples, the tension stubborn against her attempts to relieve it. "I'm sure many people would be proud to call a notorious assassin their Queen."

"It's not like they would know."

"Putting myself into that position risks that secret even more."

"Fair." Robert's eyes wandered to the common room window where streams of midmorning sunlight filtered in, highlighting specks of dust dancing in the air. "But remember, choosing Rowan would mean lying to your future spouse for the rest of your life."

Christiana leaned forward, resting her elbows on her knees. "I've been prepared for that for years."

"You may think you're ready to carry that burden," Robert said, his face softened as he turned back to look at her, "but the more years pass, the heavier it will become. Before you know it, you'll find yourself crushed under the weight."

"Wise words." It was a thought she had barely spent time on. She had always been prepared to keep a secret from her future husband, but he had a point. Zander knew the truth. A barrier she was ready to have in her marriage would be nonexistent with him. "Well, what do you think?"

Robert hesitated. "I don't know if that's a question I should be answering."

"You know me better than most, Robert." She leaned back, shifting to face him. "If anyone can decipher this tangled web of feelings, it's you."

"Well." He sighed, letting a few moments pass, his forehead wrinkling in thought. "I haven't seen you interact with either man. I don't know how they look at you or how you react to their presence."

"But ..." Christiana prompted.

"I think you've had to spend most of your life hiding who you truly are from most of the people around you." He rubbed his chin, then his cheek. "It's a burden you've carried gracefully as long as I've known you."

"Thank you." She smiled.

"But that doesn't mean you have to carry it with everyone. Especially the man you hope to one day call your husband." He reached out, taking her hand in his. "You should surround yourself with the people who make you feel authentically yourself. People who encourage you to never be anything less. The only way to gain that is to have complete honesty in a relationship."

"So, you think Zander is the right choice?"

"I do." He nodded. "I know his lifestyle comes with complications, but they are complications you can try to handle together."

Christiana stared off into the half-empty space of her common area. Though Robert's words held wisdom and truth, she still struggled to accept them. Ever since she took control of her life away from her father, she made sure to meticulously plan every part of her future. When she had a plan, she had clarity and calm. A courtship with Zander, the potential to become the future Queen of Viri, was never part of that plan. It would throw her life into a chaotic unknown that she wasn't sure she was strong enough to handle.

"Ugh," she groaned, tugging on the tangled ends of her sweaty ponytail. "I don't want to think about this right now."

Robert rolled his eyes. "Then what do you want?"

Christiana hurried to the kitchen area. "I want to distract myself by making a deadly poison."

She pulled out her prepared ingredients, the jars clinking as she carried them over to the counter. She couldn't make a decision about Rowan and Zander; her heart and mind were not working together at the moment. The one thing she could control, and focus on successfully, was making the Purgatory poison. She needed to take the next step in the case she had been neglecting for far too long because these men decided to complicate her life.

Robert stood up from the couch, throwing his saddle bag over his shoulder. "Do you need assistance with anything?"

"No." Christiana shook her head and opened a few of the jars. "Thank you, though. For everything today."

"I'll see you back at the palace, My Lady." He bowed quickly and took his leave.

Christiana pulled out her mortar and pestle and dropped in a few of the ingredients. "Stupid, stupid men." She grumbled under her breath, her frustrations pushing through the pestle as she ground the mixture. "Ruining my plans, distracting me from my job, keeping me from what's important. I. Hate. Men!"

She kept grinding the Golden Chain pods, the juices forming a thick paste. She couldn't control what was happening with Rowan and Zander right now. She didn't want to have to deal with the overwhelming thoughts and feelings that came with them. She wanted a moment where a plan came to fruition as it was meant to.

That was why she loved the art of poison making: everything came down to following a precise plan. As long as you completed each step correctly, you would finish the task with a glorious concoction. Emotions, issues, and outside complications had nothing to do with it.

Her instincts took over. Each step was perfectly timed as she moved around the kitchen, filling her cast iron pot with a generous helping of water from the in-house tap. She focused on what was important, on what was supposed to be her priority this summer: killing Julian and helping Eliza.

Her heart was heavy thinking about how much time had passed since she last saw Eliza. Her stomach rolled at the memory of the Chancelloress's alabaster skin spattered with purplish bruises; she was supposed to put a stop to it, it was her job to make Eliza's pain go away. Even though she had yet to attempt a killing strike on Julian, even though it was an unavoidable ramification, she still felt like a failure by letting things drag on.

Her hands shook as she lit the pyre and placed the full pot on the stovetop. The heat rolled over her and she pulled in a few deep breaths, waiting for the water to simmer, the tiny bubbles bouncing along the side to signal it was time to start adding more ingredients.

She could do this. She was going to kill Julian. She had a plan now. She was working to bring it to pass, grabbing the first few jars from the counter and sprinkling their contents into the pot.

She was used to jobs being easy, repetitive sometimes when her marks became more and more predictable. But nothing about Julian was typical. He was a military man, respected and loved by many, and fawned over by the rest. Christiana knew from the beginning that he wasn't going to be easy to kill, but the longer he stood in front of her alive and well, the more she doubted her abilities.

She needed to push those dark thoughts away. One moment of doubt could cost months of planning. If she was upset at herself now, she would be devastated if she lost her chance because of her anxious thoughts.

She mixed the effervescent liquid, her wooden spoon scraping the sides to make sure all the leaves were rolling in the center. The scent of anise wafted around the enclosed space as Christiana poured the golden chain paste in. This was the final step, the poisonous plants fusing together to create the base liquid for the perfect poison.

"Enjoy your final fitful rest, Julian," she muttered, staring at the mesmerizing liquid. "I hope you have enough time to reflect on the heinous acts you chose to commit in your lifetime."

Chapter Thirty-Six

A FEW DAYS LATER, WITH THE SUN SETTING IN low, dusty purples and blues, Christiana and Dorina stood in front of the palace doors. Christiana's family would arrive any minute, and her stomach fluttered as she kept her eyes fixed down the long path disappearing through the forest. The clomp of horse hooves approached, two large animals barreled into view, their shiny coats glistening in the setting sun. The carriage they pulled came to a halt at the base of the steps, the footman opening the door as Isabelle's smiling face looked up at the palace for the first time in five years.

"Ana!" She caught sight of her sister, jade eyes wide as she jumped down from the carriage. Christiana opened her arms, and Isabelle launched herself into them. Christiana's chest swelled, her smile as full as her heart when Isabelle buried her face in her shoulder.

"Hello, my beautiful daughter." Maria smiled as she stopped behind Isabelle, her petite frame accentuated by the tight fit of her marigold day dress. Wisps of blonde hair peeked out from her cream hat, a tight bun set at the nape of her neck.

"Hello, Mother." Christiana allowed herself to be embraced, pulling in a deep breath of gardenia perfume.

"Your Highness." Maria swept herself into a deep curtsy, her eyes downcast as she greeted Dorina. Isabelle tried her best to mimic her mother, lowering her shaking legs.

"Please, call me Dorina." She smiled brightly. "I'm so happy you were able to come out for my birthday!"

"I'm so excited to finally attend a ball!" Isabelle bounced on the balls of her feet, her dark magenta dress skimming the dirt road. "I was too young the last time we were here."

"Well, I'm even happier my birthday is going to be that special occasion for you." Dorina touched Isabelle's shoulder lightly, and the young girl blushed.

"Your Highness," Maria greeted once again. Christiana's brow furrowed as her mother lowered into another curtsy.

"Dowager Marchioness," came Zander's deep voice from behind them. Christiana's breath caught at the sound. "It's wonderful to see you at the palace again."

Maria rose, smiling at Zander's approach. "Thank you, Your Highness. It's exactly how I remember it."

"And you must be Isabelle," he greeted. Isabelle's spine pulled upward, her shoulders straight under Christiana's arm as she gazed at the prince. "Christiana has told me a lot about you."

"She has?" Isabelle narrowed her eyes at her sister. Christiana narrowed hers right back.

"Of course." Zander flashed his charming smile. "She's missed you this summer."

"I've missed her too." She touched her head to Christiana's shoulder briefly, then turned her intent gaze back to Zander. "Do you like spending time with my sister?"

"I do, all the time." He glanced at Christiana, and her jaw tensed. "She's become a close friend to me."

Isabelle nodded, her shoulder bumping against Christiana's ribs. "I'm glad she wasn't alone. She doesn't have many friends back at home."

"Belle," Christiana chastised.

"Don't worry, she's had plenty of people to spend time with here," Dorina replied.

"We've kept her quite preoccupied with other things besides her Marchioness responsibilities." Zander looked at Christiana once again, her eyes catching his for a brief moment before her gaze turned away. "Now, if you beautiful ladies would excuse me, I must take my leave. But I look forward to seeing you again at my sister's birthday."

"Your Highness." The ladies curtsied, waiting for him to leave.

"Are you ready to go inside?" Christiana asked Isabelle, seeing her excitement to explore.

"Actually, my darlings, I'm tired from the ride here." Maria removed her hat, fanning herself with it. "I think I'll retire to our room. If a servant could show me where it is, that would be helpful."

"Christiana, why don't you go with your mother and help her get settled?" Dorina suggested, turning to Isabelle. "I can show Isabelle around!"

"Please Ana? Can I?" Isabelle begged, tugging on her arm.

"Of course." She smiled. Dorina looped her arm through Isabelle's, beaming as they made their way down one of the long hallways.

"This way, Mother." Christiana gestured, leading her with a smile to her new room at the palace.

***

"I'm happy to see they're treating you so well here," Maria said, taking a seat at the dining table in her generously-appointed guest quarters. The common room has a similar layout to Christiana's, with an elegant navy-

and-gold couch and chaise situated in front of a stone fireplace. Two doors connected to the bedrooms, one for Maria and one for Isabelle.

Christiana nodded, the stem of her wine glass rolling between her fingers, her eyes fixed on the dark burgundy liquid. "They've been wonderful to me here."

"Are you all right, my dear?" Christiana's mother grazed her cheek. "You've barely written to me all summer."

"I've been busy is all." Christiana leaned into her touch for a moment before pulling away, and Maria's hand fell to the dark walnut table.

Although she had been diligent in writing letters to Isabelle, full of tales and exciting moments around the palace, she neglected to include letters to her mother. It was not deliberate, but with the chaos currently erupting in her life, she felt it was best to keep her mother uninvolved. The less stress Maria had to deal with, the better.

Maria leaned back, her wine cup lifted to her lips to take a sip. "Are you sure that's it?"

"What else would it be?"

"Well, I received a letter from Madeleine a week ago with some interesting news." Maria stared at Christiana, her eyes glinting off the reflection of the candlelight.

Christiana rubbed her temple. Of course Madeleine had been spreading gossip. "Did she now?"

"She wanted to congratulate me on how well your marriage prospects have been. She assumed I knew that both Rowan and the Prince had offered courtship for a potential marriage engagement."

"I'm sorry, I should have written you." Christiana took a sip of wine, letting the mix of cherries and oak roll around on her palate. "It all happened so quickly and recently. I've been taking time to process everything."

"I would have preferred to hear it directly from you, but it made me happy nonetheless," Maria said softly. "Have you made a decision yet?"

"No."

"Well, you should have written me." Maria patted her daughter's hand. "I can help!"

"With all due respect, Mother," Christiana said as she pulled her hand away, her fingers cold, "I can make my own decisions. I haven't needed your help since I was a child."

"I know." Maria's jaw tensed. "But you've never been in this situation before and I have. I could give you advice."

Christiana looked out the window, the moon finally rising into the twilight sky to welcome the night. She knew her mother meant well, that all she wanted to do was help. She knew deep in her soul none of what happened to them was Maria's fault, but it was hard to take advice from a woman who had put all of them in such danger by making the wrong decision in a marriage.

"To be honest," Maria said, standing up to refill her wine at the gold-and-glass liquor cart, "I've thought you and Rowan would be a smart match from the beginning. His lifestyle is so similar to yours, you would barely have to make an adjustment."

"Hm." Christiana couldn't stop herself from scoffing. "You know, most noble mothers would push their daughters into Zander's arms if they had the chance."

Maria put the wine bottle down harshly, the impact rattling the other bottles on the cart. "Yes, well, most mothers don't have daughters who have the same...history as you."

"History?" Christiana whipped her head toward her mother, nostrils flaring. "Is that what we're calling it now?"

Five years had gone by since her father's death, and never had she confronted her mother about the abuse. It was easier to ignore the problem and move on with a fresh start to their relationship. But every once in a while, after a horrific nightmare, she couldn't stop herself from feeling resentment toward Maria for letting everything happen. It was trying it's hardest to crawl to the surface now, but Christiana pushed it away; she wasn't ready to have that conversation.

"Yes." Maria sat back down, her chair creaking. "And with that history, I know you deserve to have a simple, quiet life pursuing the job you've done beautifully over the last five years. I'm sure Alekzander has grown to be a wonderful man..."

"He is," Christiana interjected, leaning back in her chair, arms crossed tightly.

"Nevertheless." Maria narrowed her eyes. "He is to be King of this country. You are an amazing businesswoman, Christiana. Do you want to go back to living in a man's shadow?"

"I wouldn't live in his shadow!" Christiana's voice rose, a flush spreading up her neck. "He already told me he wants me to be his partner, not just an ornament to stand next to him."

"Men say pretty things to catch a woman's attention." Maria's fingers mindlessly played with a loose curl of her blonde hair. "It doesn't mean they will follow through."

Christiana couldn't sit still any longer, striding over to stare out the tall window overlooking the palace's front entrance. A few more carriages were lined up, the rest of Dorina's birthday guests finally arriving for the ball in two days.

"You don't know Zander the way I do." Christiana refused to turn around. "He is a man of his word."

"You're right, I don't." Maria's voice drifted closer, heels clicking against the wood floor until she was directly behind Christiana. "But I know you. You deserve to have peace in your life. Now, I will stand by you no matter what decision you make, and I will be happy for you. But can you honestly tell me that your life as Queen of Viri would be a peaceful one?"

Christiana bit her lip hard enough to draw a drop of blood, the spread of dirty steel filling her mouth. Peace was a word she had never related to her life, even after her father's death. It was a pretty thought, to live simply with a caring man who let her lead a life she chose. It was the life she would have with Rowan, the life her mother apparently wanted for her.

But even if she chose Rowan, would her life truly be peaceful? Robert was right, she would crush herself under the weight of her secrets. Chaos was destined to follow her anywhere, it was just a matter of what chaos she could live with for the rest of her life. She had finally found the real question she needed to answer to find the path she was meant to go down.

"Don't worry, Mother." Christiana looked back, a smile back on her face as she forced herself to relax the tension in her neck. "I have everything under control."

"If you insist." Maria frowned. They stared at each other for a few fleeting seconds before she glided out of the common room into her bedroom, leaving Christiana alone with her thoughts.

Chapter Thirty-Seven

CHRISTIANA COULDN'T STOP SMILING AS SHE watched Isabelle twirl in front of the mirror in her latest dress, the soft blush color of a freshly-bloomed rose. Chiffon enveloped her torso to form a high V-neckline before cascading down her arms and cinching at her elbow. A gold sash sat above her hips and broke free into the full blush-and-raspberry tulle skirt, complete with crystals sewn into the hemline, twinkling in the candlelight with each twist and twirl—and Isabelle did plenty of twirling.

This whole morning had been Dorina's idea, but Christiana had made sure it was perfect for her little sister. Isabelle had spent most of her life having dresses and outfits picked out for her, but for her first formal ball at the palace, it was only fitting that she chose a custom dress design.

Luckily, Christiana had Lorraine as her new favorite dressmaker, and the young woman was eager to show off more designs. The rainbow of different dresses and fabrics was strewn across Christiana's four poster bed, the room's energy so lively and full of laughter that it was impossible to sit down. Isabelle refused to leave the mirror as she tried on each dress, while Christiana and Dorina sipped on rosehip tea and gushed over each new outfit she tried on.

"So," Dorina said as she stood next to Isabelle, adjusting the flowing sleeves of the blush dress, "have you made your choice?"

"Yes!" Isabelle squealed, clapping and bouncing on the balls of her bare feet.

This morning surprise not only gave Isabelle joy, it brought a lightness to Christiana's chest that she hadn't felt in weeks. It was moments like this that allowed her to forget the weight of her responsibilities. The case was not her priority, the clashing of Rowan and Zander in her heart was muted, and she could focus on enjoying a moment with people she loved.

"Perfect!" Lorraine exclaimed, milling around Isabelle. She pulled pins from the cuff of her dress, placing them in certain spots as she twisted and tugged the looser edges of Isabelle's petite form. "I need to take it in at the hips and it will be perfect for the ball tomorrow."

"Good!" Isabelle's soft blonde curls bounced around her shoulders when she twirled again.

"Her energy is infectious," Dorina whispered in Christiana's ear, leaning against the side of her bed.

"Tell me about it." Christiana smirked. It was her favorite quality in Isabelle, one she prayed her young sister would never lose.

"All set." Lorraine stepped away.

"Do I have to take it off?" Isabelle pouted.

"Yes, Belle." Christiana moved forward, removing the raspberry ribbon laced up the back. "You need to get dressed or we'll be late for the garden tea party. We promised mother we would be there on time."

Christiana swallowed a lump in her throat as she mentioned her mother. Ever since last night's conversation, her mother had barely spoken to her, deciding to rest this morning instead of attend Isabelle's first dress fitting. She knew her words had hurt her mother, but in the end it was for both of their own good. Maria didn't need to add any more stress to her life and Christiana wasn't ready to let her mother back in. Not with the important decisions at least.

Christiana and Dorina helped Isabelle put her cream-and-lilac day dress back on before the left the apartment for the rose grove. With many new nobles coming to the palace to celebrate Dorina's birthday, the King and Queen had decided to host a welcome tea for all the new guests. The rose grove was filled to capacity, with tables and chairs for people to sit in. Servants milled through the crowd with trays of steaming tea and assorted pastries. Laughter and chatter mixed with the sounds of nature in the grove.

The minute they arrived, Dorina was pulled away by people eager to wish her a happy early birthday before the ball. Christiana weaved her arm through Isabelle's as they made their way through the crowd, searching for their mother while they each took a cup of fresh tea to sip on. It was only a few moments before they spotted her, blonde hair perfectly pinned back as she embraced her dear friend Madeleine.

Christiana led Isabelle toward them, then caught sight of someone hiding in the corner. She halted, her vision tunneling in on Eliza, full red lips set in a frown while she sat alone at a table in the corner, half-concealed by a cerulean rose bush.

"Why don't you go over to Mother and I'll meet you there in a moment." Christiana pulled her arm from Isabelle's.

Isabelle shrugged and hurried away. Christiana took a deep breath and made her way to the secluded table.

"Good afternoon, Eliza." Christiana curtsied when she reached the table.

Eliza's head turned sharply toward her, a tight smile spreading on her face. "Hello, Marchioness. How are you today?"

"I'm lovely." She took the seat opposite Eliza.

Everything about Eliza's posture came off as happy, her shoulders pulled back, spine straight, hands placed in front of her. But all Christiana could see were her eyes, lifeless and dull. She knew that look well—it was one she used to wear every day she went out in public. She learned how to present herself as perfect, but somehow the eyes were the one feature she could never control. It seemed Eliza was the same.

"I haven't seen you since the masquerade," Christiana observed.

"Oh, well, my husband and I have been travelling frequently the past few weeks." Eliza's teacup shook when she picked it up to take a sip.

Christiana loathed herself in that moment; here she was shirking her responsibilities, torn between two men, enjoying a morning of carefree dresses and time with her family and friends while Eliza suffered in solitary silence. She could barely look at Eliza, every inch of her perfectly presentable down to the last ruby pin tacked in her hair, when she knew what real pain weighed her down each day, kept her up at night, and struck fear deep inside.

Christiana knew, not because she was the Maiden, but because she had been in that same place five years ago. She had sat at these parties, surrounded by dozens of nobles yet still feeling alone. Isolation in plain sight was the worst kind, because people assumed they knew you. They would see you and think everything in your privileged life must be perfect, but they couldn't be more wrong. No one would reach out to help, and you certainly couldn't reach out yourself unless you wanted to risk severe punishment.

"That's too bad." Christiana reached across the table to pat Eliza's hand, but she flinched, pulling her hand away to rest in her lap. "Dorina speaks so highly of you, I had hoped to invite you over for tea."

"What a kind offer." Eliza's cheek twitched. A servant interrupted them to offer a tray of raspberry chocolate cream puffs, and the two women politely declined, turning back to each other. "Life as the

Chancellor's wife is certainly a busy one."

Christiana tilted her head, her fingers tracing the pattern of a vine etched into the metal table. "I'm sure."

"I can certainly reach out if I ever find the time." Eliza's eyebrows rose, her gaze lighting up for the first time in the conversation.

"I would love that." Christiana smiled back.

"My darling!" Julian's voice broke through the cacophony of the nobility as he approached their table, arms opened wide. "I'm sorry I left you here alone. I hope you can forgive me?"

"Of course, darling," Eliza echoed, her voice strained. Julian clutched her shoulder, leaning down to kiss her cheek.

"I see the Marchioness has been keeping you company." He looked down at Christiana, eyes icy.

"I thought I would say hello." Christiana kept her shoulders pulled back, forcing her hands to stay flat on the table though she wanted to lunge across it and slap his hand away from the young lady that was too good for him. She wanted to steal someone's dagger and run Julian through. She wanted to do *something*.

Her thumb twitched against the table, rattling her teacup. Heat crawled up her limbs, sending pulses through every inch of her. Every second this man continued to breathe was another second she was a failure. She was determined not to be a failure for much longer; the poison was already forming perfect crystals when she checked it last night. It was only a matter of time before he was forced into a terrible, nightmarish coma to live out his last days.

"Well, if you don't mind," Julian interrupted her visions of the future, pulling Eliza up beside him. She winced at the sudden movement. "I would love to take my wife for a fresh cup of tea. I would hate for people to think I'm neglecting her."

"Of course, as you said before: image is important and rumors can destroy it." Christiana stood and curtsied to them. "It was lovely talking to you, Eliza."

"You as well, Marchioness," Eliza said before Julian hustled her away.

Christiana's pulse raced as she watched them, his hand tightly around his wife's waist. She had been distracted for too long. It was time for her to make a courtship decision and move on. There were more important things to focus on, people's lives hanging in the balance. She was done letting her own selfish desires get in the way of helping a person truly in need.

Chapter Thirty-Eight

CHRISTIANA STOOD IN HER APARTMENT ALONE that afternoon, her mother and sister retiring for a nap before the three of them took dinner together. The silence was overwhelming, nothing but the flickering of the candles to distract her. She couldn't stop thinking about Eliza and the anguish deep in her gut when she let that gracious woman walk away with a monster.

She should have stopped them; she should have insisted to stay by Eliza's side during the party. It reminded her of her childhood and the countless times she wished someone had insisted on saving her.

Her mind wandered, remembering all of the worst parts of her father. It wasn't just the beatings that twisted Christiana's insides, but the words he spoke as well. Her memory flooded with so many post-beating days, a seclusion so mind-bending she was never sure how she survived.

The cool summer air blew into Christiana's wide-open window as she sat silently staring out into the sunny day. The morning was almost over, yet she hadn't even changed out of her nightgown. There was no point since she wasn't in any condition to show her swollen face. The tender skin around her eye and lips stung with every movement. Last night's beating was certainly not the worst, but it kept her from being able to go out in public. Even if she wanted to, her father would never allow it. Her heart sank as she saw people setting picnics out on the lawn or strolling through the rose grove, their laughter floating in with the wind.

A knock from the doorway broke her depressed thoughts. She shifted in her chair, groaning and clutching her bruised ribs. Without a word, her father entered, a tray of spiced broth in his hands. He stared at her, face softened with concern, before placing the tray on her blanket-covered lap. She gazed down at the delicious-looking meal, her appetite non-existent.

"How are you feeling today, my darling?" Her father knelt in front of her to examine the wounds with a gentle touch of his hand.

She winced, his warm hands inflaming the bruised cut on her forehead. "It still hurts."

"Of course. Let me help." He picked up a jar from the tray and slowly applied a cooling salve on her face. His tender hands moved slowly so as not to irritate her face anymore. "Does that feel better?"

"Yes." She nodded slightly.

He smiled, moving down to rub the salve on her neck, his fingers still imprinted on her pale skin like a necklace. "Eat. You'll feel better."

"I'm not hungry," she replied monotonously, her head spinning.

"Trust me, you need it. So, eat." He offered the spoon, and she took it, gripping the cold metal tightly and bringing spoonfuls to her mouth without tasting the broth. With a pat on her knee, Francis stood and walked to stand behind her. "I wish I didn't have to do this to you, but you know it's for your own good, don't you?"

"Yes." Christiana's food struggled, a lump in her throat blocking its passage.

"Everything I do for you is to make you the best marchioness I know you can be." She felt his gaze on her, the heat beating against the back of her neck. "It will all be worth it one day, when you hold the title. You'll finally understand why I pushed you so hard."

"I know." She closed her eyes, her stomach threatening to release all the food she just ate when his hand rested on her shoulder, rubbing a tight knot out of her tense back.

"You'll take the morning off." He patted her on the back, the vibrations shaking her bruised ribs. "You need rest before returning to work."

"All right," she agreed, her exhausted body wanting nothing more than to escape in the comfort of her plush bedding.

"Let me take that for you," her father offered, pulling the tray from her lap. "Now rest, I'll make sure no more distractions come to you."

"Thank you." She stared down at her now-empty hands, her pale fingers limp in her lap. The joints popped as she curled them inward.

"Of course, anything for my little girl." Francis smiled, placing a sweet kiss on her forehead before leaving her alone. She stood on shaking legs, her hip radiating pain with each step as she limped towards her bed. She crawled into her warm quilt, tossing and turning for a while before settling down.

A knock on the apartment's front door drew her attention, her eyes opening again. Grasping her torso, she pulled herself up, straining to hear the voices drifting through the cracked doorway.

"Can I help you, Your Highnesses?" came her father's voice from the common room.

"Can we see Ana, please?" Zander asked from what Christiana assumed was the doorway. She couldn't help but be curious, so she tiptoed to the door, pressing her ear against the strong wood.

"I'm sorry, but she is too sick to see people."

"She was fine when we saw her the other day," Dorina argued.

"I know, Your Highness, but her migraines are uncontrollable sometimes. She gets them from her mother. She can barely talk with the pain, let alone socialize. It would be best if you left."

"Please, Sir," Zander interjected, "I'm leaving tomorrow and I wanted to say goodbye to her."

Christiana's heart tightened, her head pressed lightly against the door as she realized she wouldn't see Zander again this summer. Her body tingled with the urge to walk out of the room to see him one last time.

"I'll let her know."

"I'd prefer to tell her myself."

"I'm sure, but I can't control when she wants to be left alone," Francis said firmly.

"Come on, Zander, we need to respect her privacy." Dorina sighed.

"Fine, but can you at least give this to her?" Zander asked. "It's how she can reach me if she wants to write."

"How kind, Your Highness, I'll make sure to pass it on."

The heavy sound of the door closing signaled they were finally alone again. She cracked the door open to see her father standing by the fireplace, a piece of parchment in his hands. He stared down at it for a moment, studying the brown paper and black ink, before tossing it into the flames.

"You wouldn't want it." He turned toward his spying daughter. "You both are too busy to write anyways. Now go and rest like I told you."

Nodding, Christiana closed the door on him and ran back to the comfort of her safe bed.

A swift knock interrupted Christiana's thoughts, her eyes tearing away from the window.

"My Lady?" Natalia called from the doorway.

"Yes?" She turned her head, eyes still downcast.

"There is a steward here to see you."

Reluctantly, Christiana rose to follow her. If a steward was here, a noble or royal person must have sent them for a good reason.

"My Lady," the stalky steward greeted her with a deep bow. He must be new to the palace; Christiana didn't recognize his face as she did others.

She crossed her arms, her brow furrowed. "Forgive me, I don't know your name, but what can I help you with?"

"My name is Jay, My Lady. I'm here at the request of my Master to deliver this to you." He offered her a long dagger box, but Christiana couldn't help noticing a smaller square box with an envelope stacked on top. Her heart thundered at the sight.

"Thank you, Jay." She took the package from his outstretched hands, the smooth wood soft in her grasp. With one final bow, the man departed, and Christiana stared down at the packages, feeling as if they weighed as much as her horse. "Natalia, I'd like to be alone for a while, please."

"Of course, My Lady." She curtsied and hurried out. Christiana sighed, dropping the two packages on the table and curling up on the couch, her fingers sliding under the hard wax to open the letter.

My Dearest Christiana,

I've spent the last few days unable to get our last conversation out of my mind. Your fears for our future are certainly real. We will be putting ourselves in a dangerous and difficult situation. Although I understand your calling, if for any reason your secret was discovered, I would be putting my crown, my legacy, and my life in unimaginable peril. But even with all of that in mind, I can only think one thing - I don't care.

For a woman who puts such a strong and confident shell around her, you have a hard time seeing the beauty I and others see in you. You are strong-willed, smart, and utterly witty. When I look at you, I see the Queen this country needs.

The main reason I chose you is simple. I look at you and I see my future. I see a potential marriage that I always craved but never thought I would be blessed with. I need someone who will challenge me and push me to think. I need a partner, not a dutiful subject standing by my side for the rest of my life. There is only one woman who comes to mind who can set my world and heart on fire: you.

A few days ago, I presented you with a dagger to show you I accept the side of you that you keep hidden. But I think in the excitement, I forgot you are so much more than the secrets you shared with me. You are a beautiful, caring, and passionate woman who wants to prove to the world she is strong. I gave you a gift to show your strength; now I give you a gift to show how beautiful I find you. I accept all sides of you, Christiana - the beautiful, the strong, the dangerous, and the vulnerable. I hope you see in me a man who will support your choices. If you decide that this is what your heart wants, wear this gift to my sister's birthday ball tomorrow. I hope to see it accenting the beautiful woman I hope to one day call mine.

Forever Yours,
Zander

With shaking hands and tear-stained eyes, Christiana reread the letter over and over. Never in her life had she read something so passionate. She didn't realize how much she depended on the armor she kept around her heart and soul. Even soldiers took off their armor at the end of the day.

Mind still spinning, she opened the unknown box and gasped at the beautiful piece of jewelry inside. The two silver hair combs were molded to look like delicate leaves surrounded by flowers, encrusted with diamonds and joined by a double strand of creamy, iridescent pearls to give the whole piece an ethereal air. It was unique, delicate-looking, but crafted strong. It represented everything Zander saw and adored about her.

She wiped her eyes to regain her composure and brought the beautiful gift back to her room, placing both it and the note in her dressing table. She still had a full day to decide if she would wear the headpiece at the party.

***

"I can't believe you get to do this every day!" Isabelle squealed, spinning in front of the mirror in her flowy new dress. The blush fabric perfectly complimented her blonde hair, the long curls pinned to one side of her head and cascading down the off-the-shoulder sleeves.

"I certainly don't do this every day, Belle." Christiana laughed.

"You get to do it more than me!"

Christiana smiled and shook her head, but didn't argue again. Her sister was no longer the young girl curled up in bed with her; she was a thirteen-year-old lady and she was ready to join society tonight.

"You look absolutely stunning, Lady Isabelle." Natalia brushed shimmery blush across Christiana's cheeks. She had gone to great lengths getting Isabelle ready, even putting cosmetics on her face for the first time. The rosy lipstick and soft gold glitter across her eyes made her look grown up. "You'll even outshine the Princess with your beauty."

Isabelle stopped in her tracks, gaping over to Christiana's dressing table. "I wouldn't want to do that! It's her birthday after all."

"I think Dorina will be fine sharing the attention with you," Christiana teased, rubbing lotion between her hands.

"The Princess is the kindest person I've ever met! She even let me borrow this necklace!" Isabelle played with the diamond chain Dorina had given her yesterday.

"How could she not like you, little one?" Christiana watched Isabelle through the mirror as she went back to twirling, almost knocking herself into the plush chair near the window.

"And the Prince is so handsome," Isabelle gushed, clutching her chest and swaying side to side. "I wonder how women get any work done with him around."

"They don't, trust me." Christiana snorted, and Natalia shot her a

308

pointed stare to stop her from moving. She mouthed an apology and let her maid put the finishing touches on her.

Isabelle sighed, wrapping her arms around Christiana's bedpost. "Well, I would be one of them if I was allowed to stay here."

"He's more than his face, Belle." Christiana closed her eyes as Natalia swept champagne glitter across her eyelids and cheekbones. "He's smart and caring too. He's going to be our king someday; you need to respect him."

"Have you really gotten close with him?" Isabelle shuffled closer, and Christiana peeked over once Natalia's hands moved away. "Or was he saying that for my benefit?"

"No, we have," Christiana admitted, not ready to tell her younger sister about her dilemma. She had made her decision now and it was time to move forward with it.

"Well, don't my two little girls look absolutely breathtaking!" Maria clapped her hands in the doorway, her satin-and-silk lavender dress wrapped beautifully around her. The long bell sleeves opened at the elbow, adding a touch of drama to the simple corset and A-line skirt.

"Mama! Look how much older I look!" Isabelle bragged, spinning for their mother. While they were distracted, Christiana opened the drawer in front of her, revealing the two new pieces of jewelry she received over the summer: a stunning necklace and a luscious headpiece. Both from men who wanted to love her, but only one held her heart, and she was ready to let him in.

Christiana had woken up that morning after a long night of overthinking with peace in her heart. She thought back on the words those closest to her had spoken and the advice they gave. After thinking about the two lives offered to her, only one was the right step forward.

Tonight, she would wear the piece of jewelry that man had offered. She would show him she was putting this whole matter to rest once and for all.

"So, are we ready?" Christiana stood and turned to face her family, Isabelle's arm already linked with their mother's.

"Are you?" Maria asked.

"I am," she answered, pulling the finishing touch from the drawer and securing it on herself. With one final look in the mirror, she walked out of her room with her head held high, ready to celebrate.

Chapter Thirty-Nine

THE BALLROOM ONCE AGAIN LOOKED spectacular when Christiana entered with her family. Unlike the masquerade, it was obvious this entire party was planned with one girl in mind: Dorina. Everything in the room sparkled with Dorina's favorite colors of deep gold and pale blue, encapsulating it with her personality. Different-sized tables displayed foods and pastries while servants passed around flutes of her favorite sparkling wine. Christiana smiled as she took in the scene, happy to see everyone finally celebrating such a selfless girl.

"This is amazing!" Isabelle breathed, wide eyes darting between everything. Christiana laughed; her sister's reaction was exactly how she imagined.

"How about something to drink?" A kind servant offered her one of the delicate flutes.

"What do you think?" Christiana asked, nudging her shoulder.

"It's delicious!" Christiana was pretty sure that would be her response to everything for the evening, and nothing could break that trance of happiness.

"Why don't you and Mother go and try some of the treats on the food table?" Christiana pointed at the overflowing pastries around the four-layer cake covered in ice-blue frosting and gold leaf.

"You aren't coming?" Isabelle's arm tightened around Christiana's.

"I have to go and find someone first. Don't worry, I'll find you soon." She squeezed her sister's hand and released her. Isabelle shrugged, disappearing into the crowd.

"You look beautiful, my darling." Maria touched her arm, then frowned when Christiana pulled away. "I especially love the necklace."

"Thank you." Christiana smiled, touching the delicate chain around her throat. "I'll be back soon."

She swam through the throng of people, trying her best not to get distracted by everyone inviting her into conversations. She had a goal in mind to achieve as soon as possible. Now that her decision was made, her heart was pulling her to find him. She couldn't wait any longer.

Almost to the front of the room, she finally saw him talking kindly to a few other guests, his smile gentle and sincere. She had made the right decision, there was no question in her head or heart anymore.

His eyes found her, his smile spreading as he took her in. Unable to contain her excitement, she hurried to join him.

"Marchioness," he greeted with a deep bow, a sly grin twitching at the corner of his lips. "You look breathtaking tonight."

"Thank you." She curtsied in return, her stomach fluttering just looking at him. Heat crawl up her arm, her heart thumping loudly in her ears.

"I can't believe you're wearing it." He smiled, touching the pearl headpiece, then pulling his hand back to his side. "I was afraid your late arrival meant the worst."

Christiana bit her lip, looking down at the floor. "We took our time getting ready. I'm not used to having Isabelle with me."

"Oh, of course, I'm sure that's the only reason." He nodded, his brow furrowing as if he didn't quite believe her.

"I also might have wanted to keep you in suspense," she teased, shoulders shaking with laughter.

"Come with me." Zander grabbed her hand to lead her through one of the doors in the back of the room, into the antechamber where the music and crowds were drowned out.

"People will gossip if we stay away too long," she whispered as he leaned her against a wall.

"Let them," Zander challenged. "Are you sure?"

"Well, obviously." She laughed, gesturing at the pearls wrapped around her hair. "This wasn't put on because I thought it was a pretty piece of jewelry. Well, at least that's not the main reason."

"I know it's terrifying, but I promise all I want is to make you happy." He pulled her hands to his lips and pressed a firm kiss on her fingers. "I can't spend the rest of my life feeling like something is missing. What you bring every day...it's worth all of the risk."

"I'm done denying myself happiness because I'm scared of what comes next. Take that away, and there was no question. It was always going to be you." She grabbed his face and crushed her lips against his. He kissed her back deeply, his arms encircling her waist to pull her closer. Free of her doubts and fears, her lips exploded with tingles, the wildfire burning unchecked inside her.

She pulled away at last to look up at him, his eyes swirling with desire. "All right, we can keep doing that if you'd like." He laughed, his forehead falling against hers.

"Stop it." She laughed, playfully pushing him away. Even though they were hidden, her stomach still twisted that someone would barge in on them; on the other hand, the danger of being caught did send an extra spark of desire down her spine.

"You do look beautiful tonight." He took in the burgundy dress. "I'm glad my mother taught me the proper way to pick out jewelry, because it worked in my favor. The headpiece even matches your necklace."

"It was a gift from my mother." She touched the delicate string of pearls around her neck. "She gave them to me when I was officially titled."

The loud ring of horns interrupted them, the herald's distinct voice traveling through the walls. Zander gave her hand a tight squeeze and placed it in the crook of his arm, escorting her back into the room and through the large crowd in time to watch Dorina enter, her parents close behind her.

Christiana smiled at her friend, their eyes briefly catching as she walked to the front with her head held high. Her face lit up, an excited question forming in her eyes at Christiana's arm in her brother's. Christiana smiled and slowly nodded, and Dorina's shoulders tensed quickly before she returned to her parade, stepping gracefully to the ballroom's front dais.

The entire crowd gathered around, champagne flutes in hand as the King and Queen gave a tenderhearted speech about their little girl. Zander's arm snaked out from his side to wrap around Christiana, tightly grasping her waist while he kept his sparkling eyes on his sister.

"To Princess Dorina!" The Royals rang out together, their flutes held high. The crowd mimicked their words, the sound of clinking glasses ringing throughout the room. Zander touched his glass to Christiana's, giving her a quick wink as they sipped the bubbling liquid.

The music began again, the crowd's laughter and loud conversations buzzing through the room as King Lucian led Dorina into the center of the dance floor. Zander leaned in, his lips grazing Christiana's ear. "I should probably dance with my mother for this one."

"Of course." Christiana patted his hand, but her heart twitched at the idea of having to let go. "I'll find my family."

"And I'll find you after." He winked one more time before striding away to the dais to offer his hand to his mother.

Christiana smiled at the four royals on the dance floor, their smiles and laughter swelling her heart. No one else danced around them, the entire court watching the Royal Family put on an opening show. Her heart leapt as she realized for the first time, they could be her family one day, too.

Christiana scanned the crowd in search of the two blonde ladies she was looking for. The heat drained from her face when she made contact with Rowan's hard, tight-jawed face instead. She wasn't exactly sure what she was doing, or what possessed her to move, but without thinking she scurried forward, her shoulders barreling through the crowd until she reached him. He tried to walk away, but her determined grasp reached him first, hands wrapping around his blue velvet coat. "Rowan, please. I want to talk."

"You said enough this morning." He looked down at her, his posture rigid, his words laced with steel. She had gone to him this morning to tell him her decision; the words were barely past her lips when he slammed the door in her face. She felt the cuts deep in her chest; she deserved this, but it didn't make it hurt any less.

"Please, let me explain..."

He pulled his arm from her grasp. "There's nothing to explain, Christiana. You chose him."

"I know, but..."

"Look." He tugged her off to the side, removing them from the group of people beginning to stare at them. "I'm not going to stand here and pretend I'm all right, because I'm not. But tonight isn't about us, it's about Dorina. She doesn't deserve her party ruined because two people she cares about caused a scene in the middle of it."

"That's true." Christiana shoulders went limp. She had already caused one person pain tonight; she didn't need to hurt anyone else trying to fix it.

"Now, I suggest you and Zander stay away from me tonight." He pulled himself straight, his gaze narrow. "I'll come to you when I'm ready to talk. I think that's the least I'm owed at this point."

A lump filled her throat, her fingernails biting into her palm as she tried not to let a tear fall. "Very well."

He nodded, his face falling as a whisper of pain escaped through his eyes. "My Lady." He bowed to her.

She curtsied, her legs shaking. "My Lord." She pulled herself up in time to watch him walk away from her. She couldn't seem to find the strength to move, her hand pressed firmly against her chest as she pulled in deep breaths. Her pulse quickened, her heart fracturing as she tried to remember all the happy moments tonight had promised.

She wasn't sure how long she stood there, but when she felt the pressure of hands on her shoulders, she knew it had been too long. "I thought you were going to find your family," Zander whispered in her ear, his head resting against her temple.

Her hands reached up to grasp his, eyes still fixed on the empty path Rowan had walked. "So did I."

"We'll make it through this." He squeezed her shoulders. "How about a dance?"

She pulled in one final deep breath, forcing the tension out as she released it from her lungs. She allowed herself to smile once again, turning to stare into his sapphire eyes. "How about many?"

"As many as it takes to keep you happy." He kissed her knuckles before leading her out to the now-crowded dance floor.

Chapter Forty

ZANDER HELD TRUE TO HIS PROMISE, AND THEY stayed on the dance floor for as many songs as they could manage. He twirled, spun, and lifted her through the room, his grasp firm as they laughed and stepped through every song. Her heart was finally light, the weight on her shoulders releasing with each step they took together. He guided her through everything, his eyes never leaving hers.

Halfway through their fourth dance, Christiana caught sight of Isabelle bouncing through the patterns, twirled around by a baron's son around her age, a smile painted on her face and her jubilant energy extending through each limb and movement. The young man was clearly enamored with her, watching in awe when she spun and holding on tight when she came close.

Christiana shook her head, her heart singing at her sister's joy. She stood on her toes as the song started to close, the last few steps slowing all the dancers around them. "Why don't you ask Isabelle to dance the next song with you?" She nodded as Isabelle curtsied to her partner in closing.

"Your wish is my command." Zander bowed to her, and she rolled her eyes, watching him walk to her sister. Her stomach leaped when he extended his hand to Isabelle with a charming smile. Her shoulders almost vibrated with an enthusiastic nod, her hand clutching his as he pulled her close, the next song already wafting through the room.

"I think I'll have your next dance." An arm encircled Christiana's waist, turning her around by the hips to face her next partner.

"I see you came out from under your rock." She sneered up at Edgar, his dark hair slicked back from his face. She could easily escape his grasp, walk away and leave him alone, but she was too elated with the whole evening to let him sour her mood. Besides, she had bested him more than once this summer, she could afford to be generous tonight. And she couldn't stop herself from being curious about what idiotic thing he would do next to try and make himself look better.

"Funny." He twitched his eyebrows as their feet slowly began to move. "So, I see you've made a choice." He stared over her head at who Christiana could only assume was Zander.

"Technically it isn't public yet."

"Please." Edgar scoffed, jerking her closer as the flurry of other dancers pressed in around them. "You two haven't left each other's side. No one will be surprised when the formal announcement comes in a few days."

Christiana rolled her eyes as he twirled her around. "And you thought I would regret denying you. Once again, you couldn't be more wrong."

His expression went sour, lips pursed like he had tried to eat a lemon rind. "You will come to regret it."

"Forever a coward." His empty words rolled off her back.

"Oh, my dear Marchioness." A smirk slowly snaked up his face. "My plan has already been set in motion."

She scoffed. "What plan? Rumor has it you're leaving the palace early this summer." She had heard it from Dorina and a few other ladies during teatime two days after their sparring match; his claims that one of his farms needed him was a weak excuse to leave after Dorina's birthday.

"I have responsibilities, too."

"Very few."

"Well, enough to keep me away after tonight." The music reached the crescendo, their last few steps bringing them chest to chest. "But don't expect me to disappear forever. I'll be back in a few months with my revenge firmly in my grasp." His gaze glimmered wickedly down at her.

All she could do was roll her eyes again. "If you say so." She tugged her hand from his.

"Enjoy the rest of your night, Marchioness." He gave an ostentatious bow before turning away.

The dance floor was packed, everyone in their best gowns and jackets, a flourish of color filling every space as she pushed her way to the outer edge of the dance floor, the tune of vivacious instruments mixing with the revelry of laughter while the guests drank expensive wine and feasted on delicious canapés and sweet treats. She caught sight of Isabelle waving her over to the side of the room where she stood with Zander, and her smile returned, her steps guiding her to two of her favorite people.

Zander's smile welcomed her, one hand offering her a glass of wine while the other wrapped around her waist. "Welcome back."

"Exactly where I want to be." She smiled up at him, sipping the sparkling liquid. The fizz danced down her throat, sending a shiver through her limbs. She looked over at Isabelle, who was happily enjoying another plate of treats. "Are you going to share at all?" She playfully slapped her sister's arm, skillful hands stealing a chocolate truffle from the overflowing plate. She popped it in her mouth, the bittersweet flavors melting on her tongue. She let out a satisfied groan.

"I see you still have the same sweet tooth." Zander laughed, bright teeth shining as he shook his head.

"That was one thing you should have known would never change about me." She shrugged. Whenever Zander would meet her at the willow tree for some peace and quiet during their childhood, he always made sure to bring some kind of baked good or chocolate decadence for her to devour.

"I'll never forget it again." He winked, setting her heart fluttering.

"Your Highness?" Isabelle interjected, her plate discarded on a nearby table as she leaned in to join their conversation.

"Yes, My Lady?"

She tilted her head. "Are you excited to become King?"

"Sometimes." He nodded, his hand releasing Christiana's waist. "But can I tell you a secret? Sometimes it scares me."

"Really?" Isabelle's eyes widened.

"Of course, it is a lot of responsibility to hold."

"How do you make yourself feel better?"

"I study quite a lot. My father has been teaching me since I was your age. He wanted to make sure I would be comfortable."

"You have to study too?"

"Of course. I may have been born into this role, but that doesn't mean I was born with the knowledge for it."

"Oh, well, I'm glad I'm not the only one forced into studying," Isabelle complained, glaring at her sister.

"I had to study a lot too, Belle." Christiana rolled her eyes. "I don't understand why you think I do it to torture you."

"Anyway," the Prince continued, "I feel prepared. And I'm hoping to have a good partner by my side when I'm crowned."

"Like a Queen?" Isabelle giggled.

He smiled. "Yes, exactly, a Queen."

"I have quite missed dancing." Maria smiled as she joined them, her powdered cosmetics already breaking apart at her hairline from the sheen of sweat forming there. For her first ball in many years, she was doing an excellent job at remembering all of the dance steps; she had barely sat any of them out, enjoying her time with multiple dance partners.

"I'm glad you're enjoying yourself." Christiana clutched her wine flute tightly, her fingernails scratching against the crystal pattern etched into the side. It took all her will power not to squirm under Zander's touch, knowing her mother wasn't completely approving of their potential union. Luckily, Maria had been cordial with him all evening, especially since they had yet to make the formal announcement to either of their families.

"It's wonderful to be back." Maria looked at her daughter, her defined cheekbones catching the candlelight where the gold shimmer dusted across them sparkled. "Some of my favorite memories of your childhood took place here."

"This was always a place of safety for us, wasn't it, Mother?" Christiana's sharp tongue took control, the words escaping before she could think them through.

"Safety?" Isabelle's face creased, her gaze darting between them. "What does that mean?"

"Who couldn't feel safe here, little one?" Christiana forced a smile, stealing another truffle off her sister's plate to distract her. Isabelle stuck out her tongue.

Zander cleared his throat. "Who were you dancing with?"

"Chancellor Marlow!" Maria pulled a handkerchief from her décolletage to dab her face. "He's just as charming as I remember all those years ago."

"We hear that a lot," Zander responded coolly.

"And it was an absolute joy to dance with you as well!" Julian nudged in, and Maria's hand flew to her chest as she blushed and giggled. Christiana's stomach churned. "Your mother is light on her feet, Marchioness. Makes me wish I had danced with her more over the years."

"You're too kind." Maria played with the diamond and pearl pendent laying below her throat.

"Where is Eliza tonight, Chancellor?" Christiana asked, trying her best to shift the subject away from the vile man flirting with her mother.

"Unfortunately, she had to travel at the last minute." Julian fiddled with the collar of his gray-and-plum velvet jacket. The colors matched him well, making his bright blue gaze even deadlier. "Her mother is ill. She wanted to be by her side."

"What a thoughtful daughter," Maria cooed, but Christiana's stomach riled against her at the news. She knew the real reason Eliza wasn't here: she must have gone through a punishment last night and wasn't in any state to be seen. Christiana only hoped it wasn't because of their conversation yesterday. She would never forgive herself if that was the case.

"That's my Eliza." He stared off into nothing. "She is a special woman. I'm lucky to have her in my life." He shook himself, smile returning. "In the meantime, would you care to join me for a dance, Marchioness?"

"Oh, do it, Ana!" her mother interjected. "I don't think Prince Alekzander would mind letting you go for a few minutes."

"Not at all." Although he was smiling, his muscles tensed under her hand resting on his arm.

"It will be my honor." She allowed Julian to bring her to the center of the dance floor, going silently through the motions while the music played.

"I see now where you inherited your grace on the dance floor," he observed, breaking the uncomfortable quiet between them.

"Yes, my mother was my tutor in the subject."

A wicked grin spread across his face. "It seems you and I will be lucky enough to get to know each other even better now."

"Excuse me?" A chill ran up her spine as he pulled her closer, moving her to the edge of the dance floor, the crowd thinning around them.

"By the way the Prince has been spending time with you tonight," he said, his hand firm on her back as he leaned in to whisper, "I can only imagine that you've accepted his courtship proposal. The whole ballroom is buzzing about it."

"I should apologize to the Princess. I would hate to think I stole the show away from her." Christiana's jaw tensed as she looked around the room. She had been so wrapped up in enjoying the evening with Zander and her sister, she hadn't noticed the sideway glances and jealous stares pointed at her. Typically, she would brush them off, but with Julian's arms around her, she felt like a prized steed put up for sale.

"You know, Marchioness, I have dedicated my life to this country." He tugged her attention back to him, his face dangerously close. "I spent countless years serving it as a soldier first, rising up the ranks to prove my worth. When I was lucky enough to be named Chancellor, I worked tirelessly to make sure that everything I did was for the greater good of our nation."

"That is very selfless of you." She tried to contain her sarcasm, not sure if she was successful.

Julian plowed on, ignoring her biting words, "That it is. But even though I have spent twenty-two years being part of this Council, I've barely enough time to finish everything necessary."

Her brows pinched together. "What do you mean?"

"I'm not quite ready to give up my position yet." He twirled them apart for a brief moment, then forced her back to him. "I have many years ahead of me and I think you'll agree they would best be spent assisting this country in a job where I thrive."

"You certainly have the...qualifications." She hesitated for the best word. "But I don't understand why you are telling me all of this. I don't have a say in your future employment."

"Ah, not yet." His eyes glinted. "But it seems that one day, you might. When Alekzander takes the crown, quite possibly with you by his side as Queen."

"Possibly. However, that doesn't mean I have a large say in his future council choices."

"I think we both know that's a lie." He smirked. "The last thing you are known for is your docile nature. I'm sure you have a lot of influence over our future King's decisions. And I think it would be in your best interest to convince him that the greatest thing for him and this Country is to keep me exactly where I belong, in the Chancellor's position."

"*I* don't think it is your place to make such demands, Julian." Christiana struggled to control her tongue. "Besides, I would never want to force him into something that made him uncomfortable. And it seems to me that is exactly what you are asking of me."

"You're not his wife yet."

Her skin prickled, anger flaring in her chest. "What are you implying?"

"This is just a courtship, which means your union has not been solidified quite yet. My reach is far, Marchioness. I would hate to see you lose such a happy ending, so much potential power, because you couldn't follow one simple instruction like a well-behaved Lady of your standing."

"Are you threatening me?" she asked through clenched teeth.

"Of course not, My Lady." He spun her around, her back against his chest as he leaned down to whisper in her ear. "All I'm saying is, I wouldn't want to see you suffer any more than you already have."

Christiana's veins ran cold as he jerked her back around to face him.

His gleeful eyes bore into her as the song came to its final crescendo.

What was he trying to imply? Perhaps it was a scare tactic with no real merit, but she couldn't help think he knew more than she'd ever realized.

"It has been an absolute pleasure, My Lady." He made one final bow, giving her hand a light kiss. "I look forward to our potential partnership over the years."

She strode away from him quickly and hurried to Zander, eager to put the conversation out of her mind and enjoy the rest of the night.

Chapter Forty-One

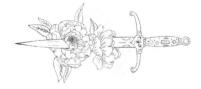

THE MORNING WAS EASIER ON CHRISTIANA THAN after her last ball. Although her mind was foggy, she tried to contain herself while Natalia finished the final lacings of her navy-and-cream lace day dress. After the ball, Christiana and Zander had decided the best way to announce their news to their families was together. Since hers was leaving by midmorning to return to Tagri, they had a small window of time; breakfast was the only way to follow through.

"Tight enough, My Lady?" Natalia asked.

"Yes, thank you." Christiana smiled, holding her stomach while Natalia tied off the corset. They walked to the dressing table and Christiana took her place in front of the mirror so they could put the finish touches on her daytime look. The surface was still littered with cosmetics and jewels from the night before.

Christiana caught Natalia trying to contain a smirk in the mirror. "What?" She laughed.

"It's nothing, My Lady," she replied, a glint in her jade eyes.

"We've known each other five years Natalia. You can speak freely."

"I just think it's kind of His Highness to invite you and your family for breakfast." She twisted one of Christiana's curls away from her face, securing it with a pearl pin to create a halo around the rest of her free-flowing hair.

Christiana rolled her eyes. She wasn't surprised Natalia was listening to Court gossip. "I think it should be obvious why he's doing it."

"Perhaps." Natalia leaned over for the silver brush on the table, running it through Christiana's hair. "But have you said it out loud to anyone besides him?"

"No." Christiana tried not to shake her head, not wanting to ruin all of Natalia's hard work. She was a combination of excited and nervous, her insides trembling. She knew some people would be excited for this moment, that they would revel and celebrate with them; it wasn't an official proposal, but with all of the pressure for each of them to marry, the step of courtship was certainly the right direction. Yet after her mother's obvious desire for her to choose Rowan, she wasn't sure of her reaction, even if she did say she would be happy with either choice.

Christiana also wondered what the King would think. She and Zander hadn't been shy together last night, so she could only imagine Lucian had inklings of what this breakfast was about. Yet something gnawed at Christiana; though Lucian had been kind to her most of the summer, she couldn't help remembering his wary gaze in the game room when he saw how close she was getting to Zander again.

All she could do was hope their parents didn't ruin this day for them.

Natalia pulled her out of her daze. "This is a happy moment, My Lady. You deserve to revel in it."

"Thank you, Natalia." Christiana patted her hand. "It is certainly thrilling to say that I am...courting with Prince Alekzander."

"That's how I know you made a good decision." Natalia placed a simple sapphire pendent around Christiana's neck. "If I'm not speaking out of turn."

Christiana tilted her head. "What do you mean?"

"I can't say I've ever seen you smile quite so brightly, My Lady." Natalia smiled, fiddling with the end of her braided raven hair.

"Thank you, Natalia." Christiana stood and gave her lady's maid one last smile.

The walk to her family's apartment was quick, the room already half-packed when she walked inside. "You work quickly," Christiana commented as her mother strode into the common room, her lady's maid carrying her trunk.

"I don't want us to get home too late." Maria slid on a pair of cream lace gloves. "Isabelle has her mathematics lesson tomorrow morning."

"And she is so very excited for it." Isabelle entered from her bedroom, blonde hair contained in an intricate braid wrapping around her head and flowing down her right shoulder. "So, Ana, what's this special breakfast about?"

"You'll find out soon enough." She kissed her sister's forehead.

"I'm sure it will be a happy surprise." Maria patted Christiana's shoulder, and she winced. Hopefully her mother was true to her word.

By the time they made it to Zander's room, the whole Royal Family was there, sipping their morning tea and enjoying the fresh-baked cinnamon and blueberry pastries stacked high on the dining table.

"Oh, Maria!" Queen Penelope was the first to stand after the three ladies curtsied to their Royals, moving swiftly to embrace her old friend. "I'm so happy I'm able to say goodbye before you leave. It felt like old times having you here."

Dorina slid next to Christiana, her wavy brown hair tickling Christiana's neck as she leaned in to whisper, "Should I be prepared to celebrate in a few moments?"

"I have no idea what you mean." Christiana gave her a quick wink and walked around the table to a smirking Zander.

"Seeing as you've invited us all here this morning, is there something you would like to tell us, Son?" The King's distant stare sent a shiver up Christiana's spine.

"As most of you have probably heard by now, I gave Ana a token of my affection a few days ago." Zander slid his arm down to grasp her hand. "It came with a formal courtship proposal to ensure she was aware of my intentions. I wanted to give her time to think it over, but it seems she didn't need that long."

"I told him last night without a doubt in my mind." Christiana took a deep breath. "The answer is yes."

Dorina bounced on the balls of her feet, brown eyes alive with joy. Isabelle's full lips parted as she clutched her chest. Maria and Penelope clutched each other's arms, grinning at their children. Lucian's face was like stone, his eyes never leaving Christiana and Zander.

"Thank you for making my son so happy." Penelope stepped forward, pulling Christiana against her. Although the Queen had always been kind to her throughout the years, she had never been so personally affectionate. Christiana couldn't help but melt into her motherly embrace. "That's all I ever wanted for him."

"I'll try my best to always make him happy," she promised. The Queen's smile softened as she patted her arm and pulled away.

The King still stared at them, his posture rigid. Zander's grip on her hand tightened, his palm sweaty. "Are you both sure about this?" Lucian demanded.

"Yes." Zander pulled his shoulders back, defiant gaze locked with his father's.

They stood there for a few fleeting seconds before his cold gray eyes moved to Christiana. She dipped her head. "Yes, Your Majesty. I'm quite sure."

A smile spread across his face. "Congratulations to you both, then."

Zander let out a breath of relief, but Christiana struggled to do the same. Something about the way the King looked at her made her certain he wasn't as excited as the rest of his family. She shook it off, trying her best to enjoy the moment.

"Well." Penelope clapped her hands. "Since this is obviously an important development, I think our families need to get reacquainted! Maria, why don't you and Isabelle stay a little longer at the palace?"

"Really?" Maria clutched her old friend's arm, eyes wide.

"*Really?*" Isabelle squealed, her fists squeezed together.

Christiana's vision blurred, her ears ringing. This was not good for her investigation. "Are you able to, Mother? Do you even have enough clothing? And what about Isabelle's tutoring? She can't fall behind on her studies."

"I disagree," Isabelle chimed in.

Christiana didn't want to break her sister's heart, but she needed to keep her family away. She just removed the complication of two men fighting over her; she couldn't add a new one of her family noticing she disappeared too often. It also didn't help she had chosen the man her mother wasn't too pleased with. Now she would have to continue her courtship with Zander under Maria's watchful eye; not exactly how she pictured it.

"We can send a letter to the household and to Isabelle's tutor to travel here with some more of our things. We have plenty to wear for an extra day or two." Maria handed Christiana a cup of steaming tea. "And you grew up having lessons at the palace, I'm sure Isabelle will be fine."

"Yes, but..." Christiana started to protest.

"Besides," Maria cut her off, "you were lucky enough spend summers here growing up. Let Isabelle have that same opportunity. Do you want to take that away from her?"

Her insides turned into a bundle of knots. "No, of course not. I would love for you to stay."

Isabelle cheered, wrapping her arms around Christiana. She tried her best not to spill her tea, patting her sister on the back with her free hand.

The conversation flowed again with the matter settled, everyone distracted by planning activities for their families to enjoy over the last three weeks of summer. Christiana could barely hear any of it, though she nodded along like she was as excited as everyone else. She already had plans for those weeks—plans she had no intention of sacrificing. Her pastries and tea felt like bland paste on her tongue as she tried to weave together different excuses she could use for the rest of her time here.

A knock at the door took everyone's attention; Jay opened it, and Natalia entered, panting as she walked over to Christiana. "I'm so sorry to interrupt, My Lady." She curtsied deeply to everyone in the room. "But this letter just arrived for you and the messenger said it was urgent."

Christiana dropped her plate on the table, taking the palm-sized envelope. "Thank you, Natalia." She gave her maid a slight nod before walking over to Zander's desk, using one of his letter openers to shear the seal free.

My Lady,

Please come to the cottage at once. There has been an emergency that can only be explained in person.

Your Humble Servant,

Sir Robert

Chapter Forty-Two

*C*HRISTIANA'S BREATH CAUGHT THE MINUTE SHE walked through the door. Every inch of the cottage was overturned, the furniture flipped and torn, her possessions strewn across the floor—some broken, some still intact. But none of that mattered; her vision tunneled in on the most important item in the room.

The Purgatory Poison that had taken her months to find, the perfect weapon against Julian, was shattered across the countertops, the half-crystalized liquid dripping off the sides.

"What..." Christiana grasped Robert's arm. Zander crowded next to her, mouth gaping as he took in the scene. "Robert, what happened?"

"I'm not sure, My Lady." Robert held her forearm tightly. "I came to check on the poison like you asked, and the place was already destroyed."

Christiana wandered forward, her arms limp as she took in the rest of the damage. Her table was flipped, her couch had a wide gash slashed through the cushions, and all her cabinets were open and rifled through.

"Did they take anything you notice?" Zander asked, brow furrowing as he lifted the table and chairs back into place.

"Some food." She noticed as she stood in the middle of the kitchen, peering into each open space. "A bag of pratas I kept here just in case..." Her heart dropped as she saw the far-left cabinet wide open, half of its contents strewn on the countertops. "Oh, no. No, no, no..." she climbed on the counters, desperately feeling around the top shelf, reaching as far back as possible. "Oh, thank goodness!" she gasped, her fingers tingling as they pulled out Zander's letter of intent. His eyes went wide when she handed it to him, the muscles in his forearms tense as he took it from her. "It would have been disastrous if they found this."

"Tell me about it." He muttered, fingers crinkling the page as he clutched it tight.

"Take it back to the palace with you."

Zander gave her a grim nod and shoved it in his pocket. "Good idea."

"It looks like just a common robbery." She turned her eyes to the ruined poison. "At least, I hope that's all it is."

"I think if anyone was on to us, they would have made themselves known by now," Robert said. "With what was taken, this looks like a hungry person looking for some food and money to loot."

"That doesn't even matter right now." Christiana shook her head. Everything in the cottage could be replaced, she didn't need to worry about that; but her insides tightened, the pit deep in her stomach hollowing out when she looked at her weeks of planning wasted. "The one plan I had is *gone*! What are we going to do now?"

Her feet tingled, numbness settling on her cheeks as she swayed. "What are we going to do?" she chanted, pacing around the creaking floor of the rampaged cottage.

"It's going to be all right." Zander stepped forward, motioning her to halt. But she couldn't, desperately scratching at the crawling skin of her arms, red lesions forming on her alabaster skin.

"No, Zander, it isn't. Everything we've been planning for is ruined!"

She couldn't slow her thoughts down; she couldn't slow anything down. Her heart raced, her body unravelling as she saw everything falling apart at her feet. She wanted control back, she wanted everything to go back to before the summer started.

"I can't do this. I can't do this. I can't do this." Pacing didn't alleviate the pressured weight on her chest. Her breathing sped up as she thought back on all the wasted time, weeks of planning the perfect way to get to the Chancellor, now pointless. Head spinning, she dropped to her knees in defeat.

"Christiana, calm down." Zander put his hands on her shoulders to help soothe her, but she didn't feel comforted at all. She pushed him off, and he pulled his hand away, wide-eyed.

"I can't calm down! I don't have time to calm down. This is an absolute disaster. I can't do this. I can't do this. I can't..." She dropped her head into her hands, shaking in utter defeat.

"My Lady, look at me." Robert knelt in front of her, forcing her hands off of her face to see him. "I want you to count backwards from ten. Count with me. Ten. Nine. Eight..."

"Se-se-seven..."

"Six..."

"Fi-five..."

"Four."

"Three." Her breathing slowed with each focused number she spoke, finally allowing her head to come back to equilibrium. "Two. One."

"Feeling better?" Robert asked.

"Yes, thank you." She rubbed her numb face with her hands, trying to massage some feeling back into her cheeks.

"Christiana..." Zander's voice came from behind her. "Did you...have a panic attack?"

Christiana's heart fell. She had wanted to hide this from him for as long as possible. She didn't want him to see the damage her father had done to her. The scars and bruising on her body were one thing; she could easily ignore those. But the damage he had done to her mind over the years was a burden she had worked hard to overcome. Although she had made many strides to control it, these fits still crept back into her life.

She took a deep breath and pulled herself up from the floor, turning to look at Zander. "Yes," she said, and his eyes softened as he reached for her hands. "I get them sometimes when I'm overwhelmed."

He pulled her close, his arms wrapping around her. She took in a deep breath, the scent of cedarwood surrounding her as she heard his heartbeat through his chest. A new wave of calm washed over her, her mind slowing as it focused on what was right in front of her. "I get it. I've had a few over the years too."

She looked up at his smiling face. He wanted to understand, he wanted to relate to her. But what was happening to her was more than just panic attacks. It was also her nightmares, her desperate need to be alone, and her inability to get out of bed some mornings. It was the anarchy of her mind revolting against her, feeding her dark thoughts and forcing her to overthink. It ran through her brain and buried itself into the deepest parts of her mind. It was more her than anything else.

"Then you understand." She couldn't tell him the truth, not yet.

He kissed her forehead. "I do. I'm here if you ever need to talk about it."

"I know." Her heart splintered as she turned around. Even when she chose a relationship because of the honesty between them, she still found herself keeping one of her darkest secrets.

Robert's eyes were filled with concern. He was one of two people who knew the truth of her episodes and the real reason they happened. Marek was the other, having discovered the issue during training one afternoon. He had taught her more than how to kill someone—he taught her how to take control of herself and her life. That was the only way she found relief from her symptoms: control.

She could see Robert's confusion spread across his face, not sure why she had chosen to lie. But the answer was simple; she wasn't ready to lose Zander. If he knew how truly broken she was by her father's abuse, he would never be able to look at her the same again. How could the Prince of this country even desire her, let alone think she was stable enough to become his partner and Queen? She couldn't lose him now, not after risking so much in choosing him.

Shaking her head at Robert, she took a deep breath. "I'm fine now, I promise."

"The summer is three weeks away from ending." Zander rubbed his chin, leaning against a wall. "If we don't do this before the Council reconvenes in a few weeks, we'll have even less of an opportunity."

"How?" Christiana moved on shaking legs over to the table. "It took me two months to even start on this plan! And with everything that happened last night..."

"What do you mean?" Zander knelt in front of her. "What happened?"

Christiana grimaced. "He threatened me."

"What do you mean, threatened you?" Zander seethed. His hands were balled into fists, chest rising and falling with rapid breaths.

She talked through the dance with him, trying to remember every word Julian spoke in his mocking tone. "And it was the way he threatened me that disturbed me the most. He said, 'I wouldn't want to see you suffer any more than you already have.'"

"Unbelievable," Zander muttered. "Any idea what he meant by it?"

She shook her head. "I've been thinking about it all day and the only idea I've come up with must be impossible."

"And what is that?"

Christiana hesitated, then admitted, "That he knows about my past and the relationship I had with my father."

Zander sat silently for a few minutes, rubbing his jawline. "But how would he have found out about that?"

"I'm not sure. I never told anyone growing up. I was too scared it would make everything worse. And my mother certainly didn't tell anyone." Her skin crawled thinking about the fear she once lived with. "That's not even what's important right now. What matters is I need a new plan, but I think this kill is out of my skillset."

"You're better than this, My Lady," Robert urged, shaking her shoulder. "Just breathe and think. What would your mentor say if you were giving up after one failed attempt?"

"He'd tell me there was a logical solution, I just wasn't looking in the right place for it." She tried to think back on the advice Marek gave to her over the years. "When you're out of your depth, try the impossible."

"What does that mean?" Zander asked.

"That if you can't conquer something, attempt something you never would before." Her fingers tapped against her lips as she forced her mind to push through the fog to think of the weaknesses she had learned about Julian. "Try to execute a move that pits your enemy's weaknesses against them."

"Any ideas?" Zander asked.

Looking up at him, she said, "Zander, I think you should go."

"What? Why?"

She sighed. This could be her last chance at getting Julian, and she wouldn't be able to properly think through this plan with Zander in the room. She needed to do this right. "Because I think Robert and I need to be the ones to figure this out."

"But I can help," Zander insisted.

"I know." She grasped his hands. "But before this courtship began, you trusted the Maiden to do this job. So please, let me do what you hired me for."

"All right." He sighed. "But please let me know if you need anything from me."

"I will." Taking his face in her hands, she bent him forward to place a delicate kiss on his lips.

"Please take care of her," Zander said to Robert.

"Always, Your Highness." He bowed to Zander, who nodded before disappearing through the front door. "So, any ideas?"

"Not really." She slumped lower into her chair, staring up at the bland ceiling. "I know I'll have to try and execute something out of my comfort zone, but I don't even know where to start."

The chair across from her scraped against the floor as Robert sat. "Start where you were planning to go next." He nudged her hand on the table, and she peeked over at him. "Pay a visit to Tobias this week. See if he knows anything that could help formulate a new plan."

Christiana sighed. "That's probably the most logical next step." Exhaustion overtook her, her limbs feeling boneless as she tried to clear the fog from her mind.

She couldn't give up. Eliza was relying on her; she was putting her hope in the Maiden. She would do whatever it took to help—even if it meant risking her own life.

Chapter Forty-Three

*C*HRISTIANA *NEEDED TO KEEP HER MIND* preoccupied, away from stress and overthinking her collapsing plans. Ultimately, there was nothing she could do until she paid a visit to Tobias. For several days, she occupied herself with whatever she could find, doing her best to keep her anxieties at bay.

That was how she found herself in Dorina and Isabelle's company, their bright smiles and effervescent personalities the perfect distraction as they played their next round of lawn bowling. Multiple courts were set up for the nobles to enjoy, laughter and clamor filling the air as people aimed for the tall pins.

"I knocked them all down for the first time!" Isabelle cheered, bouncing back to join Christiana and Dorina.

"Wonderful job, little one!" Christiana wrapped her arm around her sister. "You're a natural at this."

"I still don't believe she's never played." Dorina narrowed her eyes at Isabelle, a smirk playing on her lips as she tossed the magenta ball between her hands. "She's even beating you, Ana, and I remember you being pretty good at this game."

"Are you letting me win?" Isabelle crossed her arms, pouting up at her sister.

"No." Christiana playfully shoved her away, shaking her head. "I'm just out of practice. I haven't played since my last summer here."

She knew that wasn't the real reason; her mind was still foggy from the day before. Her fingers ached to get back to work, ready to figure out the next move on Julian. But her job took patience, something Marek had instilled deeply into her. She needed to lie in wait to make sure this went off perfectly so she wouldn't risk Eliza's life. But tension was already building in her shoulders, the ache burrowing deep. It would only worsen over the next few days. The anticipation of ambushing Tobias rested on her heavily.

"Oh no," Dorina whispered as the servants approached to offer them a glass of chilled citrus water.

Christiana pulled out of her darkened mind, turning to look at her friend. "What's wrong?"

"Um." Dorina bit her bottom lip. "I think Rowan is contemplating coming our way."

Christiana turned around and spotted him nearby, watching their game. Her heart sped up at the sight of him, her mind racing as she remembered their last encounter at the ball. She had been ready to talk to him then, but she wasn't sure she was ready to face him now.

Still, if he was ready, she owed him the chance.

She sighed, dropping her black ball. "Excuse me for a minute."

"You don't have to go, Ana." Dorina grabbed her arm, doe-eyes full of concern.

"I know, but he deserves better than this. He deserves answers."

With an encouraging smile, Dorina released her arm. Christiana's steps led her toward Rowan, his face flushed with heat.

"Hello," she said weakly, unsure of how to open what they both knew would be an awkward and heartbreaking conversation.

"I didn't want to interrupt you." He crossed his arms. "But I knew I would lose my nerve if I didn't approach you now."

"I'm glad you did." She rested against a stone bench nearby. "I know it must have been a shock."

"A shock? That's what you think this is to me?" His eyes wide, he gaped at her. Her spine tingled as she tried to keep their eyes locked, her body desperate to turn away.

"Well, no..."

"Try heartbreak. Utter embarrassment," he spat, his eyes flaming with each word. She clutched the side of the bench, the cool stone biting through her palms.

"I'm sorry." It sounded pathetic when the words left her mouth. She felt it deep in her soul, the sorrow over hurting someone she cared about, but she didn't know what else would make his pain go away.

"I don't want your apology." He shook his head. "I want to know what he did to make you so sure."

"Do you really want to hear this?" she asked, not sure how this could possibly help him.

"Yes. I won't believe this is happening otherwise." Body rigid, he stared down at her, refusing to sit in the empty spot beside her.

Christiana's head hung, her mind searching for the best words to describe the whirlwind her heart had faced over the past few weeks. "It wasn't something he specifically did, if that's what you're expecting. It was something deeper, a connection drawing me to him. And when it came time for me to make my decision, I realized happiness was more important than comfort."

"Was that all I was to you?" Eyes fluttering shut, he rubbed his forehead. "Comfort?"

"No, of course not." Her hands grasped at her dress, searching for something to keep her rooted. "But that's what I pictured when I thought of a future with you. And that wasn't the life I wanted anymore."

He shook his head. "I never wanted that, either. But I never thought that about you."

"I know."

"I held back my heart to make you comfortable." His eyes were glassy, his cheek twitching as he stared down at her. "And you broke it anyway."

She bit her lip, not sure if she should speak the next sentence. "It's killing me to hurt you, but I don't feel the same way."

"So that's it?"

"That's it." She finally looked up at him.

His chest rose, a deep breath pulled through his nose. "Thank you for your honesty, but I should leave."

"Rowan, please." She shot up when he turned away, trying to grab his arm, her fingers barely grazing his satin doublet before he yanked away, his back still to her.

"I'd like the necklace back."

"What?" Her hand fell to her side, her stomach dropping.

"It was a courtship proposal gift, which you have now denied. So, I would like it returned."

"Of course." Although she understood, it still hurt to give up something she had quickly come to cherish. "I'll have Natalia bring it over to you once I return to my apartment."

"Thank you, Marchioness." He grimaced, abandoning her beside the bench.

Her eyes followed him as he walked away, the burn of tears rimming her eyes. A piece of her was walking away with him, but she had to let it go. She needed to move on, to focus on the coming weeks and the dangers ahead. But though her focus was needed elsewhere, it didn't stop the dull ache in her chest as she walked back to join Dorina and Isabelle.

Chapter Forty-Four

*T*HE NEXT NIGHT, CHRISTIANA FOUND HERSELF restless, watching the moon join the darkening night. Her encounter with Rowan had shaken her even worse than she already was. She needed to find peace somewhere, to be with someone who could help her unload what weighed her mind. For once, she wanted to talk.

But this time she didn't sneak out the window or don her darkest outfit. No longer did she have to climb a tower to see Zander or be inconspicuous with their time together. She walked with her head high through the public corridors, even giving the guards a gentle smile when she entered the Royal Wing. Her feet were quick, finding the door she was eager to walk through.

"Well, this is a wonderful surprise." Zander grinned, opening the door wide and allowing her to pass the threshold. The room was still well-lit, the night young and plenty of time for them to be alone before it was deemed too improper for most.

She needed this. She needed him.

"I wanted to talk to you about something," she said, though he didn't seem to hear her as he rushed to her side. Wrapping her up in his arms, he gave her a deliciously-passionate kiss. "And what a wonderful surprise that was." She giggled against his lips. He continued his sensual exploration, planting kisses all along her jawline and face. "Zander, I do have to talk to you about something."

"Mmm." He sighed.

"Zander..." She laughed, trying to no avail to get her infatuated suitor's attention. "I want to talk. Typically, that involves your lips being apart from mine for a few minutes at least." Pushing his face away playfully, she smiled at his behavior.

He pouted. "I can't help it." With a final kiss on her forehead, he took a few steps back. "I'd do this to you all the time if I could."

"Zander."

"I'm kidding." He laughed, sitting down on his couch. Her wobbling legs followed him there. "What do you need to discuss, my dear?"

Christiana sighed deeply, shifting in his arms. "Rowan talked to me yesterday. He finally wanted answers."

"I heard." He sighed.

"I figured the gossip would find its way to you." Christiana nudged him. His arm wrapped around her shoulder, tugging her to his side. "I wanted to tell you sooner, but my family kept me preoccupied last night."

"Actually, he told me himself when I saw him in the halls this afternoon." His face grim, he stared into the dying fire flickering inside the dark stone fireplace. "I tried to control myself, but something...pulled me to try and get him to talk to me. I basically ambushed him in public."

"I'm assuming your conversation went about as well as mine." She had been so focused on her own anxieties and pain over Rowan, she didn't realize the loss Zander was mourning now. His best friend was no longer in his life. If she was splintered, Zander must be shattered.

"It wasn't good, I can say that."

Christiana rubbed circles on his knee. "You miss him."

"Every day," Zander massaged his temple with his free hand. "He barely even acknowledges me now. He treated me like a prince, not like..."

"A brother?" she finished for him. He gave her a slight nod, his face twisted in pain.

"He's the only person I've ever felt to be a true friend." His leg twitched, his eyes unable to hold focus anywhere. "Everyone else I always felt some kind of...ulterior motive from their friendship, because of my title. But never Rowan. He was always there for me."

Christiana's hands trembled. The loss of Rowan was written in every line creasing his brow as he stared into the firelight. It was because of her both these men were suffering; it was because of her they had lost their friendship. This was her fault and she had been too self-absorbed to notice.

"We had so many plans for the future," he whispered, looking down at her as the first tear escaped, staining his red cheek. She reached up, brushing it away. "He was going to be one of my council members. I had already asked him to be my best man at my wedding, even when I didn't have a woman in mind. We all knew it would be before my thirtieth birthday and there was no one else I wanted standing by my side."

"I'm so sorry, Zander." She cupped his cheek in her hand, a few tears slipping between the cracks of her fingers from his glassy blue eyes. "I'm so sorry for everything you lost because of me."

"But I gained something just as special." He smiled slightly, leaning down to place a warm kiss on her lips.

She stared at him when he pulled away, his face creased. She wanted to believe his words, but her chest still felt heavy, her feet twitching against the soft carpet. She had let this situation get out of hand, drawn it out unnecessarily and made these men suffer the consequences. It didn't sit right with her.

"Do you think I'm selfish?" she couldn't stop herself from asking. "For choosing you?" Her tingling legs pushed her up into pacing.

Zander straightened, shifting to lean his elbows on his legs as he watched her quick movements back and forth. "What makes you think that?"

"After everything Rowan's been through, you'd think I would try my best to put his feelings before my own." Her skin prickled, her steps faster and faster as she circled the table. "But I didn't even think of his feelings when I was trying to make my decision. All I could think about was how *I* felt in the situation and what *I* wanted. Do you wonder if I had chosen him, that you would still be friends? That he would be talking to you?"

"Ana, it's all right," Zander soothed, his hand catching hers and pulling her back down onto the couch. Her leg twitched as his arms wrapped around her. "First of all, I know Rowan has been through a lot in the past few years, but that doesn't negate everything you've been through as well. Don't you think after all your father put you through, you deserve a chance to make a decision about your own happiness?"

Her shoulders sagged. "Well, yes..."

"And second, do you think Rowan and I put your feelings before our own when we made the decision to tell you how we felt?"

"No." She shook her head, looking down at her fingers, the polished nails jagged where they picked at each other. "I suppose not."

"I'm sorry that this whole situation had to happen for us to be together, and that we both had to lose someone we cared about in the process. But what I'm not sorry for is admitting how I feel about you. I don't think I would have ever been comfortable in a marriage knowing I could have possibly been married to you instead."

"I don't regret it, either. I want you to know that what I feel for you is something I never thought was real." She shifted to face him, and his hand grazed her cheek. "It scared me for so many weeks, the sparks that would run through me. It was easy to convince myself it was just nerves from my secret being exposed. But when it didn't go away, I knew it was something different."

"You've never felt this for anyone else?"

"Never," she said firmly.

"Not even..."

"Never." She took his warm face in between her hands and pulled him close, sealing the word with a deep kiss. Her willingness to be so open with him, in such a physical way, was a pleasant surprise to her. She was exhilarated that every time Zander touched her, she craved more. She wondered if this feeling ever went away or if she would be blessed to carry it with her for the rest of their lives. She prayed for the latter.

"Neither have I," he whispered against her lips, their foreheads touching. "So, you understand why I didn't stay quiet?"

"Of course I do." She pulled away to cool down her flaming cheeks. "I just wish there was something we could do to help Rowan forgive us."

"Unfortunately, leaving him alone would probably be best." Her chest fell as she let his words sink in. "No matter how difficult it will be for us."

"You're right." Though she wanted to try and repair the damage, for both her and Zander, this wasn't about them. Rowan needed time to heal and the more she pushed, the longer it would take. She needed to apply Marek's lessons in patience to her personal life as well.

"Why don't we talk about something else?" Zander shook her shoulder, and a weary smile spread on her lips. "Any new progression on the case?"

Her stomach dropped. Why did he have to make this the new topic? "A bit. I at least have a way to try and move forward."

"Wonderful!" He shifted, his arm falling from around her so he could get a better view of her face. "What are you going to do next?"

She squirmed, fingers twisting into the ends of her hair as she tried to find the right words. She knew he was trying to be supportive, but he didn't seem to understand the dangers he was putting himself in if he knew the truth about her process. The less specifics he knew about her assassin life, the better for him. "Zander, I told you. You need to trust me to do this job."

"I know, and I do. I'm curious. Call it a vested interest in your life."

"Well..." She hesitated, her lips numb. "This isn't necessarily the best part of my life to be invested in. The information I carry is dangerous. You understand you can't know every detail about my cases, right?"

His face fell, confusion creasing against his eyes as he brushed his fingers through his hair. "Oh. I'm sorry...I assumed..."

"No, *I'm* sorry." She grasped his hand, pulling him back to her. "We should have talked about this sooner, I suppose we got distracted with the whole courtship complication. But I can't tell you the details about my work. It puts you, me, and my clients in danger."

"But why?" He shook his head. "You know I won't tell anyone."

"I know," she said. "I trust you wouldn't say anything. But my clients expect confidentiality for their own safety. Plus, if anyone were to betray me or find this out, your safety would be on the line too. The less you know, the better."

Silence fell for a few seconds. The air around her felt thick, her skin prickling. She didn't like this at all.

"I get it." He nodded at last, still frowning. "I won't ask any more questions."

"Thank you." She kissed his cheek lightly before he tucked her back under his arm. She curled up next to him, a place she usually found comfort. But this time, it was tainted by the awkward tension that settled around them.

Chapter Forty-Five

THE DAY FINALLY ARRIVED FOR CHRISTIANA TO interrogate Tobias and potentially move forward with her case. But she still struggled while it ticked by, each second feeling like an hour as she waited for dark so she could finally complete the task she had been anxious about all week.

She dismissed Natalia to do laundry for the afternoon so she could freely pull out her assassin arsenal, sitting on the floor of her bedroom with her false trunk top open and the contents of her secret life strewn across the floor. She had organized her poison satchel, disinfected all her darts, and checked her outfit for any spots that needed cleaning. She was working on her final and favorite task of sharpening her daggers, their blades sparkling in the window-filtered sunlight as they lay in a line before her.

The rhythmic swish of each blade against the whetstone lulled Christiana, washing her with the same calm and clarity as every moment she held them—a lesson Marek taught her at the beginning of her training, when she needed to escape from her life.

The dark night settled around Christiana as she made her way through the thick forest. Even though she had spent most of the summer stuck inside, she tried her best to sneak away after her father was asleep. If she stopped practicing her new skills, they would become too rusty for her to remember. She wasn't about to listen to another of Marek's lectures upon her return to Tagri; it wasn't worth the added headache and wasted time. Happily, their family apartment was located on the second floor of one of the palace wings, allowing an easy escape through her bedroom window like he taught her a few weeks before she left.

Finally, she came to the clearing of trees beyond the stables. Though she wished she could have gone deeper into the woods for practice, she wouldn't be able to get much done before having to turn around and head back. She hoped she was quiet enough not to wake the overnight stable hands.

She walked over to her tree of choice and quickly dusted off the target she had carved into it at the beginning of the summer. She had been practicing with her throwing daggers for months now and finally felt like she was improving; she didn't miss the tree nearly as much as she used to and could even hit the target's center more often than not. She didn't understand right away why Marek was so keen on teaching her how to use a weapon. After all, she planned on poisoning her father when the time was right. But learning to throw these daggers was more than trying to find a new way to kill; it was all about learning how to refocus her mind, to keep herself from getting distracted by her environment. It had become the perfect way to center herself after rough days or hard beatings, and the patience she was learning through these daggers would help her keep calm when it was finally time to kill her father.

Working hard for the next hour, she found her rhythm. She threw the five smuggled daggers with all her strength behind them, collected them, and tried again. Her muscles ached, begging for a break of sweet relief, but she wasn't about to waste her limited time. Her muscles would have plenty of time to rest tomorrow; since the bruising on her eyes and neck had not fully gone away yet, she was in store for another full day inside her apartment pretending to be sick with some ailment her father made up.

"Hurry up, men," a voice shouted in the distance. "We need to be on the road within twenty minutes or we'll be behind schedule."

Tightness flooded Christiana's body as she heard the clamoring of metal not far off. Sheathing her daggers, she quietly made her way through the trees toward the voices. No surprise it was coming from the stables, where a large group of soldiers prepared to ride out. But she was shocked to see Zander among them, fully outfitted in his black armor. Though she had witnessed him sparring a handful of times, she had never seen him completely outfitted as a fighter before.

He looked powerful with his entire sculpted build covered in protective metal. She couldn't help but stare at him as he mounted, ready to leave for the rest of the summer. She had forced herself to forget he was leaving today, sparing her own heart the pain of not saying goodbye. The warm fire reawakened from their encounter under their willow tree. Though it had scared her at first, now that he was leaving, she craved more.

His eyes wandered around his men, checking to make sure everyone was set to leave. Soon enough, as if they were drawn together, his eyes landed on Christiana, locking her into place. They stared each other down, a tether linking in their intense gaze. She had no idea what was going through his mind as he took her in, sweaty and dirty in the woods, dressed in a pair of plain pants and a dark tunic.

"Your Highness, are you ready?" a voice interjected, drawing Zander's gaze in the other direction. Finally released, she darted behind a large oak tree, sheltering from sight.

"Yes," the Prince finally answered. She peeked from behind the tree, watching him search the undergrowth for any sign of her. Finally giving up, he spurred his horse forward, leading the charge of soldiers away from the *palace.*

Christiana stood frozen, taking in deep, cleansing breaths to calm her fast-beating heart. It was pointless to try and get any more practice in for the night, so she gathered up the last of her strength and headed back to her family's rooms.

The knife hovered over the rock as she remembered that night. It had been equal parts calming and heartbreaking to watch Zander walk out of her life for the next five years. She had always regretted not finding a way to say goodbye.

She shook her head and finished on her last blade, the stone slick in her hand as the metal brushed against it. That didn't matter anymore. Zander was not only back in her life, but an important part of it, just as she was for him.

A loud knock interrupted her thoughts, her spine pulling straight. "One moment!" she yelled, gathering up her things and shoving them back into their hiding place. She smoothed her forest-green skirt, the fabric rumpled from sitting on the floor. With one quick check in her mirror, she hurried to the front door and pulled it open, greeted by her mother's smiling face on the other side.

"Hello, Mother." Smiling, she let Maria in.

"Hello, sweetheart." Maria gave her a quick kiss on the cheek. "I thought I would stop by and see what you were up to."

"Work, as usual." Christiana shrugged, sitting down at the dining table where a handful of her papers rested. She shuffled them around, trying to make a show as if this is what she was doing when Maria had knocked.

"Well, take a break!" She shook Christiana's shoulders from behind. "Isabelle and I are going to go riding in an hour and have dinner. Join us."

Christiana sighed. A part of her wanted to join them, but the stirring in her chest and the twitching of her fingers was a sign she needed to stay sharp for her evening activities. The entire case now rested on this one interview with Tobias; she needed to be absolutely perfect, no distractions around her the entire night. She couldn't risk going into it with the wrong mindset, potentially setting off one of her fits again. "I'm sorry, Mother." She turned in her seat to face her. "But I have a lot to catch up on from taking a few days off for the ball. I have to work late tonight."

Maria sat down at the table. "You already missed dinner with Madeleine and I last night."

"Because I was having dinner with Zander." Christiana leaned over, patting her mother's shoulder. "I'm sorry, I am, but I need to give him time too."

"Yes, yes, of course." Maria waved her hand, lips pursed. "But Isabelle and I stayed so we could spend time with you too."

"I know." She didn't have the energy to fight, not when she needed to keep her mind clear for her nighttime activities. "I can take tomorrow afternoon off to spend time with you two, but I need privacy tonight."

"Wonderful." Maria perked up in her chair like a revived flower. "You can even invite Zander to join us for lunch if you would like."

"He's busy tomorrow."

"Don't want him getting to know his potential in-laws, I see." Maria laughed, reaching across the table to pour herself a glass of chilled water.

"He has budget meetings most of the day." Christiana rolled her eyes, leaning back in her chair. "Besides, can you blame me? You weren't too keen on me choosing him in the first place."

"My dear, I told you, I'm happy for you."

"There's a difference between being happy for me and accepting my choice." Maria's cheek twitched, her fingers tracing the rim of her glass. "Do you accept him?"

Her eyes flitted around the room, refusing to catch Christiana's hard gaze. Her silence wasn't a surprise—she had expected it before she even asked the question. Still, pinpricks of sadness pierced her chest, the tingles spreading down her torso.

But it didn't matter to her.

"It's fine, Mother." Christiana broke the silence. "I haven't needed other people's approval for some time, I'm not about to start now."

"But that's just it, Christiana," Maria whispered. "Aren't you scared you'll be forced to find it on this path?"

She smoothed the front of her dress, pulling in a deep breath. "No, because only I can give people that power, and I have no intention of doing so."

She had faith in her words, in her resolve. But as her mother stood up to leave, threads of doubt sewed into the depths of her mind, leaving her wondering if her mother's words might one day become the truth.

Chapter Forty-Six

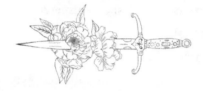

CHRISTIANA SLIPPED THROUGH A WINDOW INTO THE servants' hallways. The hour was late; most of the palace had gone to bed and the remaining were too drunk to care about the time. The only person who would be coherently awake right now was Tobias, Julian's personal secretary.

The Chancellor's office was only a few doors down from his personal apartments, making it easy for him to access it anytime during the day while also keeping a close eye on his wife. Christiana pushed the door open and peeked inside. Tobias sat at his desk, head buried deep into the pile of papers littering the large area. His half-eaten dinner sat on a tray on the floor next to him, the decanter of wine and his glass still on his desk while he muttered under his breath about numbers and budgets not working properly.

Christiana slipped through the doorway, sticking to the shadows. Removing her dagger from her boot, she crept up behind him and yanked him backward by the collar, placing the steel gingerly against his exposed throat. He froze, sweat collecting on his brow as he stared down at the pointed weapon held against him.

"I wouldn't move around if I were you. You never know where the tip of this dagger would end up because you couldn't sit still," she taunted.

"What do you want?" Panic filled his voice and his shoulders shook. A smirk brushed against her veil; this was going to be easy.

"Answers to my questions would be preferable, and if you cooperate right away, I won't have to worry about hurting you. I'm not in the mood to make a mess of things tonight." She released him. He ran for the door, but not fast enough. Jumping over the desk, Christiana slammed him against the wall, finally bringing them face-to-face.

"That's better, isn't it?" she whispered, once again placing the dagger against his fleshy neck. "Now that we've gotten your failed escape out of the way, maybe you can help me."

"I'm nobody of importance," he stuttered, eyes wild. "Nothing about me or what I know could help you in any way. Please, *please* don't kill me."

"Why would I kill someone useful to me? Besides, I'm sure you're important. Why else would you be working for Chancellor Marlow?"

"I'm just his secretary." He shook his head violently, jowls vibrating at the sudden movement. "I mean nothing to him."

"That can't be true. What exactly do you do for him?"

"I help him draft letters and reports." The words spilled out of him. "I make sure his schedule and meetings are organized, and I help him organize any travel arrangements. That is all! I swear!"

It wouldn't be a difficult interrogation since this man rambled under duress. And lucky for her, he had convinced himself she was fishing for state information, so there was no need to conceal private information about the Chancellor's household.

"Hm." Christiana stared him down, brows pinched together. "Does he happen to be travelling anywhere interesting over the next few weeks?"

"N-no, not really. He leaves for a short two-day trip in two weeks, but that's it."

"You don't say?" Her interest piqued, but she remembered something Julian said during one of their encounters. "Will his wife be going with him by chance?"

"Eliza? Of course not! She can't, not when he..." He stared at her, blinking furiously.

"Not when he *what?*" She pressed the dagger a bit tighter against him, drawing a whimper from his mouth. She said a silent prayer that he wouldn't start to move; the dagger was dangerously close to hurting him, but she couldn't remove it now. The answers she needed were at the tip of her fingers.

"Why do you want to know about the Chancellor? He's a good man who does so much for this country."

"I thought we agreed that my questions were the important ones. Now answer." She shook him back to attention, her dagger pulling away slightly as to not bite his skin at the movement.

He gulped. "He's going to see his mistress."

Christiana bit her tongue, suppressing the growl in her throat. Every time she thought this man couldn't be more disgusting, she found a new secret that proved her wrong. The only consolation was that this might be an open opportunity to make a new plan work: when he was traveling back to the palace from his time away. "Tell me, Tobias." Her grip on his shoulder tightened. "Do many guards accompany him on these trips to see her?"

He shook his head violently. "N-n-no. Just two."

It made sense. If anyone found out he had a mistress, his reputation and career could be ruined, something he had openly bragged about multiple times. The less people who knew, the better. It wasn't the perfect situation, but two guards were the best she could hope for. If she took them out, she might have a chance of completing this job.

"Just one more question." She angled her dagger so the tip barely grazed his chin. "When will he be travelling back to the palace?"

"P-please..."

"Ah." Christiana wiggled her free finger in front of his face. "Answer me."

"Overnight," he whimpered. "He needs to be back on the second to last Tuesday of the month for Council meetings."

Christiana smirked. This was the moment. She would have the cover of darkness to aid in her attack along with the minimal guards. Satisfied, and finally feeling like she could forge a new plan, she released the terrified and sweaty man from the wall and put her dagger away. Still scared into submission, Tobias stood statue-like against the wall. "Well, Tobias, thank you for all of the information you provided tonight." She pulled a dart from her armband.

"No, please, I-I-I did everything you asked of me. I answered all of your questions. Please don't kill me." He raised his arms above his head and cowered against the wall.

"Oh, I know."

He paused, arms lowering as he trembled. "Then why are you going to kill me?"

"Who says I was going to kill you?" She dipped the dart into the vial, and Tobias whimpered again.

"Well, the poison dart..."

"Oh, I never said I wasn't going to poison you. Sleep well, Tobias."

She jammed her Amnesia-filled dart into the man's neck. After only a few seconds, he went limp, crumbling to the ground. Taking the decanter and glass from his work desk, Christiana placed the glass, side down, in his limp hand and spilled a small amount of wine around him.

She snuck behind the thick tapestry she entered the hallway from. She was proud of herself for figuring out the servants' hallways so easily.

The spaces were quiet, no one around this late at night. She kept herself close to the shadows but moved with speed in search of the right window for her escape.

Halfway there, she heard the distinct sound of muffled screams.

She wanted to ignore it so badly, but her conscience goaded her to investigate. With a huff, she changed direction, following the noises until she was right around the corner from the scuffle.

"Why must you always complicate this with your screaming?" a broad-shouldered man whispered to a scared girl cowering before him. He was obviously a guard or soldier of some kind, exuding an air of self-importance in his masculinity, dressed in a plain pair of black leather pants and a black tunic with only one long dagger as a means of protection—signaling he was not on duty that night. Tears streamed down the poor girl's face as she sobbed for help. He had one of his strong arms across her chest, pinning her against the cold wall of the hallway with his hand over her mouth. The other roamed around the rest of her body, going wherever he pleased.

"Come on, beautiful, you may struggle, but I always show you a good time. There's no need for tears when I am about to bring us both pleasure, so be a good girl and enjoy what I'm about to do for you."

Christiana's stomach churned, her nose pulling in deep breaths. She shouldn't engage—she knew the rules of assassins, and trying to save this girl would break them. It wasn't a hired job; she needed to walk away. Her mind screamed Marek's teachings over and over. But her fingertips tingled, brushing against the holsters of her throwing knives. They were in perfect reach, she could end this quickly...all it would take was one well-aimed blow to the back.

The muffled screams brought Christiana back to focus, the girl red-faced while the man's hand moved under her skirt. She was traumatized enough already, Christiana wasn't about to compound that by killing the guard right in front of her or risk hurting her in the process. She had to draw him away first, then deliver the killing blow.

She drew one of her knives, poised to throw, then hesitated at the thought of Eliza. If she made this look like an assassination, or worse, a murder, the whole palace would go on high alert. She risked her case and Eliza's life if she did anything rash. Her mind raced, trying to find a solution. She drowned out the noises in front of her and thought for a moment, a spark igniting when she realized the perfect plan.

She took a few extra seconds to prepare her weapons; then, with one more cleansing breath, she threw the knife, steel whizzing through the air and grazing the back of the guard's exposed neck.

"What the fuck was that?" he growled, turning to frantically search the area. He released his victim, but she stayed cowering against the wall.

"Let her go." Christiana stepped into view but kept her distance, her hands close to her knives just in case.

"Who the hell are you?" the man slurred, staggering a few paces toward Christiana. Her feet tingled, waiting for the perfect moment.

"Wouldn't you like to know," she taunted, taking a few steps backwards.

"Oh, I certainly would." He broke into a drunken charge, and she turned and ran around a corner, out of sight from the victim. He followed her, setting her heart racing as her rash plan unfolded. She made sure to keep her pace quick enough to keep a good distance between them but not fast enough that he would lose her in the darkness. She saw the turn up ahead, the exact spot she needed to reach. Only a few more seconds and then this would be over.

A glance showed her pursuer gaining on her, his face twisted in a mixture of rage and desire, his grunts echoing after her as she turned the last corner. She stopped by another window, her shaking fingers rushing to open it. The summer air blew in, bright moonlight filtering through as she turned her back against the wall right next to it. She pulled her loaded blowpipe from her belt, clutching it to her chest as his steps approached the corner.

"There you are." He grunted, eyes wild as he closed in. She counted down, adrenaline coursing through her when he took his last step. Her lungs pushed all her air through the blowpipe, the dart sailing through the air to hit him directly in the pectoral.

He stopped, staring at the projectile sticking out from his chest and swaying as he tried to process what it was. She didn't hesitate, charging at him with all her strength and slamming him against the wall where she pinned him with her entire body and muzzled him with her hands. His eyes went wide as the poison began to activate in his bloodstream; his screams pressed against her palms, agony writhing on his face and eyes bulging from his head. His pulse stuttered as the Midnight poison reached his heart and slammed the heart attack through his system.

After a few more seconds, he slumped against her, his head resting on her shoulder. She wrapped her arms around his waist, silently thanking Robert for forcing her to do push-ups for the past few weeks; the new strength helped her close the gap to the open window. She let out a sigh of relief as she propped the guard's dead weight on the window ledge and let him go, his body falling back. Her stomach settled when she watched his head collide with the hard ground below. She stood there for a fleeting moment, giving the horrid man one last glance while his head wound bled onto the grass. She left the window open and returned to the place she found him. She needed to be quick and escape out another window before someone found her; she had been in the halls too long as it was.

She found the dark hallway, but stopped abruptly when she saw the young lady still against the wall. Her tattered skirts hung around her as she clutched Christiana's knife to her chest, lovely face turned toward her approach. "Did you...did you kill him?"

"Yes." Christiana moved forward slowly, reaching to take the weapon from her shaking hands.

"Thank you." The girl broke into tears.

"No thanks needed." Christiana turned to disappear.

"I can't believe he's finally dead."

Christiana's mind raced as she slowly turned back around. "How long has this been going on?"

"With me?" She crossed her arms, rubbing her biceps. "About four months, but I know of at least two other girls who have dealt with him over the years. He's been attacking the servants for a while now."

"Who was he?"

"His name was Damian. He was one of Chancellor Marlow's private guards."

Christiana felt the blood drain from her face. "Why were you out so late? How did he catch you out in the hallway?"

"Because the Chancellor summoned me. I knew what was going to happen...that's how it always happens." She stared down at the floor, rocking back and forth. "But it's not like I can disobey the King's Chancellor. My whole family could lose our positions here in the palace, and we can't afford for that to happen."

Christiana's fists balled at her side. "Are you trying to tell me the Chancellor knew this man was going to attack you tonight?"

"Yes."

"That's disgusting." Christiana snarled, her lips curled around her teeth. "What's your name?"

"Beatrice." She looked up to Christiana, eyes still wet from tears.

"Go home, Beatrice." Her heart softened for the girl. "Sleep easy and well and know that the man who used to hurt you can never hurt you again."

"Thank you." She ran down the corridor.

Christiana couldn't linger any longer or she risked getting caught. After a few more breaths to stop her shaking hands, she continued her journey back to her room.

Chapter Forty-Seven

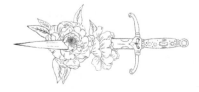

*C*HRISTIANA'S HEART LEAPED AS SHE KNOCKED ON Zander's door. She was still shaken up by the attack on the guard the previous night, and receiving Zander's letter was a welcomed excitement to pull her spirits up. Not only that, but since they would be in private, it was the best time to explain what happened. She had heard that the body was found, and she wanted to make sure Zander understood the truth. She also hoped he would consider tightening security in the servants' halls.

He answered her knock immediately, but instead of his usual effervescent smile, a thin line hung across his face. Christiana's stomach knotted. "Is this a romantic visit or a work one?" She tried to lighten the mood as she entered, her lips eager to touch his. "I can never tell anymore."

He didn't say anything, his gaze absent as he sat at his desk.

"Zander?" She stopped in front of the desk, hands resting on the smooth wooden surface. "Are you all right?"

"I had to investigate the death of a guard today." He finally looked up at her. "One of Julian's guards died of a heart attack. He lost his footing and fell through a window when it happened; at least that's what the court physician deduced."

She nodded. "I was going to talk to you about this tonight."

"Was it you? Were you...working last night?"

"Yes, I was." She walked around the desk, his eyes following her when she perched on the edge next to his chair. "Things got...complicated while I was investigating."

"Did you make an attempt on Julian and he got in the way?"

Her heart started to pound. "Well, no, but..." She searched for the right words to explain everything that happened with that terrible guard. Once he knew the truth, he would understand.

"Did he attack you?"

"Zander..."

"I'm just trying to find out what happened."

"Let me..." She reached out for his hand, to comfort him and explain everything, but he flinched away, shoulders tensing as he leaned in the opposite direction. Her heart dropped. "Are you...scared of me?"

He blinked rapidly. "What?"

"You are, aren't you?" She jumped off the desk, backing away with a hand at her chest. This had been her worst fear, the reason her head screamed at her for weeks.

"Ana, no. Stop." Zander stood, moving slowly to close the gap between them. "Just tell me what happened."

She held her hand up, stopping him while she leaned against a wall. "I went out last night to find information, something that would help me formulate a new plan. But as I was walking through the servants' halls to get back to my apartment, I came across him."

"And?" Zander's eyes narrowed.

"And I found him trying to rape a young woman." His expression mixed with revulsion and dread. "And apparently Julian helped him do it by calling the servant."

Zander's eyes widened. "Excuse me?"

"That's what the servant girl told me." The truth was out, and as expected he was horrified, but her mind still spun and the pain in her stomach threatened to overtake her body. The moment kept repeating in her mind—his body cringing at the idea of her touch. Bile crept up her throat.

His head fell, shaking slowly. "I'm sorry. I thought that horrid man couldn't get any worse. No wonder you stepped in."

"I needed to help her." Christiana felt the cracks already forming in her heart; she wanted to leave.

Zander leaned against the edge of his desk, crossing his arms as he stared at her. "See? This is why I wanted to know about what you were doing. If things like this are going to happen in the palace, I need to be made aware."

"I didn't plan to kill him, Zander!" Her voice rose an octave, fists balling into the folds of her dress.

"But if you had told me what your plans were last night, I could have..."

"Could have what?"

"I don't know!" He threw his arms in the air, cheeks blotched as the tension rose. "I could have done something! Anything to keep you safe!"

"But I don't put my safety first when I take these jobs." She began to pace around the open common area. "My client's safety is what's most important and I will do what I must to ensure it."

"That makes absolutely no sense!" He stepped toward her. "If you put yourself in danger, you might not come back!"

"And if I don't risk myself, my clients could die!" She faced him again, hands braced against the back of the couch. "I don't enjoy it, Zander, but it's a necessary evil to save people from getting hurt.

Especially in a kingdom where they are treated as the problem and not the victim."

"Now what is that supposed to mean?"

"Don't be naive. You've said it yourself; your father has been so focused on keeping peace between the borders he refuses to believe there are actual problems within his own country. Do you realize how many people try to hire me? Pleading with me to take the job even though they can't afford to pay me? I'm sure you think they are few and far between, but sometimes I am so overtaken by requests, I have to pay other assassins to take the jobs for me."

His face was frozen, mouth gaping. "That can't be true."

"We have a problem in this country, Zander." The words spilled out like a well that would never dry up. "We let people believe they can get away with anything if they have the power. My father believed it and Julian certainly does as well. It will never change unless our leaders prove they are willing to protect everyone, even the weak."

"I don't even know what to say." His eyes were downcast, his face slack.

"Of course you don't! Because you've never felt the need to think about it." She had no idea what had come over her, but she couldn't stop now. He needed to see the truth boiling over inside her. "You told me you want to listen to your people and help them when you become the King. But have you even begun to research all the problems they have?"

"Is that how you felt with Francis?"

"Yes. I was one of the lucky few who had the means to hire someone to help. Sadly, not everyone is so lucky."

He hesitated, the crackling of the fire filling the strained silence. "I am so sorry that you and so many of my people have had to endure all of this. I promise that we will help them when we have the power."

"But?" She narrowed her eyes, the pressure building in her chest as she waited for the rest of his thought.

"But as long as you continue taking these jobs, I have to know what your plans are." His words came out calm, like he was asking something simple from her.

The muscles in her neck tensed, her jaw clenching. "I already told you, I can't do that. And that is still true."

"Christiana, I cannot let you go out into our country risking your life if you aren't going to share with me what you are up to!" he exclaimed, his nostrils flaring. "I need to know you're safe! I need to know you're going to come back to me alive!"

"First off, *let me?*" Her blood boiled, tingles running up her limbs. "Second, I am a *trained* fighter with years of practice. I can take care of myself and you need to trust me!"

"I do trust you!"

"Obviously not, if you want me to tell you every detail about my assassin life!" Her fingers dug into the couch, the soft velvet scrunching between her nails. "If you were going into battle, I would trust in the skills you have been practicing for years! Why can't you do the same with me?"

"That's different." He pointed at her. "I had to learn for military purposes, so I can lead."

"And I learned for survival. You learned for work, I learned to save my own life!"

They stared at each other for several moments, the tension pushing them further and further apart. Christiana's skin crawled as if something burrowed underneath, one of her fits on the precipice of exploding. She needed to get out *now*, her mind was shutting down, her thoughts tainted by the darkness she tries desperately to suppress. It whispered to her, telling her that he was going to leave her. That this courtship was a mistake and she should leave him first. She desperately tried not to listen, but she couldn't think clearly, everything blurring around her.

The room spun as she walked towards the door. "I can't keep

arguing with you. I need time to think."

"Christiana, you can't leave!" He gripped her arm.

"I need time to think." She pulled her arm from his grasp and backed up until she hit the door, ripping it open and escaping down the hall.

Chapter Forty-Eight

THE WALK BACK TO HER APARTMENT WAS NERVE wracking. She couldn't get her body to stop vibrating, black clouds rolling through her mind, a thunderstorm of gloom making every inch of her ache for relief. She needed solitude to calm the intense frenzy; but she stopped in her tracks the moment she opened the door, every muscle tense at the sight of her mother and sister sipping tea at her dining table.

"What are you doing here?" She fought to keep her face calm and words warm as she shut the door. "Where is Natalia?"

"She let us in so we could wait for you!" Isabelle jumped from her seat, hurrying to wrap her arms around Christiana. She forced herself not to shove Isabelle off, though her touch burned like freshly-melted candle wax on her skin. She didn't want to be touched or loved; she didn't want to talk or be consoled. She wanted to be alone to keep herself from falling apart.

She pulled in deep breaths, the wave of cool air stinging her nostrils as she placed her hands on Isabelle's shoulders to separate them. "That's sweet of you two," she said as she moved forward, her mother's eyes following her, "but I'm tired and want to be left alone."

"Are you all right, sweetheart?" Maria pulled herself up in her chair. Christiana stopped to stare at her, fingers curling around the back of one of the carved dining chairs. "You look flushed."

"I'm fine, Mother." She kept her voice level, forcing the rumbling in her chest to stay down. She couldn't let Maria know she was fighting with Zander after the words they exchanged yesterday. "I had a stressful day and could use some time alone."

"But Ana..." Isabelle stepped forward, grazing Christiana's hand.

She ripped her hand away. "I said leave me alone!" Rage blackened her vision for a brief second. She despised this part of her, the outbursts that she could never control, striking suddenly and leaving her filled with shame. She didn't ask for this, but she was cursed to live with it.

She looked at her family, chest rising heavily as she took in their pained expressions, a mix of confusion and terror. "I'm sorry..." She reached out, but Maria strode to the door, her fingers twisting around her lace-trimmed handkerchief.

"No, we pushed in and that was rude of us," she said. "Come, Isabelle, we'll see your sister another time."

"All right," Isabelle whispered, her lip quivering.

"Belle, wait..." Christiana stepped toward her, but Isabelle was already at the door, neither of them looking back as they let themselves out.

Christiana's throat burned as she screamed into the empty room, eyes stinging with tears. She clutched her head in her hands, weaving her fingers through her hair as she shook it, trying to make sense of how everything had spiraled out of control. Her body pulsed as she stumbled into her bedroom and slammed the door behind her, rattling the wooden frame.

She couldn't calm down. She tried all her tricks: pulling in deep breaths, holding her hand to her heart, even punching a pillow a few times. But nothing worked; her body wanted to be in constant motion. She tried to distract herself, finding anything besides her fight with Zander and her family to dwell on. But her mind spiraled, her sister's anguished look reminding her of the last time she saw her sister in that much pain.

She heard muffled voices coming from her sister's room as she walked toward her own. It was obvious one voice belonged to her father, an immediate cause for concern. Practicing some of her new skills, she slowly opened the door to the drawing room adjacent to Isabelle's bedroom and grabbed a carved wooden chair from one of the tables, dragging it over to the adjoining wall. Standing on it, she cautiously opened a golden vent hidden in the upper corner, added in right after Isabelle was born. It was a peephole of sorts and allowed their nannies and governesses to keep an eye on them when they were alone in their rooms. Now, it was the perfect way to make sure her little sister was safe.

"Do you understand what you have done, Isabelle?" Francis asked his younger daughter.

"I'm sorry, Father. I was trying to give you a present," she whimpered. Through the slats of the vent, Christiana could see Isabelle standing at the edge of her bed, staring at her shoes, unable to look their father in the eye. Francis's back was turned, so Christiana was only able to see how upset her sister was.

"You have ruined multiple important documents I need to send to the King in only one week!" His voice was soft, but each syllable laced with anger. "Why would you bring wet and muddy flowers into the house?"

"I wanted to give you something pretty for your office!" She was only eight years old. In her little mind, it was all so simple.

Francis stopped pacing, looking down at Isabelle. "It's time for you to learn some valuable lessons, Isabelle."

"Like what?" She sniffled.

"Look at me." When she did, he swiftly raised his hand and slapped her across the face, knocking her into the bed behind her. Christiana clapped her hand over her mouth to stop herself from screaming, heat crawling up her face.

"Daddy, what are you doing?" Isabelle sobbed.

"Teaching you that all actions have consequences, young lady." He grabbed her by the collar of her nightgown and lifted her back to her feet. Trembling, she stood there and waited for what was coming next.

He backhanded her, the force once again sending her down onto the plush mattress behind her. At the fear in her sister's eyes, it took all Christiana's power not to storm into that room and take her father's life right there.

"Now." Francis composed himself. "It's time for you to go to bed and think about what you have done. Goodnight Isabelle."

Christiana shifted her focus to the sounds in the hallway, listening to her father's retreating steps. Once she was certain he had left, she quietly knocked on Isabelle's door. After waiting a few seconds with no response, she quietly entered. Poor Isabelle was lying on her bed, face buried in a pillow to drown out the soft sounds of her weeping.

"It's all right, Belle, I'm here," Christiana whispered, sitting next to Isabelle on the bed. She stroked her sister's back in hopes it would calm her down.

"I don't know what happened. Daddy was so mad. Why was he so mad?" Isabelle spoke between tears.

Christiana leaned her cheek against the top of Isabelle's head. "I wish I had an answer, Isabelle, but I don't. He was angry."

"But hitting is mean. Why would Daddy want to be mean to us?"

"I don't know."

"Has he ever hit you?" Isabelle asked, her large eyes bearing into Christiana like daggers, trying to hold on to some sliver of hope that their *father wasn't the monster he revealed himself to be. The fear and pain that honesty would inflict on her sister was something no eight-year-old should have to endure; but lying felt like betrayal, as if she would break the bond between them. There was only one thing she could do to help Isabelle have a normal life.*

She slowly nodded. "Yes, Isabelle he's hurt me too."

"Oh Ana," she wailed. "Why does Daddy hate us?"

"I wish I knew." Christiana shifted Isabelle out of her arms to lie down on the bed. "Wait here, Belle. I'll be right back."

"Where are you going?" She clung to her sister's torso.

"I'm going to get something to help you relax. I'll be right back, I promise."

"Fine." She sniffled, letting Christiana go.

Christiana tiptoed to her own room. Shutting the door softly behind her, she headed straight for the trunk at the foot of her bed. With a deep breath, she opened it up and broke into the false top she had carved a few weeks ago and pulled out its only contents: a small wooden box.

Marek had finally convinced her to keep an arsenal of poison with her at all times, but she couldn't believe she needed to pull it out of hiding so soon. The colorful vials swirled from the movement like tiny hurricanes. She took out the milky white one and a dart to go along with it. Dread filled her stomach at the thought of poisoning her sister, but it was the only way to keep her innocence intact.

Dipping the dart, Christiana made sure it was well-coated before storing the wooden box back in its hiding space. She concealed the dart between her nightgown and dress robe, grabbed a doll off the windowsill, and quietly made her way back to her sister.

"I thought Miss Lulu could keep you company while you sleep tonight, to help you feel protected." Isabelle had always loved this doll, but Christiana was fairly protective of it. It was the first gift she ever remembered getting from her mother and father; it reminded her of her

innocence, a time when her father would smile and twirl her around in his arms. She clung to that doll so many sleepless nights while she tried to remind herself that her father did love her, that he didn't mean to hurt her, that it was her fault anyway and she deserved the punishment.

This doll represented all the pain, suffering, and lies she had been wrapped in for too many years. It was time to let it all go.

"I used to sleep with Lulu when I felt scared. She has the ability to bring courage to those who are too scared to fall asleep."

"Really?" sniffled Isabelle.

Christiana sat down next to her sister and handed her the doll. "Really. All you have to do is hug her tight and she'll handle the rest."

Silent tears slid down Isabelle's face as she tucked the doll under her chin. Christiana rocked her back and forth and stroked her glossy blonde hair. Taking a deep breath, she removed the dart from her sleeve and pricked Isabelle in the back of the neck.

"Ow," Isabelle yelped. "What was that?"

"Shhhh, it's all right, Belle. It's medicine that will help."

"I'm so sleepy," she whined.

"I know. Just go to sleep, you'll feel better in the morning." Returning the Amnesia dart to her sleeve, she rose and tucked her sister into bed. The poison had worked quickly on Isabelle, pushing her into a deep, dreamless slumber. She would never remember that their father had abused her. If any soreness or bruising appeared, hopefully she would just assume it was from playing around the grounds.

Placing one final kiss on her sister's forehead, Christiana slipped out.

As she stored the dart back in its box, she examined the black vial inside. She had concocted this mixture a few months ago, putting her poison lessons to the test to try and devise the right one to use on her father. She's combined wolfsbane and belladonna, two toxic plants to create one deadly poison; she had no idea what it would do since she had yet to test it on anyone, but that didn't matter. Whatever its effect, this poison had been made custom for Francis, and nothing was going to stop Christiana from using it.

Grabbing a fresh sheet of parchment and quill, she wrote a letter she had been waiting to write for a year.

My faithful tutor,

It is finally time to show my Father everything you have taught me. I will complete my task by week's end. Keep me in your thoughts during this difficult time. I will return to you soon with many stories to share.

Sincerely,

Your Dearest Maiden

Chapter Forty-Nine

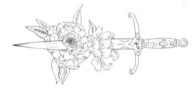

*I*T WAS DIFFICULT TO PEEL HERSELF OUT OF BED the next day. She had finally exhausted her body, collapsing into bed and resting for a few dreamless hours, then spent the morning hiding in her room before grudgingly sneaking out to the stables and taking Willow to her cottage. She had been so upset the night before, she forgot to send along a letter cancelling her latest training session with Robert.

"Stop leaving your chest open!" he barked over the clash of their sparring, the hot sun beating down on their backs. "Hold your weapon with more tension! You aren't giving it all your strength!"

"Yes, I am!" she screamed back at him, not in the mood to be taught something new.

He gave a sharp blow to her sword, sending it flying from her hands, "If I can disarm you that easily, you aren't holding it with enough strength. Your muscles were barely contracting."

"I'm tired." She slumped, the weight of exhaustion resting on her shoulders, her mind fuzzy as her vision tunneled.

"Pick up your blade." He pointed to her lost sword.

"No, I'm done for the day."

"It's only been twenty minutes and we practice the sword for an hour before we do our hour of strength training." He rattled off the training schedule they had followed all summer like she had forgotten.

"I don't care. I'm too tired today and I want to stop." She turned her back on him, striding to the edge of the ring.

Robert smacked the back of her knees with his sword. "Pick up your blade."

"Robert!" She whipped around to face him, his cold gaze daring her to disobey him. A shock ran through her as she finally saw the power of the soldier before her; he had warned her at the beginning of the summer that he would treat her differently in the ring, and he was holding true to his promise today.

She scooped up her sword, palms sweaty from holding it for the last twenty minutes. With a roll of her eyes and a nod of her head, he charged her. He had obviously been holding back for weeks, his well-toned arms bursting with veins as he slammed his sword toward hers. She struggled to keep up, her mind racing but her body one step behind him. She was barely able to keep up with his movements; it only took a handful of seconds before her sword flew from her hand again, but he didn't stop there. His free hand grabbed her wrist and yanked her to his chest; he threw his own blade to the ground, trapping her arms behind her back.

She struggled, the back of her shoulders crashing into his broad chest, "Robert, let me go!"

"Not until you tell me what's wrong!" His grip held firm, his words raspy.

"I told you, I'm tired!" She didn't want to talk about last night. She didn't want to remember or find her mind wandering back to how she felt. She wanted to ignore it.

But Robert persisted. "I know you're lying. Something is wrong and you need to talk about it."

"I had one of my..." her voice trailed off, struggles dissipating as she relaxed under Robert's grip. "*Attacks* last night."

He let go of one of her hands and turned her around to face him, his face no longer that of a warrior but of the friend she loved. He gripped her shoulder, his brown eyes staring deep into hers. "Are you all right?"

She shook her head. "And I didn't sleep because of it."

He pulled her to their hay bales and pushed her to sit down, handing over her waterskin. She took a few large sips while he crouched in front of her. "How did it happen?"

"I had a fight with Zander last night when he found out I killed one of Julian's guards." She wiped sweat from her stinging eyes. "And to make it worse, my mother and sister came to my room and I lost my temper with them too."

"Did you resolve either of those arguments?"

"No." She shook her head, the sweaty ends of her ponytail swishing against her neck. "I walked out on Zander when I felt the fit coming on and when my family left, I didn't stop them."

"No wonder your muscles are so overworked." Robert chuckled, taking her hand in his and rubbing her palm with his thumbs, breaking the strained tension buried in her muscles.

"I need to apologize to my family," Christiana mumbled, the rhythmic push against her palm helping her focus. "They didn't deserve my anger last night."

"And Zander?"

She sighed. "I don't know what to do. He pushed me to tell him about the guard and got upset that I don't want to tell him every detail about my cases."

"Why would he even want to know the details?" Robert's brow creased.

"To know that I'm safe, apparently." Christiana shrugged her heavy shoulders. "But I had to make it worse by bringing up Viri and its abuse issues and how I put my clients' safety before my own. I don't know what came over me, the words just started spilling out."

"Hm." Robert released her hand, leaning back. "Can you isolate your catalyst?"

"Yes." The more she thought about it, the more miniscule she realized it was. "He flinched when I reached out to him, like he was scared of my touch. Just seeing even a whisper of fear on his face made my heart...splinter. My mind started feeding me such dark thoughts and all I wanted..."

"Was to put your guard up and run away?"

She rubbed her neck. "Yes."

"Look, it sounds like you both said things that weren't the best." Robert took another sip of his water. "But the only way to resolve it is to talk and figure out a solution."

"I know." She groaned. She hated unknown confrontation, especially when the weapon of choice was words.

"My advice?" He nudged her shoulder. "Since you were the one to run away, maybe you should be the one to approach him next."

"You're right." She sighed.

"Maybe you should also consider telling him the truth about your episodes." He rubbed her back. "The real cause behind them."

"No. I'm not ready."

His eyes narrowed. "Christiana, you know it's not a bad thing. Your condition isn't your fault."

"Technically, it's a disorder," she mumbled, although the words were not helping. "But my fault or not, it's an unstable part of me. If he found out that I have..."

"You can say the words," Robert whispered when she hesitated. "You shouldn't be scared of them."

"If he knows that I have Battled Brain," she said, the words shook against her lips, "I'm scared he'll never look at me the same again."

It was the final gift her treacherous father bestowed on her, even after his death—a disorder that swirled inside of her, hidden in the darkest corners of her mind. Marek had been the one to discover it, to notice the warning signs during their training five years ago. He explained that not only had her body been scarred, but her brain as well; and just like the scars that marred her back, the scars on her mind would never go away. They showed themselves in her fits of anxiety, angry outbursts, and scream-filled nightmares along with a myriad of smaller symptoms. But Marek had shown her coping mechanisms to help her take control of herself and life.

Robert had learned a year ago when she told him the truth of who she was. She hadn't wanted to seem weak in front of her employee, but the pressure in her chest had built up too far until she couldn't keep the attack at bay. Her mask had strangled her and the hood buried her in its depth. She had no other choice, it felt like, than to rip them off in front of him. He had recognized her quickly, but that didn't stop him from running to her side and helping her calm the attack down. He had seen it many times before in fellow soldiers, enabling him to help her quicker than she ever thought possible. Ever since, theirs had been one of the most honest relationships in Christiana's life.

"I'm not ready to tell him. Not yet." She swallowed a lump in her throat. Zander had always praised her for her strength, a strength she built herself and was proud of. She never doubted it—it was an essential part of who she was—but her Battled Brain also was, and it challenged that strength every day. She couldn't bear to think how he would look at her when he learned the kind of weakness she truly fought within herself.

"If you're sure..." Robert's voice trailed off in question.

"How about we make a deal." She looked up at him, desperate to change the subject. "We skip the rest of sword training, but I do an hour and a half of strength training. My mind is too fogged to focus on more than one task."

Robert hung his head for a moment before lifting it back up, his eyes glimmering. "Very well."

***

After taking a nice long bath to scrub off the hot sweat and dirt from training, Christiana walked through the gardens while the sun was setting, her dark navy silk dress billowing in the light twilight breeze. She had sent Natalia to find out where Zander was while she bathed; when she said he was spending the evening in the gardens, a smile had crept across Christiana's face. She hoped he was in their favorite spot—the willow tree.

She knew exactly what she had to do to make this better. She had let her doubts and her troubled head get the best of her last night, overtaking her rational side; he wasn't scared of her, not in his heart at least. And that was what mattered to her. He was trying and he wanted to support her through this. She couldn't fault him for such a typical reaction to hearing someone admit they took another life.

She internally chastised herself for blowing such a fight out of proportion. She should have let him talk, let him explain why he flinched. Maybe she wouldn't have become so...

Christiana let out a sigh as she walked down the path, whispers of lavender and blood red filling the sky while the sun sank below the horizon. Her eyes wandered around the open space, over a handful of paired people enjoying the outdoors before dinner. Pebbles ground under her shoes on the way to the back of the garden, determined to find Zander—until she spotted him sitting on a bench a few feet ahead, and he wasn't alone.

Her heart sank at the sight of his relaxed smile while he looked down at Elaine's lovely face—the woman his parents wanted him to court. Her head was tilted, her musical giggles ringing through the garden.

Christiana couldn't hear what they were saying, frozen in her spot while she stared at them.

He seemed so relaxed with Elaine, at peace with his night—something Christiana might never be able to give him.

His eyes flickered up, catching hers and snapping her out of her frozen state. Her breath caught in her throat as she slowly backed away, ignoring the plea in his eyes. She couldn't stand there any longer feeling like a fool; she turned her back on him and walked away, swallowing back tears that desperately tried to escape.

She didn't know what to do anymore. Her mind desperately tried to convince her that he was replacing her. He had decided she wasn't worth all the trouble after all; he did want a pliable woman instead of the stubborn one she was.

She was so desperate to make her mind stop spinning she collided directly with a hard chest, hands catching her arms to keep them both from falling. Christiana looked up, her veins running cold at the sight of Julian's icy blue eyes.

"I'm so sorry, Chancellor." Christiana averted her gaze, shaking herself out of his arms.

"Quite all right, Christiana." A sly grin crossed his sharp face. "Are you well?"

"Yes, of course." She finally looked up at him, her shoulders pushed back to try and show some form of confidence. "I was lost in my own thoughts. The sunset does that to me sometimes."

"Well, since it looks like you were heading back to the palace, may I escort you?" He offered his arm.

"Oh, no, that is quite alright…" She tried to step around him, her skin tingling with the urge to run away.

He stepped quickly, blocking her path. "I insist."

A smile still stretched across his face, but his eyes swirled, sending fear racing through her. She hadn't been the type to be subjected by fear since her father's death; she was known for her stubborn behavior and need to control things. But there was something about the Chancellor's eyes tonight; she hadn't felt so deeply scared in her soul for many years.

She tentatively took the crook of his arm, her grip as loose as possible.

They walked in silence for a few moments, the palace turrets growing with each step that brought them closer to its walls. Her nerves were shaking to her core. She tried her best to pull in deep breaths silently, her racing heart refusing to slow down. All she could do was pray he let her go when they reached the palace doors.

"So," he said, breaking the tense silence. "Have you had a chance to think about my offer?"

She tried not to groan. She'd had a feeling this is why he wanted to escort her. "I'm sorry, Julian, but it still makes me a bit uncomfortable to think about."

"Of course, of course." He patted her hand. "I know it can be a lot to handle. But I have a feeling a smart, lovely woman such as yourself will find a moment to think about it."

"I need more time." Even with the overwhelming stress of the last few days, she had found a moment of clarity during her bath to plot now that she had information from Tobias. However thin, she had a basic idea of what she could do to lure the Chancellor to his end. Hopefully, this threat of his would be pointless in a fortnight.

"You shall have it." He grasped her hand tightly as they entered through the glass doors, tugging her by the wrist so they were chest-to-chest. "Just not too much more."

His breath crawled down her neck. A shiver racing along her spine when his lips touched her hand, his eyes never leaving hers. "Have a lovely evening, Marchioness." He gave her one last smirk before he strode away, leaving her frozen behind him.

Chapter Fifty

OR THREE DAYS, CHRISTIANA REFUSED TO
leave her room. She made sure Natalia brought her
plenty of food and kept any visitors out. Zander and her
family came by a few times, but she refused to see them, claiming she
was too sick for visitors; she heard the disappointment in Zander's voice
through the door, but she had no desire to get out of bed. All she did for
seventy-two hours was sleep, eat meals, and stare out the window. Yet
another repercussion of her Battled Brain coming to torture her; she
couldn't seem to get her energy levels up enough to warrant getting
dressed and rejoining the bustling of the palace halls.

By midmorning on the fourth day, she was wrapped in her large
quilt, a cup of tea in her hand as she stared out the open window into the
gardens. She felt the weight of the entire summer crashing on her chest,
smothering her heart and soul with the sheer size of it. It had been so
easy to ignore her problems since her father's death by all but secluding
herself from society. She had focused so hard on healing from the abuse,

she had forgotten to strengthen her heart in the process. Now that she was trying to break down those fortified walls, she wasn't sure if the pain was worth it.

A knock at the door interrupted her racing thoughts. She ignored it, knowing Natalia would send away whoever it was by her order. But two sets of footsteps charged at the door and it burst open, ushering Dorina into her bedroom.

"Dorina?" Christiana craned her neck, following her friend's sharp stride to the closet. "What are you doing?"

"I am getting you out of bed!" She rummaged through Christiana's dresses, sorting through each bustle of fabric.

Christiana's eyes turned to Natalia, wincing in the entryway. "I'm so sorry, My Lady. But she was...insistent."

With all her energy, Christiana pulled herself out of the chair, the blanket still wrapped around her and the thin nightgown she'd worn for three days. Face creased, Dorina pulled out one of Christiana's day dresses, the deep plum decorated with a gray floral pattern.

"Dorina, I do not feel good enough to leave." Christiana sagged against one of the bedposts as Dorina laid the garment across the bed, her hands smoothing the silk skirt.

"I don't believe you." Dorina rested her hands on Christiana's shoulders and pushed her to sit at her dressing table, the lines of her face exaggerated in the mirror by her frown.

Dorina chose a brush and combed through Christiana's knotted hair. Silence fell for a moment, broken by the rough scrape of the brush, the weight on her chest finally started to lessen. Dorina's gaze caught hers in the mirror every few moments, amber eyes swirling with questions.

"Why are you here?" Christiana whispered, hands limp in her lap but fingers twitching.

Dorina sighed. "I know you and Zander had a fight."

"He told you?" Christiana stared wide-eyed at Dorina's reflection.

"Begrudgingly." Dorina snorted. "He's been sulking as much as you over the past few days. He didn't say much, only that you two got into it."

Christiana's pulse slowed. "Oh."

"At least he opened the door for me when I went to talk to him." Dorina gave her a pointed stare, a smile teasing her lips.

"I'm sorry." Christiana dropped her gaze to her lap.

Dorina set the brush back on the vanity, her dress fanning over the side of the bench as she sat next to Christiana. "It's all right, but you can't hide forever." Her arm snaked around Christiana's shoulders, pulling her in.

"But it's easier this way." She leaned her head against Dorina's shoulder, wishing all of it would go away—the struggle and pull she was feeling inside.

"I may not know much about marriage and relationships, but I know enough to say ignoring the problem won't fix it. You need to talk to him."

"I know." Christiana groaned. "That's if Zander even still wants me at this point."

Dorina peeked at her sideways. "He said he'll be waiting for you at your spot at noontime."

"He sent you?"

She shrugged. "I offered. If anyone had the will to rip you out of your bed kicking and screaming, it was me."

"True." Christiana laughed weakly.

"Now, can we let Natalia get you ready for the rest of the day?"

"I suppose so." Christiana sighed, collecting her cosmetics on the table to prepare.

***

Christiana's heart lifted when her beloved tree came into view, the long strands of its branches blowing in the wind. She didn't see Zander, but he was most likely hidden deep within those sheltering boughs. Her

386

heartbeat picked up as she approached; she had to apologize, but she wasn't sure how to explain her actions that night without revealing her Battled Brain.

"Hello, Christiana," Zander greeted as she pushed their willow tree's branches aside. A large blanket was spread out at his feet like he hoped for a picnic or a long conversation.

She stared at him, the man who had been so open with her, who had been willing to try the impossible and attempt to love her. His eyes were filled with emotion as he took her in for the first time since their fight.

"Hello, Zander."

"Christiana, I'm sorry," he said. "I understand why you were so upset with me."

"You do?" She moved toward the trunk, keeping her posture straight and her eyes on his.

"Of course, I do. You've spent your life hiding secrets. I can't expect you to admit all of them to me whenever I ask you to."

Shaking her head, she looked up at him. "You shouldn't be the only one apologizing. I asked you to do something impossible and expected you to accept it right away. Of course you were shocked and had questions, it's a natural reaction. I killed a man."

"A rapist, Christiana."

"I know, but to be honest, that's not even the point." She took a deep breath. "I blew that whole argument out of proportion. I think I was trying to find a reason to fight with you."

"What?"

"I've been...away from society for so long, I forgot how to form bonds. The only two people besides my family who stayed in my life are my mentor and Robert, and originally, I kept them for necessity, not friendship. I eventually formed bonds with them, but it was never planned." Looking at Zander, she realized how difficult it was to open up to someone else, to make peace with telling secrets. She needed to try and break that habit. "And I think a part of me was trying to protect myself from forming a new one by finding a reason to push you away."

He took a step forward, grazing her arm with his fingertips until her reached her hand. "It's understandable."

"I'm still going to keep secrets about my jobs and my clients," she warned him. "They put their safety and trust in me and I know how hard that is. I can't betray that by telling you everything."

He pressed his lips together tightly, his nose scrunching. "Very well."

"But," she continued. "I do want to be able to start opening up to you."

"I want that too."

Everything inside her tightened, trying to shy away from what she was about to say. Still, she forced the words out of her lips. "I want to talk to you about my father."

"Oh, Ana. We don't have to until you're ready." He squeezed her hand.

"I am ready. I want to be able to open up to you. I want to show you I do trust you with secrets." And this was not only for him, but her as well. She needed to see how he reacted to her horrific past, if there was even a possibility that she could tell him the truth of her scarred mind. "You can ask me questions, I'm ready."

She pulled him over to the trunk of the tree, sitting them down on the blanket and settling her back against his chest. His arms wrapped around her torso, pulling her close, his face buried in her hair. "When did it start?"

"I was twelve," she began. "Isabelle was an infant, but my mother was already pregnant again. He was so disappointed when she was born, because he was without the son he thought he deserved. He didn't care that it was unsafe for my mother to be pregnant again so soon, but he never wanted to put the baby in danger, so he controlled himself around her. But he was angry all of the time, it seemed like. That's when it all began.

"Even though I didn't understand why he was doing it to me, it started as quick, precise punishments. A backhand across the face, a punch to the stomach." Tears rolled down her face. She tried her best not to sob. "But as I got older, and he grew angrier, they lasted longer and he started using other things besides his fists."

"Other things?" His arms tensed, tucking her closer to him.

"He'd whip me or flog me. Sometimes I would be bound down and other times he would expect me to stand still until he finished." Her throat tightened around each word. Keeping the past locked up inside and speaking it out loud to someone were completely different forms of pain. The tears fell freely now; there was no point in trying to control them. She wanted to believe that her only mask was the one she wore when she worked as the Maiden, but in reality, she wore one every day she didn't speak about what she endured as a child. She put on a show, letting people believe she was the luckiest girl in the world with the perfect childhood and a family that lost their father far too soon. No one knew the truth. "Eventually, I became so numb to it all. I couldn't care anymore...about the pain or the catalysts or life in general. I kept hoping that one day he would put me out of my misery, but it never happened. Even though he despised me, he had put effort into grooming me to take over, and he didn't want me to be a wasted effort. So, he was always able to stop himself."

A wet feeling slid down the back of her neck. Although he made no noise, Zander shed tears for her as well. "What changed in you? What made you decide to kill him?"

She took a deep breath, the vivid memory of that dew-filled morning flooding her mind. "One day, we were outside practicing archery, another weapon he was so keen on teaching me. I missed the bullseye on my eighth shot even though my goal was set at ten. He was livid. He sent me to retrieve the failed arrow. When my back was turned, he picked up the bow himself and..."

His fingers moving to the lace sleeve of her shirt, grazing the spot where her jagged scar was hidden. She always made sure to hide it in public, but Zander had seen it many times while she wore her sleeveless Maiden outfit.

"He was making a point about war and defeating the enemy, but I was barely listening. Because for the first time, he actually hit me with something used to kill people." She remembered it all: the blood spraying across the grass, the arrow tip coated in red, her mind finally coming out of the fog. "It's like it woke me up from a coma. I finally realized I wasn't ready to die."

"How could a father ever do that to his child?" Zander whispered through his tears. "I don't know what else to say. Saying sorry seems so pathetic after all that."

"I don't need you to say anything. I just need you to listen whenever I'm ready to talk."

"Always and forever," he vowed.

"Sometimes, people around court don't realize the weight they put on me every time they compare me to my father." Her fingers shook over Zander's.

"What do you mean?"

"They tell me how I look like him or how I'm my father's daughter. But they didn't know who he truly was. All they saw was the mask and show he put on for those around him." She shook her head, her braided updo scratching against Zander's velvet coat. "But I listen to people compare me to him and I wonder if they aren't as far off as I would like to believe."

"You are nothing like that man." Zander grasped her trembling hands tightly.

"Aren't I? His solution to problems was always violence. And what was my solution to my problem with him? Violence." The weight of that admission pierced a part of her heart. She had never said this out loud before. "And then I continued with it long after he was gone. I could have returned to my life, held my title and been content with it. But I chose to continue my training and start taking clients. Maybe I could have made an excuse for killing my father, but what about all the others I chose to harm of my own free will?"

"Why did your father hurt you?" He turned her around, her body still curled up against him, looking into her eyes. "Tell me."

She sighed, her cheek resting on his chest. "Anger, frustration, annoyance. Anything that he felt had a negative effect on his life."

"Is that why you hurt others?" His hand grazed down her back, sending a chill up her spine.

"Of course not." She sniffed, wiping away the many tears she had shed today.

"Why do you?"

She hesitated, not exactly sure how to explain her passion. "To bring peace to those who didn't have the opportunities I did. Everyone deserves to have the same chance, especially when it's their life hanging in the balance of surviving or breaking."

"That's how I know you're not your father." He kissed her forehead, finally coaxing a smile to her face. "Your motives are pure while his were for his own selfish desires."

"I never thought of it that way," she admitted.

"I'm still sorry that I tried to force you to admit secrets you didn't want to tell," he whispered. "And I'm sorry you had to see me with Elaine."

"What was that, anyway?"

"She cornered me while I was reading in the garden." He groaned, rolling his eyes. "I kept trying to find a reason to leave, but she has this unnatural talent to keep talking until a person feels the need to resign themselves to it."

Christiana finally laughed, her heart light as their bond forged stronger than before. "Well, sounds like it was more of a punishment than a betrayal."

"That it was." He laughed with her.

"I guess I forgive you, then." She shrugged against him. "And I'm sorry that I escalated the fight just to keep from being vulnerable with you."

"I'm not going anywhere, Christiana," he whispered in her ear. "I made you a promise weeks ago that I don't plan on breaking. Even with these extra complications, you are still more than I ever expected to deserve. There is no one else I can imagine running this country with. I don't want this courtship to end. That is, if you will still have me?"

"Of course." She smiled, staring into his loving gaze.

He bent down swiftly and took her cheeks between his hands to seal their newly-made promises with a tender but passionate kiss, enveloping her in a wall of heat. Then he slowly pulled away and shifted her so they lay next to each other on the blanket. "There was one more thing I wanted to talk to you about."

"Oh?"

"The reason I wanted you to tell me details is because I'm scared for your safety, but I also know that I have to find a way to be all right with that. I think I may have found a compromise for the situation."

Her eyebrows peaked. "Really?"

"Yes. It also may help with your concerns about being Queen while maintaining your...side job."

"Well, do tell." She propped herself up on her hand, her elbow digging into the blanket as she stared down at him.

"Kings typically hand-select their personal guard, a man he trusts with his life to be by his side as often as possible. Queens in the past have had their guards chosen by their husband."

"Yes, I know all this, Zander." Christiana narrowed her eyes.

"But you technically have every right to pick your own personal guard. And if Robert came out of retirement..."

Christiana's mind blazed with ideas. Why had she never thought of it before? Every King and Queen has one head guard in charge of assigning their protection detail. Robert already knew and guarded her secret and he was one of the few people she trusted her life with.

But her heart sank at one part of the plan. "What if he doesn't want to come out of retirement?"

"I see how loyal that man is to you, Ana." Zander shook her leg. "If he knew it was to protect you, I think he would consider it."

"That's true." A smirk twitched at the side of her lips. She hated the idea of having to assign some unknown soldier to protect her, especially since she knew few in the military currently. But Robert was a man she would never be uncomfortable around. "I'll talk to him about it."

"Wonderful." He grazed her cheek with the back of his hand. "At least this way, I can find some comfort knowing Robert will be looking after you when you have to take a job."

"Thank you, Zander." She leaned into his touch. "For trying to find a solution that could work for both of us."

"I trust you. I promise I do," he whispered.

"I trust you too." She settled herself back into his embrace, not wanting to leave the protection of his body. She didn't know how long they laid there, but to her, it wasn't long enough.

Chapter Fifty-One

THERE WERE TWO MORE PEOPLE CHRISTIANA owed an apology to. She went to their room as soon as she left the willow tree, the cream-and-gold carpet dulling her footsteps when she arrived at the door. Her fist hesitated for a moment before knocking, the sound echoing off the empty hall. The door opened slowly, Isabelle's face peeking out.

"May I come in?" Christiana asked.

"I guess so." Isabelle frowned, opening the door wide. Christiana rarely saw her sister so subdued, her energy dulled as she walked over to the navy-and-gold couch and curled herself up.

"Is Mother here?" Christiana sat on the edge of the matching chaise lounge across from Isabelle.

"I'm right here." Maria emerged from one of the bedrooms. Her face was stern, a frown settled on her lips as she sat next to Isabelle. "Something you need?"

Christiana's chest stung. "No, but I'm here to do the right thing. To apologize."

"Good," Isabelle pouted.

"Belle," Maria scolded, "don't be mean. Go ahead, Ana."

"I am so sorry to both of you about the other night." She clutched her hands around her knees, trying to keep them from rattling together. "You didn't deserve to be on the receiving end of my ire. That was unfair to you and unwarranted from me."

"But why were you so angry?" Isabelle stared at Christiana, eyes wide and glassy.

She hesitated, her eyes flickering to her mother. She didn't want to admit this, her pride swelling in her chest, but she smothered it down. "I got into a fight with Zander. I was still angry when I got back to my apartment and you two took me by surprise."

"I'm sorry, Ana." Isabelle slid off the couch, her bare feet padding against the floor to join Christiana on the chaise.

"Thank you." Christiana gave her a weary smile. "That's still no excuse for the way I acted, though. And for not coming to apologize to you sooner. I was sad about the fight and buried myself in my work." Her excuse was thinly veiled, but she had no other one to give. She couldn't tell her family the truth: that she had sulked in bed for days, her Battled Brain pushing her into a pit of despair that was an intense struggle to crawl out of.

"Are you well?" Maria bit her bottom lip.

"I am now. I just got back from talking with Zander, everything is fine between us again."

"That's good news." Maria smiled. "I'm happy to hear you're both all right."

Christiana's heart leaped at the honesty of her mother's words written on her face. She reached over to grasp Isabelle's hand. "Can you both forgive me for my terrible actions?"

"Of course, I do." Maria nodded. "I know how stressful courtship can be."

"Thank you, Mother." The muscles in her cheeks relaxed, the warmth of a flush spreading across them. She wasn't sure exactly what stress Maria was referring to, but she was slowly starting to realize her mother understood more of her struggles than she had given credit for. They might not agree on her courtship choice, but their shared past linked them in ways beyond understanding. Maybe one day, they would be strong enough to talk about it and leave it behind them once and for all.

"What about you, Belle?" Christiana knocked her shoulder against her sister's. "Can you forgive me?"

Isabelle pondered, index finger tapping against her lips. "Can you stay for dinner tonight?"

"I have to work with Robert, little one." Christiana smiled, squeezing her hand one last time. "But I'm going to spend plenty of time with the two of you this week."

"Promise?"

Christiana kissed Isabelle's forehead. "Promise."

***

Robert stared at her with stunned eyes, his face relaxed and his body sat completely still in the chair across from her. Her stomach churned, unsure if this was a good or bad shock to his system. They sat alone in her cottage, the silence deafening after asking him such an important question.

"Robert..." She tried to break the tension. "Are you all right?"

"I'm just..." he stuttered, his fingers tapping the table in front of them. "Are you sure?"

She nodded. "There's no one else I trust more with my life. I know it's a lot to ask, you would have to come out of retirement and reenlist, but..."

Robert's chair scraped back, interrupting her as he stood. His eyes bore into her as he knelt down on one knee before her seat. "I would give my life to protect you, My Lady." His steady hand reached for hers and he placed a gentle kiss of fealty on top. "I swear to you now, I will guard you with my body, my mind, and my soul. I will gladly take this position."

Christiana gaped, eyes misting as she looked down at Robert. She had come to care about him over the past year of friendship, but a part of her always questioned how much he cared for her in return. After all, he did work for her, and she had been the reason he now had the life he wanted. But seeing him now, the surety in his eyes as he swore his life to protect her, she realized the depth of the relationship they had grown together. He was not just her friend; he was the older brother she never had, much to her father's chagrin.

She patted his hand. "Thank you, Robert. You have no idea what this means to me."

"I've told you many times, I would do anything for you." He smiled, returning to his chair.

"I know." Her cheeks flamed. "You've been my rock this whole summer. I don't think I would have survived it without you. Especially now."

The threads of her new plan were finally starting to come together, and if she could execute it perfectly, it would use Julian's weaknesses against him. Unfortunately, the risk of her being hurt in the process was higher than anyone wanted.

But she made a commitment and chose to take this job. She would see it through to the end even if it killed her—or worse, exposed her.

"I know it's frightening." He reached across the table, squeezing her forearm. "Your plan is risky, but if anyone can execute it, it's you."

"Thank you." For once his reassuring words didn't stop the swirling pit in her stomach that tried to swallow her whole.

Chapter Fifty-Two

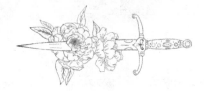

THE NIGHT OF JULIAN'S RETURN TO COURT, Christiana excused herself from the public, claiming to take a last-minute visit to one of her tenants in the area. She left early, arriving at her cottage for the evening to prepare for the ambush. She had found the perfect spot earlier in the week along the main road, a few miles from the palace.

As dusk approached, she donned her favorite outfit. She had always admired the fabric of her coat; although it looked delicate and feminine, it was durable against even the roughest jobs. She smirked at the thought of how it represented who she was as a person. People only saw her beauty and completely underestimated her strengths. Tonight, she would prove they were all wrong. She would prove to herself her weaknesses did not negate or define her strength.

Though her nerves tried to defeat her, she continued to dress, sliding the coat over her head and lacing up the front. Just as she finished, a slight knock on the door drew her attention. "May I come in?"

A smile crept across her face at the sound of Zander's voice. "Of course."

"Hello," he said quietly, lingering in the doorway.

"I thought we agreed it was best for you to stay at the castle?"

Her heart pounded at the kind smile etched on his face as he approached her. "I couldn't let you go into this without seeing you one last time."

"You don't have much confidence in me, do you?" she joked weakly.

"Of course I do. But what you're about to do, the risks you are about to take, are terrifying." Her stomach flipped. She had kept some details about her plan from Zander. He knew she was going to face Julian head-on, but he had no idea what was in store for her during the attack. "If anything were to happen to you tonight...I would never forgive myself if I let you go without saying goodbye first."

"Thank you." She breathed, wrapping her arms around him and inhaling his delicious scent of cedarwood and cloves. With each cleansing breath, she released all the tension in her body, allowing herself to be enveloped in his comfort.

He kissed the top of her head and pulled away. "Besides, I have a present for you, and I wanted to make sure you got it before you left."

"Oh? And what is that?"

"This." He unlatched the sword from his hip. "I know Robert secured one for you to use tonight, but I thought this one would bring you luck."

"What do you mean?" She took the sword from his hands, the balance perfect for her grip.

"Look closely." He smirked, his eyes tracing her as she stared at the weapon.

It clicked in her head in a matter of seconds. "Is this the sword I've been using in the training ring? The one I defeated Edgar with?"

"I sharpened it for you." He smiled, pulling a strap from his pocket, the sheath perfectly sewn along its length. "This holster was designed differently. I worked with the weapon's master to perfect it. Instead of going around your waist, you secure it around your torso. That way, it's strapped to your back and won't make any noise."

"Zander, I can't believe you did this," she said as he strapped the belt around her, crossing over her right shoulder to secure it taut against her body. Adding in the sword last, she moved around to get used to the extra weight. "Thank you." She embraced him again; she still could not believe how far the two of them had come over the summer. Through the secrets, lies, and shocks, they had withstood so much already.

But tonight was the true test of their relationship. In the end, it would be a battle they would never forget, full of unknown endings.

"I don't want to let go," he whispered, stroking her back.

"But you have to." She buried her face in his chest. "And I have to do this."

"I know." He pulled away, his forehead leaning against hers as their eyes met. "I hope you know how much I believe in you."

"Thank you." She laughed, pulling away to look up at him.

His face softened and he smirked, staring into her hauntingly beautiful eyes. "I love you."

Her breath caught in her chest. Although they had expressed their feelings in many ways over the past few weeks, they had yet to utter those three weighted words. After discovering everything she had been through, Zander was kind enough to take things slow and make sure she was comfortable with each step. But with so many unknowns ahead, Christiana couldn't walk out that door without finally telling him the truth.

For too long, she had been scared to be betrayed by someone. But she knew how she felt about Zander and she knew he deserved to know the truth. "I love you too."

Taking her face in his hands, he lowered his to touch their lips together. "Come back to me." His murmur against her mouth sent a shiver down her spine; she prayed she would be able to do just that.

"Of course." She kissed him one more time, her lips tingling as she tried to remember the softness of his touch. She took a deep breath and unwrapped herself from his embrace, holding back her tears and giving him one more nod before turning her back on him and walking out the door.

She was no longer the Marchioness; tonight, she was the Midnight Maiden, and it was time to finish the job she was hired to do.

***

The night air whispered around Christiana as she rode through the abandoned forest, the full moon sitting high in the sky to light the path. Her weapons were secured, everything she needed to get this job done, but it didn't stop the anxious shivers from running along her skin as she slowed Willow down in a thick grove of trees and dismounted, winding the reins around a thin trunk.

She took the rest of the journey on foot, arriving at the open path where carriages and caravans passed through. It was one of the only routes leading directly to the palace entrance. She was sure this was where Julian's group would come through.

Taking one last look around, she pulled in a deep breath and began her ascent into the treetops. Her newly-developed strength pushed against her, the muscles in her back and abdomen contracting as she scaled the tall tree, flipping herself up each branch, wrapping her legs around and swinging her torso up. The leaves were a perfect cover, but she had to make sure she was low enough so she could jump down when Julian passed below.

After a few more branches, she stopped, settling herself to wait. Her mind wandered, trying to distract herself from her nerves. There were few jobs in her three years as Maiden that made her body react so violently. Robert's case had certainly been one of them, mostly because it was her first solo job and she was trying her best not to ruin it; but there was only one other death that had made her this nervous. And it wasn't because she was concerned about her abilities, but who her mark was.

The night was still as Christiana lay in her bed. The moment was finally here, one that seemed impossible to reach two years ago. The only issue she faced was her inability to kill her father while her mother and sister were around. For their safety and her own peace of mind, she needed to get her father out of the house before finishing the job.

She had decided to use the ruined reports as an excuse to get the two of them alone. The less people around them, the better, she insisted—not only so they could finish their work, but so she could finally finish the plan she had worked on for so long.

She forced herself out of bed and to her trunk with the false top. Slipping into the plain black pants and long-sleeved tunic she stole before they left the estate, she took deep breaths to calm herself. She was making the right decision. Not only was her life at stake, but the lives of her sister and mother. She had to do this, if not for herself, then for their peace of mind.

But that didn't stop her from hesitating when she grabbed the pouch of poisons. This man was still and always would be her father. She held the memories of her lost childhood deep in her heart, when she was happy. What if her parents had had a boy? What if her father had never changed? What if she had never been abused?

But that life would never happen. She was proud of the woman she was becoming in spite of her father. The cruel and cold-hearted act she was about to commit would allow her to move forward with a life she deserved. She had chosen herself this time, not the happiness of others. She was ready for this future, to be the Marchioness and run the family business.

It was her time now. Her father was getting out of hand and it was time to bring the tyrant down.

The house was silent as Christiana opened her bedroom door and peered out into the hallway, the still air sending a shiver down her spine. Although this house was a fraction the size of their estate, her father's room still felt like a mile away. She had memorized the servants' schedule to ensure they wouldn't wake up before she finished, but she was still terrified that someone would see her.

She pushed herself forward, clinging to the walls like a spider weighed down by the pouch on her hip. All too soon she stood in front of his large door, the grandeur of the wooden slate towering over her. With one final deep breath, she slowly pushed it open to reveal the master bedroom; it was a decent size but just held the necessities for a visit. The most impressive part was the large four poster bed in the center of the room. Her father peacefully slept in the bedding, his face soft and his breathing filling the silent space.

Pulling out one of the darts, she quietly dipped it into her special concoction and padded over to the bed. Without giving it a second thought in fear of talking herself out of this, she plunged the poisoned dart into her father's neck.

"What the—" he bellowed, shocked awake by the sharp pain. "Christiana, what the hell are you doing in here?"

"Something I should have done a long time ago." She backed away from the bed, legs shaking as she put distance between herself and her father.

"What is this?" He sat up, yanking the unadorned dart from his neck. "What did you do to me?"

"To be honest, I have no idea. But I guess we'll find out soon enough."

He stumbled out of bed after her. "You little brat, get back here so I can..."

He doubled over suddenly, screaming in pain and clutching his chest. The poison had reacted quickly to his bloodstream and raced straight to his heart. If she didn't know he was poisoned, she would swear he was having a heart attack.

"Wh-why?" he spit out.

"Because I'm done with you." Face contorting, she stepped toward him. "I'm done watching you hurt me and the rest of our family. I'm done allowing you to tell people that we are perfect when you are nothing short of evil. And I'm done letting you control my life. It's not yours anymore, it's mine. And I'm taking it back."

"You...will...fail." He tumbled to his knees.

"No, I won't." She grabbed him by his sweat-drenched shirt and pulled his reddened face inches away from hers. "I'm going to be stronger than you ever imagined I could. Without you to hold me back."

"Fuck you..." He gasped with his last breath, slumping against her forearm.

"Fuck you too, Father."

Dropping the dead body on the floor, she picked up the dart and stored it back in her pouch. Leaving behind every piece of her past self with him, she snuck back to her room and prepared to be woken up by the screams of the servants in the morning.

Christiana rubbed her temples, her eyes squeezed shut. She always tried her hardest not to think back on that night, but the still air, full moon, and impending fight pulled it from the depths of her mind.

Killing her father had been the birth of the Midnight Maiden. She silently prayed that killing Julian wouldn't be her death.

Chapter Fifty-Three

CHRISTIANA HEARD THE DISTINCT SOUND OF HORSE hooves racing against the packed dirt. Pulling herself into a squatting position, she prepared to attack. Soon enough, the large, ornate carriage came into view, both guards sitting on the driver's perch. The time had come to see if the last-minute plan would be executed properly. She pushed the branches away quietly, licking her lips and placing her blow gun between them. With one deep breath, and final moment of peace, she forced the dart flying through the air.

It shot true, the second following swiftly into the guards' jugulars. They swatted at the sting, yanking the horses to an abrupt stop in the clearing. By the time they ripped the darts out, the Amnesia was already taking affect, setting their bodies swaying and eyes rapidly blinking. Confusion settled on their faces as they slumped forward, limp against the seat. Hopefully, she could finish off Julian before they woke up.

She jumped from the branch and into view, ready to face her mark head-on for the first time.

"Seamus, what the hell is going on?" the Chancellor yelled from inside the carriage. He stumbled out, weapon already drawn, surveying the scene in front of him; then he raised his sword in protection. "Show yourself, coward."

Christiana threw three knives in rapid succession, hoping one would pierce Julian, but he dodged the first two with superior military prowess and deflected the last with his sword like a twig falling in his face. Just as she had expected, there was no way she could get out of this from a distance. Time to start the next part of the plan.

Drawing her own sword, she moved forward, allowing him to finally come face to face with his attacker. His gaze assessed her, deducing at once she was a woman.

"Now, who might you be?" he asked playfully.

"You've hurt a lot of people, Chancellor." Christiana fell easily into her assassin's tenor voice. "Did you think you would get away with it unscathed?"

"I can't say this is the first time an assassin has tried to take me out, although whoever decided hiring a woman was a good idea must be my most foolish enemy yet." He laughed. "So, tell me, who sent you?"

"Now what kind of assassin would I be if I revealed my client's identity?" Though most of her clients wanted the truth revealed to their abusers so their last dying breath would be spent thinking of how their own actions led to their demise, this time was different. She wasn't sure how well this would end for her, each step of this plan more dangerous than the next, and if for some reason the Chancellor walked away, she would be risking Eliza's life by admitting she had sent her.

Christiana threw two more knives, trying to distract Julian. He once again deflected them, and she charged for the upper hand.

Though it was years since his last military battle, the man still fought as if he was in the thick of war. Every block and parry were fluid, sleek, his face never contorting in stress as she struck at him. Her breath deepened as she tried to take in air with each strike. *Damnit.* This was harder than she'd anticipated. It was becoming clearer she would have to execute the last part of her plan.

Though her concentration never wavered, it still was not enough to make her a worthy opponent for such a well-trained man. But she refused to back down or run away for her own protection. Giving up meant failing Eliza and Zander, something she would never let happen.

She struck and slashed with all her strength, but he looked bored while she tried her hardest to put a scratch on him. *No.* A growl scratched against her chest as her arms began to tire.

Soon enough, he was finished letting her have the upper hand. Grabbing her wrist when she went to strike again, he pushed her back with all his strength, sending her stumbling away. "Now, let's see exactly who you are, shall we?"

Bile rose in her throat as he advanced on her. She no longer had the offensive as his strength revealed itself in a powerful strike. She screamed loudly and blocked him, the blow shaking through her arm. His face no longer looked bored, it was twisted in determination and sick pleasure as he pressed in, gouging her bare arms in shallow slash marks. She had not been so scared for her own survival since her father was alive.

Julian threw one final blow, forcing her blade out of her hand, and backed her against a large oak tree. "Let's take a good look at that face of yours."

He dropped his sword and pressed a large dagger against her stomach, burning where it rested as if it had been placed in a flame. If she moved, he would gut her in a matter of seconds. She was stuck as he raised his hand and pulled down her mask, the silk fabric ripping away every last bit of her protection as it fell. His face lit up as he took her in.

"This is just too good." Eyes bright, he shook his head. "Well, My Lady Marchioness, I must say this is one of the best surprises I could have ever imagined. To think you would be courageous enough to try and kill me. So, what do people call you? Maybe I've heard of you."

She wanted to stay silent, to keep her identity a secret from him. If he had heard of her, if he knew who she was, he would know Eliza hired her instantaneously. But he wasn't having her silence, his grip on her tightening against her chest. He moved the dagger up to her exposed throat and pushed in enough to release a drop of blood down the shining blade.

"I don't have a name," she stuttered, refusing to take her eyes off the blade. Her last hope was her divine move, a move that could be the end of her or save her. She silently wished for the latter.

"Really? I don't think I believe you." He yanked her from the tree, one arm wrapped around her throat while the other moved the dagger to rest against her stomach again. Sweat formed on her forehead as he casually walked them back to the abandoned carriage. "With this attire, I highly doubt this is your first time trying to kill someone. I can't say I'm surprised with how your father treated you before he died. I'm assuming that was your doing?"

Her veins ran cold. "What?"

He shoved her against the side of the carriage, the knife still gleaming against her skin as his free hand rummaged inside the carriage door. "Well, if this is what you do, I can only assume you killed your father too. What with his tendency to take his fists to you." His hand emerged with a few yards of rope, the coils wrapped through his fingers.

There was only one reason he would need that much rope. Her hands trembled at the thought. "You knew about that?"

"Well of course I did, dear one." His body was flush against hers, hands pressing the rope gently against her jugular. He smirked when she gasped for air. "Your poor weakened mother told the Queen about it when you were only twelve years old. Did you think she didn't try to fight back?"

"Then why—"

"Well, the Queen tried to help her old friend." He bound Christiana's arms behind her and secured them tightly against the top of the back wheel. "But since the King and I were away on the battlefront against Amarglio, she was forced to write a letter to her husband immediately. You should have seen the King's face when he showed it to me. We had a good laugh rereading it over drinks that night. It was truly an amusing situation."

Christiana shook her head. This couldn't be true, she didn't want to believe this about the King and Queen, the people who led her country. The parents of her best friend. The parents of the man she loved.

"Oh, yes. He wasn't going to risk one of his most powerful titles being wasted away just because your father liked to hit you." He leaned against the carriage, his hand raking down the side of her moist cheek. She tried to keep her head straight forward, to keep his disgusting face out of her vision, but he grabbed her chin roughly, forcing her to look at him. "The next morning, he wrote back to the Queen and chastised her for suggesting such a heinous idea. He told her if she ever brought it up again, he would have your mother arrested for treason. Luckily for him, he has an obedient wife; she never spoke of it again."

Christiana could barely believe it; she had been right all those weeks ago when Julian first insinuated his knowledge, but it was even worse than she originally thought. The King and Queen had known the truth. For years they sat in silence and allowed her father to push her closer to the brink of death. They had betrayed her and her family with their actions. She had no idea how she was going to face them for the rest of her life...if she even got the chance.

"Now that all of this is in the open, what am I going to do with you?" Julian mocked, resting his hands on the carriage frame just above her shoulders and leaning himself into her. They both knew he could drag her back to the castle and have her arrested for murder, but the glimmer in his eyes struck terror deep inside her; she had the feeling that wasn't going to happen. "You have certainly given me a great gift tonight, My Lady. Not only will I be responsible for taking down a corrupt noble, but I will ruin the Prince's credibility. Once the King finds out that he chose an assassin as a potential wife, he'll never allow him to pick his own bride. He will be forced to marry an obedient woman, loyal to me and the King. And even when Alekzander takes the throne, the King will never trust him to truly rule. You just solidified my job for the rest of my life. Thank you for such a treasured gift. I am forever in your debt. Now, I suppose we have some time to waste until my guards wake up. What should we do with it?"

His fingers traced the line of her jaw, his eyes dancing at the sight of her tearstained face. She forced herself to remember to stick to the plan. She was not the weak one here, he was. He leaned in and kissed the tears off of her cheeks, and she cringed with each gentle touch, vomit climbing her throat. "Please..."

"Shhh," he whispered. "Don't worry, My Lady, I'll be kind."

"Just take me back to the palace! I'll plead guilty to everything."

"But we have all the time in the world right now, why waste it?" His cold hands cupped her fiery cheeks, perversion and desire swirling in his eyes. Pressing himself fully against her, he stole her lips with his. They moved methodically, forcing her to mimic him no matter how hard she fought and gagged, burning bile crawling up her throat. "Now isn't that delicious? How could you not want more?"

"I don't!" She forced her leg upward, her knee making contact with the tender flesh between his legs.

He doubled over at the impact, grunting and clutching his middle. A few minutes passed before he could stand upright, his face full of rage. "Now, that, you will regret."

He shifted his dagger under the lacings of her coat, releasing it from its tether. Without even removing it, he slipped his hand inside, pulling up her undershirt to expose her torso. His hand began to explore, taking in every piece of her. She squeezed her eyes shut as his roaming touch finally find its way to her breasts. A whimper of misery escaped her lips and a passionate moan escaped his while he teased the tender spot.

"You may be playing scared, but your body is telling a different story," he whispered, nipping at her earlobe.

She thrashed, banging her head against the carriage to make the misery end. "Please stop!"

"Beg me more." He steadied her head in his hands, staring her down.

"I don't want this. I want to go home."

"Open your eyes," he demanded, and the fear for her life forced her to look at him. "You are one of the most beautiful women I have ever seen. I'm going to take care of you tonight." He grabbed her roughly by the lapels, pulling her close for a deep, passionate kiss while he tugged the ruined garment from her shoulders.

"Ouch," he cried, pulling one hand away. Three of his fingers dripping blood. "What the hell?"

He grasped his linen shirt and ripped it off his own chest, looking down at his body with wide eyes as red blisters formed all down his arms and torso. He screamed when his skin bubbled, flushing his entire body crimson.

Frozen, Christiana watched the Crimson Fire poison make its way through Julian's system. She had witnessed its effects a few times, as it was Marek's signature when he worked as the Crimson Knight. Even without the Purgatory poison, she wouldn't let him off easy. Eliza had asked for him to suffer, and this poison was certainly doing the trick.

The forest swallowed his screams, his skin crawling with the fiery sensation of the poison. His face was completely red and covered in blisters, eyes fixed on Christiana with confusion.

"Your wife will be pleased to hear I succeeded," she spat.

He screamed one last time, falling to the ground like an extinguished torch, his lifeless body reeking of sweat and burned skin.

Waiting a few seconds to guarantee he wasn't moving anymore, Christiana finally let out the long breath she was holding in. Tears still streamed down her face as she tugged at her bonds. Staring down at his lifeless eyes, she could hardly believe it worked.

She had done the impossible. She had killed the unkillable man.

Chapter Fifty-Four

CHRISTIANA COULDN'T LINGER. SHE STRUGGLED against the rope and lifted her leg up behind her, barely able to grasp the short knife hidden in the heel of her boot. She worked swiftly, rubbing the blade against the rope until it broke free from her sore wrists. Her arms shook as she gingerly shrugged off her ruined coat, careful not to accidently prick herself with one of the many poison needles she had sewn into it over the past week and a half. Any place she could find in the bodice that didn't risk her pricking herself had a drop of poison waiting for Julian to discover.

Dressed down in just her black undershirt and wrapping the skirt around the bodice for safety, she hurried back to Willow's hiding place, the forest floor crunching under her feet. She tried to forget the feeling of Julian's rough fingers caressing her skin; instead, she focused on her success tonight. While searching for his weakness, she realized he had one obvious pleasure: demeaning powerful women. If he found out who she was, it would be like handing him a prized turkey on a silver platter.

He wouldn't be able to resist, which made it the perfect way to get him close to the hidden needles. The plan was risky but it had worked.

She wished she were swelling with pride, but as she approached Willow, she already wanted to forget everything about tonight. Her loving mare whinnied as she approached, nuzzling against Christiana's cheek as she shoved her coat into her riding satchel and removed the new one to wrap around her gooseflesh-covered arms. She mounted, urging her horse forward so she could leave this now-haunted place behind.

The ride was swift, Willow's gallop quickly bringing the cottage into view. Christiana's heart thundered, her palms sweaty as she slid down from Willow. All she wanted to do was take a long bath or crawl into bed and sleep.

She quickly led Willow into her stall and fed her an apple before heading to the house. She stopped in front of the door, grasping the handle but frozen in place. She wanted to see Zander and tell him she had finished the job, but something stopped her, pushing her to run away and leave him behind—a voice whispering Julian's words about King Lucian's knowledge of her past.

She took in a handful of deep breaths, trying to banish the terrible whisper back to the depths of her mind. She pulled her shoulders back and pushed the door inward, her eyes immediately finding Zander pacing back and forth. He looked up when the door opened, their eyes catching. They stood there, seconds passing while they stared at each other; her heart yearned for him, wanting her to desperately run to the man she loved. But she couldn't move. All she could do was stare and feel the rush of relief that she had made it back to him alive.

"Thank goodness." He charged toward her, gathering her into his arms, and she tensed at the feeling. She usually craved his touch, but tonight, it felt wrong. She didn't want anyone else's hands on her until she cleaned the dirt and grime of the whole night's events off every inch of her body.

She forced her body to relax, reminding herself that she liked his touch and embrace. She wrapped her arms around him, her heartbeat steady as she took in her favorite scent of cedarwood from his clothes.

He pulled away at last, looking down at her. "Are you all right? Everything went correctly?"

"It went perfect." She smiled up at him. "It's all over."

"I knew you could do it." He kissed her deeply, and her stomach churned as she forced herself to kiss him back. His lips were not the last to touch hers, and that thought made her sick.

"Yes, you did." She buried her face back in his chest, the steady beat of his heart bringing her a sense of calm. She wanted to be there. She wanted to be with him. She never wanted to leave his side again, no matter what the whispers told her.

***

"My Lady."

It felt like her eyes had barely fallen shut when Natalia shook her awake again. By the time she had returned to the palace, it was just past one in the morning. She hadn't cared about the hour, all she cared about was getting herself clean. She had called Natalia to her room right away to draw a bath, making up the excuse that she had fallen off Willow for her dirtiness and cuts. It was well past four when she crawled into bed, and as she looked out the window now, she could tell it was close to seven in the morning.

"What is it, Natalia?" She groaned, her sore body screaming at her to go back to sleep.

"My Lady, the King and Queen have asked all nobles to assemble in the throne room." She pulled the covers off Christiana, ignoring her loud moan at the exposure. "They want everyone there right away, no matter what state they are in."

Christiana finally looked up at Natalia's worried face. Her pulse sped, knowing full well what this was about. She pulled herself out of bed and allowed Natalia to wrap her damask robe around her, the heavy fabric settling on her shoulders as she tied it around her thin linen nightgown. She slipped her feet into a pair of matching slippers and walked from her apartment into the throng of tired and confused courtiers. Every single one walked with exhaustion on their faces; no one knew what was going on or why their servants had just ripped them from their comfortable beds so early in the morning.

But Christiana knew, and her skin tingled as she tried to keep her pace with everyone else, ready to hear the fateful words from the royals.

They finally made it to the throne room, lit only by the morning sun. It was already packed, families and friends huddled together, waiting for the Royal Family to arrive. Christiana stood alone, eyes wandering, keeping as close to the front of the room as possible. She caught sight of Rowan, his sullen face etched with exhaustion as he leaned against a pillar in the back. She wished she could go stand next to him, to have someone by her side while she listened to the story. But she stopped herself from approaching him.

"Ana!" Maria's voice cut through the crowd as she pushed her way toward Christiana, Isabelle in tow. "Do you have any idea what's going on?"

"Not at all." Christiana shook her head, fighting to keep her voice level, and wrapped her arm around her little sister. Isabelle's eyes were barely open as they walked deeper into the crowd

Horns blew out through the room, the entire hall falling silent as the Royals entered from the back antechamber. Unlike the rest of the nobles, the Royal Family was already dressed for the day, the richly-colored fabrics of their daytime outfits standing out in the crowd of pastel nightclothes. The King and Queen stood in front of their respected seats, flanked by their children.

Adrenaline raced through Christiana's veins when she beheld the

King's cropped dirty-blond hair, ice-blue eyes, and face aged from years of ruling. Her fist curled at her side, knuckles white; King Lucian stood tall before the people he was sworn to protect and rule, but it all felt like a lie.

Her grip on Isabelle's shoulder tightened, blood rushing in her ears as she tried to breathe herself calm. Julian was a manipulator, his words rarely the truth. She shouldn't believe the secrets he whispered to her last night—that Lucian was aware of her family's problems. But it didn't stop a small voice from whispering corrupt thoughts in her head.

If Julian knew the truth, maybe the King did as well. It could be because of him that she lost her childhood, that she had lived so many days wishing she would die. It could be because of him that she became a killer.

"My dearest Lords and Ladies," Lucian's voice boomed through the room, captivating every set of eyes. "I apologize for the early hour and for pulling you away from sleep. But an emergency came to our attention this morning, one that affects all of us." Murmurs spread through the room as the King continued. "We didn't want to hide it from anyone. It's best all of you to hear this straight from our lips. Chancellor Julian Marlow has been killed."

Gasps flooded the high ceilings. Women clutched their chests and men gaped at the news. Christiana tried to make her reaction believable, clapping both of her hands to her mouth, her eyes widening. She hoped there were enough people surrounding her that no one would notice her lack of genuine shock.

"Oh my." Maria breathed out, her face ashen. Christiana grasped her shaking hand and pulled her close.

"How could that happen?" Isabelle shook under Christiana's arm, hugging herself tightly.

"I'm not sure," Christiana whispered in her ear. "Keep listening, the King will explain."

Hopefully. She still wasn't sure if she should believe any of his words.

"Please, settle down!" The sounds of shock died down as he continued, "Julian's body was found a few hours ago by his guards, abandoned in the woods. They have brought him back here and we are preparing for his burial later this week."

Questions pelted the King and Queen from all sides. *How did he die? Who killed him?*

"Please, everyone!" Lucian's voice echoed off every surface, the deep baritone silencing them all. "I assure you, every single person in the palace is safe. We have some of our strongest military men stationed here and they are all on high alert to keep everyone safe. We are launching a full investigation into the death, and will bring this great man's murderer to justice."

Christiana knew she should be scared about the investigation. But she had cleaned everything up, no trace left behind to incriminate her. She hadn't even used her signature poison or calling card on him, a necessity she regretted. That calling card was the marker of an abuser; no one would have ever called Julian a great man again if they knew the truth.

Her eyes drifted, resting on Zander as he reached out to clutch his father's shoulder in comfort. Her heart fell, only just connecting that the King was more to her now. Not only had her real father been a monster, but her potential father-in-law might be one as well.

Even worse, she had no idea if she should tell Zander what she learned. She didn't have any proof it was real, but her soul stirred at the thought. A part of her already believed that the King was capable of such a heinous act.

But anger wasn't proof enough. Did she want to ruin Zander's relationship with his father because of an uncorroborated story told by a known liar? She needed to keep it to herself until she knew if it could be true.

The stirring in her stomach settled, her eyes wandering during the rest of the King's announcement. She was desperate to find Eliza, to see how she looked.

She finally spotted her by the front of the room, supported by two other women as she stood off to the side of the dais. Tears streamed down her face and she shook as if she could barely hold herself up. She looked like a true, grieving widow. But Christiana knew the truth, and she forced herself not to smirk.

Eliza was finally free.

Epilogue

A WEEK LATER, THE PALACE WAS STILL ABUZZ and in mourning over the murder of Chancellor Marlow. Rumors flew around like birds infesting the rafters of a church. Everyone speculated what drove someone to the heinous act of killing such a beloved member of the Council. Christiana tried to ignore all the pointless gossip. She didn't need to listen when she knew exactly what happened to the loathsome man.

To help get her mind away from talk of Julian, Zander had invited Christiana on a walk around the grounds. A cooling breeze cut through the humid air, the first sign that summer was coming to a close and autumn was about to arrive. A new beginning for a new time.

"Are you all right, love?" Zander asked, stroking her hand nestled in the crook of his arm. "You seem somber."

"Yes." She sighed. "I'm just tired of listening to more stories about how amazing Julian was for our Kingdom. I'm concerned I'll burst if I keep hearing such lies."

"It is baffling how people who used to consider him an enemy now talk as if they were the best of friends all along," Zander observed. "They seem to think if they disparage his name, his ghost will try to haunt them."

"That's preposterous." Not one person in this court would understand the horror of being haunted by Julian Marlow. She couldn't stop her eyes from darting around, her mind playing tricks as she felt his specter hover near her every once in a while. It made her spine shiver thinking about it.

"Obviously." He kissed her forehead as they continued forward, the late afternoon sun hid behind a speckling of feathery clouds. It had truly been a moment of elation when she finally felt clean enough to let Zander touch her again.

"Have you seen Eliza since his death?" She didn't have the nerve to approach Eliza at all, especially since she did not know the truth about who her husband's assassin was.

"I visited her a few days ago." Zander led them across the expansive lawn, the perfectly-manicured grass crunching under their feet. "She played the part perfectly, but I saw through it. The constant fear that plagued her eyes before is gone. They sparkle a bit more than they have since Fredrick died."

"That's wonderful." Christiana's heart sang. This was why she put herself in this place. This is what made all her hard work worth it. "She deserves to be in peace the rest of her life."

"I know you regret not exposing him, but I hope you still see the good you did for someone."

"I do. I just wish I could have saved her from the constant reminder." She brushed her hand along a row of bushes, the leaves rough against her fingertips. "Every time someone mentions his name or the *great* things he did, it will just remind her of all the horrific acts she endured."

"I'm sorry, Christiana."

"Don't be." She changed the subject. "Where are you taking me anyway?"

"To our favorite spot." He smirked as their willow tree came into view.

Pushing through the feathery branches, Christiana smiled wide at Zander, forgetting the troubled feelings of only moments ago. The filtered sunlight hit his light hair so certain strands reflected like gold. She was so blessed and fortunate to have met someone who accepted her, insecurities and all. A man she planned to spend the rest of her life with.

"I love you." He smiled at her.

"I love you too."

The first time those words had been said was a moment of uncertainty when they didn't know if she would return. But now, with the case behind them, they had the time to focus on the strong feelings that had developed between them over such a chaotic summer.

"I'm extremely lucky." Zander stared down at her, passion swirling in his deep blue eyes. "Every day with you, I feel like I finally know what full strength feels like. I've discovered what kind of king I want to be. I didn't get to do this right before, but I'm going to do it right now."

"Oh, Zander..." Christiana gasped as he knelt in front of her.

"Christiana Santinella, will you marry me?" He opened his palm to reveal a gorgeous rose gold and opal ring. The colorful stone danced with light as the sun reflected off of it, highlighting the cluster of diamonds around the center stone.

"Yes!" She launched herself into his arms, knocking them both laughing to the ground. Somehow holding onto the ring, Zander picked up her hand and slid it on her finger. She grabbed his face and pulled him into a deep, celebratory kiss.

Throughout her whole life, Christiana had worried about this moment. Since taking back control, this was the one unknown she always had to live with—until today. Her fears and doubts had controlled her for so long, but she was finally ready to move forward with

Alekzander. Marrying the Prince, becoming the future Queen, maintaining her Maiden identity and figuring out how she would fit into society were all things that she would have to face.

But somehow, with all those fears and doubts swirling through her mind, the answer was yes. It was time to let go of the past, no matter how hard it would be to move forward. It wouldn't be easy, she knew that; but she also knew that the man lying next to her would never let her give up. He saw her strength, even when she was convinced of its non-existence.

He would never let her forget who she was and just how much she was able to survive.

End of Book One

The Story Continues...

CHRISTIANA AND ZANDER'S JOURNEY DOESN'T END
here! Keep reading for a sneak peek of Midnight Revenge,
book two in the Midnight Duology!

Midnight Revenge

A Fighter.

A Survivor.

Rebuilt Through Strength...

Sneak Peek of
Midnight Revenge

THE HUMID SUMMER AIR CLUNG TO Christiana's cheeks as she stumbled down the moonlit forest path, searching for a way back to the Palace. Her silk burgundy dress was caked with mud and ripped along the skirt from twigs biting her skin like feral animals attempting to capture their prey.

Yet she didn't let that stop her. She pushed forward, back to where she belonged, back to her best friend's birthday ball, to the event that would change her life forever.

"I need to get back!" she yelled into the emptiness ahead, her fingertips raw and chafed from pushing through the thicket of leaves and branches that blocked her way. "I need to tell Zander I love him!"

Her heart flooded, pressing against her chest as she saw the first glimmering outline of the palace turret along the horizon above the treeline. She pushed onward, forgetting the sweat melting her cosmetics and her mud-crusted hair half pinned back. All she could think about was getting back to the palace, to where she belonged.

To Zander.

"Don't worry, My Lady, I'll be kind..."

Christiana froze, her spine crawling, skin numb. Her eyes darted, squinting into the darkness to find the man who spoke, his venom-filled words shaking her to her soul. She knew that voice all too well, that phrase whispered into her ear on a night just like this.

The words repeated, over and over, filtering through the trees with the summer breeze. They pressed in all around her, smothering her screams down her throat before they could escape. She wanted to find him, to fight, to kill, but the coils of roots burrowing up from the ground trapped her feet and ankles, keeping her in that spot.

Her gaze lowered slowly, her breath shallow. Her hands were no longer her own, but bound together with a cord of rope, the rough, taupe bindings snaking around her wrists and rendering her useless. She struggled against them, twisting and tugging, desperate to get free, but it was useless. She wasn't in control anymore.

He was.

He emerged from the thicket of trees, his black doublet and pants ripped and burned in spots. His usually pale, smooth skin now mottled with angry red blisters and charred black skin. His injuries didn't stop him though, it only strengthened him. He stalked toward her, each movement full of purpose, until he was directly in front of her, his sour breath filling the inches between them, his body flushed against her own.

She wanted to run, to escape, but it was no use. She was at his mercy.

"You belong to me now." Julian laughed in her face, his twisted, diabolic grin and bright icy-blue eyes filled with glee as he rushed her, ready to devour every part of her: body, mind, and soul...

Christiana woke with a scream still lodged in her chest, her throat scratchy, body covered in a thin layer of sweat that stuck her nightgown and sheets to every inch of her flushed skin. Her blood pumped loudly in her ears, deafening as she looked around, disoriented and panicked for the few seconds it took to realize where she actually was.

She was not in the forest or back with Julian. She was safe in the palace walls, where she belonged.

The nightmare had been plaguing her for months, ever since she returned home for the fall season to pack up her belongings and prepare for her official move back to the palace. The sleepless nights and panic attacks over that time were almost unbearable, but she fortified herself to fight through them. She had hoped when she returned to the palace last night—the place she was so desperate to get back to in the dream— the images would subside. Yet it seemed her subconscious, and her Battled Brain, had different plans for her.

She stretched her tired, aching muscles, peeling herself out of bed, the seasonal winter chill still biting in the air as she waited for her stone fireplace to heat the space. She wrapped the comforting fabric of her wool robe around herself, her fingers still shaking as she tied it around her waist. The vise in her chest eased a bit when she gazed at her bedside table, a steaming cup of cinnamon black tea waiting for her to wake.

Her bare feet padded against the plush carpet, her fingers warming against her teacup as she moved to stare out the window. Her guest room was nothing more than an oversized bedroom, with a giant bed, a two-person table for eating, and a corner of elegant, sage green chairs placed by the window. Christiana pulled in a deep breath, the spicy steam infiltrating her senses, a rush of peace flooding her body as she watched leaves dance in the wind across the garden lawn.

She was home.

Acknowledgements

I CAN'T BELIEVE THIS DAY HAS FINALLY ARRIVED and I'm actually writing this section of my very first published book. There are so many people who have been a part of this journey with me. Who have stood by me, cheered me on and pushed me to follow a dream I doubted would ever come true.

First and foremost, I would like to thank my older sister, Elizabeth. Without her, this book would not be in existence right now. Thank you for convincing me all of those years ago to pick up a pen and create my own stories. For sitting with me while I was stir crazy from bed rest and showing me that reading may be magical, but writing was an entirely different source of fantasy.

To my wonderful husband, Nathaniel. Who puts up with me and my crazy writing schedule and doesn't question me when it's well past midnight and I'm only halfway done with my work. Who shows me every day that he loves me and who helps me smile even when the stress is bringing me down. You push me to always work towards my happiness and make sure I don't find complacency in my comfort zone. You are the Heartmate of my dreams.

To the rest of my wild family who would yell from the rooftops with banners and horns if I gave them permission. Especially my parents, Ellen and Mark, who have always wished me nothing more than fulfilment and happiness in my career. Thank you for accepting this crazy dream of mine and for constantly showing me what hard work and dedication to a passion can really achieve. I love you Mom and Dad!

To the greatest CP, BFOTA and best friend a girl could ask for. Meaghan, you have been a constant support throughout this whole process. You believed in me when I didn't seem to believe in myself. You pushed me through Christiana's journey and made sure I didn't let my fear keep me from telling her story. When I needed you most, you were right on time.

To my other Disnerd/Whovianerd ladies. Alyson and Chelsea, I hope you both know just how special your constant friendship is to me. You were both brought into my life during a time of uncertainty, a blessing from God to let me know that I could never be alone. Because I knew the two of you, I have been changed for good.

To Miss Renee, the first lady who helped me feel welcome in the indie author community! Thank you for answering all of my questions, being a life-saving copy editor, and helping me feel safe through the process of self-publishing my first book. Thank you for giving me constant encouragement, even when I felt unworthy of it. God was looking down on us the day I won your ARC giveaway of Darkwind.

To all of the other amazing authors that I have met through this process: Bayley, Bri, Dani, Lina, Sydney, and Yasmine. All of you welcomed me and showed me what it meant to have the support of a community cheering you on. Once, I thought I would have to go through this journey alone, but you all proved to me that it is even better when celebrated with other writers by your side.

A huge shoutout and thank you to my Beta Readers: Alli, Alyson, Anna, Ashley, Bailey, Brianne, Calvin, Danielle, Emma, Erin, Jennifer, Jennifer, Jonathan, Laura, Midoria, Rebecca, Renee, and Yasmine. You have no idea how much your feedback helped me. This book came alive after all of your advice and encouragement. I hope you all enjoyed the finish product as much as the first time you read it many months ago!

To my Liberty Ladies, Ashley and Rebecca. For listening to me when I was frustrated and ready to rip my own hair out. For making me smile with kitty pictures of Leo or wild stories first thing in the morning. You both deserve a medal for all of the times you had to listen to my 'fake laugh' while talking on the phone. I miss our morning coffee talks and after work drinks at HG!

To Celin, the cover artist of my dreams! You created a cover so perfect, it was even better than the concept I had in my head. You helped to take a simple idea and make it come alive. Christiana and her journey are lucky to have your beautiful artwork representing them on the cover. I cannot wait for book two!

To my fabulous editor, Fiona. You pushed me to be a better writer, encouraged me, and helped me see just how often I could overuse actions. You helped make this book so much better than I ever thought possible. Thank you for helping me begin Christiana's journey.

Finally, to you amazing readers. Thank you for giving MIDNIGHT MAIDEN and Christiana a chance. I hope this book brings you to a place that you never thought possible. I hope you find escape through these pages when reality just isn't the best place to be. Above all else, I hope you see that no matter what, you can find your own strength if you are willing to work for it.

Thank you so much for reading and I'll see you in the next one!

*K*ATHRYN MARIE BEGAN WRITING AT THE young age of thirteen, when she was stuck in bed recovering from spinal surgery. Ever since then, she's loved creating stories and characters for others to enjoy. When she is not at work or busy writing in her home office, Kathryn can be found spending time with her wonderful husband or friends, experimenting with new makeup techniques, or watching reruns of her many beloved TV shows.

Follow Kathryn on social media for updates on all of her projects!

Website Newsletter: www.authorkathrynmarie.com
Instagram: @author_kathrynmarie
Facebook: @authorkathrynmarie
Twitter: @author_kathryn

CPSIA information can be obtained
at www.ICGtesting.com
Printed in the USA
BVHW070818290621
610724BV00007B/141